To Never See Heaven

Garrett Garland

Cover art by Hillary Crivello

ISBN 978-1-960903-58-7 (Digital)
ISBN 978-1-960903-59-4 (Paperback)
ISBN 978-1-960903-60-0 (Hardcover)

Publify Publishing
1412 W. Ave B
Lampasas, TX 76550
publifypublishing@gmail.com

Dedication

I would like to dedicate this book to my beloved Sam for his steady hands and mighty heart.

Sara for her courageous edits and long walks.
Kathy for being the most original person I know.
Hillary for her art and therapy.

Tess and the Alexander family for their unconditional love.

Deborah for gifting me the first journal where I began to write this book.

Felicia for Liza and Judy binges.

Vicki Goodwin for her edit's guidance and lasting teaching.
Andrew Smith for mentoring me and encouraging me to write.
Cat Mike and Emily for being true blue people.
Kimbo for looking at the seagulls.
Erica for being the purest soul I know.

I would like to dedicate this book to all the Antony's of the world, in the hope we all tend to and take care of people of fragility. They are often the most complex and the most beautiful.

Reviews

"An incredible representation of an under-represented population with characters so real, readers will be captivated and intrigued."

"Love, rejection, fear, empowerment…this novel takes readers on a ride through every emotion imaginable."

"A triumph in young adult LGBTQ+ literature. This book deserves a place in the spotlight as it shines a light on real, 21st century issues."

"Garland's poetic prose paves the road between torturous adolescence and the enduring soul— a captivating and cathartic love story of the self"

"To Never See Heaven evokes a temporal shift from contemporary writing, resurrecting a melodic narrative to challenge our wit…and our hearts, to create a new genre in its own right "

CONTENTS

CHAPTER ONE

The Gray Headed Albatross

"I can't imagine life without you." This is a sentence I never wished to utter to myself. Now I am facing the abyss and there is no net with your name to catch me should I choose to fall in after you. I'd sooner fall into the brilliant chasm of your mind and get lost in the folds of your thoughts. I looked forward to hearing those beautiful thoughts woven into words every year. Words to send off the next generation and see what greatness they might discover and offer up to our world. Now the burden falls upon me to inspire and I have nothing to say. I tried to think of what you would say as I stared out at the sea, wondering how much time I would have left with you. I've never had to write a commencement speech before, not once in my years as a professor. As the head of the department chair, the burden always fell to you. I remember the day you addressed my class at the end of the year. I was your student, and I could not stand you. I did not appreciate the awesomeness of what you were trying to impart. I've sat through so many of your speeches as your pupil, your lover and your husband. If time betrays us, am I to address them as your widower or what new term could I use to describe the survivor of the departed that was of the same sex? Year after year, I counted on you standing at the podium, so strong and sure of the wisdom you would award the future youth. Never have I known you to be weak or falter, and now here you lie defeated and ill. I'm trying to remember what you have said, but these words have grown fainter over the years, and I can't even ask you what they were. This is one of your bad days.

I try listening to the waves upon the coast, hoping they would carry me somewhere else, to a better time when we were young, to the first time I, Antony Shrader, saw you, but I find my fantasy interrupted by your chest expelling razor blades with every cough. I walk out to the porch I watched you build all those years ago. The weather-beaten boards need to be stained, but I don't have the care to do them. The chair next to mine is empty where you should be. The cushion is worn in the middle and the pattern is faded where you sat. The wind comes up the rocks of the northern coastline and creeps inside the threads of my sweater, pulling me back to when it all began, and reminding me of how much I don't want our journey to end.

I was such an angry child. Practically a man on the outside, but this could not cloak the scared boy I was when I met you. Your hair was darker, your tan skin unblemished and you walked taller... I'm interrupted when Henri calls me to help him sit up. He can smell my cigarette lying beside the typewriter, practically burnt to the end having never been ashed. He always lit one of many roll ups to get the blood flowing to his mind before he wrote. I thought lighting one myself might have the same effect, not realizing what a stupid gesture it would serve to this dying man. I rose from my seat and passed a mirror for the first time in what seemed like ages. When someone you love becomes ill, you care less and less about your appearance until you forget that you once cared. I stared at the lines on my forehead where they met white hair and took off my specs and tucked them in the pocket of Henry's cardigan. The one he's had since I've known him. Sometimes he was Henry to me other times Henri. I don't know why except I knew that he'd rather be called Henry if you weren't going to pronounce Henri with the french accent it deserved. So, most of the time, I probably called him Henry to save time, a valuable thing I can't afford to waste these days. I notice the missing button on his sweater before I take a breath to walk over to the living dead man.

As I adjusted his pillows, he touched my arm and asked what was in my hand. I told him it was an espresso. He pulled at my arm, and I told him, "Just a sip."

I was afraid to give it to him because I knew the triggering effect it might have on his addictive personality and subsequently, painful hacking.

"Is that one of my *papirosas* ?" He sniffed the air and closed his eyes.

This was one of his signature rolls. Its history is traced back to the Russian Revolution, when leaders of Lenin's party smoked, despite their leader's abhorrence of the ritual, a rolled cardboard tube with tissue paper, because they had no access to manufactured cigarettes. This became known as a Bolshevik roll up. I think aside from the strength of the powerful smoke they produced; he felt a kinship to the thought of himself as an intellectual revolutionary smoking a rebel's cigarette.

I finally had to answer him. "Yes, it is. I thought it might help me."

"Might I at least have a taste?"

"Why must you ask me? As you lay here, knowing I could never say 'no' to you?"

"Please."

"I thought I was going to spend the whole day unable to reach you and you only awake now for one thing when it is I who needs you the most."

He let go of my hand and turned the other way.

I came back to his bedside with an ashtray in hand.

"It isn't much," I said.

He took it from the tray and sucked in my re-creation of his favorite thing.

"Your paper is too tight, but a valiant effort." He took another inhale and handed it to me. I almost began to cry and blew the smoke back at him like Bette in *Now Voyager*.

"Reminds me of us in Paris. Do you remember Paris, Henri?"

"How could I forget?"

"Because you are slipping away from me. I can see you dissolving like a sphinx in the desert until you're buried under sand and time, and how am I to bring you back? With these words? Words which I can't seem to find?"

"Even beneath the sand you know how the sun warms everything. Think of that when you feel it on your face. And know that I can feel it too." I grabbed his hand and pulled it to my cheek and slid it down to my heart to squeeze it.

"Do you remember Paris?" I whispered.

"Every day of my life." He smiled. "And every day after."

"Be there with me now Henry, I have so much to say, and we have no time. It's as if trying to remember is killing you."

"We have been so happy, there is too much for you to remember. It is a blessing. It is far worse to have been miserable and you can only remember three times you were happy."

"I remember when we were happiest."

"You think that because that was the beginning, and now, we are coming to the end."

"Please tell me what you remember."

"Alright my sweet Antony, come here." He motioned me with his arm to lay beside him, "But you must help me fill in the blanks."

"I will, but you must promise not to leave until I have finished what I must. I must do it for you," I pleaded.

"In so many ways you are still a child."

"I am almost as old and as ugly as you."

"Less than old, and never ugly. But adults aren't usually afraid of the dark."

CHAPTER TWO

Little Lion Man

The outside of an east coast prep school looks like the setting of an Agatha Christie novel where everyone inside starts getting knocked off one by one. The vines, the cobblestones and etched glass windows were magnificent mortuaries for youth, independent thought, and sexual freedom. It was in these confines that we thrived because we argued against everything we had heard that day until the wee hours of the morning and started the brainwashing all over again.

I wouldn't call myself a happy youth. However, I was happiest when I was doing academia, but I tended to only express it through anger. It was not as if anyone was going to read anything that I had written, but every paper I wrote sounded like an op-ed for the Times, rather a collection of rejected op-eds for the Times. That did not stop us from staying up late reading the casualties from the *Salon de Refusés*, an exhibition of intellectual rejects, all under the age of eighteen.

"If that Nazi had not already stolen that title for his own book, so that no one may ever use it again, then this very essay would be called My Struggle. Then I think upon it and realize he can have his struggle. Despite what a narcissistic syphilitic ridden corpse, like Hitler might think of his own struggle, the struggle is something we all carry. No one has the market corner on human suffering, and if someone says they do then they are selling something far worse than pity. They are marketing the human experience as a commodity that can be put to words and sold for a profit. They are raising themselves up above the corpses of human suffering that have thrown themselves across the train tracks for having heard such a sad story. And yet, why should it not compare to anyone else? Because it's sad. Because someone died. And someone cried. And someone tried but failed to meet the eyes of God before they perished and kissed the sunrise before the full glory of its light could shine upon the world and heal itself with the softest words of tenderness and affection. Besides, once the story has written itself, then anyone who continues upon the path of eternal recurrence has not the audacity to echo the struggle of a former living being. And why? Because the movie remake is never as good as the original? Or pain, once inflicted, is one of those things that over time you can live with and thus loses its power? We try to get so close to pain so that we can understand it and we try to recreate it to make sense of it, but do we ever succeed? Do we ever..."

"For the love of Christ, shut up!"

"What?"

"You just-- you just keep going on and on and it never ends like the eternal recurrence of a nightmare. Sidenkrantz gave you an 'A' for that? I wouldn't even wipe my ass with it." Lucien never liked it when I went in my darkness. My words always seemed to peel a page back into his own book that he would rather forget.

"Oh, and what does that make you then my Marxist friend? You, who have yearned for the realization of the new state until all the pages of *Das Kapital* have stuck together in the fleeting moments of your wet dream fantasies of anarchy."

"My dear Antony, while I appreciate you that you have not reduced me to a complete cliche by not making my book of choice, *The Manifesto,* this would be a good time to let you know that you can go to hell and that I will be needing a new copy for Christmas."

The whole room of New England trust funds and bought for educations was in a roar of laughter that circled in the swath of cigar smoke, stolen fathers' brandy and congratulations for having finished their first semester of their last year at the preparatory school that would stick both feet through the door of some ivy league institution.

"Oh, but you are such a cliché Lucien. You drip in pretension. And you don't cover it up with your vinyl's and your thrifted black rimmed glasses." Zackary smugly pointed out before he took a final swig of his father's brandy and went to go turn over the Green Onions Vinyl. He continued with the flogging. But he stopped short of his wit to pause for a belch.

"Well, I'm just glad you're no longer trying to hide the fact you're a faggot with that cashmere turtleneck and powder blue Porsche," Lucien retorted.

"At least I can afford it because my dad isn't being investigated by the IRS." It was a cold truth that needed not to be pointed out, only because almost every guy in that room had a relative who had been investigated since the crash.

"It's fine. You don't have to get upset. Your sister told me she helped you pick it out right after she blew me."

Lucien turned his head to the side and took a swig and puff of his cigar as the room joined in on a congratulatory

"OHHHHHHHHHH BURNNNNNNN!!!"

I, of course, turned my head, and did my own, "WAH-WAH" in solidarity to our friend Zachary who did not see that coming. I myself remained in the quiet to partake in unrequited adoration for my friend Lucien. He was gay and confident, and had the whole world wrapped around his finger in a way that allowed for him to float in and out of circles invisible and regarded as acceptable to the high guard of an institution sold to the highest bidder and painted to the preference of a dead relative.

I, myself could never be so lucky, as I could never hide anything. Maybe it was the fact that I was a Libra born on October the second. I always had to express myself in a way that one could never hide from oneself, even though my own self wanted to desperately.

I was one of those kids who when I was born before my two sisters, was the exception. I never cried, colored on walls, threw tantrums or even freaked out the way babies do when they see something they recognize but don't have the name for yet. I was just cute and quiet. My mom even brought me to the doctor because she thought I was retarded or deaf or something. They said I was normal and responded to stimuli, but for some reason didn't want to talk. My mom prayed that she would receive a sign that I was alright. Then one day, when she had taken me to see the bonsai gardens near our house, a woman came up to the stroller and told my mother that I was such a beautiful child, and she could tell I would have a lot to say. My mom has told me that when she looked down in the stroller and back up, it seemed as though the woman had vanished. Ann Shrader to this day, still swears that the woman was an angel. My father, Tony, of course said she was nuts.

Oh yeah that's right my mom's name is Ann, and my father's name is Tony. That's actually how they came up with my name. You see, my parents were both so happy that I was a boy, and that both of them could each create such a special thing that they put both of their names together to create the perfect name, because they had made the perfect thing. At least, that's what they always told me.

It wasn't until a little later, when I was eleven months old, which is still very young for an infant to even form words, I came out with a whole sentence, "I want milk." My mom dropped the bottle in her hand; It shattered, and for the first time, I, Antony William Shrader, cried. Later my mom cried because she was so happy that she hadn't given birth to Satan's baby. I had real emotions, but my sisters Lauren and Ashlyn were different. Lauren the Scorpion, as I always called her, not only because she was a Scorpio, but because she could always sting she never had a deep need for people, but always was very concerned for the needs of herself. Ashlyn was different. Ashlyn could never hurt or harm a soul, and always loved everyone. She became my favorite and while both would grow to become beautiful women, Lauren allowed heartbreak during her adolescence to turn her heart cold and bitter, yet Ashlyn remained a loving energy that would radiate all over me until the end.

"What are you doing out here?" Lucien asked. "Are we being a *doopidkitty*?" He said in his mocking voice with lower lip extended.

"You're fucked up."

"And you aren't? So, what's wrong with this picture? Why are you being a sad kitty?" He said while grabbing my face and pursing my lips so I could taste the brandy that was dripping from his breath.

"How is your cat by the way? Isn't Chester like a million years old?"

"He's fifteen and thank you for asking. He's stupid and fine. What are you doing out here?" He asked as he handed me a hard cider and sat down beside me.

"What are you worrying about? Going home?"

"Yeah, I am always worried about home." I said

"Well just be grateful your sister is the fuck up and they don't know their son is a little cock sucker." He said putting his arm around my head and rubbing my hair, which he knew I hated because...well I have great hair and it needs to live up to its owner.

"Oh, fuck you. It's not easy getting it to look like this, you know."

He lifted his arm, "Yeah okay, I see you do it every morning. Takes you five minutes."

"I'm just not in the mood, Lucien."

"Sounds like you're a grumpy kitty."

"I just don't know what to do. Do I tell them? Do I..."

"What for? You're only going to be home for a little bit anyway and then it's right back here where we learn how to become masters of the universe."

"Easy for you. It doesn't matter if your father hates you. Your mom got half of everything in the divorce anyway and she loves the shit out of you."

"Well then do what she does and take a box of wine with quaaludes and you'll be set."

"I'll need a muumuu first." I laughed right before he socked me in the shoulder.

"Fuck you my mom is hot."

"Yeah....When she's conscious."

"Ughhhhh..... that's so true." We laughed, but then I drifted off in my thoughts to that place far away from myself where I can see myself being happy, but then the thought retreats to the back of my throat, and I just want to find a place where I can cry.

"You're going to be okay." Lucien said as placed his head against mine.

"What if I'm not?"

"Well, then you come and get fucked up with me. Speaking of, let's go inside and rail some lines."

"What did they bring?" I asked as I got up.

Lucien turned to me like I had just changed colors before his eyes. "Does it fucking matter?"

"It never does."

CHAPTER THREE

Sigh No More

I remember going to the bathroom of my childhood home the last time I visited for the holidays, and I held a razor over my wrist and cried as I practiced how I would do it. I knew the beauty of love itself could be found in the sounds of nature or in the lyrics of songs, and yet love was a reality that existed as something I could not see or be a part of. As I made these tiny incisions on my arm, the curved nature of the safety razor made my arm sting like a son of a bitch, and yet at the same time, I could feel immense release from my pain, as if I was bringing what I felt to the surface of the skin. Truthfully, I could never press hard enough to make the final commitment, but the slightest abrasion to the skin would bring up all these emotions that would make me cry until I was exhausted. Afterward, I was so tired I almost felt high, and I could finally fall asleep. I think part of the reason I felt so sad was because my world felt so small. There was nowhere to run from the people and places that traumatized me, scared me or pissed me off. I wanted to drown in something, go through the looking glass or wake up somewhere else. I think self-harm can sometimes be a way to go deep without truly looking inward while searching for the escape exit.

The powers of youth largely rest on the physical surface and the wisdom of knowing and understanding one's pain is granted by time. Some youth cannot wait that long and so we make breaks upon the surface to find a way in and pull out the cancer from the chest. We stare at it, roast it in the flames and walk away from the ashes before the cancer of memory returns.

Now sitting in the train station, ready to go back to Connecticut, I am wondering how I can evade my parents, my emotions, and the whole thing all together. I decided, as a promise to myself, that I would not tell. You see, sometimes bad things happen to you when you're young and then it resurfaces in the person you are now but that doesn't mean it is contingent on the person you are presently, although other people may not see it that way. I don't mean to be purposefully coy. I just can't talk about this right now as the memories churn in my head.

As soon as I see the black Jaguar pull up to the curb of the station, I feel a sigh of relief to see that tiny, beautiful woman with her raven hair and green watery eyes get out of the car to hug me. Her face changes from joy to sadness as soon as I ask, "Where's Dad?"

"Where do you think? It never ends Antony. You know that. And why do you look so thin, what the fuck are they feeding you up there?"

"Knowledge Mother. Latin for dessert."

"Oh, don't use Mother to me to criticize my fucking language. It's the best *fucking* word there is and that's why I am fucking use it so…"

"Shut the fuck up…" We finished the sentence in tandem like every child in the Shrader house always did. After the first time my dad left us, back when I was starting the second grade, we never heard another sentence that didn't end with "'shut the fuck up'" ever again.

She laughed at first and then would always get very serious. Then she would have to say how she was a good Christian after we completed the sentence for her. She was never angry. Only embarrassed.

"Now Antony, you know I'm a good Christian, it's just sometimes adults need to express themselves in a certain way that children can't understand."

"I know mom, you've been saying the same thing to me since...doesn't matter."

"Well never mind about that. I wanna know what you've been doing in your last year of school. I know you're going to be hearing back from colleges soon, and I wanna make sure you have everything. You have to tell me if we need to get anything before you go back."

"Is Dad still giving you money or was he late again this week?"

"Don't worry about that. Your mom will always be fine." As always when she wanted to change the conversation, she looked over to the driver's mirror, looking for cars in her blind spot that weren't there.

"Well now, you didn't tell me, what did you get on your SAT's? You took it four times now; you have to be done by now."

"You know me ma' I always try to shoot for perfection first."

"And did you...?"

"Did I what...?"

"Are you fucking kidding me ? What did you get?"

"Perfect."

"Ok now don't be passive with me. Tell me what you got on the test, your father and I..."

"I told you. Perfect." Cracking a smile across my face, I could feel the glow rise from my stomach to my face.

"Oh, my Gawd, that's great!! Oh, that's so wonderful!! Give me a tissue quickly."

"Oh, Gawd mother." I whined as I reached into her purse.

"Now don't make fun of my accent if you're not even going to do it right."

"Mom, you do tawk like that."

"I say 'cawfee' and 'wawta', but I don't 'TAWK' like that."

"Okay Ma, whatever you say." Turning her head to the left mirror, she started talking out loud to herself. A Show of her thought processes that everyone in proximity is forced to listen to, but no one wants to, whether it's relevant, or not.

"Well, we need to stop over here and get the prime rib for dinner. I'm not sure if your fatha is going to be there or not… so I guess it doesn't matter what size because we always have leftovers anyway. I suppose he could give me a call and let me know if he will be joining us or not."

"I'm confused," I began with a breath of exasperation, "when did he leave?"

"September, after you went back to school. He has very good timing, your fatha." She laughed to herself with a pained smile.

"But he was just here for Thanksgiving. I don't understand."

"No one does Antony. I just pray and that's all I can do."

"Oh my God. No, it fucking isn't! You can leave him if you want. I won't stop you."

"And who's going to pay for school? He doesn't give a fuck. If it weren't for me he would never write the check. He wouldn't pay the mortgage. Like, I don't know where his head is or what he cares about anymore. He used to always say he cared for you kids, but I don't know anymore. I know he doesn't give a fuck about me, that's obvious, but with you kids, I just don't understand. Ashlyn is still finding her way and is still young yet. You think he could have just waited at least until she graduated high school. That's why I had you Goddamn kids two years apart, so one of you could always be together since he has to destroy everything."

I could hear her voice choking on its pain, and I tried to intervene, "Well then let's just have a good time with or without him this Christmas. You make the holidays what they are anyway."

"Oh, you don't know Antony, I do everything for you kids and especially for you. You coming home is the only reason I even put up a tree this year. Your sisters don't help me do anything. Lauren you can't talk to because she's so wrapped up in her art, and Ashlyn is so angry with your father, I can't even ask her anything without her taking my head off!!"

"Well mom you can be intense." I tried slipping that one in without going unnoticed, but it wasn't going to happen.

"What the fuck did I do? I do everything for you kids!! Are you fucking kidding me? All I ask is for is a little help and I get yelled at? I'm so fucking done trying with you people." She threw off her seat belt and then said, "Come on, let's go get the prime rib I'll be slaving over because I don't do anything right?"

"Okay… that definitely doesn't prove my point." I said laughing as I got out of the car. And then it came without fail.

"Shut the fuck up. Let's go."

"Mom, I love you." I couldn't help but laugh. To me she was the funniest person when she was angry.

"I'm glad you find me funny, Antony. Just remember my salmon-colored roses when I go deep six."

"Oh my God. You act like you are going to die tomorrow. I can't believe we're doing this in a parking lot."

"Well one day I am just going to die and you're gonna feel bad about it."

"Well then could you hurry up and spare us the suspense."

"Oh...Shut the fuck up"

"Look Ma'. They are having a sale on roses." I pointed out as we passed through the entrance that always blew death's icy breath on you when you walked in.

"Well perfect. Let's stock up. We can buy them now and then use those that dried up as wreaths and centerpieces."

"Ma', I'm kidding."

"Do I joke around?" She walked over to the florist that sat in one of those awkwardly placed octagons in the store and took out the roll of mad money she always kept on her. "I'll take three dozen of your salmon roses."

"Mom," I laughed, "I was just kidding. You don't have to buy them."

"Well, why not? I was going to make a nice centerpiece anyway using the leaves from outside and this orange and pink color will just make them look perfect."

I didn't say anything. I never tried to stop her when she was immersed in moments of happiness. Her smile was something contagious.

"You look so pretty Mom."

"No. I'm old and wrinkling. Stress will do that to you."

After we purchased the roses and the primes rib, we drove home to a big empty house plopped in the middle of 'Stepford Ville' or at least that's how Mom always described it. The same sized white colonial houses, painted in the same three colors of trim, blue green, or black, and diabolically spaced so that you could hear your neighbor turn the shower on while his wife took out the garbage.

"Trapped like rats," she always said. Growing up it felt normal; however, over time we all became aware of how abnormal it was when we couldn't hide what was going on inside. White sepulchers built to hide the rotting stench of unhappiness that comes with too much money and too little time to spent with your kids and wife who never seems to have enough poison to pump her face with to hide the fact she's dying on the inside. My mother always wanted to keep the family together and she suffered through my father's frequent exits from the marriage with tremendous courage.

The house was quiet, but it filled itself with light up to the rafters of its vaulted ceilings from the tree and decorations that my mom put up every year. We had helped every year when we were younger, but as soon as we went away to school, my mom was left on her own. Lauren became obsessed with herself and her emotions, and Ashlyn had become so withdrawn, that there was no one left to help her. Sure, my mom had a husband, but he left right after I went to school and disappeared for over two months. The only way we knew he was alive was that the money to keep his house intact was regularly deposited every Saturday. I wept for my mother, for she, as I too, although far from her, could feel the fragility of our world unraveling. Our family was hanging from a single thread of moral fiber that, for some unknown reason, kept Tony Shrader from abandoning his family completely. Whether it was because I was the oldest or the only male in the family present, I could not fight with nor hate my father because I had to play mediator. It was a sort of self-appointed task. There were things I wanted, and that the family needed. So, when he was going to pay the mortgage, my tuition or come home, he always seemed to, for some reason, listen to me. I don't know if it was because I was his only son, or because he felt guilty for what happened to me when I was younger, but he always leaned on me for advice. Even if I disagreed, and he told me he was happy with his new flavor of the month and Mom always made him feel so guilty, I had to say they just needed to communicate and that they both just needed to take some time. Despite the fact that I wanted to scream into the phone how much I hated the bastard for his selfishness, I too was trying to keep the family together, like a mother, like a son I suppose.

"The house looks amazing Mom. Every year there's always some way you manage to sneak an extra hundred lights on the tree and another hundred on the house."

"Well, the only reason I did it was because I wanted you to come home to a nice house."

"I love it. It's amazing. I just don't get teary eyed." She always cried when she was feeling sentimental and cute.

"I'm not." She said, even though her eyes welled.

"Ok then, why don't you make me happy and reheat the Thanksgiving food I've been dreaming of since I left."

"It's going to take a while so go set the table and I'll start reheating. We should be able to eat by 7:30."

"I forgot that's early for us."

When my Dad started drifting away from us, he started coming home later and later each week until we never ate with him. We used to eat by six, but by the end of middle school we were waiting for him to come home later and later. One night we had to wait until nine o'clock before my mom let us eat; that eventually became the norm. She said we were being European, but I knew she was trying to make us feel normal by eating with the entire family together. Even if he had come home at a reasonable hour, eating together as a family was impossible, when we were so broken. I guess it didn't matter that my mom made every meal from scratch and from memory; it wasn't the food that was keeping him away. I think it was too painful for him to be around us knowing that he was being unfaithful.

"Where are you going? Aren't you going to set the table?" Mom called as I ran up the stairs.

"I will. I promise. In a little. I promised to call Lucien after I arrived."

"Well come hang out with your momma instead and I'll play some records."

"Okay in a second!"

I failed to mention this, although this may have been clear to many of you from the beginning. Lucien has been my best friend since we were five. He lives down the street from me. Also, I was in love with him, and I apologize for any future asides. I think I have a condition where I think in asides.

"Hello ugly." Lucien always had something uplifting to say.

"Thanks, building esteem one step at a time as always I see."

"How was the train?"

"Longer than imaginable."

"For reasons other than the time it took, I take?"

"There are literally too many things going on in my life that can't be eclipsed by who I like to fuck. My family is falling apart."

"I didn't say tell the bitch. I've met your mother. Go have a fight with yourself inside your head and leave me out of it."

"I just wanted to see you was all." I couldn't help but stare at the floor like a wounded thing piling on rejection the longer I stared at the floor.

"And you will. It's all good. You don't have to be brave. Wait until next year. Spring break. Honestly, who gives a fuck. Wait until you're dead. In fact, don't even go home next time, because before you know it, you'll be back in school."

I knew he was right. The fall out that would come from honesty probably wasn't worth it, but my thoughts were like a cage made of kryptonite. The more I thought about everything, the weaker I became. The weaker I became, the more I didn't want to live to the point where that voice enters in your head. It sounds like you, it tells you that you want to die, until it becomes the reflection staring back at yourself in the mirror holding the razor. I did not want to be that person anymore. A person who is afraid of the voices in their head. Instead, I want to be guided by them, to a place where I could trust myself when everything was still. I wanted to relish in the quietness of evening, anticipating the morning with a desire to see what would come next.

CHAPTER FOUR

Shutting Down and Turning Up

When I returned to school from break it was very late. My eyes were practically shut, and I couldn't even begin to think on how I would continue through another semester, when I opened the door to see my supposed best friend, Cecilia Bennett, on my bed, getting eaten out by one of the guys from down the hall.

"Dear mother of fucking God? WHY?" Standing with my back against my door, with my eyes to the ceiling, and as much as I tried to sound mad, all I could do was laugh. Of course, she would be in my room, with her legs in the air, waiting to greet me, and why? Well, that's easy, she's a fucking sociopath with a sense of humor, in other words, my best friend.

"Hey man, do you think you could like, give us a few minutes? We're almost done here I promise."

"Um… We are if you think we are?" Cecilia retorted. "It's called tongue, two fingers and press down. Okay. Fuck this. I'm not here to play teacher to some boy at an all-boys school who's probably homosexual anyway."

"Hey I.."

"It's okay sweetie." She said, placing her finger on his lips while she searched for her underwear around her, "I'll tell all your friends you were sublime." She rose from the bed to come and hug me for being a tramp. She never apologized to anyone except to me.

"Um… okay. Well nice meeting you." The boy only looked at the floor.

"Any time Schlomo-bibbidy-bobbidy, whatever your name is."

"It's Brian."

"Yeah whatever. Get the fuck out."

"Jesus. Such a bitch." Brian said as he got up ready to walk out the door.

"And I'm sure your mom takes it like one too. Thanks for your time." And she slammed the door.

"Ugh, I've missed you so. You think he'll tell his friends?" She crossed her arms and winked.

And with what we could hear coming from outside the door in the hall, "Nice man! Way to bag one from the prep school!"

"Oh well. Too late." She pulled a cigarette from her bra.

"You can't smoke in here!" I said as she laid back down on the bed and lit one up.

"Don't worry about it!" she said pointing to the detector.

"I disabled yours as soon as I got here."

"How did you get up here? It's no girls past eight."

"One of the boys let me in at six, and I've been trying to get off with what's his face since seven. I seriously doubt the likelihood of any of these prep boys being able to produce let alone give a woman an orgasm after they graduate from here."

"Won't that student narc with the bad haircut you're always complaining about notice you're gone?'

"Nope. Not after I caught her and the other narc on the fifth floor having an intimate shower session at 3am last week. No, it's smooth sailing for me and Ci's vagina from here on out."

"You're a horrible person." I said as I attempted to unpack.

"And you look like shit. What's this all about?" Rising from where she lay, she walked over and turned my face from one side to the other as her cigarette was hanging from her mouth. Swooping my hair back, she looked at me with a squinted glance, blowing the smoke through her nostrils like a dragon, and then leaned forward with her hand on my shoulder.

"Well, I think you're suffering from acute anxiety and exhaustion brought on by a suffocating closet, mother, and broken heart."

"You're such a bitch."

"And you're such a little pussy. Why don't you just blow him and get it over with? I'm sure he wouldn't mind, and you could see what all the fuss is about and move on."

"God help the patient that comes to you, should they ever let you become a shrink."

"And just think. One day, that person will be you. Except, I'll be charging you one-fifty per hour to tell me how your mom fucked you up instead of letting you do it for free, like I do now."

"So, I'm guessing you didn't go see your dad in prison like you were planning on doing over break?" I asked with a slight laugh as I unfolded my clothes.

"Nope. Because I don't give a fuck, and he's getting out anyway. They could never really prove anything."

"How many fast food chain holders do you know that need a bodyguard? He was obviously a front for the mob, or drugs or illegal immigrants or something."

"All my dad ever wanted to do was help people. The government is just after him and..." Ci stopped to continue to look under my bed for a bottle to drink.

"There's nothing under…"

"HA! Right where I left it the last time. Remind me to replace this one before I leave." She pulled the whiskey from under my bed and took a swig.

"My dad is old news. Let's talk about you. This whole you and Lou. This life with Lucien fucking fantasy you got going on, it has to stop. He doesn't like you and trust me it's not you. I'm not sure if he likes anyone, but you're just not his flavor. You need to look for someone who actually gives a shit about you and thinks of you as the amazing person I do. The person who puts up with my shit, my drinking problem, and accepts me for who I am. Don't you deserve the same?"

"Hey, I don't even know if I am gay or want to be gay. I feel like one of those kids, ripping their hair out, being forced to do neuro-sci, when all I wanna do is paint."

"Wow, that was probably the dumbest, ill-informed metaphor I've ever heard outside a church revival in middle America. Look honey, I don't know what your starting position is, catcher, pitcher, but you're not on the swim team; this is fucking baseball, and you're as queer as a three-dollar bill. Hey, if you wanna take the train into NYC and get your dick sucked to make sure you know what I have known to be true since I've known you, then we can do that."

"Well, maybe we can just go out and get a feel for the scene. I don't necessarily need to do anything."

"Perfect."

Venturing out, we went into the madness of the city. Promptly, we set out on the 10 o'clock train with an air of contemplation and silent resilience to accomplish the task at hand. Getting my dick sucked was the remedy for removing Lucien from my heart, though I could seldom believe it. You could tell what people are thinking by the way they breathe on trains. Mine shortened and unsure, like the onset of a stroke, while Lucien sucked in great chestfulls of confidence and self-assurance. He had made this run before. He knew what to expect. This was our lifeline to escape moral superiority and social rigidness. We were to leave that all behind and venture from the platform into the biting cold air of excess courage and tobacco smoke and find our suspecting prey or become the prey ourselves. This was the part I feared the most. It was such a strange feeling to wake up every morning to the stranger living inside you. You go through your whole day trying not to vomit it out, managing to conduct your exterior across the limited social cues that one is most likely going to encounter throughout their day. Then you go home to sleep and hope you don't wake up with that same person inside you in the morning.

As we approached the platform I found myself wondering how I was going to communicate to those I have never met and still be able to hold a conversation that would result in sex? This thought terrified me, but what I looked to more than Lucien's confidence was Ci's enduring spirit. She was an explorer by nature; she possessed no fear but was instead driven by an unknown uncertainty that was the god that ruled her existence, and with cooler heads than ours, she pulled her fur coat around her neck and said, "I can smell blood in the water, and Mama is hungry."

As we had done before whenever dusk turned to twilight, we strained our necks like cats to the moon as we knocked back the flask of Stoli's that Ci never came without. Making our way down to the part of the city where the moon could still make you crazy. I turned to Lucien and said, "You look nervous."

"Don't project my dear Don Won Anton Crouton Markus Augustus Caesar Mother Fucker, you."

He pulled me to him, and we stopped. He whispered in my ear, "The tigers may be out, but at least I brought my gun" cupping his hand undermine before pressing it against his crotch and said, "Where's yours?"

Every thought seemed to fade from my mind and then suddenly re-illuminated as we approached our first establishment.

Ci pulled me close and then whispered, "Don't let him get to you. Lucky for you, God gave peacocks the ugliest voices, and unlike him, you my dear, talk like a dead poet that could melt the ears off any romantic."

"I don't suppose you're susceptible, are you?"

"Not even for a fucking second. Tonight, shall be the unveiling of my creation. The one person I have nurtured for all these years. Tonight, I shall sacrifice you to the Gods and you shall be immortal."

"Jesus Christ! What did you take?"

"Something Lucien brought that came in little plastic baggies. Now shut up and pay the cover since I'm apparently here as your date."

As I paid the large bouncer in the tight suit with a cigarette behind his ear, I looked up as we crossed the threshold of no return and saw the glowing neon tiger above the door swallow us whole before disappearing into the swath of smoke, vodka, and enticing noise.

Without fail, the heat of the room, along with my nerves, made me so grateful that I wore my usual costume of all black. I wear it every day to avoid indecision, and to avoid others. My ice blonde hair and effeminate ticks were already attention enough. Looking back, I think that black became my daily mourning for the little piece of me that died every day for wanting to express myself.

Inside the Tower of Babel, I found no problems connecting to where on the food chain my kind resided. The entrance of any gay establishment is always the same: the entrance is a long corridor of blackness, condoms, and emptiness that forces you inside the stomach of the beast. If it weren't for the esophageal entryway of blackness and curiosity, the snipers would all stand at the periphery of the entrance, and pick off all the insecurities of the married, closeted or possessors of a painfully blank stare that would have sent anyone running for the exit. In the hallway set up, all the fresh meat came charging out into the arena, before the tigers could feast. Ci shielded me from the first volley of stares when we entered. Shirking me to the right, steering me with her arm wrapped around me; we made a wide circle like a pony show at the fairground, before moving full steam ahead towards the bar for that liquid courage.

"Oh God. I'm sweating dicks in here!" I exhaled, as I leaned on the bar sending a potential suitor scurrying away with a scoff and raised eyebrows.

"Well, that was artful." Ci said as she lit a cigarette.

"I'm sorry. It slipped out."

"Oh honey, no one here gives a shit, but the situation isn't starting off good. So, stick with the tequila tonight. I can't have you being a sad drunk."

"I'm not a sad drunk."

"Two shots of Jose and two tequila sodas please. Honey, you are the Edgar Allen Poe of sad drunks. If your drunk were like Emily Dickinson, then we would all die of tuberculosis like her five closest friends, a disease that she probably gave them so she could have something sad to write about like the miserable cunt she was."

"That is so unfair." She put her thumb under my chin, handed me her drink and said, "Drink up, bitch."

After slamming the shots down on the bar, I looked up at her with watery eyes and started to slur.

"I think you're trying to kill me, and where did Lucien go?"

Then she slapped me. "HEY! No sad drunk bitch face, okay? Sometimes I feel like I'm the only son of a Holocaust survivor when I'm around you. I say, 'I'm cold,' and then you remind me of the cold at Auschwitz. I say, 'I'm hungry' and you remind me of the fucking hunger. I get it, life's shit for you, but now we have to move on and drink as much as possible because life is too short, and the camp is fucking closed. Two more please and throw in some lime. Fuck him." We clinked glasses and down the hatch they went. I was about to correct her on how culturally insensitive her motivational and misguided analogy was before I could still feel her love sting from before and decided against it.

Once the agave and liquid nitrogen had officially kicked in, I felt unstoppable like every light in that place was heating the floor beneath me and sending me higher and higher. Higher and higher I did go. The night club was built in tiers with a spiral runway that went up for three stories. I stumbled with Ci up to each level from which each bar projected its own music and vibe, which drowned out the main music trickling upwards from below. When we stumbled onto the third floor, it looked like an upscale gentlemen's club with clear glass tables that glowed with the vibrant purple tubes of light that lined all the furniture. The bar was high and had no stools. The only places to sit were white tufted couches and pillows that were placed around the ultraviolet furniture. As for the clientele: an assortment of gentlemen whose ring fingers stayed firmly tucked in their pockets, single business men who weighed success by the amount of cologne they wear; and a few recluses who lingered in the corners or sulked at the bar until the young and limber came from the pit below to empty the pockets of their patrons, who more than willing to pay for an evening of plowing the tenderloins they could not enjoy in their youth.

It was here that I caught the attention of Leon Rathepan. Salt and peppered hair with a strong jawline, barrel chest, large hands that could cover your entire face, and gold rings that he rolled against his thumb while he talked. Too drunk for the air of the room, Ci and I stumbled up to the bar to order our tequila, soda water and lime: our version of a skinny, otherwise known as our sadness remedy. Turning to face each other to toast, Ci held my gaze as she sipped to let me know that someone was behind me. Someone of interest I hoped, but then after taking a quick sample of the room's age, I started to panic.

"We should go."

"Keep your shit together or I'll twist your dick off."

"Doesn't it just reinforce the idea that all gay men have daddy issues if I go home with someone my dad's age?"

"Uhh, no. First of all, you only long for the love of a father whether he loved you or not. Secondly, you fucking hate yours so that notion is irrelevant. Also, an older guy just means you get to skip all the awkward bullshit of foreplay that young guys use to apologize for the horrible sex that's about to commence. With an older guy its wham, bam, in the morning wake up to green eggs and ham, thank you Sam. Now hurry up and light my cigarette because he's about to talk to you."

Taking my lighter from my pocket, I flipped it open ready to strike then from behind my ear, I heard a click and saw a flame move right past my face.

"My mom always told me pretty girls shouldn't light their own cigarettes."

"And if you didn't have the after taste of cock on your lips you'd already be in my pants, but a girl can't have everything," Ci retorted.

Leon laughed and closed his eyes to absorb the shock of her statement, "I'd assume you didn't come here with a date because then you'd be in the wrong place."

"Yeah well, sometimes a girl has to come here to get away from all the wild men hunting and chanting with their pointy sticks."

"Well, there is quite an armory of those here, lucky for you, you're immune. Unless you're a drag queen, but then I would be just as impressed."

"I'll keep that compliment, the one about pretty girls and cigarettes I mean," she said as she rested her thumb between her teeth and paused to take a drag from her cigarette, "well I hope I didn't disappoint you, sir, if you thought I was one of those two for one he she deals. Although most gay men do tell me there's a five-hundred pound black drag queen mother by the name of Kiki who lives deep inside me who only comes out at night."

"No, I'm afraid my intentions were much more insidious from the start than I have led you to believe."

"Oh? Do tell," Ci said to him while looking directly at me. It was at this moment that I thought the odds of choking on the straw between my teeth far outweighed the odds of choking on the ice in my drink.

"I was hoping I could buy your friend a drink, but then again, it seems I've spent too much time in conversational foreplay with you. Shame that all of my hopes of success are only to be for a loss."

"Could you show me the evidence that says that's true?" I interjected.

"Ah, it does speak."

"I see of course you've tested this theory before; I suddenly don't feel so flattered."

"Truth is, I have. It's an age-old dance full of acrobatics and linguistics when a man approaches a girl as the "in" to her handsome friend at the bar until the pass off can be made."

"Age and experience. Do you ever come down from your castle to mingle with any of us peasants down below?" I posited the question to see the ease or difficulty he would have answering.

He answered, "Well history does make it customary that the peasants come to be received by the king."

I was barely able to make my swallow look graceful, "Excuse me?"

He leaned in, "I own this night club."

I lifted my glass in a toast of acknowledgment, "Your majesty, thanks for the drink."

"I've yet to buy you one. You shouldn't impose on royalty."

"We never do." Ci said as she slammed her drink down between us.

"I'm going to go and join the other peasantry; you stay up here where the altitude is preferable. And should you, my lamb, wonder from the flock, you know the name of our hotel should you come wagging your tail behind you." She touched my face and blinked.

"I fucking hate you!" I called out as she made her way down the staircase.

"That's fine because Kiki loves all and ain't nothin gonna keep her down." She walked over to the fledgling gays, "Excuse me, would you two be so kind as to help a poor drag mother find her way back to her sisters?" And with one arm over each shoulder, two men helped her down the winding descent as she raised her middle finger with one hand and waved back to Leon and me with the other.

"Jesus Christ, where did you find that crazy bitch?"

"Ya know? She's like a dark fallen angel sent by a god with a sense of humor to save my life. I would die without her, literally."

"Well, everyone does need someone like that. Two vodkas please."

"But not everyone has someone like that."

"True, it's always important to maintain perspective."

"Perspective told me I'm supposed to sip tequila only tonight, or I'm at the peril of becoming a sad drunk."

"If you're with me," he began and took out a silver cigarette case with one half lined in Parliaments, and the other with a small clear bag and a razor, "you won't have to be. In fact, I think it would be almost impossible." He put his coke on a clear, clean ash tray and began to cut two lines with the razor.

"Where did you go to school?" I thought I should start there.

"Haha, so we're playing that. Harvard Business school." I hated the way older men always resisted answering any personal questions, as if the less they told you, the more they kept their facade of mystique, yet in fact, they always come off very Jack the Ripper-ish. Despite this, they still do it anyway.

"So, how did you get into the night club owning business?"

"Gosh, it's been so long." He licked the edge of his razor while he looked at me.

"Well, my family had money, they died, were into machinery works or some bullshit like that. I sold it. Divorced the wife. She hated sex almost as much as she hated me, and I used the pocket change from the divorce to build this place. Take a line. That one there has your name on it, unless you don't do this kind of thing".

"Ha," as I took the rolled hundred from his hand, "I go to an all-boys prep school, what do you think?"

In one swoop the line was gone, and I was taking off.

"I went to one of those a long time ago, lost my virginity there."

"To a guy?"

"Of course. You can't put that many guys together and not have something happen while the RA sleeps, or while you're sleeping with the RA. Here, take the next one." He said as he pushed the glass ashtray in front of me, "Well, what about you? Things still go bump in the night when it's lights out?"

"Oh god," I creased my face as the line hit me square in the brain.

"No, hardly. I'm always studying. My friend Lucien, he's the one all the guys are climbing on top of to get at. I'm too aloof. I think I care too much. Like I could listen to any argument, no matter how stupid and not say a thing. But if I say something logically and factually and someone disagrees with me, I implode."

"Because you can't be wrong?"

"No, because I'm not wrong. No, no. They are fucking retarded, and I let them talk, you see, and I don't say a word. Then I say something unrelated to whatever fucking thing they said before, and it's always the same asshole who wants to say some shit about the logically sound thing that I said."

"But maybe you're actually wrong."

"No, no I'm not. Saying Anne Frank is the second most read book to the bible does not warrant contention from a little WASP neo-Nazi east coast prick."

"Well maybe it isn't…the most read book."

"I've read it. I have a photographic memory. I got a perfect score on my SAT's, and I most likely will be attending Yale, Harvard, or one of those schools you casually wiped your ass on, as you made your way through. So, when I dictate a fact, I'm not wrong."

"Okay."

"Okay what?"

"I'm just listening and you're talking."

"Is that a problem?"

"I'm just a simple country boy from Ohio just listening."

"Then why are you smiling?"

"Because I don't care about anything you just said. All I want to know is if you want to come home with me."

"Are you fucking serious?"

"I have night clubs all over the world: London, Paris. Do you really think I give a shit about some prep school spat? All I want to know is if you're going to start sucking my dick when we get in the car, or if you want to wait until we're up fifty flights of stairs in Manhattan."

"You're a piece of work. I can leave right now."

"You can, but it's a long drop from up here."

"I hate this."

"What? When you finally run out of things to say? I like it. Skip the bullshit, and I don't have time for it." He gulped the remainder of his drink, and gummed what was left on the plate before placing his pewter case in his jacket pocket.

"Are you coming?"

"I don't know."

"It's up to you. I'm just a simple country boy from Ohio."

"I'm anything but simple."

"Clearly. Coming?"

Against the bounding beating inside my chest I followed, so scared I wasn't going to be good enough, unaware that my youth was all that was required for him.

You are not exceptional, you are not the coveted prize, nor the diamond in the rough. You are a warrior on a suicide mission who has assumed all of the risk with none of the reward. He doesn't have to call you tomorrow. He is not young and ideal enough to wonder who you are doing during the day. In fact, he doesn't care. The reason you feel so spent and vile all the next day is because he has taken your youth, and you have made him immortal. As soon as he lays you down and enters you the first exhale is the sigh of your own regret. Your youth.

CHAPTER FIVE

The Morning After

I admit I was not strong enough to walk with giants. I wanted love and passion, and I nourished my soul short of what it craved. I can admit the sex, which I had three times prior to that point, was not bad. Indeed, he was exceptional, which was spoiled by the fact that he knew that he was. Although, in each instance of my youth, their plowing felt/or was like taking a generic prescription for sex. They were not terribly concerned if you found it pleasing. Their standup rhythm either worked, or it was excruciatingly dull: a later realization that made me wish I had met my husband sooner.

I can only recall a few instances of physical discomfort from the man being too large. You see, they liked to take it out, and then put it all the way in, deriving no pleasure except for themselves in-seeing your discomfort. It gave them satisfaction to see you withstand the entire weight of their manhood pressed against your body.

Despite age, men of many years are usually the first to rise in the morning. The earlier they rise; I assume the closer they are to death.

He pulled the sheets from my body, and a shaft of morning light rested on my buttocks glorifying his latest conquest, to be worshiped at the altar of his bed, "How did you sleep?"

"On my stomach. I'm too sore to roll over."

"Ha-ha, I'm sorry. But your body just pulled me right in, so I couldn't help it if it was too much for you last night." He leaned over to kiss my back and the nape of my neck and said, "but I'm not really that sorry."

"Neither am I. It was nice to be attended to so thoroughly after such a dry spell." Slapping my buttocks, he rose to get his robe.

"Are you being reserved on purpose after being tended to so thoroughly? I'm pretty sure I fucked your brains out."

"Do all your simple country boys come with a temper?" I asked.

"If you didn't enjoy yourself that's fine."

"Did you want a written letter of recommendation? Does my quip underscore the usual amount of cock worship that is required for so low an interlude as this? I'm sorry if I come off as unappreciative. If I came just once more would that have sufficed? I don't know if I'm ever going to see you again, and you want me to kneel before you as God?"

"You're a cocky little prick, aren't you?"

"I'm sorry I'm not the simple single celled organism you usually take from your bar. I have never quaked in the presence of a man, and I am not going to start now. I've wasted enough time chasing boys my age who don't know what makes them hard yet, but an older man knows what he wants. It's the difference between boys and men, but it doesn't make you a conqueror. The gate was already open, and I let you walk right through it."

He shrugged and then tied his robe.

"What?" I spat at him as he turned away in dismay.

"Nothing."

"Of course. Right! I forgot that older men never have to apologize."

"I don't know what I did."

" It's not important, but can I ask you something? Do you know how to disappear?"

"No, I haven't wanted to try that one yet." He replied, putting his hands in his pockets.

"I'll tell you. Fuck one of these sad confused boys who you go to school with, who you grew up with, and then you see them the next day and you become completely erased. So please, please, forgive me if I do not drop to my knees in your presence."

"Okay, I'm sorry." He said, holding his hands up.

"Oh, I'm sure, excuse me." I arose from the sheets and went to the bathroom to have a silent cry.

"Hey look," Leon pleaded from behind the door.

"I'm sorry, but I'm not going to bed and run."

"Ha! It's okay." I said as I opened to door and touched his face, "I should never have expected the greatest lessons from life to come from the consequences of one night. I'm going to get dressed."

"Well, if you want to make it a one-night stand that's up to you. I never said that. It doesn't have to be."

"I know, but perhaps it needs to be," I laced up my one shoe and threw my jacket over my shoulder.

"Before you go, do you have any life lessons to leave me with?"

I turned to leave, rolling my eyes because I knew he was mocking me. The door opened, and then slammed shut from behind me like it had done a thousand times before in my nightmares. I turned back to face him while he breathed, "Tell me," to the side of my face. Opening the door again with my hand behind my back I said, "There are two things that have eluded you all of your life: sincerity and humility. Now go about your day and forget me."

I found my way back to the hotel, and I opened the door to find Ci and Lucien passed out on their two respective beds. Somehow, the sight of them made me feel normal again. I began to breathe a sigh of relief. I went to the bathroom door ready to take a piss, and then pouring out from the door, comes six feet of black hair with olive skin dripping wet.

"Good morning." Seeing this stranger in my present state just made me angry.

"Hello, but sorry. Can I just get by?" I asked.

"Sure, no problem." He said.

As he walked past I closed the bathroom door but then reopened it just a crack to see him as he dropped his towel to get dressed, giving me a frontal and backside inspection, before shutting it again. He was hung, with an ass that was smooth and divine. My chest tightened and I wanted to die. I felt like crying, but once I heard a knock at the door, assuming that the tall jackass had forgotten something by the toilet or shower, I quickly composed myself. Instead, it was Ci, "Oh, it's you." I said.

"Who did you think?"

The nameless demi-god passed by her silently as he shut the hotel door. His evening is now finally complete.

"Oh, right. That. Don't worry about that. I want to know about your evening. Confess your sins to me my love! I want to know everything."

"It was good."

"Oh god, I can only imagine. I knew I brought you two together for a reason."

"Save it. That guy was a complete ass. So, full of himself and self-congratulatory."

"Were you guys talking about me last night? Yes, I was an animal. Did you see him go limping out by chance?" Lucien had emerged to proclaim his conquest.

"Yes, as a matter of fact, he crawled out of here. If you hurry there's probably still enough time to fuck him through the lobby floor." I was ready to slam the door in his face, but Lucien braced it with his arm.

"Hey, hey, I hear you had a good night as well so you can't be mad at me."

"Why would I be mad? I just hope he didn't put his herpes on my toothbrush, but I did see him naked, so, well done"

"He was a total bottom. So, submissive. He was begging for my cock all night."

"Probably because he never got a chance to get off, premature ejaculation is a real epidemic." Ci laughed and then slumped on the bed to remove her evening mask from the previous night.

In retaliation Lucien said, "Hey Ci, I heard you got mistaken for a drag queen again last night."

"Kiki came out again last night to make an appearance."

"Now you're black?" Lucien started. "Since when?"

"Suck my black, proverbial, fat dick."

"Fat chance."

"Too bad, you did last night while you were passed out."

"Anyway, now that the facial deconstruction has commenced tell me about your night. Who was he, how big, and did you get a number?" Lucien always liked to go over the spoils of war.

"He asked for it and I obliged, but I doubt I'll be hearing from him again any time soon."

"So, who was he? Ci said he was older," Lucien said as he placed his tongue on the inside of his cheek biting down.

"Yes, older. In fact, he owns the club we were at last night along with several others."

"Oh, shut the fuck up. You went home with Rathepen?"

"You know him? Or you fucked him?" I asked.

"Oh no, two tops don't make a right. But he did hit on me once. He told me all about his money and his clubs, but I told him as a trust fund brat; I shit money and could care less. It didn't work out, but good for you. Was he hung like a fucking horse, or does he use all that money to compensate?" He asked with a side grinning smile; almost in pain thinking about the possibility.

"Calm down. It's like you can't even conceive of anyone having a bigger dick than you and being compatible with that person at the same time."

"Sometimes you need something to steer while you drive." Lucien said.

"One of these days you're going to wake up with me standing over you, so prepare to be dick slapped."

"Doubtful, but if that were to happen in some parallel universe I would return the favor and have a black eye shaped like my cock."

I turned my body away from the door while maintaining my intense stare of disapproval, took out my toothbrush, applied the toothpaste and proceeded to brush my unsatisfied teeth, unfazed, my stare transfixed on the boy standing behind me.

"Okay, so we're going to play that game where you pout like a twelve-year-old girl until I apologize for the imaginary line I crossed that you've drawn for yourself in your head. Let's put a pause on that for now shall we while I take a shower."

Dropping his shorts to the floor, he looked down at his creation as if it had been crafted out of marble. Then he looked back up at me condescendingly, and squeezed my cheek as he walked past to hop into the shower. With the first shot of cold water he exclaimed, "Damn! It's good to be alive."

I nearly bit off the front of my toothbrush when a calm, small, warm hand came up behind me and said,

"Spit."

"There," she said. "It's not worth getting angry over, now, is it?"

"No. You're right."

CHAPTER SIX

Back In The Summer of Lucien

I t has come to that point where I have to explain myself if I am to be made clear. Self-made victims only warrant their existence in story books for the purpose of perpetuating some plot that is usually headed for an abysmal end unless the author is merciful and something good comes from nothing. This is true of romantic comedies, but not so of life, where agency and fate work like wheels and brakes against each other, creating black treads that form some sort of path. I can only speak for myself, but I will for this part of my story, sympathetic yes, and I should be kinder to my younger self for thinking... I was not good enough, but there is not one person who doesn't look back and cringe at the ignorance that comes with innocence. I myself was so naive, and thought that my best friend, whom I had convinced myself that I had admired so much, would serve to be my salvation. All I had to do was show him who he had been looking for was in front of him the whole time. But if it sounds like a cliché, then it is a memory not worth keeping alive, but it's history nonetheless and it's mine.

Foolishly, I followed and pursued him every day during the summer of my sophomore year in high school. I didn't realize I loved him until I was sitting in the back seat of his lover's car, as his boyfriend at the time was driving us back to school after a night of binge drinking in the city, because we had our exams the next day. It was late. We were wasted. I thought I would fall asleep until we woke up in front of our dormitory, but before I closed my eyes, I saw Lucien lean over and say, "Thank you," as he kissed him.

My chest tightened, and I thought I was going to have a heart attack. From that moment, any time I would even think about Lucien kissing another person I would feel this intense shortening of breath, and a seizing feeling in my chest. I thought it meant I loved him.

Even though he lived just a block away and I saw him every day; I felt as though I were losing him. I never referred to myself as gay, and I never confirmed to him that I was. When I told him, he laughed like I was insane.

"Is the sky blue? Is the grass green? Are you fucking gay? Come on Anton, you must be kidding me?" In a moment I burst into tears.

"But I don't want to be. I can't be. This wasn't supposed to happen."

"Happen? Look, you are one the smartest guys I know! Top of your class. But this isn't something you can reason your way out of like some thought experiment."

What a cruel irony.

"Well, that would be a cruel truth. God, give me the one riddle I can't solve to carry with me until I'm dead. Thank you."

"Antony, we are how we are perceived. It's how we know we exist. You are how I've always seen you."

"Then why do I feel so ugly?"

"What do you mean?"

"If I'm gay, then he wins."

"Who?" Lucien moved closer to me as we sat on the floor inside his den.

"No, forget it. Your mom will hear us."

"Do you see how big this house is? She's probably passed out in her room. I can't even hear her half the time when she's up for her refill."

I laughed.

"See, I can see a smile in there. Now, tell me what's going on inside your head."

"Look Lucien, we're best friends, and there's not a bone in my body that believes you weren't made exactly the way you are."

"To be honest, I can't believe I'm this good looking and hung either."

"Obviously," I began and paused with an eye roll, and he struggled to be serious, "Obviously, you have no problem embarrassing yourself, but what if everyone can't be born the way you are. What if you could *be* made?"

"Made? Who the fuck made you? I don't buy into that overbearing mother crap. I mean my mom doesn't even know what day it is let alone where I am half the time. No one can make you want to suck cock Anton. You're gay if you're smothered or if you have a neglecting mother or father. That's a contradiction that makes no sense. One or the other and they call it science. What about logic?"

"It's not like how you're making it sound. Look, maybe since I was eleven, I would catch myself looking at men, but I would control it. And then during the fragile stages of my development, I was damned without any hope of repelling the feelings of confusion that lived inside me."

"Antony, I respect that you are being vulnerable, and you're trying to tell me something, but what you just said is bullshit and you know it."

My eyes welled up, and I could feel myself choking on my own words that seemed to fall back down my throat.

"Well, it isn't to me. It wasn't my fault, and he made me. I could have been fine, or at the very least I could have chosen what I wanted, but he took away any hope of me being able to know without uncertainty if this is who I am despite what happened, or if I'm a fag because of what happened."

"Who? Who did this Anton?"

By this point I don't even know if what I was saying was making sense because I was crying so much, but the words kept coming out anyway. I would have rather died then to have told anybody, but in the back of my mind I thought, if I could just make him understand me, to truly know every depth of myself, then he would love me, and I wouldn't have to feel alone, and so, out the words came.

"Frank. My cousin Frank. I was eleven and the whole family was over for Thanksgiving, and he was like nine or ten years older than me. He was actually supposed to get married that Christmas. When we were younger all the kids would usually go up to the attic to play while the older kids drank bourbon, snuck from the table, in the corner. Feeling alone, like I usually do, I went over to the far window to be away from the other kids to watch the snow and try to be happy. Frank came up to bust all my cousins trying to get wasted on half a bottle and sent them downstairs to help clean up or he'd tell. Then he sent all the little ones down so they could open the presents that his fiancé had brought for all of them. I remained at the window, aware of him but not really hearing him, until he came up behind me and touched my shoulder.

"Watcha doin?" he asked.

"Looking at the snow." I said and shrugged.

"It's pretty, isn't it?"

"It's beautiful." I said.

"You like being up here alone all by yourself?"

"I'm always by myself. I like it that way."

"Hey me too. I can't think unless I'm all alone."

"But you like being around Jane, don't you?"

"Oh yeah, don't get me wrong, I love Jane, but even she knows when to give me my space."

"That's good. I hope you two are happy."

"Thanks man. Hey, can I ask you something?"

"Sure." "Do you think she's hot?"

"Yeah, I think she's pretty." I replied slowly, unsure of the intention of his question.

"Well, I know she's pretty, I mean do you find her sexy?"

I could feel the blood rising to my face, "Yeah, sure. I guess so."

"You guess so huh?" He paused to take a swig from the confiscated bourbon. "Would you fuck her?"

"Would I what?"

"You know man, fuck her?"

"I don't know, I guess so."

"You guess. Jesus man, haven't you ever popped a girl's cherry before?"

"Her what? No, I don't think so." I was conceivably too young to have the thought enter my head.

"Have you ever been with a girl, man? Slide your dick in a tight, warm pussy?" He tipped the bourbon bottle into the cup of hot chocolate I had been nursing since I came up to the attic to be alone.

"Sure. Lots of times."

"Haha, you are so full of shit. It's okay. Drink up, I won't tell anyone." Every few sips he would tip the bottle, and I would drink until there was more bourbon than hot chocolate and the taste became unbearable. We sat and talked about nothing that I can remember. It all seems so vague, but I remember feeling sick.

"I feel sick."

"That's alright cousin, that's how you're supposed to feel. I wouldn't lie to you, would I?"

"I don't know. Would you?"

"Awe come on; how could you say that?"

"Because I think I want to puke all over you."

"Haha, come here," he pulled my head against his and looked down my empty cup almost as if to speak into it.

"You know, I'm actually really nervous about getting married. Being with someone for the rest of your life is a real commitment. I'm worried she won't be enough for me, and I won't be enough for her."

"Don't feel that way." I said, slapping the side of his face with my slightly tipsy hand, and then grasping the nape of his neck.

"You're going to be a great husband."

"I know. I'll try Antony, but I have wandering eyes and wandering hands." By this point I would feel the pressure of his big hand squeezing my thighs, "Because until you've been with a girl, her shaking legs wrapped around your torso as you give to her your throbbing cock, it will never be like the first time you were with her."

"He put my hand on his crotch and then he kissed me. I tried to pull away but he kept his hand pressed against the back of my head so I couldn't see him move his hand. Before I knew it he was violently and abrasively rubbing my gentiles through my burgundy Christmas khaki's. I separated my pursed lips to let out a gasping cry, but then his hand moved from my crotch to my mouth. He took his hand from the back of my head, and squeezed my torso, picking me up and then laying me down behind some old boxes. I was so scared that I couldn't move, and I became as limp and lifeless as one of my sister's dolls.

Before I could even understand what was happening, my pants were off and around my ankles; too far away to retrieve and prevent the inevitable crime. He was stroking my cock as he began to undo his belt. As I saw him remove the hard flesh from his pants, something in me let out an indiscernible cry that sounded like I was trying to throw my soul out of my chest. Before my cry could even go beyond the boxes that he had me pinned behind, his hand was over my mouth, and he was crushing me under his weight.

I could feel his penis taunting the entrance of my body, and I could feel myself start to uncontrollably shake. He turned me to my side and told me it was going to be okay and to relax. I watched as he gathered the spit in his mouth, which was less than dry from his adrenaline despite his face dripping sweat, before he released the evaporating white foam in his hand and rubbed it all over his cock. Then his head moved over mine, and he was inside me. I writhed and moaned and squirmed as tears rolled down the hand he kept firmly over my mouth while his other arm kept me in a firm vice grip. I, who had felt love from no one, partly because I had closed myself off to the world, was receiving the attention I had longed for, but it was dirty and ugly. He could never love me anyway. It was an unforgivable crime. There was no purpose; only the deceiving nature of the crime, that poisoned the perpetrator to expect the climax of the assault to feel as a reward masked with the sole infliction of pain. Because even after it was over and I wanted to die, when he left the next day, I cried myself to sleep because I missed him. How fucked up is that? It snapped me into the present of that bathroom and seeing his lover's passing glance. That felt like its own assault I had conflated as equal as I would do with all betrayals."

"Did you ever… have you seen him since?" Lucien asked.

"Oh, that's the best part, I along with my other cousins were supposed to be in the wedding, so I had to stand next to him right before Christmas and watch him kiss the bride."

"Antony, I'm so sorry… I"

"Oh, you thought that was the end of it? Oh no. You see, at the wedding, it was an outdoor wedding, near a lake on this country club estate, and there were all these tents set up. At the reception, I found myself in the one where they were keeping all the wine and spirits. I decided I was going to drink as much as possible. I didn't care. He found me. He was drunk too.

He had this dead look about his face, but his eyes were full of tears as if he sold his soul and had come in the tent to look for something that could never be found. He said his life was over, and he needed me to help him.

He said, 'I don't know how I let this happen but now, I can't go on like this. I need you. I need you.' He came towards me, and I hit him across the mouth as hard as I could.

'Get away from me! I hate you!'

He grabbed me from around the waist. He was angry but he was crying also. I was terrified just looking at the emotions on his face change as fast as faces in a whore house. It was as if all the different versions of Frank had risen to the surface, playing across his face like a projection upon a screen. I laid there frozen in terror as he held me down on the crates. I saw the masks of his visage change from anger, sorrow, pain, agony, regret. He pulled back for a moment as my face became distorted in utter repulsion at this sad tormented thing that stood before me. Then along came that mask of evil, the mask that doesn't quite take no for an answer or stop until total devastation has been exacted.

Unable to look at me, he turned me over. Of course, I struggled but he was too strong. This time he plowed right into me, and all the air left my body in a cry of agony. It was as they say. I went completely numb. My body absorbed every grunt and push he made, but I was not there. I felt like I returned to my body when I saw a shadow make its way from around the tent to the entrance flap. I heard the gasp of his bride, and then she was gone. He went chasing after the person that had driven him to me. At least, that was what I felt about it at the time. He was the illness that sought me as the cure so there would be no repercussions for seeking a solution to the mistake of his birth within the family.

I don't feel special, I think I was just convenient. Being the outsider to myself and to my own kin, he found his prey in me. Born crooked from the ground where nothing grew, he saw me as prey in a memory he couldn't kill in the pit of my pupil but only saw himself in the blackness of a hell made in his image, unable to hear the sounds emanating from beneath the body from where he chose to bury his sin. They were divorced within six months. I never knew what she had actually seen. If she saw it was me he had been with. Every day that goes by, I am visited with the shadow of that memory. A darkness forms around the periphery of my vision, and I wonder if I was punished for my own nature rather than for a sin I may have committed in a past life. Did I not try hard enough to push those sinful thoughts out of my head, thereby bringing this assault upon myself? Or was I so wounded inside that I left a blood trail with every step for predators to follow, while knowing the might of God and the difference between the weight of the ignorant and willfully ignorant sinner?"

"Antony, you've done a lot of talking, and now I want you to hear what I'm saying. You are without a doubt, the bravest person I know, and I have been so honored that you have told me all that you have confessed to me. I want you to be my best friend until the day I die, because no one understands life the way you do. To be so gifted and to have suffered as you have and sit across from me with two legs planted firmly under you as you are now, I love this person that sits before me. You have all my respect and admiration. You've always had it."

It was at this very moment, which has both endured in my heart with warmth and pain at the same time. It is one of the purest memories I have that I go back to with agony for never being able to relive it again. I have felt as though every moment spent with Lucien since, has been trying to get back to the place of vulnerable, pure, unselfish love. I reveled in the validation of being seen in that moment. I harkened back to the moment when he saw me for all that I am, for all that has happened to me and yet he still loved me. It is with great pain that I have come to fear that revelation would never come from my parents, and the moment shared with Lucien could never be repeated with another soul. I had no more tragedies left. No more ugliness to share. At the time, I found love to be synonymous with suffering. I didn't believe in regression and tried to outgrow the shadow of my sapling self, by speaking to the light of wisdom at the end of my tunnel, never speaking like a case study, trapped in a voice, reassembling an infant, like a flair signaling to a judgmental society, the presence of sickness within the family lineage.

If I could not share my pain then I feared I might die from the inside until my blood turned black and my skin turned to ancient papyrus. Having run through the past events that I have recounted on these very pages, I promised to set myself on the course to release myself from my own bondage. I would no longer be half a son or a partial brother. I couldn't be a whole anything without the truth. The storm would come, I, its soul creator. Yet the damage could not have been foreseen, before the jaundice or the death of a limb would present itself in a manner resembling someone dying from an undiagnosable illness, whose source was only known to the carrier, whilst lying to every professional in dismay, I would have to wait for the clouds to lift to see what future could be born from telling the truth. But our futures are not forged in truth. The truth is the end of a journey guided down a path of honesty creating a map for the fullness of time left for others to follow with complete agency. Knowing this, the responsibility vested in the blueprint; it was the journey that terrified me.

We returned to the city and school went on as usual with the anticipation of the upcoming winter break. I sat in class many days not feeling present, but wondering if I could pick a day or moment that would be a good time to tell my family about the double life I have been living. When I wasn't in class, I was sneaking Ci into my dorm to keep me company and my mind off the future. During one of her visits a new family came to tour the academy. They had recently come into new prospects and in their move, had decided to place their son Anderson Underhill, we called him Andy, into the academy. As fate would have it, he moved into the vacant room across the way from mine and down the hall from Lucien; and my god, what a specimen: gray eyes, black hair, broad chest, with coarse black hair that peaked over the back collar of his polos and sweaters. In the matter of a glance my heart sank into my stomach. My agonies over family and Lucien were now being funneled into this new prospect. "Oh god, have you seen what has come into our mists, Joe DiMaggio is batting for your team." Cecilia said, peering through the hole in my door.

"You think?" I always felt as though Ci had to have been a fabulous queen in another life because her powers of perception were impeccable. "How on earth can you know that? You haven't even talked to him yet."

"Honey there's two things you have to be able to smell in this life, smoke and who's a flamer. Both have to do with fire. Both can kill you."

"What's he doing now?" I asked.

"Hugging mom and dad. Oh... And now we see where he gets it. I want to climb dad like a tree. Something about older men with a kid clinging to them makes them so much hotter."

"Maybe it's the challenge."

"Not with that ugly bitch. There'd be no challenge. He definitely traded down. Somehow they made a hot son. A gay son. His only defect according to the American Mental Health Association manual. Oh good, they're leaving."

"Do we have to go out this minute?" I protested.

"What are you going to do, knock on his door with a muffin basket? We can't lose this opportunity."

"How did this turn into 'We'?"

"Because 'We' is the only way we can get you laid."

"Oh, hi there," he started the conversation first, so naturally, I took this as a good sign. As soon as she opened the door, there he was.

"Oh, are you new to the floor?" I was a bad actor and had no knack for playing ignorant.

"Well yeah, and to the whole entire school actually."

"Oh yeah, it's gotta be rough starting in the middle of the year like this." Ci inserted.

"Actually, it was the perfect time to leave, I didn't like my other school."

"Why, were you...?" Before she could say anything, I shoved her in her ribs.

"You know," Andy began, "I believe the heart of politeness lies within subtlety. You possess none." He walked back to his room and shut the door in our face.

"Well, he's for sure gay," Ci said. "Well, we will never know because of how obvious you make everything. Most people don't just share that. Lucien was the only person I've ever known who just told people because he doesn't care about anything."

"Wow," Ci said, a gasp with a hand to her mouth, "I believe that is what we call a bit of progress."

"You know I can still hear you." Andy said when he opened the door in dismay for the two stalkers lingering by his entry way.

"I'm sorry, please forgive me. My friend is an idiot."

"Hey," Ci burst into her own defense but in recognition of her previous blunder, she found herself for once with nothing to say.

"It's inbred within her to gather as many homos as possible for herself. Much like a harem."

"Well, I have no desire to be collected." Andy was determined to be as indignant as possible to deflect Ci's gaze which was like having scalpels for eyes, constantly peeling layers.

"So you are gay. See, I always guess it!" Ci explained in her own personal triumph.

"I'm sorry darling for putting you on the spot but please don't be angry. My name is Cecilia."

"It's Andy. Anderson if you wanted to know, and you?" He looked directly past her and straight to me.

"Antony, or Anton"

"Really? Your parents just had to leave off that 'th'. Well, that's certainly different from what you hear nowadays."

"Yeah, my parents, the romantics."

"So, you like it here then?" Turning to me, he looked at Ci. "I assume you dear are not a resident."

"Haha oh no. Of course not. I go to the school for Nuns and Dikes across the street."

"Neither of which, you are then?"

"Well maybe the latter after I've had enough to drink."

"I like her, I see why you keep her around." Andy nodded. "I would never be bored." Andy cocked his head and then gave me a little jab in the ribs.

"Well, she's supposed to be my best friend but she's always getting me into trouble."

At this point, Ci couldn't help but interject with her qualities of a matchmaker that resembled that of a dark fairy.

"But without me then, you'd still be emotionally handicapped, thirty pounds heavier and probably still a virgin, so you're welcome."

"I didn't think they really condoned having homosexuality being open for discussion at this school." Andy paused when he said this and then turned his head from side to side.

"They don't!" I realized that it sounded like I was yelling and then brought down my voice a few octaves. "They just know that everyone here has a wealthy uncle in the business or dearly departed homo in the family who donated enough money to this school in his lifetime, and that any future transgressions should be forgotten or forgiven."

"Therefore, the school will look away unless directly challenged. Got it."

"But I would add, that despite the policies of administration, I find that most of the guys here along with the faculty don't seem to care, even when we have more 'expressive' colleagues than other schools. And with perfect timing Lucien came down the hallway as I had just finished my sentence. In his towel, dripping wet, opened his door, and just before closing it, removed his towel, looked back and then slowly shut himself inside his domain. Knowing he had made a successful and vivid first impression.

"Like him I suppose." Andy was very good at putting pieces of a puzzle together.

"Just like him." I replied. My voice is full of dissonance and apprehension.

"Friend of yours?" Andy inquired.

"Yes, we have been for years."

"Well then, I think this shall be an interesting school year for this floor, won't it?"

"Lest we should perish during the pain of completion and be sucked into the void."

"My, aren't we the poet?" Andy responded. And as I turned down the hallway and put a cigarette in my teeth, I turned to correct his statement, "No, not a poet. For we are all pessimists."

Fall semester, as it always did, sped with the impending break that we all looked forward to. And even though Andy would not begin classes until next quarter, he came by often enough to make an addition to his room or join us for our lunch hour. Like an idiot, I entered myself into a race I couldn't win. I could see that Andy had an eye fixed on Lucien. He was so fuckable, that he forced me to keep my teeth clenched. I saw Andy almost every other prep period I had. The one class Lucien and I did not share. Upon his visits, he'd catch me before I even had a chance to enter the room. He'd pull me by the arm and away we would go. One day I told him, "Alright, I'll come with you, but we have to do something that's not our usual. And while I don't mind our usual place under the tree in the back of the courtyard, I have elected it should be your turn to surprise me."

"A challenge I see. Have I grown dull?" I could tell by the tone of Andy's question he didn't believe it himself.

"No, but monotony is the first step toward insanity or extinction."

"Or solipsism. Who knew? You could be a brain in the vat, and I am a mere subject projected onto your subconscious."

"But if that's true, then I give you my full permission to change the channel."

"That's it. I have it. We'll go to the coast and sit at the foot of the ruins. The bridge to a collapsed civilization where you can sit and set all your troubles out like ships in a bottle lost at sea."

"That sounds marvelous but what the fuck are you talking about?" For once I felt as though he was trying to make me feel like what it means to be friends with me and hear me talk at the same time. In response to his embarrassment, he began to question if I were truly the reincarnate of the fallen soldiers of the 1870's Paris revolt.

"I thought you were a poet, a revolutionary."

"Oh, you're mistaken, just a pessimist." I raised a finger and bounced it off his nose. He squinted his face up in a cute way, like a boy trying to get his way.

"Then I propose a Renaissance. No more are we able to be stale relics or realists. From here on out, only romantics and slaves to the theater of the absurd."

"Fine. Then you go get your car and pull it around the front where I will be standing waiting for Godot."

"Alright," he said as he started on a run for his Porsche. "But you will let me know if he arrives."

"Piss off."

"Well, I can try to save you from the ending, but it never comes." By that point he had gone beyond shouting range but the anticipation that filled me as I approached the front of the school made my heart pound in my ears. I thought to myself as he pulled his champagne blue Porsche from around the corner. This is what makes it all worth it. No longer will I have to linger over the man who can't be mine. Or wait for those older vultures to come and pick me off. I could finally exhale on the shoulder of Anderson Underhill. Whatever would come, no matter how hard the waves crashed, I could withstand the blow with him at my side.

"So where to?" I asked as I got in the car and slammed the door.

"It's a surprise. Don't worry, I have the fuel we will need for our adventure." He pulled a small plastic bag from his pocket.

"What the fuck is that? Is it acid?"

"Wouldn't you like to find out?" In a moment, we were off in a race toward the coast. Right where the rocky bluffs kissed the shore, I asked him if he had a plan.

He said, "All will reveal itself as we become part of the plan." We laid down under where this grove of trees ended. I wasn't sure if we were going to do it here or if he was going to try to lay the groundwork for it later. As soon as I placed the drug on my tongue I felt a pit in my stomach, full of anticipation for something to happen. And then we waited. From the surface of the earth I sank, deep into the grass, until I felt like a wall had been erected between Andy and me. I reached out, but I could feel nothing.

"Are you still there?" I called out.

"Of course, I am. Come on, you didn't even take that much and I don't want you to freak me out."

"I won't, but have you done this before?"

"Yes, now just surrender to the moment."

"Oh God. My cardinal rule."

"What's that? I'm sure you're going to tell me." I could hear the irritation in Andy's voice grow but I couldn't help myself.

"Nothing good ever came from a cliché being uttered. You've jinxed the whole thing."

"No, you're jinxing it. Here." He reached out from what felt like 1000 miles away and held my hand. I inhaled. I could hear my breath like a wind tunnel swallowing itself into the back of my own head. This set into motion, at least what I saw to be, a direct effect to my breathing. The leaves whipped past my head from the tree above. Flying past my face they went like we were now soaring into the sky, moving toward the tree above, but never reaching it. When a leaf finally touched my face, this tingling sensation passed over me like an ant hill had just opened up on my face.

The colors were rich. The sky was vibrant. But soon after the initial shock, time slowed down. We both became entrenched in deep thought, introverted, but awake, alive, and more conscious than ever about being alive.

"I feel," Andy began with the first exegeses, "I feel like it's all circular, like the way we're moving, the way we are right now, like the end of this is the beginning of something else. Is that how it is to be then, from now until eternity?" Andy sighed with a breath of relief.

"Well deluded talks about the planes of eminence we all exist, which are just made of infinite folding planes composed of time and space. The only thing separating the planes from each other is distance." My eyes widened at the speculation of his thoughts.

"The end and the beginning of it seems so conceivable, but so unimaginable at the same time."

"I feel like time is like this tree." I began my sermon. "From its earliest seedling, it sprung forth. Its branches reaching for a million diverging possibilities."

"Whoa. That's... fuck my head hurts."

"I feel full and empty at the same time. Can I have some water?"

"Sure." Andy reached for the bottle and threw it against my side. I took a sip and it all dribbled down my face and down the back of my neck, until it soaked the nape of my neck, where my hair stopped, and skin began.

"Can I ask you something Andy?" I spoke with a certain trepidation.

"Obviously, I'm paralyzed from the waist down, but my ears are still working."

"Well, I was just thinking, if time is like a tree, does that mean that like a tree, time too shall die?"

"If it does, I think the end of time shall signify the beginning of everything that has yet to come or be done. To be as the universe has aspired to be: fixed in certainty but rooted in its own contempt."

"Ha! So, apart from your pun, the cure for time is for the universe to be happy, free of contempt as you put it?"

"Well, I suppose it's like this; if our place in the universe remains fixed, should we not aspire to be as what the universe has yet to achieve?"

"I suppose, but you talk about the universe as if it were a person in a way."

"I, myself, have always believed that miracles as they are known, are the universe's benevolent attempt to restore balance to itself as a whole, because we are part of its composition where even the smallest morsel matters."

"Despite the smallest morsels, what about flood, famine, disease? Those are all pretty big morsels."

"Damnit, compared to what? What constellation, what galaxy? Know how the heavens above delineate who lives and who dies, but I remember when my mother was in stage three breast cancer and we got a miracle, I always felt that she lived for me so that I could do something great because I'm supposed to be a part of something greater than myself, and I'm the extension of her as her mother was before. As you said, it's all circular."

I knew I was treading in water, but I couldn't help myself. I had to poke this sleeping philosophical bear about his conjured fantasy of logic.

"You said it was all circular and if she dies, the world turns with or without her? You could be great without her."

"She didn't die. Who is to know what the alternative would look like? Being that she lived, I couldn't imagine getting this far without her."

"I guess that makes sense, but I think you would have found a way." I turned over and found him already turned over facing me in the grass.

"Can I ask you something?" He was biting the inside of his lip and his eyebrows had come together on his forehead to pose a question that I could see him writing across my face.

"Yes, of course."

"You are so smart, like one of the smartest people I know, but you are always saying yes to everything. You never say no, and I don't know why."

"I think people who say yes to everything are waiting in a bread line that has no water at the end of it but when we… finally get the chance to slake our thirst, there's no water and the well next to it is empty. And on top of that, Ci makes me do a lot of crazy shit." We laughed as we struggled to not lock eyes with each other's lips.

As he neared my face he said, "I know what should follow, but I know how much you hate cliches."

And then with a matter of seriousness I said, "Then let it be terrible and something I will never forget."

"Terrible, I am. Forgetful, I am not. That's a chance I'm willing to take." In a moment, his lips were pressed against mine. I closed my eyes and braced myself in tandem to the waves crashing against the shore below us. In my head, I was screaming: the chance is his, the risk is all mine. The logical equivalent of cleaning your house on speed.

As the drugs raged on we became physically enthused but mentally lethargic. We snuck below Lucien's window and told him to come down. We were going to break into Cecilia's school and kidnap her. Lucien's was down in a flash and in minutes we were below Ci's window begging her to come down.

"Wait, Tony, are you actually fucked up?" I laughed in one big breath and in a vacant expression of content replied, "Yes."

"Oh, my god. I'm so proud. My little Gay-bee is growing up. And how are you fucking doing drugs without me?"

"We're sorry, it won't happen again. Come down and do a tab of acid with us."

"Shut up!" Lucien said as he pushed me aside to take the reins of where the evening should go.

"Hello darling, and might I say your tits are looking full of life this evening," Lucien smiled.

"Thank you kindly, and may I say I have often dreamed of a horde of gay men gathered below my window ready to declare me as their leader." That dream had come true.

"What should we do this evening?" She yelled like a corrupt den mother reenacting a scene from Shakespeare.

"Accciiidddd!" I yelled, jumping on Lucien's shoulder before he shook me to the ground.

"Oh God, that sounds too severe." Ci stood with her hand clutched to her breast while the other handheld together her silk kimono. "It is the third to last school night before semester officially ends, so I propose we go down to the Jacuzzi room that they use to calm down the retarded, take a bunch of Molly that I just scored from the lesbian janitor and do shots of Jäger from my cleavage."

"I like everything except the Jäger." Andy loved parliamentary procedure.

"It's alright." Lucien assured him. "I brought vodka."

"Perfect!" Ci shouted. "I'll be down in a second." Down she came with her ombre bleached hair, black leotard she had cut outs made at the mid-drift, resembling a skull face, leggings, and heels for reasons, to this day I could not tell you. Into the belly of the school we went until we came to the French doors that led to a room that resembled a Turkish bath. "Fuck! Could I come here if I pretended to be retarded?" Lucien moaned.

"You wouldn't have to pretend, darling. You might have to tuck or something because no boys are allowed, remember?" Then she hit a button that started the bubbles. Steam began to rise.

"So, when did they start letting the retarded come here anyway?" I asked.

"Just last year. I guess there was enough of a demand from rich white folks with downsies that they were compelled to build them a whole separate wing. They probably needed to with all those years of inbreeding and cousin fucking. A litter of downies was bound to turn up in one of the generations."

"You know my sister has . . ." Andy just let his sentence die off. We were so damaged, like framing the picture of a car crash, that we couldn't see how we resembled the ghosts of the kids looking at a car crash, while those who lived in driving school took pity on the stupidity of those spoiled kids in the picture as we ignored their breath, focusing only on the position of our corpses, the testimony of our surviving relatives, as we tried to remember if we wore clean underwear that day. I'm still embarrassed when I think of the money spent on selective generational stupidity. It is times like this when I regard recollection to be the equivalent of aiming a gun at a mirror while wearing a blindfold, before calling the ambulance to pick up shards, after recollection fails conveniently as to the owner of the gun.

"Oh, I'm sorry." Ci said, through biting her lip. I'm such a stupid bitch, I'll say anything without thinking. For what it's worth, I'm obviously retarded too." And then a pause lingered before she let the words, she had just said sink in, "Oh shit! Fuck! That's not what I meant either."

Andy cracked a forgiving and glazed smile. "It's alright, let's just get so fucking smashed that I don't remember anything you just said, and then I won't have to remember forgiving you either."

The red color that had risen to her face had begun to fade. She grabbed his face and kissed him. "Thank you. Oh, and Lucien, do you have a charge card? Because Molly isn't going to cut herself. Mirror is in my bag."

Lucien began to work on the drugs as Ci pulled me aside, "What the fuck is going on between you and Andy?"

"I'm sorry, I can't focus right now. You're being really intense."

"Getting fucked up in the middle of the day so you can have sex with strangers is my thing. Who are you these days?"

"My face is tingling and I'm happy. And we didn't fuck, we just made out."

"Oh, my god. But that's great! He's not old enough to be your father, and he's actually gay and available. This is growth."

"No one grows and no one changes. Calm down. We're just hanging out. Don't make this a thing, or I'll make it a thing and freak out."

"But…"

"No, you don't get to interfere on this one."

"Come and get your lines bitches." Lucien called from the hot tub's ledge. He was already three lines in and the water that huddled beneath felt like a warm enveloping hug.

Ci and I came to the edge and stripped naked because we were so used to being naked around each other all the time. It was then we realized we were the only ones who were naked at the time. I had probably seen Ci's vagina more times than I have seen women in my life and that includes their acquaintances and their vaginas. To be fair I had hardly noticed until Andy raised his nose from the mirror with a 50-dollar bill still lodged in his nose.

"I'm sorry for being free and feeling honest." And then Ci and I jumped in the churning pool and stayed under until the bubbles that tickled my face got the better part of my curiosity to see Andy remove his trousers but propriety made me look away and reach for the lines of drugs that laid across the mirror. Before I could regret my decision to turn away the bubbling fizz had swallowed his torso, placing him next to me. As I strived to keep my eyes up, I saw him wander from me to Lucien, undressing. Sitting himself down cross legged, he abstained from going into the water because he didn't want to sweat out the drugs before they could take their effect. He placed the vodka bottle square between his legs and proceeded to roll a spliff.

Ci broke the gay standoff with one of her interjections, "Has anyone noticed how this boob floats higher than this one?"

I could not help but laugh to see each of her breasts fully submerged as one act dependent from the other.

"If I can say so, your breasts look magnificent tonight." It was a compliment I had paid her so often I was almost obligated to say so every time she took off her shirt.

"I don't know what to do with them, but they do make for excellent drink stands or pillows if I ever need them on an airplane or passed out at a bar."

"I can use my dick as a kickstand." Lucien had a habit of finding ways to insert his dick into the conversation.

"Or as a gag, I hope, for yourself." I said hoping to crush his attempt at showing off.

"That's usually something my dates offer to do for me."

I wasn't sure if it was the drugs, steam, or combination of all the elements around me, but before long, I began to feel sick to my stomach. "I think I need to get out of here for a second, I feel sick."

"I can go with you." Andy said.

"If you want. I need a cigarette to calm my stomach." I grabbed one of the robes that lined the hallway and took the exit to the right that led to a side door and then to a stairwell.

"I wonder if this leads to where I hope it does."

"Where," Andy called out to me, "hold on, let me tie my robe."

Andy took off after me while I raced for the top of the stairs, all while feeling like I was climbing to the sky. My heart racing, I burst forth with my eyes wide to the twinkling sky, taking in the whole universe, I somehow felt lighter than I had before. If I swallowed a star it might fill me and carry me off into a solar system where everything would feel different. Andy walked up behind me with a lighter ready to light me.

"Beautiful, isn't it?"

"I feel full. It is a wonder to look up and think when we look out, does anything or anyone look back?"

"Fuck, I think I'm rolling."

"Yeah I'd do anything for a stick of gum right now."

I turned around to him and said, "I just wanted to let you know, I had an amazing day."

"So, did I. Glad I could steal you away for an afternoon."

"I barely put up a fight."

"But then, perhaps, we should continue from where we let off earlier." He moved toward me, and I could feel his sense of urgency growing from underneath his robe.

"I don't think we should try anything while we're on this."

"But it makes it feel so good."

"I'm leaving tomorrow and I have so much that needs to be done."

"What do you mean?" He asked.

"Well, I'll be in college soon and I want to start my new life free of burden. I don't want to be a lamb going into a lion's den." He put his hand around the back of my head and looked me in the eye, "You can't tell them. Go to school. Start your life. And then do it on your own terms, on your own time."

"Is that what you plan to do?"

"I like my life and I love my parents. But there are certain things we have to give up on being happy." To me, happiness is the same as living.

"Even if that thing you're giving up is what can make you happy?"

"Who says if that's the price?"

"When we were out there today I saw my life like it was one of the many I have lived before. In this life, I felt I was born to live the life of the one who loved but couldn't and perished in the conflagration created from his own circumstances."

"Why then go home?"

It sounds crazy, "I feel as though there is a price yet to be paid. I'm afraid I must carry this cross so that what was undone could be put into effect now."

"Well then I'm sorry. I'm sorry I ever gave you this shit in the first place. Fuck man, people see purple dragons when they're on this shit and that doesn't make them one. You get a little high and now you're a fucking zealot."

"It's not the drugs. They just confirmed what I already knew."

"But you don't have to."

"I do. And then I'll come back, and you'll be here."

Leaning toward his lips I whispered, "And we will have the stars."

"God, you are tripping so hard right now."

"I guess so, because I just used a cliché and I don't even care."

We kissed and it fell upwards into the sky, lost in that moment before it all fell apart.

When I arrived home my Dad was absent, nevertheless the house was decorated to the rafters in silver and gold for me when I arrived. Mother was in the kitchen making three kinds of pie in her usual fashion of perfection and sweat. I came in and kissed her lightly so as to not steer her from her task and went upstairs. I made a point not to call upon or see Lucien. I couldn't afford any temptations or distractions. I knew he would try to stop me, and I couldn't stand to deal with his criticism he might try and lead me astray from my feelings for Andy. It was for him and myself that I was doing this for. That's what I told myself.

Sitting in my room I found myself growing restless and thought I might call Andy so that I might feel assured in myself. His voice alone could calm me; it was that sort of unwavering strength that he procured through his calm demeanor. The phone rang and rang. The second time as well as the third.

I wandered down the hall to the room of my younger sister Ashlyn who never asked for anything beyond her needs despite being the youngest of the family.

"What's up, love bug? I'm home."

"You can't come in. There's work to be done."

"Still working on that collage of artificial intelligence I see." I was remarking upon the strewn pictures of various male celebrity crushes.

"You think you're so funny but one day, one of these guys is going to happen." She exclaimed with a fiery conviction, holding up a picture of James Dean.

"I don't think he's happening. He's pretty unavailable as far as I know, being dead and all."

"He's just an archetype obviously."

"Using literary devices to sexualize the opposite sex. Private school becomes you. How's mom?"

She turned her head and then back down toward her collage on the floor. "I can't stand her. She cries all the time, but because I'm the only one home. She has to come and talk to me, but it's too much."

"She's doing her best, you know."

Looking up at the ceiling I could tell her eyes were beginning to well up. "I know that, but I'm just so tired. She should know that it affects me too. You weren't here, but Dad came home for a little bit and everything was fine. And then, just like Jekyll and Hyde, he's turned and gone, then mom falls apart. And Lauren is no help. She's just like him. She has art school; her art friends and she just runs. And…and it's not fair." The angling of her head could no longer keep the tears that began to flow down the side of her cheeks. "Maybe I wanna disappear too! But just when I get a second to myself, mom comes into my room, sits on my bed and cries. This is my room! It's the only place where I can be safe and alone."

"Oh, sweetie I know. And you've been so brave to hold down the fort while I'm gone. Holding her close to me I let her have a cry as I ran my fingers through her thick ebony locks that she got from my father's side, so different from my own. It was nuances like this that made me feel the split of separation of my family physically, when I looked at them and when I closed my eyes to think about them. "Would it help if I gave you one of your stocking stuffers early?"

She pouted up her lips and responded with a coy and quiet, "Yes." Aware of her need to appear cute.

"Okay. Wait here." I came back into the room to see a smile break her face. It warmed my heart to think I still had the power to do that for my little sister. I entered with my hands behind my back before bringing them out for a final "ta-da."

"Oh, it's pretty! What is it?" She paused between her excitement and confusion.

"It's a sign that says, 'Princess's Room' because, well… you are and then this part says, 'Princess is AWAY' and you can rotate it to say, 'DOING NAILS, SLEEPING IN TOWER, SHOPPING WITH HER PRINCE' and…well it's fucking pink so here you go! Oh, and here's the string of pink pears it comes with so you can hang it on your door, and it may even deter mom from coming in for a while."

"You're the best brother!" She laughed and wiped away her attempt at doing eyeliner and then we both started laughing because she looked like John Wayne from *"The Longest Day"* or a pirate. I couldn't decide which, so I just kept laughing.

"Yeah, well every time I go downstairs Mom tells me I look like a street walker, so I just keep piling it on to piss her off."

I looked at her as my laugh began to subside. "Now, when did you get that cynical?"

"It's in our blood Antony and was bound to happen. Anyway, I feel better now."

"I'm glad Shmaboobs."

"You're the Shmaboob!" I laugh to this day thinking about it now because I have no idea what that word means. It was our word and we made it up. That's all I know. "So how long are you here before you leave me again? You know mom is going to cry all through Christmas. I don't think I can make it through without you."

"Well that all depends I guess."

"On what?"

"I have to talk with mom about something."

"What? School? You can tell me. Mom did tell me you got a perfect score on your SAT's but that's about all I know. But we all know you're so freaking smart. Jesus Christ, compared to you I must be an idiot."

"No you're not."

"No. I am. I think reading is stupid, but I admit I must not be that stupid if I realize that's a stupid thing to say."

"It disturbs me that what you said makes sense."

"Anyway, what do you want to tell her?"

"I don't think I should tell you. I love you but the timing isn't right."

"Oh, my God are you dying?"

"No. It feels like it though."

"You can tell me anything. I won't tell. And besides, you can practice on me and say what you want to say to see how it sounds out loud."

"And you said you weren't smart."

"I, like others, have my moments."

"You have to promise not to say anything to anyone."

"Who am I going to tell?"

"Ok…here it goes…I could whisper it to you."

"If you think it would make it easier."

We were sitting on the floor of her bedroom when I leaned over and let the secret fall from my lips like water falls from a pitcher, each drop filled with thousands of molecules of information to send the synapses firing in a million directions. As soon as the full secret was out, Ashlyn pushed me back and slapped me. "That's it? That's the big secret? Fuck! I thought you had cancer. You kept me in suspense for that? Next I'll be sending you a postcard for when I get pregnant at the prom."

"Will you keep your voice down? And this was a big deal," I touched the side of my face that was pounding. "And that hurt!"

"No! No! Climate change is a big deal! Russia is a big deal?"

"I thought you didn't read?"

"I hear things sometimes! And I've been crushing the dating dreams of all my friends for years saying, 'he's intellectually sensitive.' What a bunch of crap! You're such a shmabooby!"

"I guess I should thank you for taking this…well?"

"I never got what they saw in you. I just told them I thought you were gay. I guess I was right."

"What? How could you do that?"

"You should be thanking me. I just saved you the trouble of having to tell all those people, who told their friends, who told their siblings, who told their parents that you're gay."

"Holy shit, you're a little cock sucker." Lauren sounded it out like a holiday greeting as she entered the room.

"I just looked up to the ceiling and wailed, "Oh lord and heavenly father…"

"Yeah, yeah homo be thy name blah blah. Now I owe my friends a bunch of money! Thanks a lot." Lauren turned in a huff and lit one of her pink cigarettes.

"My friends and I have been taking bets on whether you were gay since you were thirteen. And now that it has taken long enough, I'm going to be paying interest. Thanks, ya' little shit."

I had to put an end to this. "Wait! Hold on! If everyone knew then why didn't anyone tell me?"

"Well…" Lauren only searched for a second before she found the answer. "There's Mom."

"And there's Dad." Ashlyn added. "And because we love you."

"Yeah and we couldn't derail the family protégé from discovering the cure for cancer while he was jerking off his schoolmates. I always told mom and dad they shouldn't be wasting all that money on an all-boys school."

"Or maybe you were too busy being the family fuck up for mom and dad to notice," Ashlyn added in my defense.

"My shift has just ended and now apparently, it's his turn to be the family fuck up. If we're lucky, then Ashlyn will get pregnant, and we'll all be one big happy fucked up family."

"Lauren, sometimes you're so disgusting that even a sinner like me is repulsed by you."

"Fuck you!" Lauren screamed.

"Ha! Fuck you!" I could always get Ashlyn reved up despite being the quiet one. "I've read your diary, and it wasn't that interesting. Although the pages were soaked from your panties."

"Fuck you too then!" Lauren hissed trying to assert some long lost older sibling dominance. Don't come crying to me if you need help getting that cherry popped. Better to consult some homo-rabbi and his disciples."

"Okay, can you psychos hold on for a minute. I need to know if you guys think I should tell mom."

"Wait! Back up!" Lauren was now the last remaining influence of law and order. "Is that why you came home? To warm our hearts with an update of where you've been sticking your dick since you went away to boarding school?"

"Well, who am I supposed to tell? I can't very well call Dad and…"

"Ok fuck dad! We know he's not here. Mom is already a wet bag of emotions who, if you were around more, you would already know this is not the update she needs right now. Did you think this was something we were all dying to hear? It's Christmas and if you drop this bomb in the middle of dinner or lighting the tree or if you get a little turned on while fisting your stocking and decide to release this secret into the universe, then I will wreck your world."

"I'm not here? I am one of the reasons Mom is still holding it together because she feels like she did something right. Why don't YOU, just do like you usually do and not be here?!" I felt rather powerful in my pronouncement.

"I'm here now and I'm telling you Mom can't handle this."

"What is it I can't handle?"

"Oh, didn't you hear? Antony is a fucking homo."

Mom took a vacant and expressionless pause before speaking again. "Oh, very fucking cute Lauren. You get another gold star for adding another gray hair to my head. Now all of you come downstairs to eat the dinner I've been slaving over in addition to the Christmas dinner I've been preparing since yesterday."

"They make shit that comes in a can you know." Lauren had to stick that in like a daughter tempting her mother to give up on her weight watchers diet, but our mom had too much resolve built up against Lauren to let a comment like that slide.

"Oh, you would like that, wouldn't you? Then I would never hear the end of 'Remember that one year you served Christmas from a can?' And I've thought about it but I think it would be so much better to cook everything from scratch before inviting your boyfriend to join us so he can see everything that you're not capable of. Now come downstairs!"

After mom left the room, Lauren turned to me, smug with satisfaction that her sick experiment had worked, before leaving the room herself. "Your move." She scoffed.

Ashlyn followed in suit with an appeasing but sorrowful backward glance. I was left to stare at the walls, taking in the ceiling embrace with my eyes closed, hoping it would crash on top of me. The flood of fear began to feed the beast that I could feel growing inside of me until my eyes welled up and I opened my mouth to cry to God, but the talons of the beast shot out from my throat and pulled me inside myself, lost in the dark, where I would not resurface for the next two years, until an angel would appear to save me from the depths of myself.

Some version, unknown to myself, descended to the kitchen table below where I sat and swallowed food that tasted like charcoal and went down like hot ash. The abyss manifesting inside me felt like a rock in my stomach that was giving birth to a black hole. It was like being awoken from a lie, that my body was not my own. I had disappeared and became trapped in some small corner of myself, unable to break free, completely unreachable and totally alone. I became distracted from my despair when my mother asked me if I was alright. With eyes so heavy, I looked up from my plate and asked to be excused. I didn't wait for her permission and instead just left.

"Where are you going?" She hollered.

"To call Lucien!" But I didn't. I went upstairs and found an old Winnie the Pooh Bear my grandfather had bought my mother at Disney World when she was barely old enough to hold him. He was missing an eye but then the whole world seemed to be suffering from blindness lately so for a stuffed bear he was well ahead of his peers. I pressed my face into his matted fur and cried. I don't know why. Perhaps for myself, but everything seemed to be moving too slow to matter.

Instead, I drifted into a sleep hoping that I would sleep through Christmas and wake up in my dorm at school where things made sense. Literature, Logic and Latin would all the be the same and life would go on as it had, quietly amongst the shadows. A small light made its way into my thoughts and a vague hope that was Andy, made me curl around my bear tighter. As long as he knew who I truly was then that was all that mattered. I hugged that bear like I had found my scared self in that one-hundred-acre wood. I held it tighter and told it everything was going to be alright as we drifted into a deep sleep.

Christmas came with no anticipation, only in preparation, as everyone practiced their best smile, pretending as if father wasn't missing. He had made a career out of ruining holidays when he was around, so why should they be ruined by his absence? The only thing that made it unbearable was the pain in mother's eyes and what made it even worse was the fact that she cared. The only joy she got was from her children, watching their smile from opening the few presents she had managed to stow away under the tree. The satisfaction it gave her to see us happy quickly absolved me of any notion that I might wipe away that smile by confessing to her the truth, that would ruin the planned-out world that she pretended to live in. And so, for the duration of the day, I remained a quiet, good son, while throwing myself into drink and mixed conversations between my sisters and their boyfriends. I think it comforted my mother having other men, besides me, around the house.

The ceiling swelled with heat as the good wine ran out and the shitty wine began to empty from the pantry by the gallon. Perhaps it was the mixing of the two that made me uneasy and drove me away upstairs until I found myself in the attic, staring down from the window I had looked out from all those years ago before the crime was committed. My eyes broke away from the picturesque scene taking place outside the window to that spot on the floor where it had happened. In a way, I felt comforted knowing that day would remain locked away up here, without the possibility of parole until my inheritance bid me the right to burn it to oblivion. For me, at that time, I looked at that room as, "this is the place it happened, and this is where it stays." But it stays, nevertheless and never goes away. Like Satan, you could chain him in hell for 10,000 years but in hell he remains unfettered. A lesson to us all that evil doesn't die, it just changes shape, goes somewhere else but is somewhere; in your memory, in your house, in your mind. You can't kill it. Just minimize its presence. Then it occurred to me in my pondering, that I came upon quite a disturbing conclusion. I wondered, "in what form of evil does the homosexual preside?" The perspective over whether it was or not was a split vote amongst society. So where does it go when one member inflicts their self-hatred upon an innocent one? Evil as it were can't be killed, only alter form, so through what form does evil take after the exchange of violence? Through what capacity does it survive in the host of violence who gives it to his victim? The conclusion I reached was, "incurable illness."

Mother's creaking up the stairs encroached my thoughts of terminal illness along with the smell of something sweet that was traveling from the two mugs she carried before handing one to me. "Why'd you run up here?" She asked.

"This has always been my favorite spot." I said.

"I know but you're missing out on all the fun. I wanted this to be a special Christmas. Your last one here before you go off to college." The way she smiled. She was so sad and beautiful.

"Mom, you can't cry to me every time you talk to me. It becomes too much." I said while touching her hand.

"What? I've been good all day, haven't I?"

"Yes Mom. Christmas was amazing this year. Truly. All because of you."

"Really, Antony? I tried."

"Mom. You're crying again."

"Shit! I'm sorry I'm such a mess."

"I guess there's no question we are related then." I jested, trying to make her laugh. She let out a faint chuckle like she was trying to keep air from escaping her lungs, "I suppose you're right. Anyway, why would you say that? Is everything alright at school? You've been off color since you got home, and I don't want to send you back in disrepair. You know you're the only hope your father and I have for our children becoming something someday. Lauren has art and boys. Ashlyn has…boys. She has great kindness too, but you are the one with that spark of brilliance I saw when they put you in our arms. And I don't want anything your father and I go through to take away from that. I just want you to go out there and kick ass at something."

"Thanks Mom." I drank from the cup and smiled.

"And there's nothing you want to tell me? I will try and support you in any way I can."

"I'm fine. I just want my life to start already, yah know?"

"I know you've always been older than most people your own age but that also means it's been a while, now you just have to drive forward."

"Older. Blessing and curse. Go downstairs and I'll be there in a sec to watch the Christmas tree with you.

"Alright. I love you."

"Love you too." As I saw her disappear downstairs, I could see the ice forming outside my window like the encroachment of something inexplicable on my heart, like ice forming in the fissures of my soul. I pictured myself returning to school like Napoleon fleeing from a Russian winter, cold and defeated. Cowardice is much like black ice the way it forms invisibly over the cracks of surfaces before shattering under pressure. All was beginning to feel hopeless as the snow fell around me, the night drew to a close.

"The Preparation Overcorrection," was implemented when we were old enough to be bad but not old enough to be tried as adults. Lucien and I were preparing to wreak havoc upon New Years as we had always done. I usually left the planning up to him and as he always knew where to go and once we were there, I was the one with the shit stick stirring the shit pot, trying to get us thrown in jail, betrayed by my unconscious mind. I found within the narrow straits of our planning, the time to call Ci and find out what her plans of self-deprecation entailed. She had no intention of letting any resolutions fall on the virgin steps of the New Year. In her mind, all decisions made were reparations for the dull existence she must have led in her past life, which must have been a very dull one indeed.

"How many people are you going with?"

"So far, about seven girls. Only about three of whom I can corrupt effectively."

"Is that with or without sex?"

"If you're talking sex then I will corrupt you two indefinitely. But who knows? They say tequila makes the heart grow fonder… or is it gayer?" "I don't think that's how that works." I laughed.

"I don't think that's how that works." I laughed.

"Well assuming there's a few dolls thrown into the mix, a little peyote then yeah, that is how that works."

"Not feeling men lately?" I asked. "It's an all-girls school. Not many men to feel around here. And I can't do professors. Then I have to play teacher to the teacher, and it defeats the purpose of a good release."

"So… you're going out as a lesbian tonight? Letting the big bad plaid monster out of its cage?"

"That is a horrible stereotype, and that's not just because I'm wearing plaid right now. Plaid tunic with boobs up and out. No panties."

"Do they let you in places dressed like that?"

"I think they assume only an obscenely dressed celebrity would show up like that so they don't even bother."

"How convenient for you."

"What about you?" She asked.

"Gonna ring in the New Year with a casual bang and a New Years good morning goodbye?"

"You know I'm seeing Andy, and I wouldn't do that."

"Sorry, I keep mistaking you for me. I'm just now starting to see what a mistake it is. I make a better gay man than you do on your back."

"This may be the one time I don't say anything and I just agree." "So, have you talked to Andy at all?"

"No, he's with his family and I miss him."

"Well break is almost over and then the anxiety of choosing the right college and sorting through all the rejection letters begins."

"Ha-ha thanks a lot."

"I am speaking more about myself. You're the smartest one in our graduating class. You'll be fine."

"In that case, you better start figuring out now whether or not you can get a degree in prostitution."

"I'm pretty sure anything you do well enough can be turned into an art form that you can get a BA in. And if you hear back from NYU I hear you make your own degree and then you can major in sucking dick. You don't have to worry about performance because 'C's' still get you a degree."

"I don't score average on anything." I was trying to regain some priority in the conversation above the performance score.

"Maybe. But I'm pretty sure we already established I'm a better gay man than you."

"I just decided not to argue with you."

"Well, your silence is your consent."

"I don't even remember why I called you."

"Probably because Lucien is not around, and you needed to get your dose of emotional abuse from someone. Or you were missing your boyfriend, so you decided to call your life wife instead."

"We haven't made anything official yet. I was going to ask him when he got back from break."

"If you don't ask him you won't know how he feels."

"That's what I'm afraid of."

"I'm sure you already know how he feels. I think you're just afraid of letting go of your unrequited, never gonna happen, boo thang instead of trading up for something real and tangible. You've never had that before and sometimes it's hard to accept good things when they come into your life. You always seem to be teetering somewhere between okay or sad. Never happy."

"I've gotten close to happiness on psychedelics but anything that challenges my already dismal existence would only elevate me to slightly above average. But yeah, I think you may be right about that. Time to sweep out the cobwebs and make room for good things."

"I'm never sure if I'm right. That's just something my therapist told me once."

"Regardless, I'm going to have to ask him to be sure."

"And if you don't…"

"You said it, 'my silence is my consent.'"

And with a sound as clear and with the same effect as a gunshot, I heard the phone click. "Did you hear that?" I asked Cecilia, full of panic and shortness of breath.

"Yeah, for a second I thought you hung up."

"No."

"Must have been the connection."

"No."

"No, what?" She proclaimed in uncertainty with the intent of a question to calm my ears.

"No. No. NO!"

"What the fuck are you saying?" The sound of pain and panic was starting to rise in Ci's voice.

From my bedroom, I could hear the vibrations of the house tremble with terror as the sound of footsteps echoed from the stairs to the hallway, leading up to my bedroom.

"I have to go." It was synonymous with the acceptance of the Queen of Scots before she lost everything.

"Antony, I need to talk to you." Mother swung open the door wearing the face of a person who had just discovered a body.

"I'm sorry, I have to go." I repeated. My voice cracked as it slipped between registers trying to find footing within a spirit that was attempting to escape from the body of its host. I struggled to find some rehearsed reactions but sometimes there is no preparation for a storm.

"Don't!" Ci pleaded.

I hung up the phone and stared at my mother with the receiver still pressed against my ear. The presence of its' placement was almost as powerful as that of a bridge jumper without a flotation device.

"Please explain to me for the love of God, what I just heard and why you are trying to kill me? I already have to deal with your father and this is supposed to do what for me?"

"I was going to tell you, but I decided to keep it to myself because I didn't want to burden you with this."

"Tell me what? You can't tell me something I know you are not. I just think you're trying to be sneaky so I can't stop you from making the biggest mistake of your life. You just wanted to confide in your little boyfriend while your father and I pay for school which apparently has only taught you how to be perverted and hide it from your parents."

"First of all, Dad pays for school, while you take whatever money he decides to give you for that given week, so Ashlyn doesn't starve."

"What I do, I do for all of us! A sacrifice that clearly isn't working."

"What do you do? What you're not doing is not starting over because you're too afraid too. And what you've done is sold your soul to fill this tomb of a house with pretty things to bury us all alive with you!"

"Do you honestly believe your father is going to pay for school just so you can grow up to be a cock sucking faggot?"

"Fuck you mom! Fuck you! You're obviously obsessed with just the sex. It's all you can hear instead of the words I'm saying because it's been a century since anyone has even touched you."

"Excuse me?" She seemed almost perplexed by the egregious reaction and decided that coupling it with an almost equal offensive response would save me from perpetual sin. "You wanna talk real now? Ok let's talk real. Do you want to have a guy cum in your ass or not? My sex life has nothing to do with that."

I put my hands over my face. "And we are back to the sex. How about this? You are disgusting and I fucking hate you. Why would Dad even want to be with you? You're just a miserable bitch. You're a vile, ugly, jealous, anorexic, miserable bitch. Your bones stick out so far you make me wanna vomit."

"I can't say you make my stomach feel settled."

"Why does it even matter? What has changed about me since you've known? I'm the same person I've always been."

"That's not true! You've been different ever since you've come home."

"Because of this! Because of exactly this! I've been riddled with so much anxiety, scared of what your reaction might be and then you go and prove me right. Way to go! I'm so glad this is the one time you actually followed through with something by being a complete disappointment!"

"Keep being disappointed because you're not leaving this house."

"Like I would even go out looking like this? Have you lost your fucking mind?"

"I'm calling your father." She turned to leave the room.

"Good luck getting a hold of him." She shut the door. "I hate you !!!" I screamed until every piece of my breath had fallen away from my body and my voice cracked. I heard a timid knock on the door but before I could say anything, Ashlyn had come in. "Please" I begged, "Can you please just leave me alone?"

"I'm sorry brother. I love you." She started to close the door to leave the room.

"Wait!"

She stopped. "Come here." I reached for her tiny frame and hugged her.

"Ashlyn. Ashlyn, can I ask you something?"

"Of course," she nodded with tears in her eyes and a forced smile.

"Do you hate me?"

"No! Never." She seemed shocked at first by my question. "No but I'm afraid for you. I think you just made your life twenty times harder than it already was."

"Please help me." I cried with my mouth agape with sorrow and spit falling out.

"I love you and I'm going to pray for you." I knew she meant it sincerely and not in a condescending way.

"Okay. I should make some calls. Will you tell me if you see mom come up again?"

"Yes. I better go. Love you."

"You really fucked up!" Lauren yelled as Ashlyn was coming out of my room.

The first person I thought to call was Lucien, but I called Andy instead because he was probably the only emotionally stable person I had known up to that point.

I called and his mom answered puzzled as to why I was calling on New Year's Eve. She probably thought I was intoxicated. I'm sure I wasn't making sense being so distraught.

Andy answered the phone with a confused "Hello?"

"It's me!" I sputtered.

"Oh, my God. I was so confused when my mom handed me the phone to say some drunk idiot wants to talk to you." And then he laughed a little.

"Oh, Andy, it's all wrong. So terribly, terribly, wrong."

"What's wrong? You didn't talk to your parents, did you? Because if your mom finds out who my mom is and…"

"My fucking God. This may come as a surprise to you, but I'm the one who called you because I'm the one in crisis. I didn't fucking tell her. She overheard me talking to Ci about how much I like you, because I'm a fucking idiot apparently."

"Why would you ever feel the need to talk about me when it's not safe there? That's like Anne Frank playing heavy metal while hiding in the attic!"

"I told you, because I'm a fucking idiot! Maybe if you didn't leave things so open ended before break I wouldn't have had to call Ci with my existential crisis over defining our relationship."

"Your problem is you. You think EVERYTHING is an existential crisis. You were compelled to call Ci from your own insecurities. Not mine."

"Fuck you and fuck you! I'm sorry that I'm so fucked up that I couldn't keep quiet for two weeks because I missed you, and I wanted us to be together when we got back. But you know what? It's fine! Your secret is safe with me, and I'm fucked. All nice and tidy."

"What's going to happen?" I could hear him shaking like a dealer with chips that were weighed down.

"To me or to you? I don't know!" I screamed at the top of my lungs and slammed the phone down before collapsing into a crying heap. I was so disgusted by my own pitiful state. It was like being stuck in the saddest film titled "My Life." It's so hard to try and function as a person of dignity when all you do is cry all the time. It's hard to push out thoughts of death when you live in the shadows. This character I was playing, he was stale and repetitious with no hope for redemption. I thought, "how could anyone stand me long enough to see me through until the ending?" The weight that I had been carrying felt like it had transformed from solid to liquid and was oozing from skin and hardening once it hit the air until I became this motionless, fossilized, sad thing, curled up in a ball on the floor, that was so overcome with grief that my body turned off my brain so that I wouldn't do something I couldn't take back.

CHAPTER SEVEN

Christmas Ghosts And Chains

When the morning came, I awoke feeling as though my body had just returned from another place. I looked at the clock and saw it was noon, so wherever my mind had escaped must have been a journey because I never slept past nine. This is what it must feel like to be Ci, I thought to myself. I walked down the hall and the rooms were empty. I came downstairs and all was just as eerily quiet as it had been upstairs. I came from around the corner of the living room adjacent to the stairs and found, sitting across from one another, my mother and father. At first I was happy, I think my mouth was even open at the sight of seeing my father after it had been so long. From the look being projected from both their faces I forced myself to swallow my breath with my joy and take my respective seat across from them. It felt like the morning of a debate tournament, full of anxiety, the only difference; knowing this was rigged and happy with the result.

"It's good to see you Dad." I said with a smile halfcocked.

"Sit down son." He extended his hand to the spot on the couch beside his, whilst my mother sat in a chair across from us; eyes wide and waiting.

"It's been so long that I can't even remember the last time I saw you." I tried feeding him the words slowly to level the playing field to allow for the guilt of his absence to set in.

"Well, I've been busy, Antony, trying to make money." He bulldozed right over my obstruction. I could tell by the sound of his voice that I was fucked.

"I know Dad. We just miss you during the holidays. Ashlyn especially. She's the youngest. Christmas still matters to her." My second emotional snare trap was sitting in between both of us. If he couldn't feel bad enough for me I could at least appeal to his emotions surrounding his youngest, and a general feeling of abandonment for his other non-gay kids. He still loved them I guess, and he REALLY loved the youngest one. I think he thought, being the youngest, they are the easiest when it comes to forgiveness, but still the easiest to hurt.

"I'm here now." He said. "I'm here because, obviously, I can see how much my absence has affected you developmentally. You're obviously feeling confused and abandoned and so I'm here asking you not to throw your life away over the mistakes I've made."

I took a deep breath.

"Even with the best intentions, there are so many hurtful untruths in what you just said I don't even know where to begin."

"Anton. You are not what you have convinced yourself that you are."

"If I'm in denial then it's obviously an inherited family trait because it truly baffles me to wonder what you must tell yourself to justify abandoning your family."

"I'm here, now aren't I? The mortgage is still paid. You have a roof over your head. You go to private school. The only one out of all your siblings. I bust my hole and mom takes a check and makes sure the house is running and you are all fed. Now I'm here trying to get my ducks in a row, and I'm starting with you."

"First of all, IF, if you manage to remember to send the check because you're off doing god knows what. And then, Mom stresses out as she pulls money out of the bank intended for your retirement. I truly doubt that you, for one second, believe that sending a check is as good as being a present parent. If you do then you're mental, and a check sure isn't going to save anyone from the emotional scars you've inflicted on this family, while you've been off having a five-year long mid-life crisis."

"You're mental if you think I'm going to continue to write a tuition check for my son… MY son, who wants to go to school to be a faggot?"

"Why don't we stop throwing daggers at each other for one second so we can discover exactly what's wrong with YOU, because obviously, everything that has gone wrong with this family has to do with you. So why don't we crack open a nursery rhyme over your childhood and see if we can pinpoint what went wrong. Like actually lay out, what the actual fuck happened? Mom didn't love you enough or Dad loved you a lil' too much? Which is it?

"THWACK!"

The back of my dad's hand went straight across my face, almost sending me over to the back of the couch. I went to get up and he tried to back hand me again but missed. He lunged forward but I was already gone, sprinting from the living room, heading for the stairs. I was halfway up them when my dad pulled me down.

"Get off of me! I hate you! I hate your fucking guts!"

He pulled me up by the hair and slammed me up against the wall to deliver some clear shots to my face and stomach. He connected several times, but his hits were sloppy, and I wasn't making it easy by wriggling so much so I never felt the full force until I saw him come from below with his fist to uppercut me in the jaw. I swung my hands up to deflect the blow and sent my hands smack into my own face, up and into my own nose. I lost it. I began to completely unravel. I had previously deviated my septum back in the seventh grade in woodshop, a place I had no business being in, and when my hand went back up into my nose, the experience of that pain was so intense, I saw my vision turn gray and I felt the blood began to trickle down the front of my shirt. Everything went from gray to black. Some other creature or person burst forth, writhing in pain on the floor with such anger, my father alone could not contain me. I kicked him away, sending him back down the stairs. I picked up one of the vases that lined the stairwell and threw one at him. I missed and then grabbed another and another until there was a pile of porcelain at the foot of the stairs. When I ran out of vases to throw I just stood there screaming like I was vomiting fire from my belly. It was like I was exorcizing my father's connection to me, purging it through the bulging veins of my neck and out my mouth for all the times he failed me and my family. My father stood back in horror at his creation, unable to act as I became unhinged.

"Why? Why?" I screamed. "If you don't want me anymore that's fine. Just leave me alone!"

"You fucking dare embarrass me and your mother after all we've given you." He picked up a vase that sat on an end table at the base of the stairs and whirled it at my head.

"Me! ME! Fuck you! How can you even reconcile your behavior for mine? You sick bastard!"

"Stop it! Stop it! I should have never called you!" Mother wailed as she pulled on Father's arm, trying to move him away from the stairs with the momentum of her little body.

"How did you think this was going to turn out? Did you think we were going to have a fucking bible reading and a spiritual awakening? Sing Kumbaya? What the fuck is wrong with you?"

"You little fucking faggot! Come here!" Father bolted up the stairs after me, as my mother's screams echoed behind him, begging for him to stop. I couldn't believe I was running away from my own father. This brand of fear was alien to me. It was so bizarre that I thought my father might kill me. I ran into the upstairs bathroom and locked the door. He pounded on it relentlessly, threatening to break it down if I didn't open the door. It was even more terrifying knowing he could with ease but some force of fear, perhaps fear of what he might do, was holding him back from doing so. There was a tree and some garland that grew out of the window. I could climb onto it and escape. The only thing that separated me from it was a plate glass window, but I hesitated to break it.

"Please! Please!" I screamed. "Just go away! I'm sorry! Just leave me alone please! I just want to leave!"

"Good! I want you gone! You make me sick!"

"Then just get away from the door and I'll be gone."

"Fine. I'm going."

"No! Mom must lead you away. I'm not opening the door until I hear mom's voice." With my face pressed up against the door I felt like Shelly Duvall in the Shining. I hit the door with my squeezed fists, clenching my eyes trying to imagine how my life had culminated to create this moment of terror, where I was now afraid for my life because of my own family. I tried to track in my head, despite the adrenaline clogging the airwaves of my brain, how I got here, pinned behind a door, waiting for someone to say, "Here's Johnny."

That man was my father and now he is not.

I was his son and now I am no longer.

I was a person who lived in a world where certain things couldn't happen to a person. Like a knife to the stomach, the realization that what was not supposed to happen, I've already felt in spades. This is just another occurrence, cycling to ensure my destruction. Somewhere in the stars I went wrong, and now I was paying for it. This is the turning point where people who incur trauma must decide whether they want to die by their own hand or by their own circumstances. I saw inside my mind's eye an entourage of binge drinking, sex and violence, in a war I would wage with God to try and kill his beloved creation until he would stop using the illusion of my standing corpse to prove the validity of his benevolent existence by virtue of my own endurance. Well damn you! The pillars that I stand upon that house this soul have been battered to their breaking point. No more I say! I'm taking my corpse back and my soul is coming with it. My soul no longer belongs to God! I will show them all how His indestructible miracle is going to come crashing down on their optimism, faith and comfort. Comfort is just a substitute for their discomfort should I choose to stop holding it together. I function so the world doesn't go around feeling obligated to address my problems. Now they can have all the problems. The levees have been broken, the church destroyed, and their temples decimated. I'm no longer a sanctuary to look to for strength.

All of this whirled across my brain in a second and then I was just a face pressed against a door, no longer transcended. I apologize for the rant but if you made it through and you're still reading, then I would probably consider us friends. My thoughts became interrupted by my mother's voice.

"Antony, come out! I'm here. Your father is gone."

"Mom, please don't lie to me. Is he really gone?"

"Yes, please come out."

"Alright…. I…"

"What? What is it?"

I wanted to say I love you, but I held my tongue before turning the latch on the door and we walked down the hall. I began to ask, "What should I…" but my mother cut me off.

"Be quiet and keep walking."

I saw that their bedroom door was closed, and I froze with terror for a moment too long before that door came flying open, his fist landing right across my face and the world turned to black.

CHAPTER EIGHT

Can You Hear My Heart Pound ?

When I woke, I was in my bed like Dorothy returning from Oz. Maybe it had all been a dream. It was that unknowing that it pushed me to rise from my bed and feel a moment of safeness. Then I raised my head and the blood that pulsated to where his blow had struck was pumping to capacity. It had all indeed happened despite the failed efforts of my memory to block him out as the previous attempts marked by failed exasperation

I flew into a panic. This would mark the beginning of my exodus from the life I knew. I had an old champagne blue BMW I got before I went away to school. I could wheel it out of the garage silently and then start it when I was down the driveway. I had a sock with seven hundred bucks tucked away. Anything else could remain in my room as the treasures of a tomb laid to rest since the time of death of my childhood. I crept to the kitchen cork board that held the keys and snuck into the garage through the kitchen's conjoining door. Every creek or step I made felt like a spin on a revolver.

Then there was the opening of the garage door. There was no way to do that quietly. My plan for a quiet get away would have to be a mad dash. I opened the car door of the driver's seat before kneeling to grasp the garage door handle to keep myself from losing precious seconds. The door went up with a roar. All I could hear was a recurring thud that was making me fumble as the percussion of my heart played the overture of certain death echoing in my ears. The key made its way into the ignition and then I saw there was nothing in the tank but fumes. But it was too late. Car was on. Perhaps I could wheel the car to the corner gas station if it died. I put my foot to the floor and shot straight out the street, from the corner of my eye, a man in boxers running for the car he had paid for, as I sped away into the night.

It wasn't until I was far away enough when my body finally stopped tensing and the adrenaline stopped pumping. The cold sweat was gone with the heat and blood traveling back to my face as a quivering of wavering bravery struggled to solidify a place of respect in my mouth. I surrendered my propriety to screaming out to the universe. To a distorted reflection on the windshield, I screamed "WHY? WHY?" and ended with a "Fuck you!" as I wiped tears away. Then I felt a strange euphoria. It was a familiar and distant feeling as if what was happening wasn't my body's chemistry attempting to restore equilibrium to the irreversible mental nuclear fission that was taking place.

Driving towards school I couldn't think about the students that would be there. Too many people, none of whom I wanted to see save one. Perhaps Andy would be there; Ci more than likely. She couldn't stand being home, but New Years for her could sometimes last a week. I thought about stopping several times to call someone but resisted each time. The comfort of driving into the morning served as a soothing metaphor. I was like Apollo rolling out the dawn for the rest of the world hoping to see some clarity through the virgin light of this catastrophe. Despite my lack of sleep, I saw the beautiful city emerge through the skyline, holding up the sun, while bowing in graceful silhouette.

It was just a few more hours before I would hit upstate. Knowing that gave me the strength to continue until I reached school relieved with a smoldering engine. I laughed at the irony and sold it for parts to the school groundskeeper for two hundred dollars. I knew that would piss my parents off. It gave me even more joy to see him driving it around years later.

Walking into my usual building, every step and breath taken felt like it took the strength of ten men. The whole day could be summed up as one giant exhale. Everything familiar seemed like a front, like at any moment the curtains would come up with the foot lights, and the facades of the buildings would fall, and I would find myself surrounded by twenty gestapos ready to shoot me because they knew what I had done. I didn't know what I wanted or what to do, somewhere between the spectrum of sleep and death. There were some early arrivals, familiar and new, but I brushed past them all until it was only Lucien's room and mine. I went to Andy's room first. I changed my mind and decided I didn't want to see my friend who could read my body and mind at once. Then I realized of course Andy wouldn't be here. It was too early, and I was delirious. I leaned my arm up against the door and let my head slam against the closed door. And then a creak and small aperture created by space and light became visible to me. Andy would never leave school without locking his door. The school does a walk through looking for lifted forks, recreational porn and pot but nothing seemed to be disturbed and surely, they would have relocked it. I turned on the light.

"Maybe he stepped out." I thought. "Perhaps even to call me. I wouldn't be there so how would he know where to reach me? I'd have to run into him."

I turned the light and shut the door. I slumped to the floor and thought until I heard a familiar noise. At first I was relieved, it meant Lucien was home, but I had walked in on him too many times that it would be most unsettling to my stomach to do so again with everything that was going on. But then again, I was the one in crisis. I'd seen the dregs he had brought to his room before. I decided I couldn't wait, and he would just have to turn his penis off if necessary if only to give me three minutes of his time.

I walked through the door. They quickly separated. My ears were ringing, and I stumbled down the hall until the white noise stopped.

"Antony!"

"Fuck you Andy!" I flung myself on the bed and buried my face in my pillow only to be pulled up like a turnip.

"What do you want?"

"I don't know. I thought you were supposed to run after people in these types of situations."

"Put on your shirt and button your pants. You look like an idiot." I sobbed wiping away his cloudy image with my hands

"I'm sorry." Andy looked down and fiddled with the defiled hardware of his trousers.

"Nothing to be sorry about, you like me, but you want his cock. It's been that way since he learned how to use it."

"That's not how it…We were alone. I was weak."

"I believe that. No one can resist him. Must be nice for you knowing you're now one of the lucky thousands that have had the same sensational seven minutes of the tour de Lucien."

"What do you want me to say?

"That you're stronger than everyone else, that you're better than everyone else. If I thought there was even the slightest chance of this happening, I would have NEVER pursued you to the point of this inevitability."

I thrust my hand out, gesturing to Lucien who was now standing behind him.

"Look," Lucien said. "I'm sorry this hurts you Anton. I really am. But don't you think you're being a little dramatic over one fuck?"

"If it's just fucking then why not me? Why never me? I'll tell you why, because anyone who would be stupid enough to like you needs to be kept at a safe distance while we fan your stupid ego."

"I didn't fuck you because you're too fucked up. If I fucked you, you'd be begging for it every day, and then comes the day when I refuse you and you'll threaten to hurt yourself or actually do it spare us the suspense."

"That's not true!" I screamed back.

"Ha!" He laughed. "Now who's being dishonest?" Lucien folded his arms across his chest, staring at me, waiting for a retort.

"You're a fucking sociopath. You don't get to turn this on me just because you want to keep me broken, obsessed with killing any chance of me finding happiness."

"You've had a million chances at happiness! This is just one of them. I would throw you a fucking parade until hell freezes over if you made just one of those stick without driving yourself off a cliff."

I turned to Andy. "Well, you obviously agree with him because you haven't said a fucking word."

"I'm sorry I hurt you. You must believe me when I say that. I also think you need some time. I don't think you're ready to be with someone just yet."

I got up from where I sat and hit him across the face as hard as I could. "TIME? I have tons of it. What I don't have is one solitary person in my life that I could ever completely trust!" I just fled from my house after my dad nearly killed me. Why? Because I was trying to not believe what they think is true, that our love is polluted and ill-intentioned and therefore could never work. So, what did I do? I declared my true nature to them before God because what I know to be true nature could not be corrupted by social convention. And then what do you do? You prove them right when you crawl into bed with this oily snake, acting just like the sexual deviants your oppressors think you are because you hide in the dark. Damn you! Damn both of you! You're all cowards! Cowards!"

"Where are you going?" Andy called.

"To find a crypt and close the door behind me." I left to find Ci. When I was at the bottom floor of the dormitory I phoned her hallway hoping she would be there. As soon as I heard her say, "hello" I started to cry.

"Antony, stop it! I can't help you if I can't understand you. You don't have to tell me anything now. Just come over. Can you do that?"

"Yes. Yes, I can. I'll be there in twenty. Will you meet me outside in fifteen?"

"Of course. Just come here straight away and don't do anything stupid alright?"

"Okay. Thank you. Oh, and Ci.."

"Yes?"

"I love you."

"I know." She said, "I love you too." She hung up.

When I got to her dorm she was already outside with a cigarette in hand and one hanging from her lip. She handed me the lit one from her mouth and lit the one for herself in her hand. "Before you say anything just take a drag of this first."

I did. That was not a cigarette. After a huge exhale, I just sat silent.

"Just lay it out for me. However, it comes out, just say what you need to. I can handle it."

It all came pouring out of me like a dam breaking. By the time I got to the end of my saga I felt like it had already happened to someone else.

"But you're here now. You're out of that fucked up house and obviously, Andy wasn't right for you and hopefully now you realize how wrong Lucien always was for you. At least, in that way."

"I'm going to just nod my head because that's all I have the strength for."

"Tomorrow we can go back to your room and rearrange the furniture. It'll make you feel like you're in a new place until you're mentally there."

She looked so sincere I started to laugh. "That's the gayest thing I've ever heard."

"I'm trying to be constructive here."

"Because that's what you do when your life is falling to pieces? Arrange furniture?"

"I'm usually drunk when I do it but it's always interesting to see what I come up with in the morning."

"I suppose we've been here long enough. I hope one day you can come to me when your life hits a bump."

"As soon as it stops heading down hill I'll let you know," she took a drag and held it in.

"Is it possible for us to have these meet ups and not have problems. There's always problems. Most are mine I know but…"

"My dear Antony, your very name is indicative of a life and legacy led by chaos and intrigue. And when they read about you, they'll envy you from beyond the grave."

"Ughhh! I don't even know if we have time to dissect the density of that statement."

"You talked a lot and now you just have to listen. You're an idealist. An idealist with problems. You see things as they should be, but because of all you've gone through, you can't accept things as they are. When things don't go your way, you lose it. You act as though you've already accrued ALL the transgressions a person can in a lifetime, so the universe better just let the rest of its negativity pass over you. But my dear, sweet, brilliant idealist, as brilliant as you are, you're just barely eighteen and have a lot more life to live, with the unavoidable probability that a lot more might happen. Hopefully nothing as terrible as in time past but life and loss are part of a cycle we must accept, or we become stuck. And I love you too much to see you get stuck. And for what cannot be undone, know that I, like many others, love you and will continue with endless amounts of patience to help face whatever you struggle to accept. Why are you smiling?" She asked.

"Because I love you. Because I forgot how smart you are."

"I'm so proud of you." I smiled.

"That almost sounded like a compliment." She stepped out her cigarette and kissed my lips.

"Now let's get you back, drink a bottle of wine and move some furniture."

"Can't we at least wait until after five or when it gets dark, whichever comes first?" I begged.

"Now that's the attitude of a fucking quitter. Alcohol hasn't given up on you so don't give up on it."

"Oh, god forbid! What was I thinking?"

"I saw that eye roll. Don't make me break out the white."

"That's not even funny, not even as a joke."

CHAPTER NINE

Every Second Counts

My hallway was as quiet as when I had first arrived until I turned around the corner to find every peer crowded around my door. The notice posted was the color of blood and read "Account past due. See administration immediately. Any attempt to move into premises before account is brought to date will be regarded as trespassing and will be met with the appropriate administrative or legal action."

I could feel my face becoming the color of the notice.

"See if your key still works Anton." Ci said, trying to sound calm but squeezing my hand at the same time.

"It won't work." Andy said. "I saw the guy when he was changing the locks when he put the notice up."

"Thank you very fucking much." I said through my teeth upon pondering what to do next.

One of the guys said, "What gives Anton? Your old man forget to pay the bill or something? Class starts in three days."

"I'm aware. Quick, what time is it?"

"Almost five." Lucien said.

My face was growing hotter. "And what time do most banks close?"

"Six." Ci whispered to my ear while squeezing my hand harder.

"Ok I have to… Ci, you coming?" I was halfway down the hallway before she started to run after me. She was one of those people who you didn't have to ask; they just knew what you needed when you did.

"What are you going to do?" She asked. We were both out of breath by the time we got to Ci's car.

"I don't know. I'm not even sure what's happening. There's an account that the school automatically withdraws from to pay the tuition. It's either frozen or it could very well be empty. If that's the case then there are separate accounts that I have access to, but I have to act fast, or my father may close those too. And I will not, will not be thrown out of here in my last semester before college God damn it! Now if I remember there are three separate accounts linked to a trust that would cover the last semester, maybe even some spending money left over. After that, I don't know but I'll think about that later."

As we pulled out of the parking lot Ci asked rather innocently, "What about college?"

"For fucks sake! One thing at a time before I have a heart attack."

CHAPTER TEN

The Crash

The account is closed sir."

"Are you sure? You have to be sure." I pleaded while gripping the edge of the merchant's desk.

"I'm looking at the account right now and it was closed this morning by the primary account holder."

"And my trust?" I closed my eyes and cocked my head.

"It's been absorbed and consolidated into the other remaining members of the trust."

I swallowed hard. "And my personal account, what about that?"

"Still open."

"Close it out! All of it."

"Alright sir. When you say all, you mean all? That's five thousand and thirty-two dollars and twenty cents."

"Do it!"

At the next bank, we had to wait. We were seated at five thirty while I stared at the clock hoping to turn time to mummy dust. Even if they took us now it would probably only give us fifteen minutes to get to the next bank. Sitting in front of the merchant, I was growing sweat stains the size of a lake. Until Eric, the Teller, began to answer my inquiry. "Well, you are listed as one of the account holders, but it is customary that we contact both parties of the account before closing when one is not present."

"That's ridiculous, there's no law that dictates that. I'm listed as one of the primaries and should be allowed to do what I please no questions. I'm on a tight timetable and need to resolve this as quickly as possible."

"As I have stated it is mere bank policy. Your father is an important client with a large holding, and we reserve this policy to protect our most valued patrons. You are entitled to the money, but I must notify the other patron first."

"I'm a client too! I should have the same considerations."

"And you would if this scenario was occurring in reverse. Now take your hands off my desk."

As his fingers spun on the rotary I saw how this would end in disaster and scandal. Just as I was thinking how it had all been a waste and I would never see the school year to its end, Ci stuck out her hand on the receiver. "Please don't. You don't know what you're doing."

"If this is going to turn into a police matter. I suggest that you both leave."

"No, you don't understand. I'm Jewish and his father doesn't want us to be married. We are leaving here to start a new life free from prejudice and we need a little money to make our way in the world, or at least give us a chance at happiness. So, do it if you must but please understand you'll be destroying the lives of two young people while only slightly wounding a selfish tyrant blinded by his hatred for me. I can't allow him to punish my Anton any further because of me. Maybe this is our punishment for being lovers in a past life. I don't know but…Please. Please reconsider."

Taking her lead I added, "Just help us. Our lives will already be that much harder as soon as we walk out the front door."

He put down the phone and leaned back in his chair, almost perplexed in a humorous way by the Romeo and Juliet scenario that had been put to him. Then his serious face resumed, signaling to me that we had lost it, and as he walked to the door of his office I knew we were fucked. Instead, he closed the door and proceeded to count out nine thousand dollars. "Be on your way." He said, "I don't want to see either one of you again. Good luck to you both," before motioning his hand towards the door behind us.

"Thank you Mr. Sodarburg! My fiancé and I appreciate it."

"Yes, thank you! Thank you for being so kind to both of us." Too enveloped in her character development she planted one on him before skipping out the office door.

We were gone. Full speed to our last stop. "Oh, my fucking God I can't believe we pulled that off. That was so Tony and Maria."

"You had to take it to the show tunes place, didn't you?" Ci rolled down the window and lit a cigarette. "But I agree. It was brilliant. You're welcome."

"How did you think of it? Jesus Christ that was such a rush. I almost want to do that again"

"I saw his name on the desk head and ran with it."

"And that lovers in past lives bullshit, the way you just inserted that in. Jesus Christ."

Ci looked at me and then back on the road again. "What bullshit?"

I smiled and kissed her hand as we drove the rest of the way without talking.

CHAPTER ELEVEN

They Have Closed All Roads To Switzerland

Wait! Stop! Please stop!"

"I'm sorry but we close at 6." The clerk said, who was locking the door.

"Well, we technically have one minute, and I do apologize but I must insist that you let us in. It's important."

"Come back tomorrow!"

"But we still have time!" I persisted.

"Which according to my watch expired six seconds ago, so if you don't mind."

"No please. Ci show your tits if you have to."

"Show him yours." She snapped back. "Jesus, we are not Tony and Maria."

"Move or I'll call bank security."

"What seems to be the trouble Mr. Shrader. Are you trying to rob a bank instead of becoming the president of one? It's alright Paul. I'll take it from here."

"Whatever you say Mr. Fairfax."

The merchant handed Mr. Fairfax the keys and we walked right in as the bank tower struck six times.

Mr. Fairfax was an old family friend and president of the bank. He was too boisterous for my pleasure but was always well intentioned in an almost naïve way, which was ironic for a man in charge of such a cynical institution. Having him here meant this would either go very well or somewhere in the scope of apocalyptic proportions.

I was explaining my situation as we walked to his office. "I'm so sorry to bother you and your clerk like this. It's just that I'm going abroad, and this is the only moment I've had apart from school that has allowed me to pull some funds before I depart."

"That's quite alright Mr. Shrader. Come on in young lady. Paul I think we're good here. Why don't you finish up and then you can go."

As Mr. Fairfax opened the door for us to pass, Ci unsnapped two buttons on her blouse, turning to the clerk and hissed at him before Mr. Fairfax closed the door.

As Mr. Fairfax pulled out the proper draft papers, he began to ask, "So where in Europe are you going to be stationed before you fly all over the place?"

"Paris." I said, "I do hope to do a little bit of traveling as well."

"Hence why you're here. Tell your parents 'I'm sorry' when you see them. Unfortunately, my job has left me obligated to help you get into trouble."

Ci and I laughed uncomfortably through our teeth.

"How big of a draft do you think you'll need? Is five or seven and a half enough?"

"I'm afraid not. I'm unsure of when I'll be returning to you and making a foreign bank draft would be so tedious. So, for now, I'll say all of it will do, save a hundred, and my father will replenish it in the following week I assure you."

"Well, it's none of my business but, nearly seventeen thousand seems a little steep for just one person."

"I just want to be prepared sir."

"Oh, I see, what's going on here."

"You've lost the ability to write a draft?"

"Ha-ha, you thought you could put one over on me. Is that why the little lady is here. Are gonna sweep this little tart off to Europe for some "deeper studies" just like your father. He was the same way when we were at Harvard business I tell you…"

"The draft Mr. Fairfax."

"Oh, yes well, did he ever tell you the story of when he and I went to Cambridge business school for a convention he and I would go to the pub…."

"Yes, yes and I'll bring her back in one piece. The draft Mr. Fairfax."

"That's me." Ci said. "The old ball and chain."

"See I knew it. Just the same, like your father. Quite a looker she is too. The prettiest ball and chain to come through all day." He rolled his head back and laughed like an impertinent Santa Clause. "Perhaps I can arrange to have you stay with one of my relatives, a cousin, she has a Chateau in Nice, can't cook worth a damn, but quite a property, maybe this little thing can show her a thing or two about being domestic."

I laughed, and then elbowed Ci in the ribs to do the same.

"Marvelous! Well, you can just leave the dates with my secretary, and she'll make all the arrangements, blind as a bat but knows where the numbers are on the phone at least. She used to be a looker which is why I put her out in the front you see Anton, but obviously, that's a lesson in a poor return investment." Turning to Ci, "Just make sure it doesn't happen to you or you'll have to swim back home." He gave a slight sock in the shoulder and Ci sat there with a smile as frozen as a painted porcelain doll. "Now do you want to split some of this up, perhaps a few thousand in travelers' checks?"

"Just cash in a bank sleeve will be fine."

"Now don't take this and spend it all on this little lady in a week. I know how women get the moment they get to Paris."

"I'll make sure to pack a short leash sir."

"That's my boy. Sharpest kid in his class, that's what he is right here. You're quite a lucky young lady. No one plans for early retirement better than a pretty woman." He counted out the cash and handed it over just before adding, "and I want to see you first thing when you get back, me and this little lady are gonna straighten you out partner."

He released the bag and shook my hand until I thought my arm would pop from its socket.

"Don't worry sir, I'll put him back to the books as soon as he gets back."

"Enchante mademoiselle. A pleasure to meet you. Try not to miss him too much when we send him off to university to make a man out of him."

"I'm sure I'll cry in my pillow right before touching myself every night. Meet you by the car sweetheart." Then she stormed out of the room, still with a smile frozen on her face.

I turned red and speechless.

"Are you sure everything is alright with that girl, son?"

"It's a Jewish thing I think. Banks make her horny. Excuse me sir."

If his jaw weren't attached it would have been on the floor, but I was gone before I could find out.

CHAPTER TWELVE

Don't Stop To Count: The Bonnie And Clyde Roadblock

Despite the success of our plunder, the weight of my soul did not subside. After staying the night at Ci's, I went straight to the administration office to dump ten grand and some change on their desk.

"Open my fucking door."

"Excuse me?" The woman at the front desk seemed alarmed like I woke her up from the tedium of her daily reality. She was like a bad story that repeated every generation of a spinster in a floral gingham dress, permed hair, and half-rimmed -bifocal glasses. A woman who sits at home, watching reruns with a bottle of wine as her seven cats struggle to fight off her sexual advances only to succumb to the temptation of catnip she has dangled above her genitals. Some of this could have been speculation but how much really? But there she sat, in the world of administration, placed at that exact moment by time and space to make my life more difficult.

"Well, Master Shrader, first I'm going to have to process this payment and wait for authorization from billing to be submitted to the housing authority who will send someone to unlock your dormitory. This is why we have deadlines for our students to avoid these kinds of situations."

"Ma'am, although you cannot see it, you are standing beneath a deadline. A deadline that will open beneath you and suck you down into the unemployment office. Right now, my Dad and some of the other Dads of this school are probably golfing and having martinis with the Dean as we speak. Do you know why? Because you don't work at a normal school. You work where a bunch of rich fucking entitled brats will go on to be the boss of your brats that you probably pushed out of your body and into public school, that you use as a tax subsidized day care center until they're old enough to join the work force and collect a pension I've set aside for them, from the company I inherited from my golf-playing dad. And people like me don't have the fucking time to deal with people like you, who have been given an eraser tipped size amount of power that some other idiot gave you so that you so that you didn't have to feel like you ruined your life by becoming and overpaid professional pencil sharpener. Now count the cash and give me the fucking key to my door. NOW."

She rose from her chair with a wavering pride, comprised of enough molecules to extend her hand to hand me my key, holding a clenched mouth until I left, which I'm sure ended in waterworks shortly after. And yes, I regret doing that. Ok. I regret it, but bureaucrats always pop up when you need to take a shit, but they give you a form to fill out before you can get toilet paper. It's just the way it goes.

I went to my room to count the money that was supposed to last me until the end of school, that wouldn't pay for the privilege of a week at university. I didn't know what to do. Couldn't go back and had nowhere to move forward. As brains do what they will when overheated, when the exhaustion of running circular arguments with no solutions becomes unbearable, mine let me crash into a scattered whirlwind, with the hope that the settled pieces of uncertainty would make their place toward absolution after a deep sleep.

The next few weeks of school were agonizingly quiet. Wondering whether my dad knew about the money, if I could settle into my classes without fear of being singled out as a pariah. There was a small part of me that hoped I hadn't heard anything because he was taking the time to come around. We always hope our parents will be better than our own uncensored wisdom.

In the middle of legal studies, I was pulled from my class by the Dean's secretary. Walking to his office I wondered why they called us master: "Master Shrader to the Dean's office." What was I master of? What were any of us masters of? Certainly, a falsehood imposed by generations of pathologically high-self-importance to compensate for any of the future generations' shortcomings.

Sitting in the office was a Dean, my parents and a man who introduced himself as Dr. Riley. He was the administrative director and head psychologist of the catholic run mental hospital that resided on the outside of civilization as we knew it.

"So, as the facts present themselves I'm of two minds. First, for the wellbeing of my students, that includes you. And for the wellbeing of this institution's reputation, I believe that if you remain here you are a threat to both. We have gathered here today to ask you to leave with this gentleman, to go to his institution, and upon the successful completion of your rehabilitation and a good rest, we will be more than happy to welcome you with open arms to continue down the path of higher learning as the gift that has been given to you."

"A gift? The irony of being that what I have is some kind of curse that you will rid me of. Tell me doctor, how do you turn a boy into a fag? Certainly in all your experience you have the answers. Is it from an emotionally abusive and distant father? An alcoholic overbearing mother, or perhaps being locked away year after year in this institution, and everywhere you turn there's a penis in your face; do you think that could make you a cocksucker or is it a combination of all three?"

"You're going to regret that." My father said, leaning in towards me. I tensed in my shoulders and neck and retracted from the mere feel of his breath. Mother was just sat there in stony silence.

"Son," said Dr. Riley turning towards me, "I was recommended by a friend of your parents who found themselves in a similar situation and that boy is now a happy, healthy young man. I don't think you realize that the decision you make today will not just affect you but everyone. In my experience trauma inflicted on the mind will adjust behaviorally to deal with the situation. Even though you may be using this lifestyle to reconcile the trauma of your youth, there's no way to foresee the adverse effects of your future."

"With all due respect doctor, but you don't know me. You don't know what I've been through. All you have is conjecture from the guinea pigs; test subjects given to you from feeble minded parents."

"All I can tell you son, like you and the others I've treated, is that the pain you're feeling now is only going to wind up hurting you and your parents."

"The pain you see on my face comes from the sound your voice makes."

"I think it's time that I intervene." The Dean said, "I think you're in need of a reality check of what is at stake. Either you take a leave of absence and leave with Doctor Riley right now or forfeit your tuition and your place at this institution. If you agree to accept the help being offered here today, you will also name the students, who I have learned through my recent investigation, are also involved in this elicit activity. It is my job to preserve the sanctity and safety of this institution."

"I'm sure I know nothing of this activity nor the nature of what you're insinuating."

"It's of the same nature that you find yourself in my office today."

"Just because I'm a certain way doesn't mean I have a running tally in my head of every student that has given each other a blow job. And if I did I wouldn't help you, but I will let you know it's more than you think."

"So, there is more than you?" Dr. Riley said, leaning his head in.

"Put your blades back in their Pilcher. I will help neither of you. I can't believe this god forsaken building is an institution of learning, while you conduct witch hunts amongst the student body for undesirables in the titanium age of learning."

"So, Lucien and Andrew, you've never been inappropriate with any of them?"

"You mean have I seduced any of them? No, I have not." I sat back in amazement.

"I asked if you had been inappropriate. No one mentioned anything about seducing. I want a straight answer. My reputation and the reputation of this institution are on the line. Have you been inappropriate with any of the students at this school?"

In one of my many suspended from body moments, I paused to postulate an answer and its consequences, foreseen and unforeseen. To tell would mean betraying the friends who betrayed me. In truth and in principle I could not live with the idea of helping to persecute those possessing the same nature I was struggling with. If there was ever to be a reconciliation between us it would not come from me having them expelled or sent away to institutions. In that moment, it was clear my time here was over, and the only power I would have would be to defy the system, and the only chance I could give my friends was to leave them undetected with the hopes that one day they would become the men to sit behind the same desk as our oppressors. I turned to the dean and spoke as plainly and as calmly as was possible,

"I cannot give you any names because I have no names to give. I have never seen or participated in any of the behavior you are seeking to eradicate from this school. I have always been a good and hardworking student. Any struggles pertaining to my particular nature have been kept as my own business and mine alone."

"That would be fortunate to hear, presuming you were telling the truth."

"The truth is all I have left."

"Then will you also agree to leave with Dr. Riley today?"

"No, I will not sir."

"And do you realize that by refusing the help being provided to you today I will have no choice but to expel you from this institution for misconduct? All your honors will be rescinded, and you will permanently be barred from coming within one hundred yards of this institution."

"I do sir."

"Antony please! Don't do this to us." Mother gasped

"It speaks."

"You won't get one dime son. Even if you manage to get in somewhere, I will not give you one dime."

"My dear father, knowing that will be my greatest pleasure." I turned to the dean. "Can we get on with the drawing and quartering now?"

"Moving forward, I need your signature here terminating your status here as a student and then here saying you won't come within one hundred yards of campus, or you will be arrested for trespassing. Also, because of your termination for violation of our moral code and misconduct, you are not entitled to any refund from this institution for your tuition. You are entitled to the remainder of your housing fees.

Normally this cashier's check would go to your father but as it seems your signature is on the receipt, I have no choice but relinquish it to you, knowing that these funds may very well go further to aiding you in this lifestyle."

"This may be a moot point, but can you really do that?"

"Take this as your final piece of education. Yes, we can. We are a private institution whose moral code is above those liberal public establishments. Our foundation here is tradition, in which case, you don't have a leg to stand on. You are no longer the responsibility of this school."

My eyes hurt with every ounce of my being as they swelled against the need to cry. I was relieved but at the same time I could feel the weight of everyone's desire to save me from myself. I turned back to look at the empty seat I had risen from. After signing my name, I spoke into that empty space and to no one else. "I know you all think my life will be an enduring waste due to this socially imposed technicality, but I say to you from this moment forward, no weapon forged against me shall prosper."

CHAPTER THIRTEEN

I Have Confidence... And No Money Maria

When I closed the door behind me, I left behind a world familiar and unkind but was stepping into the unknown with a sigh of relief, where not knowing where I might fall next became a comforting thought to me. I, possessing the lowest of all expectations, saw the blank pages ahead as a boundless possibility, a paradox of priceless value lying within the nothingness. For once, I was relieved to be denied the luxury of choosing what path to take. I saw the beginning of a process I had only read about, where people are shaped by the cultivation of experience, which may have led me to believe that the true meaning of experience is what happens to you, not what you choose for yourself. I saw this part of my life as one I would look back to as one of those critical moments, where at the time, I did not see the benefit of what was happening to me until given the gift of being able to look back at the adversity as experience earned.

This is the closest humans get to being like God, and they call it wisdom. Wisdom is the gift God gives you as the body starts to fail and the people you knew to be constant begin to fall like rain. As all humans are endowed, within us, the peoples of the past, so do we carry with us the wisdom of experience, rather the "how to" on how we found light during darkness. As the seers of the youths' future, we can guide them past the sirens and the gorgons they may find along their way down the path of life until they are, one day, resting in their beds waiting to be received into the palm of God for having made it past the trials that could not be sucked out of this version of this world. Laying in His palm I hope to be released into a world that knows no pain, or I shall be resigned to never wake up.

After, could He then bring us back from the world He left us and then smile when we look up with tears and gratitude to say thanks, I've made it. That is my wish for all of you as well as myself. I have no guarantee of this being true, save for what has come from my own mind, yet its own resource could only have been put there by something greater than the organ of my inspiration that interpreted it.

There, from the doors that closed, did a journey begin. It is superfluous to think of one's own struggle as a journey, but I can only write my own as a catharsis, as a letter, to every version of myself that came before me. It serves as a marker for those perpetuated into the next loop as myself who see themselves in my place, see my place as also theirs. If someone can live through something then the possibility of survival becomes that much stronger for the next to do so as well. The many souls of this earth fear annihilation from their counterparts or from unknown places above. But I laugh at these notions because the human condition has been narrated by the power of the known spirit and it has yet to perish under the persistence of fear and destruction.

As soon as I closed the door to my room, a knock came from the other side. Needless to say, it was not an opportunity. It was a failed opportunity. "Hello Lucien. What do you want? I don't have the strength to fight you."

"I heard you were taken out of class today and then someone saw your parents leaving."

"Coincidentally my dear Watson, I too am leaving."

"Are they pulling you out?"

"Better than that Lucifer, they are throwing me out." I was trying to solidify this point by removing the various pinning's on my walls and adding various letters to his name.

"Who? Your parents?"

"No! This institution."

"But they can't do that, I mean you're like one of the smartest guys I know."

"That I'm afraid doesn't matter. I have violated the moral code of this institution and I have a week to leave."

"Well, I can take this up with our professors. They wouldn't stand for it." I've never heard Lucien actually get upset over anything really, but I could hear the anxiety growing in his voice and it was making me emotional.

"I'm afraid they'll have to stand for it. I've been branded with a big "H" across my chest and have been branded a pariah so no one can come near me."

"But there's nothing wrong with you. Half of the guys they make us study were fags.?

"'Are', if you are using the literary sense," I retorted.

"Fuck the literary sense and fuck them. I'm going straight to the Dean's office, and he can expel me too if he wants."

"I'm afraid he most definitely will Oscar Wilde."

"What do you mean?"

"One of the many reasons for my expulsion was that I refused to name those from within our little circle. And while I think it's noble of you to want to stand next to Ester on the platform, I'm afraid you would only be playing into their hands. Better you should leave and then rise up to be counted once you've built your own little empire in some corner of the world. You're better at being gay than I am and always have been."

"Why? Because I fuck? That doesn't mean anything!"

"No Darling," I walked over and held his face in my hands, "Because you can pass," and then kissed his forehead and went back to packing. "You are safe while I've always been too much of one thing and not enough of something else. I mean, that's basically my problem with men. I'm in between everything. Legs that could kill, with an ass that won't quit and the voice of a screaming faggot. I can't be loved because I'm too scary to love. Fun to fuck when the lights are off, but don't like me in the sunlight because I'm the wrench you throw in to destroy the machine of everyone's masculinity."

"I love you Antony." Now Lucien began crying.

I smiled back at him, "Not the way I need to be. My dear, you know what I'm talking about. You're not in love with me. Took me until now to admit it to myself, that I wanted to be like you by being loved by you. But I've seen every man and boy you've ever taken to bed; I will never look like any of them."

"Because you aren't a fucking idiot? You're better. You're not hot, you're not sexy, you're fucking beautiful. You're better looking than most women, but you have a fucking penis so it's intimidating and scary. How does someone even approach that? And then you have to open your fucking mouth and be brilliant. Like how is that fair? If you also had a twelve-inch cock, I'd probably kill myself. I look better when I'm standing next to you because you're interesting. I just don't look like everyone else while I'm standing next to you trying not to be everyone else."

"I appreciate everything you're saying, but you have no idea what a lonely place I live in and now my petty bouts of low self-esteem don't even matter, only survival. How much is that worth in a world of cold concrete and steel?"

"What will you do, Antony?"

"Try to live and try not to die, but it feels like I'm treading on that knife's edge with either possibility."

"God, you talk like a Hegelian Shakespeare. Where, in God's name, did you come from?"

"Down into the belly of the earth from the peoples of the past?"

"You have lifted my life from the pit, though I do not know how I will carry on. I have completely taken advantage of our time and squandered it away on pettiness, jealousy; and anger."

"We learn all lessons with time. It's the only way we appreciate it as a gift the universe gives us to change what we want to, when we want to, while we can."

"I'm going to miss you." My face completely twisted, and my hand was over my mouth. "Please go." I could not keep back the emotion I had kept back behind the wall of anger I had put up against him and now, our time is up. I was terrified. He ran to my side and embraced me. "Oh that," I cried. "I'm so scared. Lucien, I'm terrified."

"Don't cry. Please don't cry." His head rested right on top of mine as he held me tighter.

"Well then, you stop."

"Fuck it! I can't either."

We both had to laugh for a second and then Lucien spoke in a way I hadn't heard before. "You're going to make it. You're not going to let them beat you. You're going to survive and when you're standing on a podium saying something fucking brilliant, I'll be sitting there, thanking God I knew that kid who lived up the block. Until then, I will not see you again but know that every day I love you like the brother I never had." I hated what he was saying, but I knew what he said was true. He was powerless to help me, and I would only cling to him like a crutch if we remained in each other's lives because that's what we had always done. I had to go from him, like when Alice fled from reality to Wonderland to discover what was real for herself between reality and chaos, only to realize that chaos is the order of things. This was the parody on which the universe turned. The uncertainty of one's own annihilation, contingent upon well organized chaos, was comforting because the world might end tomorrow, and I wouldn't have to worry about this shit anyway.

While I was hoping for the planet's destruction, I promised myself while in that dorm that I would try to minimize my worry over my own life, because if the world ends the particles of my consciousness were going to be so pissed that they wasted their time when they could have been fucking Marlon Brando: time didn't matter.

"Well," I said after we separated, "I think I'd better pack."

"Do you need some help?"

"No, I think I should do it by myself."

"Where are you going to put all of it?"

"I rented a little storage space, the one off of River Street next to the corner of Murderville and then I am going to stay with Ci undercover for as long as possible and go from there."

"Alright, well I guess I'll leave you to it. I'll be down the hall if you need anything. You're not gone yet." Lucien let out a small laugh.

"Oh yes of course." There was a pause of silence that was only broken by the last utterance I would ever make to my best friend. "I think it would help end this conversation if you shut the door."

"Right, well, bye Antony."

"Goodbye." This is the thing about final moments. They are the ones we wish we had control over. The ones that we can't change but that we always remember, lending me to believe that perhaps eternity is just infinite final moments that we would lay upon forever until we convince ourselves it happened differently. When you figure out the order, let me know.

When I left the school, I went straight to Ci's. I think this was a decision which showed my lack of years more than anything. We were doomed from the start and if I had actually thought about securing some kind of future for myself, then I wouldn't have gone where I was sure to be homeless again, which is where I would be within three-week's time. How do you ask? Well, after a slew of endless drinking and partying, now being devoid of all adult responsibility, the drinking and partying escalated to a fantastically staged break-in that involved a school flag, ripped tights, scaling walls and broken glass and straight into her Resident Adviser's bedroom. And all because Ci forgot her key and we were too wasted to realize we had broken into the wrong room. That was the end of my stay with her.

She was sad to see me go but then I think she somehow blamed me, like I had fueled the drinking that kept her away from the source of happiness that kept her sane, but I never told her so.

I told her I would contact her as soon as I found some kind of permanent residence, a promise I failed to keep. When a person is desperate, you make yourself think it will be for the best even though all the reasons are wrong. After several inhales and exhales and a few phone calls, I found the man I was looking for and met him at his front door at one in the morning with a cigarette clenched in my teeth. At first I think I scared him, but then he smiled when he recognized who I was.

"Hello cousin."

"Hello," I said.

"Long time since we last danced together."

"That it has." I said in arrogance. He walked up to the steps of his apartment like he hadn't seen me, turned the key, walked through the door and then stopped and leaned back on the handles with his body half-cocked and said, "Coming up?"

And up I went repeating the lines of the inferno in my head as the inferno grew hotter in my mind, "Abandon all hope ye, who enter."

The next day I woke up in a kind of daze, not recognizing at first the room that I was in or why I was there. The soreness brought reality back. I pulled the covers over my head and tried picturing myself calmly explaining to a police officer how I'm not fucking my cousin. As humans, we are often forced to reconcile what is nature and what is not. Murder happens in nature and humans have decided that we are above that, so we make it illegal. Homosexuality, also found within nature but banned by the fraternity of men. Fucking your cousin, probably happens in nature and was once okay, but now frowned upon but knowing we are men of conscience, canceled out my justification.

My nature told me that what we did was wrong, but was it because he was my cousin or because he raped me and if he raped me then why was I here? It seems like every path down the "road of homosexuality" as my educators and doctors would call it, I took, seemed to lead me to more perverse and deviant behavior. But that was me, those were my choices and being gay had nothing to do with it, but there was always this hanging question with everything I did which was, "If I weren't gay, would this be happening?" The scary conclusion was that you were never really sure. Maybe and maybe not. More so in certain instances and less than in others. I've read many books and in none of them did the girl ever go back to her rapist, not before killing him anyway.

Then I thought of, "Gone With The Wind," and put logic on pause just because life imitates art, doesn't make it so. A victim needs sympathy and if you're with the person who traumatized you then the trauma must not be that traumatic. Yourself as well as others could come to that same conclusion and then it occurred to me Tess. Tess of D'urberville married her rapist to save herself from poverty and couldn't live up to him or herself so painted the ceiling with brains. Brava! My future has an ending I could live with.

Looking around this palatial apartment I struggled to figure out what it was my cousin did. The apartment was of substantial size and remarkably clean. I wrapped a sheet around me and went to the door. Outside was a stark black and white interior fitted in covered red light fixtures. There was an ashtray on every table and a pile of cocaine on the coffee table, designated for high tea and entertaining. The kitchen was atrocious, but clearly suffering from sustained partying from the night before. I was startled when the refrigerator closed, and my naked cousin appeared standing behind it as he finished the last drop of milk out of the carton.

"Good afternoon Star-shine." He said, "you obviously slept well. I didn't want to wake you."

"Oh, pay no mind to me. I'm not even sure if I'll be staying here much longer."

"Nonsense. I would say from the size of your bag you're going to be here for a while."

"That's putting you through too much trouble."

"Not at all. You'll stay in my room. Maid comes every Thursday so this will all be gone by the afternoon. Just bag the drugs in the living room before two o'clock. Make sure this girl doesn't disturb the backroom. She's new."

"What's there?"

"That's where all the magic happens."

"I thought that was the bedroom." It was a stupid joke but what else was I gonna say?

"No, that's where I shoot my load before I fall asleep."

"And if you have someone there with you?"

"Makes no difference, I suppose."

"I see."

"Well, I have to be out of here in a few so make yourself at home."

"I really appreciate that Frank."

"It's what you do for family, isn't it?"

"I'm not sure what family is supposed to do anymore." I had to look away. I couldn't look at him.

"Family does what feels right." He lit the cigarette he had behind his ear.

"Ha ha, well you'd know all about that." I turned bright red. He made me so nervous I didn't know if I picked a scab or started a fight. He moved toward me and started to raise his hand and I closed my eyes preparing for a blow. Instead, he brushed my cheek softly with his hand before squeezing it then laughing.

"You turned out to be a funny kid," he said with a deep inhale.

"I didn't know I had it in me either."

"I'm going to shower. Take it easy today."

I stayed in the apartment until the maid came which in itself was an odd experience. She knocked and that was fine. I assumed she didn't have a key yet upon which I apologized for not having one to give to her, but she corrected me and said she in fact did have one. I asked, "Then why did you knock?"

"I was told to."

"By whom?" I persisted.

"The other maids I work with."

"Oh, well next time it would probably be fine if you used your key."

"Mr. Frank still lives here?" she asked.

"Yes."

"Then I'd rather just knock."

I smiled and stepped inside.

She tackled the kitchen and then the living room, sweeping away any little flecks of cocaine she came across. Before heading to the bedroom, I called out and said, "Remember not to go into the backroom."

She came back into the kitchen where I was sitting, reading the paper enjoying a cup of coffee and walked right up to the table, just to say, "I Know!" And then she walked away

I thought, "What was the point of that?" It's like she was letting me know "I know what you know so don't try to tell me what to do." Except I didn't know anything, which made me wonder what the hell was going on back there? I couldn't look while she was here but started to rule out looking. I was just trying to stay here until I could flee. For now, I would put it out of my head.

When Frank got home he was grinning with a certain delight that made me nervous. He said, "Get dressed, we're going out."

"What are we celebrating?"

"I just closed one of the biggest deals of my life and I want you to meet my friends."

"Friends? I don't even know what you do."

"When you introduce yourself just say you're one of my business associates."

"You're very confusing. I don't want to think of you as anything but…"

"Take a dime." He held out a bullet and pressed it under my nose and like a reflex, up it went.

"I see you've been learning a lot in school, you didn't even cough."

"It's a prep school." Then he kissed me passionately and slowly, resting his forehead against mine, our eyes locked.

"Take another." I did, and he kissed me again.

"I think you're crazy," I said as I wiped my nose.

"I've missed you. Can't I miss you?"

"If you can help it I suppose."

"Get dressed and let's go."

"Alright."

"Want another?"

"No, I'm fine." I said walking to the bedroom.

From the hallway he called, "So I see the maid was here. How was that?"

"She cleaned and left. How was she supposed to be?"

"Just like that I suppose."

"She was a little jumpy at first."

"They all are," he said.

"It seems as though you've developed quite a reputation with these people."

"Oh, I'm sure they've seen things they can't imagine. It's because of where they come from."

"Nothing surprises me anymore." I came out of the bedroom, and he lit my cigarette.

"All black?" he asked.

"Always prepared for my funeral," I relit the tip of my cigarette.

"That's grim. I like it," his smile was unsettling.

"Let's take off then."

"I'll lead the way," leaving the tomb behind us, I felt relief.

CHAPTER FOURTEEN

The Night Crawl

I crawled out of the car after the coke, drinking and violent fingering I received on the ride over. I didn't want to continue with the evening, but I didn't have a choice. If I did, I would have missed it. We arrived in front of nothing. An abandoned building with broken windows. However, this was not my first rodeo and while I hate clichés, I can't think of a better way to say that. Parties like this always look like nothing on the outside to conceal the music, drugs and prostitution that was likely to be taking place inside. Like I anticipated, around the back we went and appeared a doorman in a latex suit who was hesitant in his movements at first but acknowledged that he knew Frank. We went down a red velvet hallway. The walls were all black and teak wood and the center of the club opened like the colosseum that showcased several private rooms hidden behind glass beaded curtains. The music was low, filtering a heavy base that drew everyone inside, moving like they were floating in outer space, only changing course if just for another drink or accidental bump by a passerby.

"What are we doing here?" I asked Frank.

"Business and pleasure." He said.

"Where is the pleasure?"

"Pick a curtain."

I laughed. I'm not sure why. Perhaps I was nervous. It was becoming increasingly clear to my conscience that I tricked myself into believing that I was a hardened, seasoned person, who had seen it all. Clearly, I hadn't, but I was too far down the rabbit hole to admit it and too scared to turn back. Now I realize these are the feelings that you listen to when you need to get the fuck out. Yet, by the same mechanism they are the ones that keep a deer in the middle of the dark road when the car approaches. So is it that the vehicle of history that we are misled to stand in the road and receive the lessons of youth that are tiresome at best? They feed upon the soul and your denial of them accrues interest that makes you old. At my age, I try to avoid standing in the road when my legs tell me to run, and my heart is frozen painted upon the fresco of an unavoidable iceberg.

I chose the pink crystal curtain in front of me. Frank smiles, someone just repeated the beginning to an old joke that he knew the punchline to. I turned to him and asked, "Was that the wrong choice?"

"I guess it depends on your preference: The aesthetic of the drapery or the preference behind the choice of color denotes the flavor of one's own interests."

I thought to myself, "Well, what the fuck does that mean?" but it was too late, and we were in my misguided selection. We all sat in a circle. It was a group of older men with large rings, Frank and me. Their eyes were throwing longing glances at me, confused and perhaps turned on if they knew I had something to gain from my own appearance. I was without a doubt an odd duck at their gathering. There was a small stage that sat in the center of the ring of men, resembling producers crossing their fingers before the announcement of Best Picture. We were like the fellowship of the masochist waiting to get our testicles flogged before swearing our lives to the sacredness of unlimited credit among broken millionaires. That was just one possibility that crossed my mind when we sat down in this mini-fetish-theater. The lights dimmed ever so slightly to reveal a person standing from behind the beaded curtains. I almost fainted and let out a huge gasp that brought the entirety of the performances to a halt. This black studded latex head with tits and black goggles cocked her head maniacally and made her way towards me, grabbed my hands and made me feel her tits. Up and down, she moved them until her nipples were hard, along with her penis. I was sweating. She unzipped the back of her latex cap and black luscious curls fell out. She kissed me and then stepped back to the center. Then Frank threw a one-hundred-dollar bill on the stage. She proceeded to take her underwear off and stroke her sizable penis. I had never seen anything like that. I struggled to not be judgmental while maintaining curiosity and trying to look entertained and not horrified. Right before she was going to finish herself in a flood not seen since the old testament, Frank pulled me by the shoulder, and we left. We went behind the yellow beaded curtain across from where we were before, to sit down and talk with a black guy in tiny sharp-shaped-rose colored glasses, while two girls peed on each other. I have never been so disgusted. I'm sure there was someone in the room who enjoyed the sensations. As if witnessing the depravity paid for by their own lineage, was a right to be observed by the patrons of a dying family name given to a handful of mediocrity.. By the time I had my fill of the urine-soaked women procured by the members of this false church, I turned my ears to Frank's conversation. They were arguing over the gross percentage of a product's distribution, of whose nature, I wasn't entirely sure. Frank wrestled and won ten percent in the promise of more to come.

I was confused but stared ahead above the heads of the girls. It was about that time, when I saw urine start to drip down the stage, that Frank pulled me up and we left.

"I'm sorry," I said, "Fun as this all has been, can I please have a drink? I'm not drunk enough for this."

"Order from him." He said pointing over my shoulder.

I screamed and jumped back from the kinky chained, latex waiter.

"Does anyone here work with a face?"

"You want something sir?"

"Oh, thick Brooklynn? OH well you're not so scary then. I'll have a vodka double." He bowed in silence and walked away. The masked man came back in a few seconds, drink in hand to which I replied, "Thank you. That was fast. Hey, hold on, this is gin."

"Ha ha, I think he likes you Antony."

"Ugh I hate…oh as long as I'm drunk, what's the difference?"

"Come behind here. Something we can both enjoy." He led me with his hand against my back to the ruby-red curtain, but the performance hadn't commenced. Two men appeared in latex masks, something which was getting really old for me at this point in the evening. They took off their latex underwear. All of their body parts matched in size and proportion, so I felt a twinge of anticipation to see the two fat guys get it on. First it started off casual. The taller one unzipped the mouth of the submissive and put his cock in. I noticed his mask was different from his submissive. He had this oxygen apparatus, like a gas mask, but the other had his latex mask totally unzipped on his face. I found this distinction created the potential for a performance that was making me nervous, but I looked on. There was a table, and the executioner laid a zipper-latex headed man's face down and strapped him to this table resembling a scaffold. Then there was the unraveling of this leather "tool kit" shall we say. Some of these things looked like penises and some of them were household objects and others were like ancient inquisition devices. The various dildo insertions produced the expected moans of ecstasy from the audience. It was even a bit enjoyable. It was something people like to fantasize about and practice themselves. But then everything changed. The corpse began to writhe in pain. "Why would anyone let someone put themselves through that?" I thought to myself. And then my brain had to check itself, draw from its own experiences and exit from its own recording of the act itself. The combination of my guilt, that disgusting display, the screams and the smell, I grew ill. I wanted to run. I wanted to vomit. I turned and Frank grabbed me. "Stay." He said.

I was too afraid to move, and I sat and watched like a medical student at the dissection of a Cadaver retrieved from the stocks. I became angry. What was I afraid of? I wasn't a child. We were adults. Adults with our own issues, but adults, nonetheless. "I'm disgusted with all of this." I shirked my arm out from under his hand and went through the glass beads during mid-intercourse. Past the masks, the facades and the red, I was outside. The first rush of cold air hit my lungs and suddenly I remembered I was alive. Places like that were designed to make you forget so you would never leave.

"What the fuck are you doing?" said the voice from behind me.

"I'm sorry. I couldn't be there anymore. It's vile. How can you stand it?"

"I thought you'd like it." Frank reached for my cheek.

"Stop it," I spit. "Why are you trying to scare me? You frighten me!"

"Why would you say it like that?" he stepped toward me.

"Get back! Why are you smiling? Why is it funny to you? Are you trying to gaslight me?"

"No."

"What's wrong with you?" I screamed.

"I don't know, but I'm terrified, like I'm not really seeing you, only in the shadows." He pulled out a cigarette.

"I don't like when you look at me like that," I said.

"But you like when I touch you like this." His cheek graced my hand.

"And yet I hate it when you do."

"Let's go. Perhaps tonight was too much for you. Alright?" I could hear the impatience growing in his voice. "Come on, let's go. Business is done here anyway." He began to walk away as a sign I was supposed to follow.

"What business?" I called from behind him, unable to move.

"Lemonade stand." He continued to the car and didn't stop.

I followed. To hate and to love and to love what you hate and to hate yourself for loving it. There were fumes within me that I could feel mixing inside like a chemical reaction. The hatred and confusion of my youth and my wounded adolescent self was willing to love wherever its soul could find it, having leaned upon the memory of a child that made all that was left feel like something I had dreamt up. I looked at Frank, searching for what scared me ten or so years ago and I couldn't find it. Perhaps I didn't want to see it. I wanted to be loved. Down the rabbit hole I followed her, to sit down for tea and hope. I would become mad with all that surrounded me and then what I was doing would be normal, and that carcass of a bad dream would decay with the understanding of time. This was my wish. It was my fantasy but like all fantasies there are stolen moments that take us to wonderland and then we have to wake up and put the mad hatter's hat in the closet, but the madness lives inside while the hat, the fantasy, rattles in its box, begging to be taken out again.

I woke up sore and momentarily happy because I thought I was somewhere else. I did my best to pretend like I was part of a routine with coffee and the morning paper like I was playing house. Sometimes the maid would come, sometimes I would walk for hours. Sometimes I would walk to the small market that claimed to be a hundred years old that used what looked like the first register ever made. I would just go in, to stare at the fruit, the exposed brick walls, the flour that dusted the floor beneath the bread baskets and it would calm me. It was its own little world frozen in a simpler time. The exposed wood, brick and mortar like the essence of the American dream, and I grew an attachment to it. Sometimes I would buy something and other times I walked around for an hour. The owner, this petite Italian mob boss with hairy sausage fingers, would call me James Dean every time I came in. He didn't know what was wrong with me, but he knew the name put a smile across my face no matter what state I was in. One day, I must have lost track of time and wandered around until closing without realizing it. "Hey James Dean, we're closing here. What can I get you?"

"I'm sorry, you probably want to go home?"

"It's no problem, can I help you find anything?"

"Um, no. I just need a few things." I picked a flour-dusted baguette and a bottle from the display of Chianti that was next to the ancient register.

"Will that be all, movie star?"

"Yeah," I said demurely and handed over the cash.

"I'm sure something will find you."

"Yeah, maybe."

I didn't want to leave but I didn't know how to keep the conversation alive. "Could I get an extra bag please?"

"Sure kid."

"I like your store."

"From you, that's a great honor."

"Thanks."

"Of course, anything else I can do for you?"

"No, I should be getting home."

"Alright then, take care son."

Okay. I don't know, I just wanted to cry, and my feet couldn't move, and my lip began to quiver.

"Hey, hey kid, you're like twenty, right?"

"Um, I'm old enough to buy the bottle of chianti you just sold me."

"Right, here." He took out two glasses from behind the counter where he stood and poured out two glasses of Sambuca and dropped three coffee beans in each and swirled the glasses around.

"To health," he said. "When everything is gone to shit, never will you be more grateful for anything else."

"Thank you, sir."

"Of course, let me know if you know anyone looking for a job. I'm in the market."

"Thank you, sir, goodnight."

It was the first time I ever turned down an offer from a man. I think that's what they call growth. Leaving, I felt good.

CHAPTER FIFTEEN

Un Masque De Conclusion

I took that small act of kindness like a candle of hope that I would carry into the darkness. Every time I lay down and he fucked me, I thought somewhere in the world, not far away, there is kindness.

People would ask me, "That Italian grocery basically gave you a way out, why didn't you take it?"

I said, "because I would have been too afraid. It's scary to think something as terrible as being fucked every night by your cousin is more comfortable than the idea of working with the public but it was true. And I didn't trust anyone at that point." I said, "Because I would just assume that everyone was nice until the right opportunity to fuck you presented itself."

So, I stayed, and I have regretted that decision because of the memories I can't erase. Moments come creeping, triggered by the most mundane activities. I could only warn those who may find themselves in such dire situations, added only by the memories which plagued me, that pain, was their asset. It was all very cyclical, really.

There was a period when Frank was gone most the day and didn't return until the late evening except to work in the room I dared not to venture. It was fine with me, and I could buy peace for a time.

One evening I could hear them working. The sounds coming from the hallway were unbearable and lasted well into the early hours of the morning. When I came out of the living room, in the afternoon, a naked, waify blonde twink was sprawled on the couch with underwear that was clearly too big for him, wrapped around his ankles. He had a black eye and blood crusted around the bridge of his nostrils. One hand was tucked between his legs and the other teasing a pile of cocaine sitting on the table next to the couch under some tin plate.

At first, I thought I was dead, staring at myself from above, but then I sat across from this kid about my age, at the table and waited to see if my presence could resurrect him.

He stirred at the sound of my breath and opened one eye. "Who, the fuck, are you?" he asked.

"I live here, you?"

"I didn't ask what you were doing here. I asked, "Who are you?" he said.

"That you did. I'm Antony. My friends call me Anton or Tony, but I don't really like that."

"Didn't ask for your biography Tony. One word would suffice."

"I prefer Anton…"

"So, how did you get here Tony?"

"I'm just staying here awhile with Frank."

"And what's he getting out of it?"

"Excuse me?"

"You don't get anything out of Frank for nothing." He said.

My face felt hot. "What are you getting out of it?" I retorted.

"He pays me."

"To do what?"

"I'm asking the questions," he belted. I was uncomfortable but willing to see where this was going to go.

"How do you know Frank? You work for him?" he asked.

"No, um, we are related."

"Like brothers?"

"No, like estranged cousins."

"So, you're fucking your cousin?"

"Uh, no, wait…what? Why would you ask?"

"It's fine. Don't get defensive. Trust me, I've seen some shit, but that my friend is some shit."

"We are not," I tried to defend myself.

"You don't have to explain yourself. But you do have to make me some eggs."

"You have to at least tell me your name."

"Amadeus."

"No, it's not. Bullshit. Tell me your real name."

"That's the name I got, that's the name I am going to give you."

"You're quite the prick, you know that?"

"You can call me prick too if you like, but now I really do need some eggs or I'm going to projectile vomit all over you."

I blinked in dismay, "Entitled prick."

"Great, now I get to have a first and last name," he laughed.

"Oh, whatever, would you like some coffee too?" Annoyed, I was determined to find out more about him and see if I could get to the answers before my patience wore out.

"Yes. Black."

I brought him over the hot coffee as he was taking a bump.

"What do you need the coffee for then?"

"I just like the taste."

"You're the first. This coffee is shit."

"Eggs are on the table. I'm not bringing them to you."

"Yes mom."

"Hope you like it over easy. Oh, and a slice of toast to go with it."

"You know Tony, you really shouldn't wear your heart on your sleeve like that. I don't want to wake up pregnant," he snarked.

"It's just toast," I said. "I just thought the bread might absorb the poison and semen in your stomach."

"So, I guess you know what I do for a living?" He asked.

"No, I was trying to insult you."

"A guess is a guess no matter the intention."

"So, Frank pays you. You're like some kind of gigolo for him and his friends?"

"Good sir," he cried and stood from the table with a napkin in hand like it was a prop clutched to his chest.

"I am an actor." He proclaimed in dramatic fashion.

"From the Royal Shakespeare Company, are we?" I chuckled.

"No, not nearly as prestigious, but it pays."

"And Amadeus is your stage name?"

"No, he is my tortured soul, ill, passionate and fading."

"And your black eye?"

"Part of the performance, my method and my craft."

"And is the performance you give, live or recorded?"

Leaning over he touched my nose, "Boop, you are a clever boy."

"We are the same age." I reminded him.

"Looks can be deceiving. The weight of the soul is the true measure of age. Mine is dwindling towards extinction, to be recycled and renewed for the years unspent. Right now, I'm fighting with time itself, the vessel which houses the souls of the world with our expiration dates."

"Well, that is true. You can't defeat time."

"No," Amadeus said, "But you can piss it off."

"If you leave this world prematurely, time and space will spit your soul back out until you fulfill your soul's promise to itself."

"What promise is that?"

"That's the fucked-up part. The universe doesn't tell you. You have to figure it out and if you don't then you get hurled back to this god forsaken rock called earth until you do."

"So…"

"Basically, I'm the problem child of the universe that keeps getting held back because I can't follow instructions. I'm the thorn in space and time's side."

"Wow, what is in that cocaine?" I said, staring at the plate.

"Really good shit but that's not the point of what I am saying. The point is… oh, fuck it. You wanna do some?"

"Sure, I clearly need to get on your level."

We compressed 7 hours into what felt like 20 minutes. An all-day binge. We were dancing on the furniture, and I was crawling along the edge of the hall, like Perkins Gillman. When Frank got home, I was passed out in a hallway closet and Amadeus had returned to his spot from that morning. I think we parted ways after he tried to finger me, but I honestly can't remember.

I don't even think he meant it in a sexual way just as something to do. He intrigued me, and terrified me at the same time. It was fun that he was reckless and maintained a lack of fear, the same lack of fear that might send me into the same void as him as well. Yet somehow, being around his energy made me fear the void less and that's what terrified me: a shadow whom you owe a toll to.

"I guess you've had a productive day. Both of you." Frank was smiling but while his face was composed, the grinning visage, the cogs in his head were turning as if he was trying to assess whether or not this new meeting of the minds between Amadeus and I was a good thing or not.

"Daddy's home."

"Amadeus shut up," Frank snapped.

"I didn't think you'd still be here," he said.

"Neither did I, but I couldn't refuse the generous hospitality of our dear Anton. And there didn't seem to be any point in going home if we had to do a re-shoot anyway."

Frank flung his coat at me as if I had become part of the closet. "You talk too much 'A'" and he headed towards the kitchen.

"And you love me too little." Amadeus said, jumping right in front of Frank's path, dangling his naked self in front of Frank. Frank kept his eyes up and squeezed Amadeus' face.

"How could I love you more? You're a dirty slut." Two soft taps to the cheek and Frank squeezed past him to retrieve the bourbon from the freezer. I could feel the heat rising from within Amadeus' body, but his face never changed. Everything just sort of slid off him.

"You know, you drink bourbon totally wrong. Straight is poured over ice, but never chilled."

Frank took a sip and walked over to Amadeus with a particular swagger in his hip as if his world had been altered. "Is that so?" Frank replied.

"Yes, but don't worry I understand you want to feel like a man while you sip like a faggot. I promise your secret is safe…"

THWACK!!!

Frank had grabbed Amadeus by the throat and pushed him up against the wall. "Shut up! I understand that you're trying to impress your little twin by acting like you're not a little cock sucker for pay, but don't forget that I can put you in places no one ever will find you if you disrespect me again."

"I already like it rough. Your threats are like role play."

Frank laughed and dropped him. "With a face like yours, how can I stay mad? In fact, why do I have to? If I want I can bring over ten convicts and train fuck you on the kitchen table and you'll do it. So why get upset? Speaking of, lady Midnight, we're gonna need you to be ready to go all night so go wipe yourself off and I'll see you there in an hour."

Amadeus smiled and floated down the hallway leaving Frank and I locked in a stare.

"You wanna watch?" He asked.

"No, no, that's okay."

"Okay then, I guess I'll see you in the morning."

Then it was 8:15pm.

"Of course. Goodnight Frank."

"Goodnight then."

I left the room and escaped under the covers and prayed for morning. Nothing good came from the room down the hall all night. And the whole time, I kept thinking, thank God that isn't me, but I couldn't help but feel I was closer to being "A" than I was willing to realize.

CHAPTER SIXTEEN

We Could Run

The morning was like a time loop. Amadeus laying in the same naked state as I had found him from before.

"Please tell me," I said, "Why do you do what you do? You could be anything. Why this?"

"Anything?" He said. "I could be great. But how do you kill greatness before greatness kills you? That is the dilemma."

"I never thought about it," I had no answer worthy to follow up with his insight.

"Of course, you didn't. That's because you don't believe you're anyone worth of an alternative path. I could be a great cock sucker for pay, as I've been told, but I'm at war with the universe for giving me the chance of having to choose a choice. Choose anything really. Choose to be, to exist, dammit. We either choose something or the world chooses for us. So," he paused for a while until I couldn't tell who he was staring at, or looking at until he began again, "what you really you really should be asking yourself is, why do you do what you do and what the fuck are you doing here?"

"I don't know." I said.

"Well then that's scarier than knowing why, isn't it? You might as well be dust floating in the air."

"Well, what do I…" I began to think about an alternate life.

"See, there you go again. Why the fuck are you asking me for?" Ask yourself, what the fuck am I doing? Answer that and you'll have your answer. Excuse me," he leaned over and took a bump from the table.

"Come with me?" I asked.

"I'm not the meat you keep in the freezer for leftovers. I'm pasty white milk that's about to expire before you need to drink it. But then again, I'm very certain you will carry with you the words I have given you on your journey."

"Thank you, Amadeus."

"Thank me when you're gone, and I'll be thankful you've left."

I left the room to go to my bedroom and resurrect my suitcase from under the bed. I began to pack without a plan. I could stay in a hotel until I had figured the rest out. At least for a day or two. I decided I should at least call Ci. I hadn't spoken to her in ages, and it was comforting to know someone in the world knew and cared where you were. I rang her dorm, and no one answered so I rang the hall and a girl answered and said she moved out. Discouraged as I sounded, she go the girl who lived next to Ci, who told me that she was renting a flat off campus but she had left her new number with her in case I called. I bit my lip and wanted to cry. I probably thanked her a hundred times before hanging up abruptly and calling her straight away. When she answered the phone, she totally flipped. "Darling, I thought you had fallen off the face of the earth. I got kicked off campus, isn't it wonderful?"

"I don't see how?" I said, "They might expel you after this."

"Probably but fuck them. But don't you see, now you can come stay with me and come away from whatever abysmal hell you're living in."

"Oh, um, can I come by around after midnight tonight?"

"Oh, do you have to sneak out without the landlord knowing? Totally serves them right. I'll leave you a key in the mailbox, 37. 37 is also my apartment number. Get off at Voltaire and turn right on Rousseau. It's the brown stone building on the corner marked 1784. Can you remember?"

"All in my head, love."

"I can't wait to see you, love."

"Bye darling and thank you. I'll bring over some champagne if I can."

"That would be lovely. À bientôt, if you don't, I'll have spirits waiting."

After we hung up, I felt a sigh of relief like perhaps I wasn't going to die, and the course of the universe was for once working in my favor. The only thing remaining was this ache pulling at my chest like I was leaving Amadeus behind. My love burned, as my heart sank, but his belief in me propelled me forward.

I slept, rather, I pretended to while they filmed. It was at the height of unbearable chaos that I decided it would be safe to flee. I opened the hallway closet to retrieve the bag I had hidden, and when I stepped away to close the door, Frank was standing there.

"Where do you think you're going?"

Like a coward I broke instantly. "I'm sorry, I can't take it anymore."

"You're not leaving."

"Just let me go, Frank. There's nothing that I can give you that you haven't already taken, that I haven't already given."

"That's where you're wrong. Come with me." He pulled me down the hallway and continued, "I've fed you, and housed you and now you're going to show me how much you love me."

"That's just it," I was beating on his arm, "I don't love you. I fucking hate you!"

"Then you'll be that much more convincing," he stared blankly at the end of the hallway.

In the light of the red room, I could see the blood on his shirt which he removed like he was ready to fight in the boxing rink. He took a bump of coke from behind the camera and handed the plate back to the little Puerto Rican who was operating it, highly doubting that he had gone to any prestigious film school. Frank came over and threw me down on the mattress, next to my bloody and incoherent co-star.

"I told you to run!" Amadeus said, "Why didn't your run?" And then his eyes rolled to the back of his head, and I have no idea whatever became of him since. I have searched for any whisper of a boy named Amadeus that had perished from the earth, leaving this scene as my final memory of him.

"What have you done?" I screamed!

"Me?" Frank laughed. "I have done nothing. The drugs are supposed to help you do the work. Not keep you from doing it. The boys got too rough with him before they realized he wasn't responding because he was unconscious."

Two naked large men stood in the corner with their arms crossed until Frank motioned for them to remove Amadeus from where the next scene had to continue from.

"Don't touch him!" I screamed. But one of them pushed me down while the other carried him out. He began to kiss my neck and I screamed in what felt like an airless vacuum of disbelief that this all was happening in this second.

"Hold on," Frank said, "He's not ready. He needs a little help. He brought over a tray and was explaining how the rest of the evening was supposed to go. "You see, there's usually not enough money in the budget for an understudy and "A" has been such a trooper up until now but look how fortunate that we have a live-in with an uncanny likeness. We can do the rest of the scene from behind and the derelicts who want this shit wouldn't even know the difference. So, here," he stuck out the tray in front of me. "Take as much of this as you need, and if you need my friend here to rim your hole with it first he would be more than willing. But if you refuse, I will break you, then will finish you, and then I will bury you."

"Well, if these are my options," I knocked the tray square in his face and ran from the room. From behind I heard Frank scream, "Don't touch him!" I went straight to the front door and in front of it stood, the other naked but now clothed giant. He picked me up and pinned me straight to the wall. Frank stumbled out, rubbing his bloodshot eyes and knocked me down to the floor.

"I said don't touch him, fucking idiot, go to the back and stay hard. The star will be ready in a few minutes."

I crawled on the back of my hands away from him behind the coffee table. He picked up a large glass of water that was sitting there and threw it on his face. "Well, I can't feel myself blink, but I feel it's all gone straight to my brain. Better for me but worse for you."

"What do you want from me?"

"Tell me what you want." He grabbed me off the floor by the throat and held me up.

"I want to be dead. I want to be free from you."

"You don't want to be free from me. You want me to live inside."

He pressed his mouth firmly to mine and I bit his lips until I tasted blood, but it was fast and hard. Then he dropped me and decked me to the floor; my back crashed to the coffee table.

I cried out and he struck me so many times in the face I began to laugh instead of cry and then he kept going, but I kept laughing. Harder and more obnoxious until he stopped.

"What?!" I shrieked "What?" I stood up and pushed him. "Keep going. Don't stop!" But he held his hand.

"You, you, god damned coward!" And then I hit him. I hit him hard. And then again. And again.

"What? You can't do it?" I struck him in the face. "You don't want to kill me, you just wanna fuck me up until I do it for you. Well, I'm not going to help you. You're a weak, cock-sucking coward who feeds on souls because you don't have one. And now I'm leaving, and I won't let you come near me again!"

I turned around in full force and went to the door before a big bloody hand came behind me and pushed it closed, slamming my face against the wood. I could feel him try to reach around the front of my pants. I elbowed him so hard in the face that I heard my elbow crack, and he flew back and pulled me down with him. His nose was completely flat. I got on top of him and proceeded to level the rest of his face. It was dark and there was something jagged and broken on the floor that he grabbed and sliced my upper arm with. I held onto his hand and forced it above his head and beat it from his grasp. He pulled me forward and flipped me over his head on my back. I cried out and then my air was cut. His hands around my throat, my arms flailed for anything, and I felt a shard of glass melt into my hand and screamed, gasping for breath, I plunged it into his upper shoulder and completely tore my hand. I pulled my knees to my chest and kicked him as he fell to his side, crippled and in pain. I heard the door to the hallway open followed by running footsteps. I fled down the hallway, to the stairs and to the street. I stood for a moment in the light from the lamps that hung above my head. For a second I was basking in the bloodiness of my task as severance rendered, swallowed by light. From the light, I ran into the darkness that was saturated by my own clarity, through it, I navigated with an ease that felt familiar. My freedom from the demon incarnate and from the devils that had once filled myself. I flew from the light and into the dark and yet everything seemed much clearer. My bloody hand turned the key to Ci's flat and I was home.

CHAPTER SEVENTEEN

The Art Of Filleting

Ci let me sleep for almost three days for the total of which I didn't move. For me, three days felt like twenty minutes, but the panic that arose from me waking in a strange place subsided with knowing that I was indeed someplace else.

Ci was apprehensive to approach me but very softly kissed my neck and whispered, "I'm glad you're here." She was shocked to discover where I had been staying, but never questioned why I chose to go to Frank.

In retelling this story to you, I'm not sure I have the answer either. Maybe one of you will have found the reason in something I've said and use that for what it's worth to help you understand yourself and those around who are like you. Not one among you possessing the identity of an outward likeness to that of a victim, but akin to a soldier returning from war in a costume borrowed for a mascaraed that lasts far longer than the stitches holding the costumer together or the ceramic paint of your mask from peeling. Fear retreats into itself and without fear we try to find the familiar so it won't make us afraid, but if all we can know with certainty is ourselves, then good could possibly come from relieving pain if not to convince yourself that what you feared was not the thing that made you sick. However, the first time you cut yourself with a knife it's called an accident, but the next time you cut yourself then it is you who are doing the cutting and the only fear that remains is the truth that you are in turn carrying the sickness of fear and the cause of your own pain, because you don't believe in the cure.

Perhaps we hurt ourselves to punish the past for what it didn't do for us, only it makes any chance of change for the future rather slim. No one will tell you that it takes several times to learn this lesson. Only, try to remind yourself of this before you're already dead.

"So, what are you going to do now?" Ci asked, which was a poignant question I had not answered for myself.

"I don't know."

"Well, you have to go back to school." She said.

"I'm done with bureaucratic institutions."

"I have never been the practical one, but you have to do something. You have to finish school."

"I'm trying to do this thing where I don't go back to the things that hurt me"

"Being poor is going to hurt a lot worse. Trust me, and we do not work."

"But…"

"No, no sweetheart. There." And she held up my hands to my face. "These things do not work. This!" and she touched my head "This will do all the work you will ever need, but we need to get you to university first."

"Well, we have to graduate high school first."

"I know smart ass. You'll need your GED. It's a test. The universities will see you've completed high school, and you will say you took the last semester off to grieve the passing of your Datsun and then hello Harvard for you and hello Radcliffe for me."

"Do they even care about high school at Berkeley?"

"Thank god we applied there just in case."

"Can they kick you out of a public school?"

"I don't know." And we were both quiet as we pondered over it. "Damn it, we can certainly try."

"What do I do in the meantime? I have to make sure I pass my GED. I need the rest of my savings for when I get to college and then my scholarships will have to fund the rest."

"Well, you can always stay here."

"I know, but these," as I grabbed her face, "might actually have to do some work until we go away to university."

"I'm so glad you feel that way." She started jumping on the bed. "Well, the librarian I was blowing got fired for getting a girl knocked up, so the position was open, and I filled out an application with your name. I talked you up because I always have a juicy story for the hermit, Mrs. Hermelin, so all you have to do is interview with Hermelin and you'll start next week. And don't worry I already told her you're a pufta and have no interest in women which actually makes you perfectly qualified."

"Why not just hire a woman?" something I thought was a good question.

"Well, apparently, the last one before that was but that didn't stop her."

"Oh god."

"Yep, let's just say she wasn't using her hands to rearrange the Dewey decimal system."

"Here it comes."

"But she did arrange my skirt a couple of times."

"Jesus Christ."

"Honestly, it wasn't even that great."

"Good, then I'm glad you got a girl fired for mediocre foreplay. Regardless, I don't know. I'll take the job and I'll do the interview, but it sounds painfully boring."

"Oh, no doubt about it, but you'll be paid and use your lunches and slow times to study for the GED and you'll be close to me."

"And what if the boys from my old school see me?"

"Very simply say you're a pufta and you got accepted into the all-girls private school cause you fit right in."

"Nary a complaint, I'll just say no one has noticed."

CHAPTER EIGHTEEN

Stapling Your Stomach

The hum and drum of organizing, cataloging, filing, sorting, stapling, printing and copying was enough to make me want to take out the whole school and myself included. Yet contrary to most of Ci's decisions concerning herself, her advice given towards other people was spot on. I was getting a lot done. Needless to say, I already knew most of what it took to graduate high school, but I spent most of my time weeding out all of the irrelevant information. I was rather convinced that calculus, French, Latin, Geography, and Philosophy were all irrelevant to creating the average well-rounded American teenager. Apparently if I could spell my name, sort of multiply and divide, and string a sentence together, then I was prime beef for the workforce. I had been groomed for a different path entirely and despite all of my privilege and advantages in learning, my education was irrelevant.

I was the second person to finish my test after a 75-year-old Puerto Rican, but if he had come this far, then he deserved it even more than I. The following weeks were spent waiting for my results while sending droves of intercepting letters to colleges, explaining why I needed to be home with my family before I made the transition to college, having spent all my time since I was ten at private school. Ci helped me come up with that gem and I found it to be rather convincing. The majority of my tension lay in the waiting. The letters came in and for the most part it turned my admissions into a coin toss. All my public universities came through one after the other, then all my private dream institutions began to reject. Every response began with a "we regret to inform you" heading. Some gave their reasons and others did not. The ones that did, expressed their vague concern over whether I was ready for the responsibility and that I should apply again in the fall.

"We knew it would be a gamble," Ci said as she touched my shoulder.

"I feel like a Russian Czar awaiting a response from Bolsheviks. I've been stripped of title and power, convinced divine right will keep the Bolsheviks from putting a bullet in my back."

"Well to hell with them. They are a bunch of idiots."

"Correction, they are members of a joint aristocracy who have the task of telling me my membership to the country club has been revoked. I'm Sarah Crew and Miss Minchin has just told me I'm a princess no longer. It's time I faced that."

"What are you saying? You're just going to give up?"

"No. What I'm saying is that we may not be destined to be a Harvard and a Radcliffe apart from each other. If this were the good old days, daddy would make a phone call, build a new science lab and I'd be in, but that's not my reality anymore."

"How many do you have left?"

"Four."

"It's not like it couldn't happen."

"I'm just trying to accept that it probably will not."

"Antony, I…"

"I'd like to go to bed now, please?" I asked. "I'm tired." Tired as I was, I did not sleep. The news reals of WWII updates played across the screen of my eyelids that made me realize that the dissociation through transplantation could not be conjured through the power of will. It only highlighted the limited power of the human race, whereas dreams are not the blueprints to solve the stupidity of a generation, unaware of how unprepared their children were despite the I.O.U. simulated in the doppelganger of a failing line of mediocrities, who would not even claim Stonehenge or ale as the source of their lineage for fear of revenge upon a failed family line of transgressors without ramparts or country. Only a name, with a declaration of privilege and a resolve to make choices in the names of their children.

CHAPTER NINETEEN

Government Printed: The Golden Ticket

Days turned into time that was blurred and made gray by not knowing anything. The hands on the clock became irrelevant because I did not want to know. Time was slipping and I had to either accept admission to one of the public schools or hold out for the ones I had dreamt about since I was a boy.

Ci came into my room one morning and jumped on my bed holding four envelopes. I shot straight up and wiped my eyes.

She began with "Oh so I don't want you to be mad, but I wanted to wait until they all came in so that we could open them together. Each one kind of trickled in over the last month and I thought it would be best because I didn't want you to groan."

"Cecilia, it's fine. I haven't even given it that much thought."

"What the fuck are you saying?"

"Okay, I'm lying. Just open them!"

"Oh, okay, first one then…"

"Rip. Open. Drop."

"Rip. Open. Drop."

"Are you sure you don't want to open them?" She hesitated.

"Darling, it makes no difference. In fact, a 'no' from you is probably better."

"Rip. Open. Oh, my god! Yes, okay!"

"What? What?"

"We have a yes. One yes."

"Who?"

"Well, I don't like it but…"

"Dammit woman!"

"Okay, Stanford."

"Oh? Really?"

"I know, like it's nice but uncomfortable."

"Fine, just put it aside. Oh Shit!"

"What is it? Did my boob pop out?"

"No, no, dear I saw it. It's their seal."

"Oh, um, well it looks like it."

"I don't wanna know. Tear it up now."

"Tony, we are on a winning streak, we can't fuck it up now."

"Oh god, fine, open it."

Rip. Open.

"Oh Antony, oh Antony."

"What?"

"My dear Antoine, look." She collapsed beside me and stuck out the letter. "It came! It happened! You got in!"

"I got it. It! In!"

"I knew it would happen. Never doubted it."

Then I laid down beside her and buried my hand in her hair and rubbed my fingers down her face to her lips and kissed her. "I dedicate this Harvard acceptance letter to you. My light and confident."

"I love you Antony."

"I know. That's why you can't get rid of me."

"It looks like we have the next four years together."

"A marriage I look forward to having till death do us part."

"You would not leave me," She protested coyly.

"Never, unless I couldn't help it."

She nuzzled in my chest as my mind drifted to the future. It became hard for me to accept anything positive, and that I would after, always anticipate the bad to follow. I just didn't know in what form such an ugly thing could arise from a blessing conceived in a dream.

CHAPTER TWENTY

The Quality of Status

I accepted greedily and foolishly and then my tuition statement arrived. I cursed myself and my stupidity. I was not in good enough standing to receive any academic competitiveness standing that would mean scholarships and I was still registered as a dependent child. If I were to refile, I would have to concede my spot and reapply the following year, but I would have no place to go. Regardless, I refused to reside in this city any longer. Too many families and unfriendly faces, whispers, and in-discretionary glances.

I told Ci "I will kill myself if I stay in this town another year. I have to get out of here."

"What did the admissions office actually say?"

"I've missed the deadline to refile my financial aid, as an independent, and since I'm declared as dependent on my parents taxes the only way I could prove independent status is by showing individual income and residence dating six months. Which I don't have and despite your hospitality nothing in this fucking apartment is in my name."

"How could it be?"

"Exactly! I was fucked before I even got accepted and I didn't even know it! And as a private institution there are no income exceptions unless you've been abused, homeless or a welfare of the state."

"Two out of three isn't bad." She said, trying to offer help.

"If you're a fag it doesn't count. If my parents beat me because they hate me that's bad. If they beat me because they hate I'm a fag then that's understandable and I need help."

"Do you know that for a fact?"

"Well, they hung up right before they said, 'I hope you find help,' so yes! I would say my conclusion is valid."

"Well, perhaps I could convince my father to extend the lease on this place as an investment and you could stay here and just join me in the fall."

I reached over and I grabbed her face, "You don't understand, I need to get the fuck out of here. I want to go to school! And I don't want to wait. If I don't go then they've won. They win everything and then I will die."

In a stream of tears, she grabbed my hands and pressed them against her face. "Don't say that. You're not going to die! We're going to figure it out!"

"No, No we're not! I just want to go to school. Why won't they let me? What did I do? I wanna die. I can't get up these many times. It's too hard."

Then she slapped me. "Stop it. You didn't die. I don't want to hear that anymore! You don't realize that what you say hurts other people. You mean more to me than anybody in the world and you're going to throw it away because of what name of the university will be on the diploma."

"But I've worked my whole life."

"You've only been alive for seventeen years. You might be alive for many more and things will continue to happen, and I can't be worried about you every time a tornado comes and picks up your house. You know I'll follow you to the end, but don't be so damn selfish and think you can leave before the finish line, or I will hold a séance every day for the rest of my life to torture you. That's a promise stronger than eternity."

"I feel sick."

"Then we need to find you a cure."

"For my homosexuality? Yes please. Born into a fate worse than death must be a joke God plays so you'll reach for salvation."

"Ok, if you could be a little less Proust right now I will try not to think about killing you."

"Ok, well, what do you got? I'm pretty much running on empty."

"Clearly, you began to talk in clichés."

"Ugh, kill me." I rolled over and pressed my face in her pillow. "Is this what must become of me?"

"Okay, reign it in Taloula."

"God she's fabulous. She really doesn't get the credit she deserves. You know Bette Davis could have at least paid her a tribute for basically giving her the role of Margo Channing."

"I think you're having a gay stroke. Will you fucking focus?"

"Fine, fine. Shoot."

"Oh, I think we have to face the fact that it's too late and too expensive for you to go to any of the private schools." My face turned red, and my eyes were filling up again. It's hard medicine to swallow when there's nothing you can do, and your choices are ripped away from you.

"Don't cry. We know this and we can't change it. Now, what public schools did you apply to?"

I shifted through the pile of papers sprawled on the bed. "I don't know, a couple in the tristate and one of these new public universities they're building in California."

"Here. Look."

"Oh my, California, you lucky bitch! Can you imagine all those sun-kissed blonde boys that will be begging to bend you over? Is that a smile I see through those tears?" Her voice shot through that *Baby Voice*.

"You know I hate the baby voice."

"But then why are you smiling? Cause you know how much I 'rub' you?"

"Oh, my God, I'm going to pinch you!"

"Say it."

"No"

"Say it. I know you want to."

"No."

"Say it or I'll rip your dick off and shove it up your butt with rubber glue."

"Oh…I rub you too."

"Haha, you little bitch. And I rub you too" Then she kissed my nose. "You give in to me too easily. Well, it says it's an accredited university. So, it's not a state school. It's in northern Cali, right by the ocean in some fucking town I've never heard of and let's see…Oh fuck you! They don't give out grades. Just degrees!"

"What does that mean?" In all sincerity, I was seriously confused. Either this institution was a joke, or my ship had finally come in. "But what does that mean, like you never take a test?"

"Well hold on, I'm reading. It says the course work is divided into the new quarter system of a ten-week learning period upon which each class administers a final exam or final project to demonstrate knowledge of the material. The end of your senior year is a thirty-week seminar in which you will be required to write and publish a senior thesis through the public university system. Oh, my god, Fuck you!"

"Alright, well tell me what this means to you."

"Basically, you pay a tenth the price of a private school and you graduate with a degree and a published thesis that you can submit to any grad school program. Publication is huge! Fuck, I should go here!"

"But even if it's cheaper, how am I going to pay for it?"

"Did you even read any of this shit? You've been so stuck on Ivy league bullshit; you don't even see a gift when it's been given. They've already offered you an SAT scholarship and an academic competitiveness grant for being a clever little thing."

"Really, how much?"

"I'm going to strangle you! All of it! The grant pays your tuition which wasn't much to begin with and for getting a perfect score, they'll probably pay for books, supplies and even condoms probably."

"Alright. Okay. This is good. Now where am I going to live?"

"Uh…yeah they can't help you there. I'm assuming this is their offer based on the fact that you're a smart ass with well-off parents.

Even so, they're still willing to pay your entire way. I would call them. They're three hours behind so there's nothing you can do about it now, so just call them tomorrow telling them your circumstances have changed."

"But then it might be the same as all the others."

"They obviously want bright individuals because they're new and they want you. They already sound too good to be true, maybe there's something they could do for you."

"I truly hope so." I was starting to believe that all of this has been a journey to a blessing. And for once, I'd like to be proven wrong by having it be so.

CHAPTER TWENTY-ONE

The Mouse Trap

My first introduction to public bureaucracy was waiting on hold until you have a stroke and then being taken off life support with a "Thank you for holding, How can I help you?"

"Hello sir?" I heard the pause in her voice and the sound of my temple bursting.

"Yes, I'm here."

"My name is Nora; how can I help you?"

"Um, I'd like to review my tuition statement."

"I can certainly do that for you. Can I start with your last name and date of birth?"

I gave them.

"Oh, I'm not seeing you here. Are you new here or returning?"

"New."

"Okay, I've found you. Well, you aren't a student yet. All you have is an offer then we can create an invoice based on whether you choose to live on campus, which as an incumbent freshman is mandatory unless appealed on the basis of financials or health needs."

"I guess that's my dilemma. I don't know if I can accept it because I don't know if I can afford either."

"Well based on your father's income, we can either set up a payment plan for food and campus housing or they can finance a loan that will pay for the four years you are here."

"I don't know if that's going to work."

"Well honey, I don't know what else we can do for you otherwise you lose your spot or your scholarship."

"The thing is my parents can't pay for it."

"Has there been a change in income or a life changing event that would keep them from making a family contribution? Because we can file an extension to recalculate a family contribution."

"I don't think that's going to work. They can't pay."

"Forgive me Mr. Shrader, but to me it seems like you're trying to substitute an unwillingness to pay for an inability to pay."

"I don't…"

"Honey, honey, are you still there?"

"Yes, it's just my parents don't want to make the investment in my education anymore."

"Can you tell me why that is? I'm sorry, but that just doesn't make sense. I'm looking at your transcript, a perfect SAT score and an academic grant with scholarships. What parent wouldn't take that offer let alone support their child?"

"It's because they don't think it's in my best interest."

"Why? How could higher learning impact you negatively?"

"It's because I'm sick."

"Sick? As in terminally ill?"

"Yes."

"Well honey, if you need special accommodations to make your time with us easier then we will work with your needs."

"I'm afraid attending will only make it worse."

"What kind of illness would be metastasized by higher learning?"

"Something incurable. Look, I can't talk this into a circle any longer and I've pretty much lost my chance anyway, but my parents don't want to pay for my school because I'm gay. And if they pay for me to go to a liberal college on the west coast, then that would only exacerbate my current affliction."

"I see, and do you know this to be the way they feel currently?"

"All I know is the last time they spoke to me I was given two options. To be disowned financially or take classes at community college while undergoing psychiatric evaluation with treatment."

"Okay, thank you for being so honest with me. First, I must tell you that it's unfortunate that your parents feel this way. Second of all, I must also tell you…" I cringed to hear what was to follow so I closed my eyes, ready to absorb the knockdown blowout of hope that would keep me from ever seeing the inside of a university… "I must also tell you that there's nothing wrong with you."

"What?" I sat up amazed as if the Red Sea had parted over my head and the whales were flying through the sky when submerged above ground.

"There's nothing wrong with you and we are going to try and fix this, but I'm going to need your help. Because you were so honest and forthcoming with me, I'm going to make a motion for you that I must tell you is an undisclosed classification that the University of California keeps for a select group of students known as students with adverse effects. This places you in a position to receive additional financial aid as well as make you independent from your parents without filing a class action, should your relationship with them change during the time of attendance here, we must be notified. Failure to do so can result in expulsion, denial of your degree and you will have to pay all that was lent to you back. Do you understand the conditions of the application status that has been put forth to you as an alternative to the original answers of your present application? "

"I understand." I was trying to remain reserved while my insides were jumping. I was grateful but I felt as though I wasn't allowed to be. I had to pretend I was still in disbelief of any of this happening even though a part of me really was.

I moved forward cautiously and asked, "What is it you need from me?"

"I need a detailed letter describing exactly what happened from the moment you disclosed your sexuality to your parents, until their admission that they would not be paying for school."

"Is that all?"

"No, the other part is, I need some sort of documentation on official letterhead from a teacher, counselor or doctor that could corroborate your story."

"I don't know what you mean?"

"Well, for example, perhaps you disclosed this situation to a family friend who happened to work for the government. They could provide a detailed letter corroborating the events of your circumstances."

"I don't have anyone like that."

"That's fine. That's just an example. Did you receive any treatment from the doctors your parents wanted you to see? A copy of those records would be enough, and you have the right to them."

"I never saw treatment which is why this happened."

"I understand, but I need some sort of corroboration composed on official letterhead."

"I have my expulsion letter"

"From your high school?"

"What were the grounds for expulsion?"

"I was a threat to myself and to my colleague for exposing them to lewd acts and unnatural behavior."

"I'm sorry son, but you're going to have to clarify this for me before we move forward. Did they indeed catch you in such acts?"

"No."

"Then how did they know you did them?"

"My parents said I did."

"What?!?"

"My parents went to the chancellor and said I was suffering from this illness and requested they pull me from school because I posed a risk by exposing myself to my classmates. I refused to acknowledge such claims or give the names of other students that would also be considered high risk students. They expelled me and then my parents signed my expulsion letter acknowledging the school's right to do so."

"And you still have this letter?"

"I've wanted to throw it away or tear it up a million times, but something always kept me from doing it."

"Well now, just send those things to me by way of the prepaid envelope I will enclose with the appropriate forms. I will be sending your case to the admissions office and hopefully we will have you here in school by fall."

"Can I ask, without sounding ungrateful, but why are you being so nice to me?"

"I'm doing my job, and everyone has a right to go to school. Who you are should have nothing to do with that."

"Thank you. If this all works then I will always be grateful to you!"

"Thank me when you cross that stage to graduate. Just get those documents to me as soon as possible so we can get a foot in the door for you."

"I will. I'm sorry, but I forgot, I didn't get your name."

"It's Nora."

"Nora. Thank you."

"Thank you. Take care."

I would only speak to her one more time after that when she told me I had been moved to independent status as a student with adverse effects with my tuition, housing and materials paid for. Then one day when I was sent to the advising building to renew my status as an independent student, I saw a remembrance card on my advisor's desk for Nora. She passed in November, after I had already spent two months in attendance and didn't know she had left the earth. This knowledge would stay with me, haunting and comforting me like a familiar spirit until the day of my death. And when I was to awaken the next day, having learned of her passing, her hand was there, resting on my shoulder when the morning came and swallowed me up into its light.

CHAPTER TWENTY-TWO

Bring Us Your Masses

I was off, and nothing made sense. Life seemed far and long, and I was tired and hungry but unable to satisfy either because I would not allow myself to take in sleep or nourishment until the promise of a boat to sail was fulfilled.

It was a strange and confusing time for me while I was getting what I wanted, getting to my new school would be the end of a movie, but what they don't tell you at the end is that it isn't the end. Once you arrive and you put your bag down and smell the redwoods, see the ocean off in the distance, an invisible fence seizes control of your breath as you wait for someone to tell you there has to have been a mistake. I walked through the hallway, suitcase in hand, past parents and kids who had to say goodbye because now they had something to prove; the big reveal; when they would walk across a long stage and grasp the scroll that said they had become an adult. However, that time was not yet to pass. Goodbye is all we are given to take with us to the unknown, and an "I love you," as the only words to help you find your way. I closed my door with my back, turned away from what was happening outside, and walked to my cracked window situated above my bare mattress.

"Goodbye. I love you." What could I do but cry? It has become my solution for everything.

There was a knock on the door, and I had to compose myself. Kevin, the RA, Marvelous Kevin who was tall, Latin, and gorgeous. I wanted to die. I was too emotionally fragile to pry or to flirt or to string together a yes or no.

"Hello, I'm Kevin. I'm your RA."

"Kevin?"

"Yes? I'm just here to welcome you to the building."

"Kevin, huh? You look more like a Juan than a Kevin." Fuck me, why do I speak, why say anything?

"Well, Juan is my middle name, you can call me that if you want." He turned to leave.

"Aren't you going to write me up? I'm sorry, it was a long trip and I'm an asshole."

He turned around and rested his arm above my head in the doorway. "I have a policy of not writing people up on the first day and unfortunately I can't write people up for being assholes, then everyone would have a write up. But I can tell you assholes have a five hundred percent more likelihood of doing shit in front of me that would otherwise get them into serious trouble or expelled so I tend not to lose sleep over write-ups when they tend to write themselves."

"Sorry isn't going to make this better, is it?"

"I don't know. Why don't you try saying it in Morse code through your wall and I'll let you know if I get it." Kevin walked over to the door adjacent to mine and closed it behind him and then reappeared to say, "It's going to be a fun year," before shutting the door again.

Having begun this journey to making friends, I set out to make my own four by four space, the likeness to Marie Antoinette's Petit Trianon. I finished the style in dark wood replica, movie posters, all and every Tennessee Williams playbills (Cliché but talent leaves a taste of obligation), some Tommy Dorsey records I had mounted, my tea pots, ceramic cups, and a rolling rack of limited taste and clothing consistent to the range of A to B, namely black and white with hints of gray.

My bedding was gray with ethereal periwinkle and mint accents and then there was me, lying there staring at the ceiling fan. I laughed to myself. The build up to this moment, akin to a tsunami wave, and its climax was a closet I could barely fit a bed in. Then there was me and a smiling face laughing at my choice of what I now consider to be ugly bedding. I was hungry but totally unprepared to venture out into the world of mingling amongst the acceptees who had parents who were paying. Had I gone to my other school of choice, I would have at least had the consistency of the overlapping circles of American aristocracy, spending my first week bumping into familiar faces because we had all been groomed for the same thing. We weren't winning anything. But we held onto this notion of the gentlemen's club run by the "good ol' boys" who get you into that party or that interview room or that job at that firm. This process was consistent with the spawning of salmon, who travel to the site of procreation without purpose and inevitable death. While I was laying there waiting for the ceiling fan to click, I felt proud to be outside of the world I grew up in. I was being given the chance to make my own way and forced myself to see that I should count myself lucky when so many exist, having had their paths already planned for them.

It was such an odd realization to come when it did, but I thought and discovered within my chest a piece of myself buried within, that I had to let out by rolling over on my side, the weight of itself condensed and let out through a single tear that fell-down from my left eye, and over the hill of my nose, and down the gully of my cheek. I never wanted to fight, to be a soldier, not a child of war he waged against the world. I wanted to be a student for the rest of my life. Constantly learning and discovering, but I did not want my career to expire like men of science who name a star, or an element, and it becomes their tombstone in total. I needed, for my own longevity, the study of the human race, its history and its legacy.

The history of the human consciousness. It is the study of the process by which the human race has attempted the task to know thyself and record it for the progression of its evolution. It is our most important endeavor, and how clear we make it; through war, national identities, flags, moments and the written word and yet for all our advances, with no end in sight, the measure of our progress becomes marked as impossible and futile.

As for my own progress, I knew I had at least fifty years or more to live but the pulse of my life was beginning to grow faint by my willingness to see myself to completion. As stupid and as obnoxious as this may sound, I felt totally incapable when it came to talking to any of my peers. I could not even conceive of approaching a new subject without feeling ill, what with the accent, the hair, and the pretentious poetry like speech, I felt as though they would eat me alive. I devised a plan, brilliant in concept but cowardly in its execution. I would open my door and then lie on the bed until some curious idiot wandered in, and with some luck, perhaps a whole herd would come in. Without anyone knowing I would be holding auditions for friend replacements. I only needed one or two, to make it through four years and for each one at least four vague acquaintances would follow that would serve as conversation fillers at parties as well as study partners provided they had a mind and the occasional extra cigarette, without feeling bad because they'd be asking for one a day later.

The door opened and like visiting an aquarium, a school of fish went by, but I could not interact with them. Maybe I was the fish in the tank and didn't know it. Then I had an existential crisis over whether fish think they are viewing us through the glass or if they know they're being viewed. It was at this moment a waify little moth with fluttering lashes, pixie cut, at about five foot and ninety-five pounds walked in.

"You know if you leave your door open long enough, some little pest is going to wander in and never leave."

I stared at her, unable to think of a response for such a hyper, small and delicate creature. She leaned against my wall and lit a cigarette she had tucked behind her ear. Every move she made seemed to be animated by the clanking of the large chandelier earrings she always wore. They looked like two trapeze apparatuses, sitting ornately beside her head and nearly the same size.

"Is that a poster of Dante's Inferno? It's rather morbid but I wonder, do you, keep this by the entrance on purpose?"

"Couldn't you feel the pull towards no return the moment you came in? Once you cross the vestibule, there's no going back."

"And, 'abandon all hope ye who enter', eh?" Such an appropriate response. I believed I wasn't among just idiots, abandonment and liberals.

I laughed but found all previous rehearsed speeches stained on my brain to be irretrievable . Everything that came out of my mouth I felt had to be made up on the spot. "Well come in, but I warn you, from where you stand is the point of the pagan poets and damned infants. Should you cross the threshold you will no longer be saved by ignorance for you have been warned."

"Yet with the words of a poet, I am drawn forward like Eve."

"I'm no snake."

"And yet your wit bites like one. I like your accent"

"I like your accent as well."

"You and everyone else who's impressed by the British. You all could have had this had you stayed under the union Jack, but instead you all talk in these hybrids of…well I don't know how to describe it."

"Too much money and too little education, I suspect."

"Ha-Ha, that's marvelous." She squeaked and jumped on my bed. "Would you like a cigarette?"

"I won't refuse. I accept."

"For a price, which I must add. Can you repeat "The Calla-lilies are in bloom?"

"I can also recite FDR's declaration of war, but without a cigarette it will hardly have the same effect."

"I was only teasing, but you are so quick and darling. I'm so glad I happened to walk by."

"I'll let you in on a secret." I leaned over. "It's all part of my plan."

"Well, I guess it worked. Can I ask, but that I, and maybe I'm projecting, but what the fuck are you doing here?"

"How do you mean?" I felt like I was sitting naked in my underwear.

"You're like a black spot on a piece of white paper. You stick out. But I can say I'm a black spot too can't I? I mean, don't you think so?"

Her eyes were large, they looked like two brown entrées sitting on two large white saucers that got bigger with each expression.

"If we find any more black spots we could be a whole Dalmatian." She laughed but I could feel her prodding for a way to converse, so I tucked my sword behind my teeth and just listened.

"I came here because I wanted something different. I grew tired of Oxford shoes and plaid jackets and professor robes. I sort of took the fire escape out of my prep school window and came here but caution serves as the chains of my upbringing. I can tell you do too. You can feel them. I feel like a freak walking around here like I might say the wrong thing and I've run out of the granola I was hiding under my bed so will you come eat with me so I don't die, and we can be conspirators together?"

I was blushing because she started to ask, "Why are we covering our mouths?" I asked.

"I don't know," she said. "Why are we whispering?"

"I don't know." I laughed. "Did you just ask me out?"

She pushed my head back with her palm and got up. "Ha, well you're not euro so you must be a fag and not the one you smoke. I guess you can smoke and be both. I'll work on that one, meantime, let's go."

"Wait, how did you…?" Truly I was shocked despite what some of you reading may think.

"Well, a stranger sat on your bed for about fifteen minutes, we're in college and not once did you even bother to look at my chest."

"That's just good breeding."

She whipped around as I got up, "are you saying I'm wrong?"

"Um…no." I winked at her but was looking at the ceiling.

"Alright then, thank you for clarifying and it was nice meeting you."

"I suppose honesty works for anyone."

"My older brother is too, so I kind of had you pegged. Although looking at him, you wouldn't know and somehow that allows me to never be wrong."

"Is he bite-sized like you?" I couldn't help but ask.

"Why? Are you fishing one handed?"

"More like practicing my cast."

"Ha-ha, well go fish because you're undeserving, but you'd have to go ten thousand miles to see him."

"What does he do?"

"Professor. He teaches across the pond in philosophy and international politics, twenty-seven and a half and he's completely the opposite of you. He's a complete whale, a total Moby dick and if you know how that story goes, then you know you can't catch him.

"Perhaps you're just testing me, and this is something you do to all the men who set sites on him?"

"All the men? Does the legend precede the man?"

"Perhaps and I'm assuming in order to single me out you've had practice somewhere on a few to fine tune that instinct of yours."

"Perhaps, but he's still ten thousand miles away and that's a long way to swim but I always travel with a paddle."

"Shall we go to dinner? I'll get the door."

Holding it open I saw her give a side smile, "But I bet you've got a picture don't you."

"Wouldn't you like to know?"

I followed her in. "Mostly out of curiosity. You could at least quench that."

"I will but while you pester me for the status of the imports you've neglected to notice the specimen occupying the ground at present."

"But I only have eyes for you," I jested.

"And I have the chest of a 12-year-old boy, so if that's what you're into I think I will need to reevaluate our friendship."

"It was a joke."

"And not to be taken lightly. I've dated so many of your kind I'm thinking of getting a membership just so I can level the playing field."

We sat down and ate, and I followed her back to her room which I realized was directly beneath mine. I laughed at this coincidence for which she replied, "This is the only time you'll ever get to be on top of a woman." She was right.

CHAPTER TWENTY-THREE

The Carousel On The Shelf And The Menagerie

The time I spent at university was eye opening and strenuous all at the same time. I expected certain entry level seminars to accommodate students of nearly one hundred or more, I myself had never been in a classroom over 30, my every struggle was to pack in a fight for who wanted to sit in the front and who wanted to sit in the back to avoid being called upon, between the two groups laid a space as wide as a mile, the late arrivals would go to drown in the seats, sitting as low as possible, either to remain unseen or pretend they had been there the whole time until the professor walked up the side aisle to the midway point and picked them off one by one.

I noticed a pattern that was in all my classes; all the people that sat on opposite ends of the abyss knew each other having succeeded in cultivating superficial but adequate connections in the first week that would allow them to form a herd of foundling students who operated under the false premise that there was strength in numbers. The professor, familiar to the rouse, would strike the head of the flock by posing a question to the most disinterested.

Naturally, he would fall on his sword and hand off the question to his friend, usually stupider than he was. Herr Slaughter would go on for about ten minutes before the boredom of slaughtering spring lambs set in and the gap in his or her lecture, was cause enough for salvation, before the trauma from the using of dull words would set in and end the academic aspirations of undecided majors, forced to take entry coursework disguised as higher learning.

Having been possessed with the character flaw of investing too much in one person, I found myself as my only ally among different majors. During the day, I had to defend myself sitting in the gorge between front and back. I saw myself being called on right and left. The first few times I was called on were an accident or an act of desperation by the professor but after some time, I felt like the circus freak student. Sometimes I had things worthwhile to say and other times I thought they just enjoyed hearing a queer in an East Coast accent.

I told them, "the town I came from, almost everyone sounds like this. Too many years of inbreeding and not enough culture are the root causes."

My French professor used me as a segue to discuss the nature of how dialects form while my professor of British history used me as a segue to the formation of the class system that gave rise to the labor movement. Whether they realized it or not, I was being singled out as a misplaced elitist. It gels as though I went from one classification of an "other" to a different one, no matter which coast I resided. Was this to be the trajectory of my life? And what's worse, is that at least back home propriety, kept the curiosity of human nature at bay, where the nuances of my sexuality, though noticed or detected, where left to their own devices as I cultivated them to create the culmination of a full human being. Here, I was a different undocumented arrival. All they could hear was an unfamiliar voice drenched in years of fine breeding that was dying.

So, while I repulsed some of my peers, the other half, mostly the female half, found me to be quite a catch. Invitations to coffee or study resulted in heartbreak and scandal making me more of a pariah.

I said to one girl, "I didn't even know we were on a date. How then can I be guilty of misleading you if our feelings are not and could never be mutual?"

Her embarrassment, usually seen as passion, would sever us from ever interacting again and with that, her entire friend group became off limits too.

I was totally alone except for that gem in my doorway. Walking in, her very air and a voice announced who she was from the moment she met you. This was refreshing to most and she cultivated quite the following, mostly of men who found me to be just as confusing as my peers in class did. Women found her to be threatening so all we had around us were hetero men, none of which were interested in me and none of which were interested in her, apart from reasons being the obvious. My feeling was that she was too smart for them, a fact which she made known to her pursuers. This only made them try harder as I faded to the back. She did sustain a formidable companion. Rather she was a kind of a Persian goddess. Her western name was Hannah, and she was enticing. A transplant rebelling against her conservative Persian upbringing. She became the toast of our groups. She relished in all the male attention she received. She became the ideal diversion to the male advances made towards Jane and Hannah herself, the once untouchable becoming the one everyone touched. Yet I admired the ethics by which she operated. She kept a male who was remarkable at sex for about two or three spaced out evenings before offering the inevitable suggestion they'd be better off as friends until then all lost interest, and then for the more inexperienced, she could sustain a false relationship for months at a time until her inevitable suggestion, but by that time she had created a man from a boy. This catch and release program was as solid as ever, but she retired from conquest until she met and married a Persian doctor and had five children, an inevitable fate. She saw her college conquest as the fantasies that would sustain her through marriage and children.

Regardless, as our group remained an ever-revolving carousel of male faces, two girls and a young queer, I found myself to be the doormat of male introductions. I would have had more utility had I insisted they take a number and I'd call them when it was their turn than I did at serving as a male linguist specializing in meaningless conversations. I chose to recuse myself by rescinding most evening invitations. Instead, I found myself retreating into nature. The university sat on a hilltop that was broken up into twelve or so smaller buildings which spread out over seventeen thousand acres, if I recall correctly. From the school were several bluffs where students would lay out naked and watch the clouds or the birds cradle the peninsula. There were even classes where you could learn how to sail. Being an east coast native, I naturally signed myself up and arrived on the first day at six in the morning in my striped St. James shirt, white shorts, sperrys and knife in my waist belt. Unable to take lessons suited to my own personal history, I succeeded in once again singling myself out for ridicule and confusion. I wanted to quit, but Jane wouldn't let me, and we had a bet to see who could sleep with our sun kissed Grecian god of a boating instructor first. Somehow, I won that bet quite by accident you see. At one point towards the end of a lesson, he called me over to help tether the main sail. While we're talking, he offered me the possibility of earning extra credit if I took a few of his night boating classes that he only offered to some of his best students. However, he insisted I would attend because his classes for night boating could only operate with a minimum number of students in attendance to pose the least amount of risk, depending on the size of the vessel used, one could easily man a boat with two, but I felt obligated to make sure the class would go on as planned and perhaps in a more intimate setting I could get the other students to like me and perhaps cultivate a group of friends for myself.

I accepted and showed up with supplies at the ready. To my partial regret there was no class, nor had there ever been one. Both of us, sailors to our word, took the boat out anyway and I, as a person, practiced to never assume anything. Just when we were beyond where you could barely make out the lights of the Marina, he dropped anchor and then dropped me down below and gave what I regard to be the best sex I've ever had. Now, I've had plenty since and in some respects, I prefer others, but I think his balance as a seasoned sailor kept the course of his penis entering me as consistent and unwavering as if we were on dry land despite the obvious rocking of the boat that made the whole experience feel more erotic, knowing that while he was fucking me, we could have capsized at any moment and I will admit with certain thrusts I think we nearly did. This erotic boating continued through the entirety of the course until his contract was up and he was off to instruct at another school. This saddened me because I did enjoy our evening classes. At one point, I did ask him why he chose me. He said being an east coast native himself, he knew I either had to be from there or gay. To his great fortune, I was both.

Clumsily, on one of the last nights we would spend together, I asked him if I could ever see him again. He said he was more of a drifter and relationships even one of correspondence was not his thing, but he wanted to let me know that out of all the guys he's been with, in our evenings together, he's never cum harder. I exhaled from my cigarette and said, "That's so depressing to hear." When he asked why, I said, "Because no matter how many times I've heard that, not once has it ever given one of you cause to stay. But I don't hold it against you. You're just men. You're not God."

Those ventures in the first part of my undergrad were never fruitful or sustaining. My comfort was derived from the fact that I and one other person were not the only homo you could find for miles. I had choices. We had choices but choices don't always give you what you want. In regard to love making, I found that among a smaller population we were more giving of one another to each other because we understood choice was limited, release necessary, and secrecy vital above all else.

In the case where one has a choice, I was initiated into the humiliating ritual of going to bed with someone from intro psych, waking up next to him the following morning and then seeing him look straight through me the following day. And this wasn't because every single man I slept with in college was a sociopath, and while some did wind up working on wall street or in genetic modification is beside the point, the reason for their blatant ignoring of me was choice. If we carried our books for each other it would be a signal to all potential prospects that both were off limits, and how many people do you know are worth it just from a classroom glance? So, I adopted this libertine attitude myself. You don't see me, and I don't see you. Now what this was going to do to my soul and esteem in the long run was not of immediate concern. I was trying to plug my thoughts with ecstasy and flesh. My thoughts for others began to dwindle right around me. Towards the end of fall semester, I took home a slightly overweight science major named Trenton who asked me for a light right outside the library. His weight had nothing to do with my lack of interest as he was only slightly so and his cock didn't suffer for it, but my lack of interest was a symptom of a socialized practice I integrated as part of my character. However, the sex was rather inspiring, and I almost missed a final because of it. Coming out of that exam room I saw Trenton fumbling with his light. For a budding chemist, his complete lack of mastery over the use of flame was a total embarrassment. I walked toward him, and we met eyes when he motioned me over for a light. I took a drag of my own and tucking my head down walked by. The feeling of guilt went deep into my gut with my next inhale until the inevitable exhale that sent those feelings straight out of my head until he appeared at my door, eyes full of tears. He was huffing and puffing in a complete hyperventilated state. He pushed past me despite my protests and persistent questioning. I could see him wanting to muster up the courage to speak. His eyes said it all. The eyes always do. I knew I had hurt him and he, like me, had not known the rules.

But who was I to be for him now? The benevolent enforcer or his lover? In a quiet breath, I spoke while he paced. "God, damn it! These are not the rules! These are not the rules of engagement."

He paused in his tracks to look up at me with the eyes of a fawn belonging to the body of a bear, whose hands easily scooped me up and dropped me down on the bed and I let him. He kissed me ferociously before I stopped him, cupping both my hands around his face and moving my hand around the top of his hair and holding it from falling into his face before nodding and proceeding. And then he proceeded. He was ferocious and strong, and he never laid down but stood over me as I laid on my student bed which was elevated for storage underneath.

From where I lay, he looked rather magnificent, shirt opened and pants around his angles, we locked eyes for a moment of what significance I could not tell you and he pumped me until I was full of himself. He collapsed on me, and I stroked the back of his head until he caught his breath and then I asked, "Did we just make up or break up?"

"I don't know but that was nice."

"I agree."

"I don't want to not be able to do that, do you?" he asked.

"I'm sorry, I didn't know. College seems like one big poker game where everyone pretends like they're not bluffing while we all bluff."

"Well, I'm not bluffing when I say you're only the second guy I've been with."

"I can believe that. You haven't even removed your penis yet and I'm trying not to cry."

"Oh, I'm sorry. I'm so sorry."

"You don't have to be sorry when not every man is carrying something like that around."

He stood back and pulled his boxers on, and I sat up. "You don't have to do that. Come here." I held out my hand as his swallowed mine and I pulled him in between my legs. I ran my hand up his back and down the inside his boxers and over his furry buttocks until they hit the floor again. I kneaded my hands into his buttocks and craned my neck back to look up into his eyes. I asked, "What do you want?"

"I don't want to be alone here," he said.

"Well then, neither of us shall be."

He looked away from me and confessed to the walls. "It can be very lonely here."

I brought his face back to mine, "But never in here." We locked our eyes and our lips, and he filled me again and again until we fell asleep. I awoke in the morning and brought back bagels and two black coffees. I laughed at the giant that lay in my bed with large legs and two large feet hanging well over the edge of my double sized bed, which for both of us felt more like a twin. I left the breakfast next to him and left to go out into the dewy morning. I walked over to one of the bluffs that turned into a hill that went straight to a field where students ran track around it, but today, there wasn't a soul on it. On the bluff was a politics of religion class that sat in session. The professor had tied his shirt around his head. Typical. Below the class section lay two Aphrodite's naked in the sun reading Falkner and all while this was happening I began to hum the tune "On a clear day" and I sat down and began to undress. There was no orchestra, but I could hear them in my head. The music that was playing in my head became the hum on my lips until it was no longer a song in my head but a song that was bursting from my mouth. Self-conscious I was not, the others around me all seemed to disappear. Down the hill I went, as naked as a newborn babe, clothes strewn behind me like relics from my past. I stood at the edge of the bluff naked with arms stretched out basking in the light of my truth, soaking in the knowledge that on days like this you can see forever.

I wonder if that's true when you go to heaven. I hope it is, so Henry doesn't have to worry about me from there.

CHAPTER TWENTY-FOUR

A Clear Day

I returned back to my dorm and fell asleep next to the bear that was still in hibernation, when I was awoken by a desperate knock on the door. I tried to ignore it, but their persistence didn't waver, so I arose to answer it.

Jane came bursting through and stared at my naked body. "So, it's true, you've flipped your fucking lid. Campus security is scouring for a screeching naked idiot that lost his marbles because he failed his finals or something. When I didn't hear from you for a week I assumed you were busy but now I realize it's because you need my help."

Unable to handle nor comprehend what she was saying, I put my hand over her mouth and pushed the door closed and a voice behind me moaned, "I thought she would never shut up." Jane lowered my hand.

"Oh, Oh I see."

"Yes, my dear. I'm not crazy, just happy."

"Well, you can be naked. You can be happy. Butt naked, happy and singing and they will put you away. Those things occurring at the same time are never considered a good sign."

"Well then, maybe everyone is wrong because I've never felt better."

"What's this? Who are you and what did you do with that Avant Garde pessimist I know and love?"

"I'm not feeling like such a pessimist anymore."

"You're about to be. The deadline for turning in your study abroad papers is in half an hour. I'm going right now to save us a spot in line. Hopefully I will see you there. It was nice to have met you, sir. Hopefully we can meet again. It seems as though you've made my friend very happy."

"Don't worry, I'll send him to you and make sure he won't be late," Trenton said.

She closed the door and I let out a loud "Fuck, I totally forgot. Trenton, I have to go, but I'll make sure we see each other tonight."

"Is there any point with you leaving now anyway?

"Oh, for Christ sakes, that's not until next year and you have to be accepted first."

He rose from the bed and began to dress. "Stay in if you like," I said, "I'll be back anyway."

"There's a student rally against the tuition hikes tonight. I wasn't going but perhaps now it would do me some good to clear my head."

"Too pout whilst in protest. Fine, suit yourself. But you don't have to get so cynical. I haven't even gotten in yet."

"Then I selfishly hope they don't think you're as brilliant as I think you are."

"That was adorable, and I love you for it." I kissed him on the cheek. "I'll see you tonight."

The deadline to submit your application to the study abroad office was in 20 minutes by the time I got there so naturally, the publicly funded bureaucracy saw to it that it would take four hours by that time. In which case why even have a deadline? If you're going to have a publicly funded institution then it would make sense to fund them so they could function. After hours of waiting with all the other last-minute applicants, Jane and I decided to walk to the dining hall after being famished all day and discovered that the rally that had started as peaceful was beginning to erupt in the center of the school's plaza. The plaza dipped in the center like a naturally formed amphitheater and the surrounding buildings and tables and benches had been built into the rock, like a quarry site. During the day it was full of life, students, smoke, coffee and conversation.

Tonight, it was full of smoke, anger, noise and fire. Someone stood atop the rock formation that made the center of the quarry plaza and yelled, "Fuck the system!"

From beneath them they began to tear up the stones of the plaza and hurl them at the surrounding administrative buildings. From the crowd, someone cried out, "Fire!" and from atop one of the benches, I saw Trenton with a glass flask, light its wick and hurl it into the side of the school's bookstore. Up in flames the whole building went. I screamed, "Stop it! Stop it!" But the building was swallowed by the flame. Jane pulled my arm, and we fled up the side of the quarry plaza into the surrounding woods, where we finally caught our breath. We looked back to see the whole forest glowing in fire and siren lights. I wept at the sight of seeing my beloved school go up in flames. It was as if all my idealism, love, and nostalgia for this institution could be easily snuffed out. And yet while I stood there, holding onto the idea that no idea could die by fire, the finality of ash, its irreversible state offered no hope of return to what it had been before.

I blocked out Trenton. I couldn't look him in the eye without seeing so many other faces but I knew he loved me. It was a pressure I couldn't have. It's hard to have gifts from god and feel as though they might wither in your hand. One day I saw a sparrow hit my window and I rushed outside to retrieve it from the ground. I felt him go cold in my hand after three days and placed him below my windowsill for failing to save him. I discerned he must have been too young to fly and sailed straight into my window from one of the trees above. I couldn't release him to the elements while he was too weak and immobile so I fed him apple juice using a syringe and this worked the first few days before I must have tried to feed him too much and he drowned.

God sent me one of his creations and I killed him. If I could not care for an infant sparrow, then how could I love a man without pulling him into a pit of my own creation? I sat up from my bed where, next to me lay some version of Adonis and Iago who's particular member I would have gladly cut off by act 3 of the evening if given immunity and poetic license to do so, but alas I looked at him and thought if I lay down with one more of these, then nothing of my soul shall remain should god choose to anoint me with one of his creations. If I have no soul left, then how will I love what has yet to be given? And then it occurred to me as the candy went up my nose, "I forgot, I was already dead. I can't even save a bird"

CHAPTER TWENTY-FIVE

Preparing To Pack: Don't Call A Cab, I Drive A Hearse

Have you ever had one of those dreams where you're inside your own body? I don't know what I had been dreaming about before, but I remember at one point of sleep that I was inside my brain, and I watched someone hammer a spike through my brain while I lay on the inside of my skull. The sensation was so real I awoke in pain and nearly fell off my bed. It was then I realized the sensation had been simulated by a repetitive loud knocking on the door. It was my beloved creature Cecilia. I smiled and then she hit me. Can't remember where because I was barely awake. And then I woke up. I said hello and she struck me across the face. My head turned to the right and when I brought it back to face her she knocked me to the left. I tried to bring my head back while looking at the ceiling, but she wasn't having it. She hit me anyway. And then again and again. Until I could only see her through the water that came rushing through my eyes as hers swelled as well. I tried to hold her, but she pushed me back and I fell.

"I'm sorry," I whispered.

I came crawling to her on my knees. She attempted to raise her hands, but I held them firmly to her side as I wept into her stomach. Her arms relaxed and then I was weeping as she stroked my head. She grabbed a handful of my hair and pulled my head up.

"Look at me." She said as I shut my eyes. "Look at me." She shook my head. "You tried to get rid of me. Why?"

"I'm sorry Ci. I'm drowning."

"I called, and you never answered, I wrote and nothing. How could you do it? It's fine. I knew there was something wrong but fuck you! I'll kill you if you ever do that to me again."

"I'm sorry. I swear to God I don't know what day or what year it is. I'm so ashamed that I want to disappear. When I got here everything was beautiful and then they raised the fucking tuition and I've been working so hard, Jesus Christ I'm so fucking tired I have no relief. I've fucked everything that crawls closest to the earth and for all my effort, nothing puts me to sleep. I only exist somewhere between sobriety and hallucination, and I can't fucking breathe."

"Oh god, you beautiful idiot." She knelt to kiss my forehead. "Shut up and have a good cry and when you're done tell me where you're keeping all of it and we're throwing it away."

"What?" I raised my head and caught my breath. "What do you mean? I'm not… I'm just tired."

"I know darling. I can't have you dying on the plane to Paris."

"How did you?"

"Jane, my replacement, told me all that you've been up to. She's fragile but she cares about you a great deal, but she hasn't the stomach for this nor does she know you like I do."

"Ci, I'm sorry if you came all this way for nothing but you have to go." I got up and went to my desk to pop a few rainbows.

"That's fine and while you do that I'll go to the Chancellor's office and let him know you're selling drugs to the entire student body. You'll be expelled and you'll have to give all that money from your tutoring monopoly back."

"In what universe do you think you have a right to come here and tell me how my life is going to go when I've never had any control over anything that has ever happened?"

"You don't have control now. I got here Saturday night. It is Wednesday. You've been asleep for three fucking days. If you don't wake up to realize you've already lost it then you're going to lose everything. I know, I've been a tart and thrown myself at more heads than I can count, and I've put more up my nose with you than the number of cars that go through the Holland tunnel, but I show up. I'm here and I know what day it is, and I don't want to die. I never thought you did; you were always my fighter. And apart from sending you to a sanitarium to dry out this is the only way I can help you without ruining your life in the process and you know what? This is probably a mistake and I'll regret it later because I'm not a saint and I'm not a doctor, but you're in a lot of pain and I have to stop you before you break beyond saving. Don't make me go over your head to save you. Because that's probably what you need but the cost would be us and that's a price I selfishly am not willing to pay, but if you force my hand, I'll call you a little fool and you'll lose. Now don't fuck with me, tell me I'm right and kiss me."

I walked over to her and kissed her and then she held out her hand to spit out the pill I had pushed in her mouth with mine. "What's this?" She demanded.

"Take it. You're going to need it. It's going to be a bumpy night."

CHAPTER TWENTY-SIX

The Pentecost And Detox

Detox was a horrible and languishing illness that never leaves you. It's like reprogramming to make you sick while you're doing it so the next time you take a pill you'll think twice on it as you remember retching and sweats that could fill the Nile. Ci survived the ordeal, and I had the hallucinations, the night terrors and the pain that could only be temporarily subdued by drops of codeine or ibuprofen after we ran out. After the worst of it had passed, I began to see time like an ocean expanding on the horizon rather than divided up like a pill dispenser that could decide if I was going to be happy or not and then I saw it. The fear of the unknown. I could count on knowing the pills were there as my security, my source of income and sometimes even my friends who couldn't leave. They stayed when I needed them and went when I threw them against the wall. But they always forgave me for my flaws and lifted me up when I hated everything about myself. I made it through a 10-day detox, but there was no way I was going to set foot in a strange land without my comfort. Yes, I could acknowledge that I was overworked and the whole thing had fallen out of my control but there was no reason under heaven why I couldn't function and have my fix. Fuck, to this day I hate words like fix, addiction, crutch because they oversimplify the satisfaction the drugs provided. Just like how the word love can't contain within it, the vastness of its meaning, so has there yet to be such a word to describe the relationship between a man and his pills? Nary has such a word been uttered and yet dare I speak it; can it be love? Unhealthy as it was, the word fit perfectly.

The dawn had come with the time that it has taken for me to labor upon this period that was my life for so long, but it was necessary not only as a bit of catharsis for me, but amidst the reread with the context of what is to come. I hate the disparities that exist between the readership and their feelings towards certain characters, that whole business of I hate him, and he got what was coming and the other half who bleat and cry with Antony. You don't have to love him, but I would ask that you read no further unless you do not have a modicum of compassion for him, to the exception being that you may be allowed to proceed in the hopes that you might inevitably find compassion for him just as I did in the many years that I spent trying to forgive him. If I could go back and teach him how to exhale then I would, but it wouldn't have done him any good. First, he had to learn how to breathe.

Up the gangplank he went to prove to himself that he was fine. He buried pieces of darkness in the final essays he wrote and sold them to buy six months' worth of drugs as a precaution. The lies we tell ourselves when logic teaches us that the only thing we can be sure of is our own mind is comical. To lie to the only thing, we can truly count on as if the mind does not already know that there's poison in the glass when it gave you the idea to put it there. This is the downfall of the addict, the divine comedy divided into nine personalized rings of hell that form the path of a downward spiral until you come out repentant and clean on the other side or perish on the lake of ice trapped by disease, unable to free oneself from the vice that led him to the lake to lie with the betrayers, killed dead by his own vice he perishes upon the lake of ice. But before proceeding I will offer this, in the fulfillment of all righteousness even He could not be baptized until He kneeled in the river. Righteousness, not salvation, is something that you can not walk to nor achieve while standing. To be born again, one must crawl and scrape and kneel upon the altar of their own destruction, in recognition of their weakness before the table of the Father like in the prodigal son returned. Purity is a process not a state. If left alone the water turns brackish, the fruit to rot and the fields overgrown unless otherwise tended. How much more than must one lend to the tending of their soul let alone to one that is broken? It is then with no amount of irony that I confess that within the covers of this journal is the landscape of men at work on a mountain that overlooks a lake. Such a landscape reminds us of how hard we must work if we are to reside close to God. It is with that notion that this boy's life begins, commencing the journey that Antony's life must takes in order for him to ascend. As I have been the vessel for his pain, I hope I write to create another vessel for his healing. He is my greatest accomplishment, and this is my opus to him. The story of how I saved myself and how Henri saved me.

CHAPTER TWENTY SEVEN

A Room And No View

The arrangement that I had made with Jane was that Ci would be taking a leave of absence to attend the Sorbonne to be used as credit towards the completion of her undergraduate work all while living with us and paying 2/3rds of the rent. It was a small apartment with a bedroom and a fold out sectional in the living room/kitchen that I volunteered to be my sleeping quarters out of chivalry and for want of privacy for my things while respecting theirs. It's harder to hide stuff when you're sharing a door, I figured. Two girls cut from the same royal cloth would be too immersed in comparing labels and waist sizes that my belongings would serve little to no interest to them.

I couldn't have been more wrong upon coming home one afternoon to a catwalk of my assorted furs, handbags and leather goods. Occupational hazard of being a gay man with taste, all your girlfriends will take your shit. Thankfully, the uninteresting sock rolls, manicure and shaving kits were hiding the real treasures, a whole rainbow of uppers, downers, carpets, drapes, and other in-home mood enhancers. Since everyone's eyes were everywhere except on me I could experiment with them on when and where I could take a pill. I took my moment alone on our balcony like a love scene from Romeo and Juliet. I brought the smooth white and red and blue pills to my lips before whispering "anon" and taking them in. Part of me felt a great sense of pride for being able to hide a horde of pills, some in the colors of the French flag and the other part made my heart race, engaging in a forbidden romance no one could detect. It became an obsession all on its own. But I can concede to the extent to which a disease can tread along the boundaries of the phrase of "mind over matter." The surroundings alone were enough to distract one from your body, causing one to only look up. It's the calling card for the American tourist. Frenchmen keep their noses to the pavement while Americans have their eyes to the sky. Paris is where one goes to be seen. Large boulevards lined with cafes crowned with wicker chairs to people watch, serving as a national pastime. One wanders with their eyes to see the tops of beautifully placed and buildings resembling God's chess pieces, and goes back in time, to a place of marble terraces circled in wrought iron, paved sweeping boulevards, to broken cobblestone streets and wood paneled thatched establishments. These small edifices stood hitched under the great architectural feats of Paris, often ignored by children who can't be bothered by crooked streets, Carl Marx cafes, dusty bookstores and hidden taverns. Standing on deserted streets you find one of many lives you've lived before, passing by the life you are living now. What did I crave 100 years before and what made me stand on this abandoned avenue that made me not want to move? Walking in the sun, how familiar it all seemed to me. It felt familiar for someone else, whose memory I was keeping hidden, until now. As I turned for home, I watched the sun fall back to God behind the rooftops and the Palace of Justice and the faint silhouette of the Eiffel Tower from the Seine. All these new sensations soothed the cravings of a broken heart and a weary mind.

The body thirsts while the soul grows hungry for relief. The body houses the soul and yet in it, are the weaknesses of the flesh that breaks the covenant between spirit and body; Proof of our own humanity and, our imperfections as well as our mortality. Was it possible to find salvation in anything? For so long, I told myself it was in those little capsules. Logically all the answers I was seeking could not be found between the ends of a capsule. However, I couldn't stop until I found something to replace it with, but I would do my best to search and only take a pill until I could stand the cravings no longer. If I could cleave away from all who had done me harm, I would sow my own garden like in Candide; forge my own path and break from the chains cast around my beating heart and wilted wings. I would not make myself a slave to my own body. If I sought with all my might to heal mind and soul then perhaps the flesh would bend to the will of the two, air would leave untrapped from body and the sky would look more like a possibility than a challenge.

CHAPTER TWENTY-EIGHT

The Valley Of the Intellectual Leper And The Hand That Holds The Pen

I had to remember I used to love to learn. I couldn't believe that the world which had left me bitter could not also teach me how to be human again. The French have this method of writing where you pose a question to what you have learned, rather than the Anglican way of writing which is, "repeat to me in the most eloquent way possible exactly what I've told you." Sitting once again in a room of ten and not one hundred, the air of the professor left us more skeptical of everything he had said and of what we knew before we entered the classroom each day. In fact, the best grades were often given to those armed with reason and could break down the legitimacy of every concept of the curriculum through the exposition of a question created by the students themselves.

It was brilliant. I ate every moment up, like a macaroon wrapped in gold. I had a professor named Hubert of Persian French and

Anglican descent revealed through the red whiskers he tried so hard to hide inside his black beard. The class was titled "19th and 20th Century French Intellectual History." The first day we read Plato's dialogue written about 3000 years outside the confines of the class's title but that's where he began. He began with the word "Parrhesia," which is the act of truth telling or if you are a parrhesiast, "bringer of the truth." The stance of their writing considers ignorance to be a sin but raises the distinction of being willfully ignorant, much graver a sin above just being born ignorant. Therefore, being a parrhesiast was not only the honor of a parrhesiast but a moral occupational imperative. However, as a witness bearer of the truth one becomes the bearer of its consequences. Plato's discourse is on the trial and execution of his mentor. Socrates who as a parrhesiast carried with him the truth and burden that he knew nothing and the people of Greece killed him for it, but before they did, Socrates condemned them for condemning him to death. For to condemn a man to die, one makes the claim of having knowledge after death. If one did not know the consequences of death, then the power of the punishment is void. Socrates who knew nothing, couldn't be afraid of something unconfirmed by the natural world and for that reason chose death by suicide, living his life to the last breath as the man who questioned everything, knew nothing, and died for it. And Plato takes up the torch of his master, continuing in the tradition of parrhesia by bearing witness to the truth of the slain.

After saying to use "The odyssey to find truth" read by the master and his student as bringers of truth begins; he slaps down discourse: a syllabus. "The Problematization of Parrhesia," is how it all began. There was a series of lectures given by an avid homosexual and French philosopher whose works on sincerity and truth I had read under the covers like playboy magazines because his work had been banned. One never realized the extent of the meaning of private education until knowledge becomes a matter of taste and preference and here this man stands at the head of this flock and says, "I will show you how to be philosophers but not in the sense that you'll be sitting under trees waiting for apples to fall, but you'll be actors and critical thinkers. To be a philosopher is to bear witness to the truth. One cannot call themselves a member of the human race, unless there are some beliefs that you're willing to die for, because at some point someone will ask the person next to you, to account for your life. What is it you would stand for? What would they say? If you don't know then you're not alive. You all think you were born? Yet, you all must be born again, or rise from the passive graves that have all been dug for you. If you cannot stand for something, lay back in your cradle as it will serve as your cage. Or go home and when we next weigh in, tell me in five pages, single spaced, a truth you're willing to die for and maybe I'll let you take my class."

"Now, some of you might think from where you're sitting that I can't do that because you're paying to be here. To that I say, no one is paying you to live. You have to live by your own willpower to do so. The requirements of this class are that you connect your will to live to universal truths you find cannot exist without, just as much as you cannot exist without air. If you can't do that then don't come here because you won't pass anyway. But if you are willing to bend your will to allow me to bend your mind, then I will be proud to say that I have sent however many you are, out to the world as actors and not pacifists, not conformists, but parrhesiast, bearers of the truth. Now, class dismissed."

The 18 of us sat there in amazement of him, paralyzed and unable to move. He took out a hand rolled cigarette and breathed out thick billows of smoke that he sucked back into his lungs for a second hit before releasing it through his nostrils like a dragon. "Dismissed" he bellowed, and with the effort of a crack of a whip we scattered. A few of us, myself included, found ourselves still unable to move each of us uttering our most prevalent thoughts.

"He's amazing."

"He's an Asshole."

"He's a genius," I said.

And with hearing as sharp as his intellect, he responded and said, "When you're off the clock and away from my classroom, you can say all those adjectives, however colorful or personal about my life and taken them to Human Sexuality and Cognitive Psych. Both are down the hall. Perhaps the three of you can schedule your appointments together. Unless you need me to lead you."

Like mice we scattered as I tried desperately to avoid his eyes but failed on all counts only to be frozen at the entrance, unable to move. He stared at me with an indiscernible quandary and asked if I needed a light or a fag.

"I said neither, I don't smoke."

He smiled, "Liar," then took a drag… "dismissed."

That night and for the rest of the week I was unable to sleep as I was both kept awake by the things that I liked about Professor Hubert and the things that made me afraid. Although one is never quite sure of the things that keep us up at night. I don't think it's fear of going to sleep, it's the fear of waking up and things being exactly the same, this of course is derived from the fact that we can't see the future. It has been said that this is the reason why we can't see the future. If we did, we would all become immobile, panicking from ever going out the front door for fear of the inevitable.

Therefore, the unknown becomes, our light and our guide with the hope that today something will happen that will change one's life. It's the dice roll we make every day when we get up out of bed and play out the day on God's humor. It's amazing how life will surprise when life itself happens, breathing hope back into you as you breathe out the promise of time sealed in a kiss and wrapped in the space that consumed it.

Standing in a courtyard that acts as the buffer between all the Science Po buildings, the students and professors would congregate to exchange their thoughts sent through smoke. It really made you feel like you were internalizing what you were learning when you inhaled your assignment and sent it out to your comrades in a billow of pride. I had just finished making a grand point on French nationalism and its effect on current European relations when Professor Hubert came up to the loudest group of youths making a stink about European politics.

"Really boys you're not going to solve the European crisis before 9am and trying to do so before 9am and without coffee is unholy."

"Are you removing your politics to become a papist, professor?" A student asked.

"Impossible."

"Why professor?"

Putting out the end of his cigarette he replied, "Because I'm a fascist." We all laughed. "Good you all laughed." He said. Pulling out another of his roll-ups. "I guess that proves I am," looking straight through me, and then to my hand clutching my Gauloises. "Do you have a light Shrader?" Like looking at a game of chess, I begrudgingly handed one over and he smiled and said, "Merci, see you inside Shrader."

"Bastard." I thought to myself then smiled at the impending commencement of class session. When we sat down he asked that we take out our papers and place them upon our desk. He would walk by and collect them and then choose five at random each week to discuss causes or thoughts we would be willing to die for. By the end of the session, we might feel differently about our original arguments we had put forth, or perhaps adopt a new one altogether. The point being, by the end we would give a fuck about something. Some titles he read out loud to create suspense of coming attractions and then he came to my desk. He was about to leave my desk when he came back and slapped down the paper entitled "My truth," by Anthony Shrader, my argument. "My truth is I have no truth because the truth is a farce" in a single space, five pages repeated approximately 10,000 times.

"Read it!" He said.

"I know what it says."

"Then you should have no problem reading it. If this is the belief you're willing to die for, then you're going to say it."

"My truth, by Anthony Shrader. My Truth is I have no truth because the truth is a farce. My truth is I have no truth because the truth is a farce. My truth…"

"Good," Then he snatched up my paper from my desk before I could continue and to quell the cacophony of snickers disturbing the peace. "Now, get out."

"Go and fail me, but I did the assignment. I spoke my truth."

"Being a parrhesiast and a smart ass are not the same thing. I'm willing to die for what I believe and that is why I teach and if you don't care and think this bleeding-heart cry for help is supposed to make me sorry for you, then you're mistaken."

"You want the truth for a lie? I can't write what I don't believe because I don't know what to believe. I can't find nor think of a truth I'm willing to die for in less than a week. And if I made one up for a gold star then that would be parseshist, Professor. Why don't I take this class and see if you can make me believe in anything and then I'll write you a paper on what I believe."

"Out of fairness to the students who completed the assignment you're not allowed to participate but I concede not everyone walks in here already feeling something. Therefore, I will be seeing you in my office after class and what we discuss will determine if you will be staying in my class. That is my right. Dismissed."

I rose from the chair biting my lips and not breathing until the door closed behind me and the first of many tears hit the floor. I was right but I was wrong. I fought but I was defeated. I thought I had loved, and I lost.

Whenever I thought about how I could make my fear become severed, like an artery, with all my dreams bleeding out along with my idealism. I had changed the scenery, but when I sat to write that prompt, I realized I was living a life according to a path rather than by a principle. We live but we die knowing what we lived for. I didn't even know why I was alive now.

"I didn't want to answer the prompt until I had truly found the answer. Anything else would be a lie and not in the nature nor practice of parrhesia."

"Then why not come to me? Ask me for an extension? Communicate your thoughts to your peers? That's what adults do." Professor rested with his arms against his chest waiting for an answer.

"Do you want a reason?"

"I certainly want to understand your process."

"My reasoning was stupid and unfounded."

"Such conclusions are usually brought on by fear. What was it that you were afraid of?"

"You, Sir."

"That right there, fear disguised in formality. When we are not in class you may call me Henry, so long as you know I'm the professor and you're the student. I do enjoy that, as I have spent nearly a decade in higher learning to be acknowledged. It might be within the vein of pride, but I like the title that gives the students a place to go when they search for answers to their questions. It's for the same reason we say doctor or officer. It derives comfort to those from whom we seek help. If you need me, 'Professor', or if you need a light, Henry. Alright?"

"I must say, sir… Henry, I'm a bit embarrassed but I'm grateful for the time you've spent, teaching me as it were, on how we can move forward."

"I'll go even further and wager that by the end of our time together you will find the truth you seek. I'd wager my future as an educator on it. You will feel something in my class."

"May I ask, what is it you're reading? It couldn't be my paper as we both know what it says."

"Your file. I read all my student's transcripts and reviews. It gives me context for when they speak or ask questions."

"Does it say I smoke there?" I was being sarcastic of course.

"Yes, in fact."

My head shot back to him. "Oh, don't look annoyed. I went to an all-boys private school." He snickered.

"How did you find it? Your experience there I mean?"

"Rather gay and annoying."

"I'm assuming you found the opposite to be true, why else would you, Shrader, leave and choose to finish your GED on your own."

"I found the institution to be plenty gay just not very accommodating to those who were."

"Who are. They are gay even after they leave." He rolled a cigarette.

"That's not what I meant."

"No, it was. You're testing me to see how much I can catch onto; or how much I'm willing to tolerate."

"I think you assume me to be more calculating than I appear."

"I think the ability to appear contrary to that assumption is part of your charm and I look forward to seeing all your nuances in my class."

"I no longer find this conversation to be appropriate. I have never been talked to by a professor in my life this way. For a man of higher learning this conversation has sunk to the most debased level."

"Don't shoot up out of my chair as if you've won the moral high ground. I've made no such assumptions beyond what you've read and what you've told me. If you wanted to pass my class as a pacifist, being passed over in lecture then you wouldn't have instigated my curiosity with that farce of a paper unless I assume you were not trying to be difficult, but rather call to my attention that you were an independent thinker, a martyr for thought."

"A parrhesiastes or a pantheist?"

"Precisely but only to your first reply."

"You use flattery on me sir. How dare you?"

"Don't need to. I have the truth. You just keep drawing the line, erasing and redrawing to confuse yourself." I motioned to speak, "No, don't deny it. It's true, although it fascinates me as to the why."

"Men have suffered from wanting to learn less," I looked around the room for an escape.

"I have a strong immune system. I assure you, my pupil, you will leave my class with horizons widened."

"I'm still your student?"

"Yes, I'm afraid all my attempts to discourage you as well as shooting your own potential in the foot have failed. The only way you can fail is If you don't turn in your first assignment by the end of the term. All future assignments will have their respective due dates."

"You think you can teach me something?" I was halfway out of my chair halfway through the sentence.

"Mr. Shrader," he called, "I haven't even begun to teach you."

"Take care and save your wind for class." I thought I was being clever before he retorted.

"I'll save my wind for smoking."

With the door closed, I heard him "Oh and Mr. Shrader." I couldn't walk away because I know he knew I heard him. Opening the door, I poked my head in with a "yes professor?"

"Humility."

"What I asked?"

"That's your first lesson. Dismissed."

And I shut the door, burning with pride until I returned to our little apartment on the Seine in the third arrondissement, searching to see if I packed my humility with my pills.

CHAPTER TWENTY-NINE

The Sun Sets With A Lecture

The girls returned home from their evening classes to find strewn about the failed attempts at life's big questions in an existential mess of clothes and booze.

"I always pictured this is what it would look like to write my own wedding vows." Ci had a way of making humor converge with identity crisis.

"Is the cure for cancer somewhere in here as well? Jane asked?"

"It's actually the kindling for my funeral pyre."

"How can we help?" Ci was trying this new thing where she would become constructive after my attempted rehabilitation. She wore it like a badge as most people wear chartreuse: a dare that should never be attempted.

"Do you have a match? You can light me," I asked.

"Dramatics are not going to help in the completion of your task nor aid in your recovery," Ci handed me the light.

"Cecilia, these fortune cookie altruisms and self-help one liners are driving me up the fucking wall. In fact, you sound so unlike yourself I need a drink just to listen to you."

"Oh then, what would you like me to do?"

"Start drinking to at least appear normal. This born-again shit is giving me a rash and feels like an *Invader Of The Body Snatchers*. Just act normal."

"To be honest that sounds like a trick question Anton. Because my normal is abnormal so if I tried acting normal I'd go crazy."

"Here is a vodka soda and sit on it." As Jane hastily shoved the sticky glass into Ci's hand she moved over to where I sat on the floor and touched the back of my head. "Come on, get up. We're going for a walk."

"I don't want to." I turned to my feet that felt like anchors.

"I know, that's why I want to torture you. Now, up!"

"If you guys can remember on your way back to grab another bottle that would be divine"

Cecilia was fending for her own sanity and judgment.

"I bought one this morning," I said.

"Yeah… I know and while I live in the country where wine and bread are the two cheapest things, I'm going to need as much as possible, even if they have to charge me an extra baggage fee. My fat ass can afford it."

"You know, I'll help you carry your butt across the tarmac?"

"That's why I love you," she flipped a shekel towards me that I caught in mid-air.

"Try not to eat all the bread for the citizens of Paris, will you?" I called back at her.

"But they eat cake," was her reply.

"Fine stay here. Don't lose your head. We won't be gone long."

"I'm not sure if that was a pun but it was cheap and terrible." Ci always maintained a modicum of censorship when it came to the use of clichés around me.

"This city is so cliché, I've come to embrace it." My sigh felt like relief.

"I would say we'll grab a drink but you're going to need a clear head if I'm going to get inside that thick skull of yours. Now walk." Jane pulled me out before my coat was on my shoulders.

We were moving but in a slow, foot dragging protest of pace.

"Why is everyone trying to help me? I'm fine," I screamed. "Can't I maintain some loyalty to my east coast roots by acting like a jaded prick? It's important not to forget where you come from. These miserable French pricks are still trying to fight someone every minute. I literally had someone move me out of their way getting off a metro. Physically picked me up. I thought my entrails were going to fall out of my butt. I don't know why I am here."

"Walk, breathe and smoke and not one word until we reach the Seine."

"Seduction before sunset. I'm homosexual Jane. Changing time zones do not alter realities."

"Pull down your shirt Anton, you're showing your vanity."

"Was that your attempt at a gay joke Jane? I have one... knock, knock."

"Shut up and walk! I want to show you something."

We passed Art de Matière and a hard right down Rue de Beau Bourg. You could see the orange sun showering the tops of the Hotel and Notre Dame a pink kiss that turned into tangerine, violet and ruby. Birds were fleeing from their stone prison before they turned to gargoyles. Folly, it may have been, but an explanation that intoxicated my imagination before we reached the bank of the Seine.

"Now sit. Talk." Jane fell down with our full weight.

"Can't we just sit?" I asked.

"Ok, selfishly I might admit, maybe I have more to say at the present then you're willing to tell me now, but maybe by the end you'll hear me and have something to offer."

"I'm so sick of being told what to do and everyone's diagnosis of what they think is wrong with me." I took the largest drag of a cigarette since they first gave tobacco to the natives and nearly choked to death. "God help me." In the middle of me choking on pride and my left lung, Jane removed a small silver flask from her scarlet red pea coat. One that I fondly remembered for its brass fleur de lis buttons wishing that at the time I had a camera with me to capture the sight of her.

"What is it?" I asked.

"Bourbon. This is probably a no-no for sobriety."

"The drink has never been my vice. It does little to silence the gremlins dancing in my head." I grabbed the flask and took a swig that was like cauterizing a wound. My eyes watered but I cleared my sight and looked up into the blinding sunset, realizing I had never bothered to see Paris at sunset. Sitting on the bank of Notre Dame, the blossoms from the garden of elements that sat behind the church drifted into the organ waves of the seine, called by the wind.

"It's beautiful." I said.

"I know." Jane said, taking a swig from her flask.

"Is that why you have brought me here?"

"Partly. Have you ever seen Paris during a sunset?"

"I have now. I am now."

"But we've been here nearly a month, and you haven't until now?" You can't see what's around while you sulk and drown in your sorrow. When I first saw you at college I was enamored with your mind and your passion but you're wilting like some fruit on a vine, and I find myself unable to help."

"Did you think that forced detox robbing me of my only comfort would leave me inspired before I was dropped in the middle of a country with no common language, friends, or surroundings?"

"You would have died before you got here. Perhaps Ci loves you too much to see that you haven't stopped but we both know you haven't. If we never had intervened, ask yourself, 'why did you come here?'"

"I don't know."

"Think."

"It's stupid. A child's fantasy."

"There is no amount of hope wasted in innocence."

"Innocence? It is the death of innocence that befalls the threshold into adulthood. Except no one tells you how hard it's going to be."

"What's bothering you? I want to help but every time I try to pry, you change your shape."

"I thought everything would be different. I think there exists an expectation created when one thinks of Paris. But I live in Paris, and, well, it's not the movies."

"Yes, it is, because you can have moments like this." She reached out to touch my hand.

"Is this idealism contagious?" Looking at her with a surgeon's speculation, I was searching for her next response on her face.

"It must be. I caught it from you."

I laughed.

She smiled, "There's a reason why the poets of the past write about Paris. It's infectious, contagious, and beautiful beyond any city you can visit."

"Too bad they didn't tell us that our school French isn't worth shit to a Parisian."

"You can't think about the words you just have to say them, spit them out as fast as they, walk like your pants are on fire and start drinking at noon."

"How do you know so much about the nuances of French life?"

"Well, my brother, correction, half-brother, teaches at our school. I've been staying with him at the end of term since I was 14."

"And this has only become relevant now?"

"This coming from the most secretive person I know?"

"What does he teach?"

"He lives and breathes French intellectual history and philosophy."

"Any chance I can get into his class?"

"I'm having lunch with him tomorrow. I'm sure he can snatch you away from the other professor who's been giving you shit."

"The thing is, I don't think he's a bad person by any means. He has a fork for a tongue and a scalpel for eyes. It's like he's trying to cut me open and inside every time we talk. It's as if his only chance of getting you to eat his bullshit is if he gets inside your head and I can't stand it."

"Well, if you do meet my brother I would refrain from calling what he teaches as bullshit. I don't think any of these men can talk about this shit everyday unless they live by the principles they teach."

"I definitely would like to talk to him. Anyone would be better than this lunatic."

"Okay then, two blocks back from where you get off at, St. Germain, there's a side street with a brick bordering and wood embossed building that looks different from all the others surrounding it. Supposedly, that's where Karl Marx spent his time writing his manifesto."

"Doubtful."

"Regardless, that's where I'm meeting him after class. A small hole in the wall. Can't miss it. Owned by a little Italian and his brother who works as a server. The chef is from the previous owner who sold his chef along with the building."

"And he's still alive."

"Yes, smokes like a chimney while he prepares the food, but no one can get him to stop."

"Sounds charming." I was apprehensive about the whole thing but had to abide with how accommodating Jane was being. She's literally so hands off and I felt as if she was really trying to help me or save me. It was like living in a house that was on fire but only she could see the smoke from the chimney. Perhaps she could help me get away from Professor Hubert and show me everything that I was missing. I was an "A" exchange student and time was slipping.

As we watched the sun take its final curtain call, Jane began to speak in conclusion as if this had been a session. I know that wasn't her intention, but her delicate exterior was much like her disposition. She didn't like waves or messes. Everything had to be fine, and everyone should be as well. It would seem as though she could conceive of no other reason why anyone should drive themselves into a brick wall intentionally. Nothing could be so horrible. "You know what I think, Antony?"

"What?"

"I think you're going to be fine. I think you've had some… regrettable experiences, some of which I do not know the specifics of, but I think deep down, you want to do better, be better and feel better. Maybe once we have shaken that stress load a bit, you'll be able to see everything in the light in which things were intended."

"Getting a little born-again, are you?"

"No, just trying to make you see things without the shadows."

"You be my light then, won't you?" I asked.

"No darling. Has to come from here." She said, placing her delicate fingers on my chest. "You will meet us tomorrow, won't you?"

"I'll be there. I'll be there because you asked. And this was nice. Just this. Sitting here, talking. Thank you darling."

"Don't mention it. Just be happy."

"I can try. We can all try."

CHAPTER THIRTY

Bitter Grapes

The next day I awoke in good spirits, skipped my morning pill and replaced it with coffee until about noon when the morning pill doubled up with the afternoon's dosage and then an extra one for nerves. What did I have to be nervous about? I was always nervous about everything. The pills don't only affect your mind, they affect the body but not so much internally right away. That takes time. At first, it's gradual and then before you know it, your epidermis has become paper. The wind, the air, the rain, life, voices, people all break your skin like the soluble capsule that you put in your mouth because you thought you were hot shit who didn't have to deal with problems. Now, I took a pill to fill in the new cracks forming on the surface. I can't trace the new ones without finding the breaks beneath, made of underlying problems festering under my broken flesh.

The restaurant was easy enough to find, standing frozen in time, having survived the Haussmannization that overtook Paris all those years ago. Perhaps it was just too beautiful and picturesque to cut out of the world like an abscess. Rather it was more of a beauty blemish that was allowed to persevere upon the force of an aging beauty, the true personification, manifestation, and definition of Paris.

I walked through the small gate where half a dozen or so picaresque flower boxes lined the original cobblestone that was the entrance to the restaurant that stood on its original stone foundation, whereupon you had to step up and into this fleeting world rather than glide through.

I was the first to arrive, the owner, an old man and I were the ornaments of this beautiful world of embossed dark wood, pewter tankards, and embedded smells that were preserved in the grain of the wood as much as it was preserved in the history of the place.

To make a good impression and to appear assimilated, I took the liberty of ordering a bottle of moderately priced Bordeaux as to not appear too cheap or too pretentious. A tiny pair of hands appeared from behind me to block my sight and then disappeared to reveal this tiny and poignantly dressed creature in a blue fox trim coat and read leather gloves; she was a model of perfection and simple elegance.

"I'm very excited, you know." Reaching out, I began to fill her glass before continuing.

"I've had something to look forward to. I think I've been craving some external source of mental stimulation."

"Then you should enjoy yourself very much, because once Henry starts talking, there's no putting out that roman flare. You just have to let him burn out."

"I suspect he's been burning for years already with no end in sight."

"That pretty much sums him up. Here comes Lucifer in the flesh now."

While most of you reading this might have reached the forgone conclusions of my humiliation some pages back, I had to tell it in the same oblivious, drawn-out fashion in which the events themselves unfolded.

At precisely 12:13pm, Dr. Henry Hossein Hubert walked in and shot me in the face. Oh, not really, but at the time I wish he had come armed.

"Curiouser and Curiouser," he started out, "I've been chasing the white rabbit all this time and here he sits before me."

I could feel my limbs detaching themselves from the corpse they were attached to.

"No, please don't get up. I can do office hours on wine better than any of these other frenchies and in fact I may start requiring that students either meet me here or bring a Pinot before they even think of coming to the office. Can I roll any one of you a fag? But you only sometimes smoke, right? Perhaps before the end of this lunch, you can decide whether smoking is something you can believe in or not. Before you decide, I recommend several deep long pulls. I'm sure even the most Puritanical during the reformation could understand the benefits of a good cigarette despite it being a vice. It was also the most popular last request by prisoners sentenced to the guillotine. The most important thing to them before they lost everything from the neck up. Imagine that. You don't have to answer if you can't, right now. Why don't you take the entire semester to think about it."

"Fuck, Antony, I…"

"It's alright, you didn't know and neither did I. Goodbye."

I never did get to taste that wine.

CHAPTER THIRTY-ONE

My Tub Overfloweth

ntony. Antony, please open the door," Jane pleaded.

"I'm naked and trying to drown myself. Do you mind?"

"Antony, that's not funny."

"Call the police, just don't tell them it's an American otherwise they'll never come."

"Fuck you! Open the Door!"

"Jesus Christ! Don't have an aneurysm!" Dripping wet, I went to the door and then slipped my sedated body back into the tub."

"What are you doing?"

"Doing some self-exploration through drug experimentation."

"Stop it!"

"Or what darling? You're going to try to fix me again? If I ever complained of some minor constipation, you would probably shove the whole Eiffel Tower up my ass."

"There's no way I could have known the connection but given that you are a perpetual cry for help it comes to no surprise that you were being the impudent little shit, the bane of existence, the pinnacle of insolence."

"He talked to you about me, did he?"

"He did."

"And one of the things I can't seem to understand is why you insist on making everything so hard for yourself. I'm sorry for setting you up, but from the conversations I had with my brother I never would have been able to conclude that either of you were talking about the other. In fact, I would scold both of you for being underwhelmingly accurate in both of your personal speculations on the other. Damn both of you for your gross and unfair character assassinations of one another."

"Damn you, for your inability to look beyond the shortcomings of your own brother which has rendered you useless in discerning that such an odious contemptible ass of a man's description could only fit one single bastard in the universe and all its entirety."

"Well, damn you for starting this whole thing. It was one fucking assignment! You couldn't have chosen to die on a more important hill?"

"God damn you for not understanding either! Get out!"

"Fine! Come find me when you're not like this." She left filled to the brim with frustration that the two most pigheaded intellectuals were also the two most important men in her life. Just when remorse was beginning to sink into my heart, my thoughts became interrupted by a knock on the door.

"Jesus Christ, will you go away?" I shouted before burying myself underwater.

"Fuck you and, I'm not Jesus Christ," Cecilia came in and at down on the toilet across from the tub.

"Is there nowhere in this house where I'm allowed to be naked and alone?"

"Nope, I'm afraid not. Start talking."

"I'm really done talking about it and this intellectually frustrated old man with a power trip and small prick."

"Okay, I see where this is leading."

"What are you doing?" I said in horror as she began kicking off her mary janes and unbuttoning her blouse.

"Getting personal. Move over!"

"You're fucking crazy!"

"That's a pretty irrelevant statement for this stage of our friendship and we've already crossed this bridge, so pull the Victorian prudity out of your ass and move over." Sliding down and across from me the water and suds rose-up and around her breasts, cradled like two bocce balls on a pillow of pink bubbles. Reaching over to her slacks on the floor, she pulled out a small bottle of Stoli and a pack of cigs. Lit one and then knocked back a belt of vodka, through one of her rings of smoke. She said, "Okay, go."

"Well, seeing as I don't have a choice,"

"No, we all have a choice and the only reason you're brooding is because you're begging for someone to sit on your chest and make you talk about this and unfortunately there's not enough baguette in this country to make Jane weigh over 100 pounds, so I'm it! And between both of my tits alone, I have half her body weight so let's try this from the beginning."

"Dr. Professor Hubert, made us write an assignment."

"Yeah, babe, we already got that shit, and then the same mom, different father, mistaken identities, got it, I'm here so tell me the issue. The events are irrelevant, what's the problem?"

For once I had nothing to say.

"I'm sorry, is there an echo in this tub?"

"I, I don't know."

"Oh, so you're mad and you're ruining friendships, and you don't know? Yeah, that doesn't fucking cut ice with me, I'm gonna need to hear some shit before the bubbles disappear around my boobies."

"I fucking hate him," I said quietly while looking away.

"Okay, great start. Why?"

"Because he humiliated me!"

"Okay babe, I love you but we both know you did that one on your own. He called you out on your shit okay? What else?"

"He's arrogant."

"He has a PhD, and a big dick so that gives him the right to be. Next."

"If my answers aren't good enough then you can get the fuck out of my tub!"

"I still have bubbles left and my foot is resting right between your legs so we're gonna move on, but your efforts were noted."

"I don't know what you want me to say."

"I'm going to pretend and be the man you hate and force you to think. Why do you hate him?"

I stared down at the bubbles that were almost gone and saw a reflection I didn't like and then another and another until I splashed the water with my hand and ran my wet fingers through my hair and felt like crying. Ci leaned forward and touched my arm, "Tell me." She said, "What are you thinking?"

"That I hate myself. I hate myself for hating him. He's… he's exactly where I want to be and even though he stands a few feet in front of me where he is, what he is seems so far out of reach. I see what I want, and I feel like I don't have the steam to make it to the finish line."

"But you're already in the race, you're here and you're doing it. Why wouldn't you finish?"

"Because I'm weak. Because I'll never be able to stand up and speak the way he does, how could I ever without feeling like everyone can see through me like glass?"

"Okay, so the students that you don't have can see through you?"

"Well, he can, when he lectures, I can feel him inside my chest, and he stares right at me with these eyes like he already knows everything but he's just fucking with me."

"Darling," Ci took in a deep breath and smiled, "Now let me fill in some information for you. Truth is, he sees you, but not, in the literal way, in the way that you might think. Your past though it may feel like your present is your past and no one knows about it except you. But like me, I can see when one of my friends is hurting and honey, you have hurt faggot written all over your face, especially the fag part because Henri is a pufta as well. He can see you; he can smell you and he knows you because he is you."

"Oh…"

"Yeah, jealousy and hatred blind us to a lot and for the record, prior to our attempts to get you sober, which I'm placing in non-operational status at this point, Jane and I discussed your meeting her brother in the hopes that he might serve as a mentoring inspiration, blah blah, you get the picture."

"Well, now that's fucked."

"Hey, it's not over, you're not dead yet. Reincarnation had never been more real to me than through watching you."

"I apologize for making it look so easy while I fade from exhaustion! Je suis tres fatigue."

"Looks like we've run out of bubbles." Ci took a last drag from her cigarette and dropped it in the small bottle of tub water that used to be vodka to put out the cigarette. "Look at that. I made art. Kind of pretty, don't you think?"

I smiled and sank back down into the chilled tub water, "It's perfect."

CHAPTER THIRTY-TWO

Office Hours

As opposed to taking the metro to St. Germain, I decided I would walk through the Spanish quarter past the St. Michel fountain to collect my thoughts about Dr. Hubert. My tote bag grew heavy with each step, but I chose the hour walk, instead of a seven-minute ride underground because of the value I had come to place in deep thought.

My arrival to Sciences Po, was interrupted by a security guard that asked to see my student identification card before I entered the building. There were always labor protests and every so often a bomb threat would follow.

I showed him my card, he glanced at his counterpart then above my head and then said, "Entre s'il vous plait." As I replaced my ID back in my bag, I saw them take the ID of one of my classmates. They said, "Retires varte sai." After dumping everything out they said he could go in. His eyes locked with mine as he put each item back in his sack. I walked away with my face burning red, hating myself for having not done anything. I went to sleep thinking how could I complain about my own state when I move through everyday obstacles with ease. As humans we suffer as one, and yet how alone we feel as we do. As a white, I could enter but as a black man, every step is labored in a way mine never could be.

I walked up several unaltered and original spiral staircases and came upon a corridor of dark wood doors until I found the one I was looking for.

"Professor Hubert," I knocked. His chair spun around whipping smoke that was circulating in his office and spit out the window he had been resting his feet upon.

"Have I come at the wrong time… I thought the syllabus said,"

"No, you haven't read it wrong. Come in. What have you got there?"

I pulled out a bottle of Bordeaux from the restaurant that I had failed to taste. "I'm assuming you were serious about wine during office hours."

"You know, I never speak without intention. Did you bring a bottle opener?" He asked.

I froze in mid bend like this was another assignment I had blundered.

"No matter, I have one here. Sit down and give that to me." Like a professional he pulled the cork and handed it to me to smell. It was a test to see if I would know what to do. I smelt the cork and set it down, then he pulled two glasses from beneath his desk. He poured and turned the bottle like a spigot to measure out the perfect tasting portions. I froze to take one before he clinked my glass and took his. I smelled the glass and visualized the nodes before taking a sip. The portions were small but pungent and I curled my lips and touched my mouth to hide the smile. I sat back in the chair and he in his as if to enjoy and sit in the quiet. I put my empty glass down and his eyes diverted to the glass to me and back to the glass. He put his down and rubbed his hands around his lips before reaching for the bottle and pouring his glass and then mine. I took the glass to sip that became interrupted by his question. "Are you going to ask me something? It's not office hours until you ask me something. Otherwise, it's just an aperitif."

"Usually that's served before dinner, is it not?"

"If you want to do it in the French way. I don't need reason to drink because there's always a reason to do so."

"Is this a tradition that you acquired yourself?"

"Well, my father was a drinker, world class in fact, so I choose to reward myself with vices throughout the day in small doses rather than become utterly buried by them."

"I'm sorry, or well, I'm not sure that I should be…um…"

"For whom? My father? He's an ambassador and as much a lush as anyone who works in administration or as a government functionary. As for me, nothing to be sorry for. The father can only influence the son if the son ever cared."

"So, Jane, she's…"

"Half-sister, but you already knew that. Oh, you mean why am I brown and she's not? Ha! There's that east coast pedigree, the pigmentation police, concerned with the origin of everyone's complexion to test whether we are safe for consumption."

"Sir, I didn't mean to offend. You're barely…"

"Barely, what? Brown, you mean? Passable by the coifed hair and fine clothes, but questionable due to a Mediterranean complexion."

I turned red and looked away in case I cried but then the noise of trickling wine caused me to turn my head back.

"Drink up. I'm your teacher, it's my job to correct you."

"I didn't mean anything."

"I know, you're just trying to figure it out. So, I will take you out of limbo. A French diplomat of Persian descent finds a little English girl away at French school and they make consolation for a lovely child bride. Father could only allocate himself to work and to anyone who wasn't my mother, so she filed for divorce and made Jane with her attorney, living comfortably off the settlement she won from my father's estate ever since. Granted, I'm not bitter about it one bit. I'm sure he has children on every continent, and perhaps many more but being his first son, he showed an invested interest in me for some reason, and sent me to all the best schools to make me as polished as he was. The summers I spent with mother and Jane instilled far greater lessons in kindness and matters of the heart that would make me an ill candidate for a career in politics so here I am. I'm like a doctor and surgeon who critiques the establishment with a pen and scalpel and maintains the notion that there are five senses." He leaned back from his chair satisfied and lit another cigarette, waiting for my response.

"That certainly fills in a lot. I definitely feel like I understand you better."

"As much as one can in a brief time I suppose," he added and smiled.

"Well, you're a difficult person to place. Even your accent…"

"Half my time spent in French schools, the other half in British ones, nannies from Morocco, summers in Scotland, yes I suppose it's all one jumbled mess."

"No, no, it's nice. I like it. Like if Carry Grant and James Mason spoke both French before they learned English and did a semester abroad in Marrakech."

"You mean you find it tolerable?" He raised his eyebrow. I was beginning to catch on to his game and so I swallowed his bluff and fed it back to him slowly.

"You know for a man of higher learning; you are awfully sensitive to almost everything I say."

"I'm a professor of philosophy and intellectual history. Words, their origins, and their usages are all my business."

"Yes, but you must hear ignorant thoughts all day and if you acted like a bullet to glass every time you reacted to something that displeased you then you would never make it out of the front door." I appeared like a deer crossing over a frozen pond.

"This is where you make your point," he said.

"Well point is, you do make it out and you function in the world with as much tolerance as one can. For each person per interaction."

"And with my invisible red pen, I will underline that sentence and say, 'Thesis?'" He caressed his hand in the air with the smoke of this cig.

"My point, I have come to the conclusion that you have tolerance for every person except for me."

"An implication that I will not, not entertain, not in my position."

"Why?"

"Because that question plus wine, no longer makes this my office where I'm a teacher and you are a student."

I had him leaning forward, hands clasped together resting tightly on his desk. I leaned back. "You came so far to bring me here and now you who deem to be all knowing can tell me nothing." I was almost offended.

"I have never. I'm just a humble parrhesiast, as we must all be with the truth that we carry." He bowed his head.

"You're right sir. So, the question I want answered before the end of term is why you try so hard to provoke me the way that you do. It may not even be a conscious effort on your part, but I think we both possess the ability to make the other act to what is contrary to our nature."

"I think you are suffering from the misapprehension that anything I have ever said or passed to you has had some alternative motivation when I have only spoken in the interest of instruction. As for my nature, there are no abnormalities I can assure you. Should any arise, I would sooner tear them out like an abscess or remove myself altogether."

"That will not be necessary sir. The mistake has been mine. Thank you for taking the time to clarify yourself to me. Enjoy the wine."

Antony left the room as Professor rolled a cigarette. He stared out his office window to the street to watch his student disappear, and drifted into a lingering thought that would stay with him until morning. His next thought would be how to remove Antony Shrader from his head before he sunk down and settled like a cancer in his chest. No longer could he take in those deep inhales he enjoyed so much, before that tightening feeling would set in, causing his breath to stop short before letting out a quivering exhale.

CHAPTER THIRTY-THREE

Catching Fire Without Burning Icarus

The following weeks were hell for Professor Hubert. Hell is like a category, a blanket term prescribed to a situation so perfectly crafted that one would rather call it hell than to endure the extent of it themselves.

His classroom no longer his domain, but rather a narrowing stream of where he could place his eyes without becoming distracted. The words became dry in his mouth. His thoughts became weakened as the day lingered before gaining their second wind in the evening, keeping him from retreating to that comfortable fantasy that he would revisit in his books, his writing, or in his dreams. This feeling became part of a fervent search, languishing over choice, art and passion, over position and principle. He was a man and so was the other and why shouldn't the two converge? What would he give up by conceding? What did he have to lose after pursuing a lifetime of tedious fumbling with young flesh. The need to want to break the skin of some young thing and render him conquered, had left the professor talented and intact perhaps but lonelier as the books on the shelf grew larger as life got smaller. He saw that he was young, he was wild, he had the intellect that cut like a diamond's edge. The Professor could remove the stingers and the shards never erasing the scars but perhaps if he broke the skin on his neck, love would seep into his veins and Antony would forever remain lying in a pasture of eternity preserved as a glimmer in the professor's eye.

"But how do I make him come to me?" He wondered. "How?"

If you sent a flock of fledglings into a storm and none came back would the brethren to those who perished set flight into the next storm? The weak might be hesitant but the strong and resilient would take wing. Professor Hubert didn't do cautious nor was it that state of complacency that made him get up to the sunrise. It was a possibility.

Possibility keeps us alive. Hope allows us to wander for what we seek, believing it is possible , so that we may finally allow ourselves to breathe when we find it. To not have that thing doesn't make us sad to look at a sunset because of the loneliness that sets in when the sun starts to diminish. The sadness comes when there's no one there to witness this daily miracle with you. Someone to let you know you are alive while you are dying is a marvelous gift.

CHAPTER THIRTY-FOUR

Fruit And Nuts

The fall leaves were coming in singles, one by one they fell like the final moment from inside an hourglass to let all know that winter was approaching. Vin Chaud and Vianon spiked cider were all you could smell on the streets, and on every street corner a chestnut vendor with his hot plate selling his roasted delights in a small paper bag for pennies. I, myself, would buy a bag from the Parisian fellow next to the news stand that was situated next to the mouth of a metro entrance and the church of St. Germain. I would buy two bags, one for each pocket and grip them firmly until I reached the entrance to my school. I would share them with classmates and find myself too full and warm to move when the bell sounded to end class. So, I started this ritual of bringing one bag for class and one for the homeless legionnaire whose name I never learned whose war stories I could recite to their entirety. I never actually talked to him about his time in the trenches, only that he spent his mornings until dusk recounting his battles from start to finish. I used to like to take my seat in the back next to the window and listen to him every day like a radio serial, when

I didn't want to hear any of the professor's ramblings. I would even make sure I would get to school early to get the seat by the window. Before I would go into the building, I would hand off the warm bag on his cart of various objects and then by the time I got to the top of the stairs, he had started on somewhere in the middle of episode from his life.

It was astonishing to me to listen to him go on day after day with the same renewed passion, far more than any of my preceding educators. I saw him every day for the duration of my stay in Paris. And I often wondered and pretended if after some time, he did it because he knew it pleased me. For me, I felt like I was the only one who was truly listening and if so, then why should he not shout for me with his tales of woe and mayhem? I also wondered if he enjoyed the nuts I brought him. Truly, not just for the thought but for their warmth and nourishment. I was sitting in Professor Hubert's class, propped up against my usual spot that was the window, when the Professor's voice began to invade my ear and draw attention away from down below.

"I have, here, in my hand, the fruits of autumn. I have discerned this to be the most beautiful, largest, ripest, juiciest and unblemished apple in all of Paris. I shall walk by and show you all, lest one of you shouldn't believe me." And he walked up and down the aisles, beautiful in form, it was but it wasn't until upon closer examination that the qualities of this apple as they had been described to us didn't even do justice to its majesty, aesthetic and allure that passed itself to the viewer as we all speculated on what it might taste like. "And to each of you," the professor continued, "you might marvel at it and then simultaneously wonder as to the taste. And to each of you, how you imagine it shall taste is the culmination of your experience with apples, yet even in all your experience, you cannot conceive of how delectable this apple is until you've tasted that first bite. The relevance you may be asking? The apple is freedom. It is everything that you picture which you think of AS freedom except you've only just seen what true freedom looks like when I brought out my perfect apple. Now having seen it, experiencing it, or in this case tasting it, are two different things.

So, this is what I want all of you to do. Get into groups of three or four. Each group will give a presentation on how they will ascertain this apple, which for our purposes, works both as literal and metaphysical freedom. While you discern what freedom determines, the best group will win the apple. Assuming your arguments for why you deserve freedom align with the whole group, sharing the prize won't be an issue."

Out of convenience, I saddled myself with the peers closest to me. The black student who was stopped by security those weeks ago was in my group. Out of a sort of obligation I felt as though I should have elected him in charge of our group. At first, he seemed surprised but if we came up with the winning presentation "I would want you to have it." I said.

He laughed and his eyes rolled towards the ceiling. "White people are always so kind, giving out freedom like Christmas. We should argue freedom is a scam, a bunch of white people made up to keep black men working with no intention of ever making good on your promise."

"I didn't personally make up the concept."

"Yet here you are carrying on the tradition with a smile and your savior bullshit."

"What's wrong with wanting you to have something?" Derek asked.

"Because you think I want it, and you think it's yours to give. If freedom is God given and inalienable, why are white people always trying to put restrictions and obstacles in the way of it? Probably has something to do with the fact you have a white Jesus too."

The other girl in our group leaned forward in the air of silence that had settled in our back corner and tried being our voice of reason. "I think this is a good and healthy discussion, but it's not going to help us win that apple or pass this assignment. But I think both you Antony and you Derick have brought to light some interesting points."

I took her teaching moment as a segue to compliment as well as apologize. "And I think you're right about this notion of freedom acting like a privatized commodity that has been used to delineate, to subjugate groups for good behavior while the power structure has done nothing to earn it yet has been holding on to it like they invented it. Of course, I'm sorry if what I said seemed like an extension of that awful history. It… It was not my place."

"I know you were trying to do it as some kind of apology to me for whatever it is you think you saw and maybe I was acting out of pride, but this is my burden to bear. It's why I study social justice. My weapon against indignation. And my name is Issal. Use this information as it benefits you."

I blushed red but continued with the conversation. "Well, if freedom is an inalienable thing that I cannot be given, then perhaps he cannot either."

"Professor Hubert would do something like that. Make us compete for something we already have, create a pointless game to make a point." It was my anger turning on a light bulb in me. The girl whose name has escaped me looked between Derick, Issal and I then slapped her hands on the table. "So, are any of you going to write this down?"

"You're right um…" I took my pen and handed it over to Issal who took it and then turned it around and handed it back.

"Your writing is better than mine." He smiled.

"But I'm left-handed."

"I know, that's how bad mine is. Write it, I know you want to."

"Alright, but essentially our argument is we win the apple because it was never his to give because we already, have it? Do I have that right?"

"Think of it like this, it's like Dorothy at the end of Wizard of Oz. Sit through two hours of technicolor to learn she had the power to go back all along. So, in fact we don't even need his apple. OOO, that's good! Put that in!" Derick said as he leaned over my pad with excitement like we were going to finally stick it to the man through this exercise.

"Which part, Dorothy? We don't need any of your apples since we got our own apple tree!"

Our third party of reason, Issal let out an exasperating breath and sighed out, "Both!"

CHAPTER THIRTY-FIVE

The Ripest Wax Figurine In The Menagerie

We went around the room to the competing four or five other groups, all offering forth their bridged versions and various counterparts of democratic theory. I found the anticipation more annoying than the droning on through the various ways this prize could be attained. Which reaffirmed to me that we were the ones on the right track of this assignment because essentially what we were all competing for wasn't his to give. Quite the original idea I thought. But in all honesty, it didn't take us that long to come to that conclusion. In fact, though abstract and seemingly correct, the solution seemed too easy for someone as complex, brooding and jaded as Professor Hubert was. The more I thought about it, the angrier I got. I was going to present our argument like I had found the formula for turning copper into gold and then he was going to smite me with that look of arrogance that made me want to squirt my fountain pen into his face. I became angry and could feel my eyes burning through his skull, and I had to divest my eyes toward something like that fucking apple, that malum of death, sitting and staring at me with malice, sitting upon its axis of evil, spinning upon the lies which fed it.

Then it became my turn, and I felt a shortness of breath and a tightness of chest and collected sweat upon my upper lip. It was my turn to present for my group and for the first time I froze to the audience I faced because I became stuck, unable to choose if I should say the presentation as planned and allow him to exploit our mistake while remaining superior, or do the injunction, the codex laden inside this rigged thought experiment.

"At first I thought I was going to stand here and say to you all how we found that you Professor Hubert have no right to reward freedom because it is not yours to give. And that may be right, but then I remembered what you promised: if we could prove why we deserved it, you would give us a bite. Our argument rests, that if it's not yours to give, then we already have it. And if that were right then we'd have to taste that apple. But none of us can. None of us are right or could ever be right because we could never taste or if we did, then we know the truth of that apple."

He bit the corner of his lip and smiled. "Go on."

"It's fake. It's wax or plastic or something but it's fake. We have all been competing for something created by you for a concept that doesn't exist. To learn who rules over you , simply find out who you are not allowed to criticize, Voltaire."

"You can sit down now Mr. Shrader." My group dropped their pens and looked at me with a kind of awe that made me feel like I found the Wizard behind the emerald curtain.

"Mr. Shrader, I'm not sure what it was that inspired your revelation, but I have done this experiment hundreds of times and none once has anyone seen through its ruse. In the government, telling you, the people telling you, I have something you all possess that I will hold in safe keeping, that you all have to earn, and you all go about your various ways of achieving the taste of the promise I have set forth.

You try through various means, wealth, democracy, anarchy and some get close, and others get crushed but here I remain holding the prize, the end, and for that, no one has ever asked whose decision it was to enter the race anyway. The first day of class we talked about parrhesia, and the cost of bearing witness to the truth. Sometimes the truth we possess can bring an entire system of deception to its knees. What will you do with that truth? Watch on as an entire flock fly into a storm or be the light that guides them safely to shore before they all perish? Here," he tossed the apple to me. "There's a real one waiting for you in my office. Congratulations. Class dismissed."

CHAPTER THIRTY-SIX

In The Garden

I knocked quietly on his door that was already ajar like he had been expecting someone. I walked in and placed the apple on his desk. He spun around. "Bravo, Monsieur Shrader. Je voudrais que vous donnez votre liberté." He pushed a large round, unblemished, ruby red apple toward me.

"I thought the lesson of this exercise was to question the cost of freedom when it given like a gift from the institution that created the notion of freedom itself."

He smiled, "I am no longer the institution. I hung up that robe when I ended class. In fact, I'm glad you won the prize and saw through my exercise. Now that you're here, let this apple be like the first time Prometheus stole fire, and create something new from the ashes."

"An olive branch then?" I held the apple in my hand and stared at my reflection frozen upon the surface of the wax-like skin.

"Look, as your instructor, it's quite obvious that I like to challenge students. Yet it is so seldom that a student challenges me. I forgot that. I forgot myself and became a brute and an oppressor. Hypocritical to the kind of thinking I try to inspire from my students. And so here we are." He leaned back in his chair and pulled open a drawer and took out a rolled cigarette. His face temporarily disappeared behind his initial puffs of ignition. He flexed his eyebrows and leaned forward with his hand to one side of his face waiting for me to cut the silence.

"What do you want me to do now Professor?"

"Take your prize and bite it," he said, pausing only for a moment to take a big inhale and then blew downward. The smoke curled under my hand and seemed to bewitch my senses. Like waves, the curls of smoke seemed to push my hands up towards my mouth that made the whole thing seem like it was happening on a different time plane. I took a bite. The bite was bigger than I anticipated, and its vitals began to dribble down my chin. I diverted my eyes so I could stop the flow of juice from staining my shirt and allowing myself to maintain an immovable state of propriety. Before I could look up he snatched the prize from my hand and took the biggest, most obnoxious and obscene bite from the same part where I had taken mine. The sticky juices ran down the sides of his stubble like brackish water that sticks in the reeds of a riverbed. Smug and satisfied he laughed through a big grin, grinding the remnants of red flesh between his teeth.

"And with a kiss I have sealed our concordat at this diet of Paris in this the year of our lord…"

"You find your impertinence to be funny?" I narrowed my eyes and pushed my teeth behind my tongue until it slipped and made a snap.

"Not at all. It is with all seriousness that I made my treaty and made you see the light whatever my intention."

"Sir, with what intention do you come bearing this treaty?"

"Peace, that you may finally come to my class without dread. I want my class to be the thing you look forward to in your day."

"Sir, forgive me but your vanity is showing."

"I disagree, but it's my job to make sure everyone enjoys coming to class. But I don't lose sleep over the ones I can't win. I'm not that fickle."

"I have yet to believe."

"Then I have my task as you have yours." He looked down at some notes he scribbled on his desk, but he was really buying time trying to decide whether he had won a victory or sunk his ship. He knew well enough that sometimes it's best to let a dog lick its wounds before you pet it. Then he began to smile as if he had just found the answer he was looking for under some notes he was pretending to look at.

"You know, and this is before I let you go, as I still have another class to prepare for, I'm so glad you won today. Truly. Though I thought you might and part of me hoped you wouldn't, I really like what you bring to the table, and I hope you'll start looking forward to attending."

"Fine," I said, trying not to give much of myself away, I solidified my awkwardness with another "Fine."

"That's all? No amendments or embellishments you would like to add?"

"No, for once I have nothing to say."

"Good, well, I suppose I'll let you go. Thank you for coming to straighten this out."

"Thank you À bientôt"

"Enchante to you."

"Oh, and sir, one more thing."

"Yes?"

"You're going to hate me for this, but I like you better when you apologize." I closed the door leaving it ajar.

After he got up to shut the door, Professor Hubert sat staring at that closed door with an almost philosophical intent. He pulled open the top button on his fly and then pulled the strip of his belt to the left. He clenched his fist and looked at the door again. Still in the closed position, he slumped back in his chair and rubbed his hands up and down his face in contemplation of whether to proceed. "God Dammit." Was all he could muster as his confession as he went to work.

CHAPTER THIRTY-SEVEN

Then There Was Smoke

When I went home that day, the walk seemed to take longer as my thoughts became heavier with every step. I wasn't sad but to say I was happy would be incorrect. Even if I had a feelings chart, I'm sure I couldn't even pick out the right one. I was confused. What was I supposed to do with what I knew and felt? I liked him. He liked or at least wanted me all while trying to rationalize the logistics which seemed as improbable as a Mars landing. We were each bound by our positions. I didn't want to act on impulse and compromise him, then he would hate me. But maybe he just liked me as a person, no longer hating me, but finally accepting me as a part of the human race. It's so hard to trust your instincts when you're damaged. Was what I saw in his eyes a reciprocation of the flame burning within or had I imagined it to be so to assuage my guilt for hating him? What did I know about Henri Hussein Hubert? At the time, not much. Paris offered so many distractions visually and of the alcoholic persuasion. There were as many absinth bars as there were churches. I stopped in for a glass of that green witch's brew tinted and aged like a good Shakespearean sonnet, it reeked of trouble, but for the moment only, could clear all my troubles.

With all the traps laid against me, I spearheaded the drinks into my gut along with a pill I washed down with more green liquor. I left the bar and walked down my familiar street where the light only pierced three hours of the day but was perpetually saturated by night and all the noises and familiarities that came with the sun's setting. I could hardly look at Jane, I felt like a line hadn't been crossed yet, but one that I had over and over again in my mind. It seemed silly to worry, when the only thing worth hiding were the thoughts hidden in my head. So, the next day and for several weeks, I made it a point to see him in his office to sit with him to talk to him, pick his brain until I felt like every thought was no longer a chess move, but a fluid exchange of honest thoughts between intellectuals as friends. After a while, I would forget why I was coming there and find myself going there to forget. Time was like a balloon with an air leak any time I was there. We could talk and the only thing I had to be conscious of was remembering to breathe. If I ever got excited I would talk until my lungs felt like they would have to remind me to take a breath. I caught him multiple times during lecture staring at the clock. He would catch me looking at him and I would try to divert my eyes to something else even though I couldn't erase the smile from my face that knew that class ended in seven minutes. On a few occasions either to make me blush or to pay me a kindness, he would say "class dismissed" and wait for my reaction.

It was nice and strange knowing that someone was looking forward to seeing you as much as you were to see them. I had never had that before. I was scared to like him but liking him, liking itself didn't hurt the way it usually does. For the first time I felt like I was doing myself a kindness by liking someone who could reciprocate feelings of mutual interest.

One day, I asked him why he smoked and then he asked me why I didn't. I said I had in the past, but I didn't want to become dependent on anything.

"Frederick Neichze, a man you may be familiar with, made out with a horse, his sister was a Nazi sympathizing whore, and edited his work to make him sound like an anti-Semite to personally jerk off her husband and the intellectual members of the Nazi party, embodying the culmination of an oxymoron definition cloaked in the pun of betting on the wrong horse. Anyway, one thing led to another and upon his death, he did say that a man with no vices is a man with no virtues. Therefore, I smoke because it keeps me humble, reminds me I'm mortal and it can kill me. Those of us who go around thinking they are immune to the temptation of the flesh also see their place in respect to man as being above everyone else because they've conquered vice and addiction. I live with people. Not above them. I tend to think if we all indulged in our flaws a little bit more, we would see more ourselves in other people and perhaps be a little kinder, not to mention, it feels Fabulous."

"And that is why you smoke?" I asked.

"That's some of the reasons. What about you Mr. Shrader? What are your sins?"

"I don't know."

"I'm not going to make you say 80 hail Mary's, but I do feel as though our visits have become one sided. Now I know I've lived more life and therefore, like a television serial, I could go on and you could fall asleep to me babbling about boarding strange steamers in Morocco and hiking mountains in Tibet, but as I become more human and less entitled, might you not think that I might also want to know the student?"

"Perhaps. To what end?"

"Why would there be an end? To build a stairway to heaven, how would I know? You tell me something and who knows where it shall lead us."

"What do you want to know?"

"What do you want to tell me? Obviously, there's an arrangement of broken glass, cutlery and debris strewn about the crevices of your brain. We need not visit those compartments where all that discomfort resides, but I don't know. Perhaps I've sent myself down a rabbit hole. I'm sorry, I have to go. Don't get up, stay here. I need a moment to think."

Henri was very distraught. It was like they were both running a marathon with a plate of glass separating their path. And here he was. What was he doing now? It felt like an admission of guilt, but they had done nothing. But they had already done everything in the professor's mind. He was so drawn to this fragile, exotic, peculiar, broken thing that he could not understand how this shattered figurine of a boy could pull him with the weight of 20 men. Pulling him under like a siren calls upon a ship. And why? It's a pleasure, seeing the remains of the vessel at the bottom of the sea. He leaned up against the brick of the institution he loved so much and wondered, "Why do I feel like loving you is going to hurt? I have no problems and here I invite them in, but I didn't ask for you. You sought me out with the objectives of a virus. You lay there like a wounded serpent but you're just as deadly. Those thoughts of you, I languish over them as they are the thoughts I feel for the… Child I love…That child was me. God dammit. I have repeated my own history in my lust for flesh that is much younger and safer than mine. But his mind, like that of a dead poet, thoughts of him taint me as his prose are my weakness. Alright then. Alright God, I'll make you a deal, I will bare my soul, exposing it to the flame and then if I get burned I can drown myself in liquor, and cigarettes."

In a final puff of courage, Henri flicked his cigarette against the curb and went back up to his office to discover an empty chair. In the moment he needed to take his next breath, Antony had vanished.

CHAPTER THIRTY-EIGHT

I'm Always Afraid I Might Cut Myself On A Souvenir

Homeward bound and underground I made my way to L'art des Metiers metro stop and found it to be quite a relief to see the sun setting. Tomorrow would be Saturday and that meant no professor until Monday, which for the first time in a while, felt like quite a relief. I had a lot to process; when you spend so much of your time trying to numb feelings, it becomes rather hard to process any new ones that might come up. I went to Ci who I almost never saw anymore. She had taken up with a French man after having already taken up with many other Frenchmen and one French woman in a bathroom that involved cocaine and cleavage. Regardless, she seemed happy and was more than willing to help the process and execute my newfound feelings for the professor.

"Well, he's not going to put out on the first outing. He has too much pride and only a few weeks left until you're not his student anymore. He's going to hold out for as long as he can until he has to admit he likes you." Ci was pacing the floor as if the answer would appear.

"We don't know for sure. It's just my speculation." I said as her feet treaded across the surface.

"Ok, but that studdly, give me some air bullshit, you mentioned, he probably had to step out so he could bust a nut. I'm sure it was hard for him to contain the explosion in his pants."

"Why do you always have to go vulgar?"

"You like it when I do." She reached out to stroke my inner thigh and walked her fingers towards my now wilting flesh.

"Watch it! It's a sensitive place." I scoffed.

"I'm sure it is from your hourly jerk off sessions thinking about the professor."

"Ci, you're vile. If you were going to talk about my brother you could at least make sure I wasn't within earshot." Jane stood in the doorway of the bedroom Ci and her shared.

"Sorry, um, I can leave if you need a moment." I was trying to keep the redness from creeping up my face.

"Don't get up. I just got home. I wouldn't want to interrupt the planning for how you seduce my brother." She removed her waistcoat and slung her sunglasses on the bed. She put her hands on her waist also looking for an answer to appear on the floor.

"Jane, Darling, I really don't see what you stand to lose from this union or this inevitable shagging from taking place. Is it a British thing?"

"Nationality is not a genetic predisposition to bitchiness. But having a sleep deprived induced migraine from sleeping on a couch bed while you shag until 5 am might have something to do with it."

"Well, that's a separate problem from us talking about your brother's willy."

"What my brother does with his willy and what I do with my Wilma has always been no one's concern but our own. What does concern me is how Antony's pursuit of him will affect my brother professionally and emotionally."

Suddenly it was no longer a skirmish between two girls and the struggle of one using the bedroom they shared as her own personal fucking arena. I was starting to feel the source of Jane's sleep deprivation was not just for being banished to my little couch bed with me, but the unknown consequences that would befall her brother should I engage with the professor. "What exactly do you mean by that?" She now had my full attention.

"I don't see why we have to make this personal Antony. If you care for me at all, you'd leave well enough alone and not pursue this."

"Have you spoken with Prof… Henri?"

"No, as I said. His personal life has never been my business which is why I'm asking you to drop this before you cause either one of you embarrassment."

"You limey twat! Why don't you just say what you would like to say and dispense with your breathy insults."

"Fine! You're a drug addict and his student and I think both of you are a lethal combination for any relationship. And you!" Now she was directing her venom directly at Ci, who was ladling back scotch and soda with each breathy insult."

"What kind of friend are you? Fine, maybe living together was a mistake and maybe you never liked me anyway, but you've proven to be such a selfish slut. However, I find you siccing, your drug addled friend on my brother negligent and selfish in the least!"

"I'm trying to help my friend be happy! Showing him there's people and things worth living for. I don't think working through some personal things disqualifies him from a shot at happiness."

"First of all," I couldn't remain silent anymore, "I'm not falling apart and I'm not an addict. I'm also not trying to destroy lives or a man's career. But I don't appreciate either of you talking about me like I'm not here or a plan of action that needs revision. I have what I'm now discussing, feelings. Human feelings. Some of which I've shared with your brother, and I want to find out what it means. My pursuits are purely scientific. Like a trial test run, I have no expectations for the outcome. I'm just a youth living in Paris with two bitches, while my hormones are racing, whose interest has just been piqued by someone I admire."

"My brother is not a lab rat for you to infect with your problems and see if he lives through the outcome."

"When did I become your enemy? When I stopped coming to you for help because you only like me when I'm a mess?"

"I wanted you to get better. Right now, you're just a traveling shit storm tornado looking for a place to drop your house. Your next victim is not going to be my brother."

"Victim? He's a big man who can take care of himself." I found this point laughable.

"And you? Who's supposed to take care of you? Me? Him? Ci? You're not ready. Don't you get it? Or has your drug-addled brain convinced you that you're fine?"

"I'm fine. I haven't taken anything in weeks. I'm clear headed and present. I'm here!"

"I bet you're high right now! Are you fucking kidding me?"

"Oh, normally I'd let you guys work this one out, but I think attacking each other isn't going to make it better for any of us. We all have to live together. So, let's figure out how to do that right now." You knew it was bad when Ci was the voice of reason. It was all Jane could bear.

"Oh, fuck you! Making peace offerings when this is something you created and encouraged. Blind guides leading blind guides. Maybe if you were more focused on your friend instead of some temporary French fling you'd see he needs help before starting something a little too close to home." By this time, Jane had become overwhelmingly upset, most likely because she had allowed herself to show emotion beyond her usual tempered and controlled self. She pulled her breath back into her lungs to stabilize herself from going into a state. Then she turned to me and I saw a look of devastation transformed to anger. "You can't be mad at me for looking out for my brother. I've done my best to help you. I failed and I'm sorry. Now I have to protect my family."

"You really think you're so much better than me, don't you?" I looked her straight in the eye.

She sighed. "I think you're better than you think you are."

"From the point of privilege, the solution always sounds so easy, because the only force moving against your words is the air itself. No one has ever stopped you from doing anything or made you feel like nothing. Let me know when that happens so that the anger you feel from the helplessness and not being able to retaliate against your suppressors becomes so great you can't even swallow food. I want you to either choke on the fork in your hand before you go for that bottle just so we can all see how the person with everything manages to turn the world off using only her head."

"I'm sorry you don't like the way I feel but…"

"You're right and while you're listening, what I don't like, let's throw in your face and at your 12-year-old boys' breasts. Yeah, I don't like a lot of things, but I guess I don't get a choice. So, since you're so used to getting what you want, I'll oblige you and stay the fuck away from your brother. Better to blow it out now than to let you poison him against me with your bullshit." I snatched my coat and headed for the door.

"Where are you going?" Jane pleaded like she started a fire she couldn't put out.

I rolled my eyes and slammed the door. I couldn't make anyone else worry about me so I might as well make the shrivel left within her that did, worry sick. I had no plan, but Paris had two options. It could fuck you or kill you. Being a masochist, I went to one of the most crudest clubs you could imagine. It was amazing what you could find people who were willing to pay for. Ironically, there was no shortage of people that did. I wondered whether knowing the type of place it was, whether anyone paid under the presumption that they would leave happy. First let me explain what homosexuality and Paris have in common. The answer is nothing. Now I'm not saying this to the extent that if they see one, they are obligated to kill on site. If that were true Paris fashion week would never exist. Contrary to romance, Paris can be economically lucrative for the homosexual. However, the reputation that Paris bears for its romance and the love and acceptance one seeks as a homosexual could not be any more suitable than a polar bear is to a desert, or as cyanide is to the body. Rather, if you are a homosexual seeking love, and any of you find yourself in Paris, I highly recommend you leave your expectations at the door or you bring a hazmat suit. If you don't, then the air of disappointment will break your skin, and you will die of infection and a broken heart.

Second lesson. Most gay establishments don't allow women. Most establishments are geared towards homosexual men, there are few for women and if you're planning on bringing your sexless marriage partner, aka my Cicelia, they won't let her in. Gay clubs, bars, and restaurants are, pardon the pun, an open cock fight that operate under strict business before pleasure practices. These examples include: 1, if I buy you a drink, I can fuck you. 2, If we dance, I can fuck you. 3, If I hold the door, maybe a bj that could lead to fucking.

The art of small talk is something Americans invented to fill dialogue in movies. Behind these four walls human interaction is reduced to business for pleasure. I was familiar with the rules of engagement but wanted more than what this place had to offer and yet I paid the fee and entered through the mouth of the beast as a non-existent wall ornament. I spent the better part drinking Smirnoff over ice until this Toulouse Lautrec character came up to me. In five glassy-eyed minutes I listen to him talk about God only knows. I thought about leaving or falling asleep on the bar. Just before I could choose the latter, my concentration broke as the lights changed, and everyone's attention diverted to the center of the club to watch two Latin men engage in an entire tango striptease that ended in an almost simulated blow job before the whole club went dark. Even in this place of depravity, the French never shied away from an opportunity to create art. When the big lights came up, my bald, gap-toothed promise was standing there as if waiting for me. But for the life of me, no moment of grammar French could make me understand what the fuck he was saying.

His voice became louder as if in my head and his face began to move up and down as if it were trapped inside a nickelodeon reel. I turned away from him to leave, but my bar stool seemed like the edge of a cliff. His voice was ringing, ringing, like it was after my soul. My only option was to jump. I closed my eyes to brace for the fall before everything went dark. I did not wake until morning. When I did, I was in a stranger's apartment. To a great sigh of relief, I could see the Eiffel tower. So at least I knew I was in the same city. My shoes were missing but I was fully dressed in my clothes from the night before. Despite how abnormal this was, perhaps for most people, I thought to myself, "I could do worse." I had done worse before and that's not what this appeared to be. There was the problem of a time lapse, but that would come back, I was sure of it. Perhaps too much vodka with the benzos. It happened before. Totally serviceable. As I looked to either side of me I remembered the last person I saw. That little French gnome. That parasite. Then I heard that familiar and terrifying sound of the apartment door click. With the certainty of death, I heard the apartment door click. With the certainty of death, I held my breath until the identity of my keeper revealed itself to me. My blood congealed and then left from my shallow face to the sound of the sigh of relief when I saw the face that matched the footsteps.

"Good morning," he said.

"Good morning, you beautiful bastard." Was my reply.

"Shall I shut the door?" he asked. "Is the maid coming?" I asked.

"No."

"Then why don't you put your bag down and come to bed."

"Are you afraid of being bitten?"

"You mock me, 'STEVE?' When you know I'll do more than bite you." I said sarcastically as if I did not remember who he was.

And for all that chivalry was worth, I must confess, despite Leon's rescue of me from his night club, of which I had not a clue until now, the view from his bedroom was more impressive than he was, despite coming close several times.

CHAPTER THIRTY-NINE

My Third Journal Thoughts

Time is the thing we cannot escape, but you can delay it by putting benzos up your nose while fucking the rich and powerful.

"You know if you do that for too long, you'll wear yourself raw."

"Right. I forgot that's your job." It's easy to manipulate a man's attention span when you use his own ego.

"Then why don't you put it away and come to bed so I may continue."

"I recall meeting a certain gentleman at a bar over a plate of dust that was so strong it felt like yesterday."

"I don't really do that so much anymore. Occasionally and only socially."

"Practically the face of Algernon are you?" I smiled through my reflection in the mirror facing the bed.

"Still a bossy little shit, aren't you?" He moved the sheet like a sheath as if to provoke me into an insurmountable task. It was mountable, just exhausting taking it from a man who searches for his youth through the breaking of your body from his own over exertion. I turned around.

"I've learned a lot since last we met, but my taste in men and all the sins of the flesh have not. Men do not change, which is why the devil can make such good use of us, like the creatures of habit we are."

Like a hand too close to the lion's cage, he pulled me into him, with my hand bent in such a way I was pinned on my back. Then he mounted me and began to kiss up and around my neck like it was something he thought he was supposed to do. But then he got close to my ear and whispered in my ear with a message that vibrated through the hairs on his whiskers, "And what if I told you I'm the devil?" There I saw that familiar face realizing who I was with and where I was. That night club owner in New York, but he was here in the flesh. I turned and looked him in the eye.

"Then you've already made use of me."

"And I'll continue to do so." He slid himself into me.

"I'll wait for your worst." I closed my eyes and prayed for death while whispering to myself, "Henri."

CHAPTER FORTY

A Penny Saved ?

I walked through the door of my apartment around mid-day. Jane looked shocked, either because she thought I was dead or because she thought I was a ghost.

"Where have you been?"

"Oh, just a casual sex dungeon disguised as a nightclub where I got roofied and then rescued by a former lover and nightclub owner. So, you know, just your typical Tuesday."

"You could dispense with the dramatics and replace it with the truth for once."

"And this is essentially the knife in the spleen of our friendship. You pick the truths you like and ignore the ones you don't."

"Wait! Hold the front door but don't slam it on my testicles, are we talking about oil slick back in NY, who I set you up with?"

"Yes, he's opening another club in Paris. Some club number that sounds like a sex position, soixante dix neuf. And we found each other in the dark, by chance before I was snatched up and carried away by Nosferatu."

"Huh?" Ci who would usually read my thoughts was having trouble.

"It's fine. You can all stop worrying about me and whether I'm going to throw myself at the head of the illusive and mysterious Professor Hubert. Rather I have set my teeth upon a former lover and wealthy benefactor whom I shall use and enjoy how I please until our time here is over. Jane, why do I get the feeling you look disappointed?"

"My reaction is as much a surprise to me as it is to you. Perhaps I'm just sad because no one can save you."

"No one? Or no one amongst your relations?"

"You're high."

Ci stood motionless, unsure whether she should referee this stand off or run away.

"That I am darling, because that's how I want it to be." Jane stood poised and poured herself a drink.

She raised a smile in the corner of her mouth and lit a cigarette. "Professor Hubert's last class is in one hour. I suggest you get to it." Then she turned and left the room.

"Fuck, fucking, fuck me." And I had nothing else to offer.

Ci creeped up behind me like an imp and whispered in my ear, "If there ever was the slightest existence of tender feelings between you, now would be the time to play upon them." Then she slinked away.

Deep underground, moving past the blinking light and blurred mirage of humans, I looked within my head for the answer that wouldn't make me look like an ass hat. It was hard to do when you are an ass hat.

I arrived at class and sat down to three essay questions based on something I was supposed to have read, which obviously didn't happen, but it didn't matter because, it was philosophy, so I had the option to spin bullshit. That would at least get me a passing grade. Then my eye traveled to the bottom of the prescripts. "Please use supporting evidence."

"Fuck!" Okay, well I'm sure I could travel back in time to my prep school days and things of phrases worthy of a passing grade. My brain was so foggy a year felt like a lifetime. Then I thought about the man I watched every day for a semester who poured his life into his work. The words seemed to appear in my mind coming forth from his hands, like they had been presented to me. I guess I had paid more attention than I had realized. He was a mesmerizing speaker I had tried to push out of my head and my heart for six months and now he was going away. Now all his speeches, our conversations in his office and courtyard musings in between periods were playing across my mind like a slideshow of a funeral. How well we remember when people slip into time and space and how clear it was that time is what we squandered. I wrote my essays with such fervor I found myself apologizing by the conclusion to all of them because there wasn't enough time or paper to convey the depth of the understanding bestowed upon me by the lectures given by such an educator. It sounded like brown-nosing, I know, but I had within each concrete detail, the lecture date and snuck in details about his tie or the color of his shirt. I think about that, and it makes me turn red and I want to die, but what else could one pen into a hand-written essay when the title page, number, or author alluded you? Everyone turned in their papers and I sat on the edge of my seat waiting for the closing comments and questions section of the last lecture that took place. Professor Hubert counted all the papers and smiled.

"My comrades, to one and to all, I want to thank you for allowing me the pleasure and the honor of facilitating this course, which for me is like the handling of a delicate surgical instrument. Its effects are priceless but first you must handle it with care. I hope I have done that. Moreover, I hope you have learned and garnered the long-term effects of this course that extend beyond its prescriptive title. But that's on me. The burden of the educator dictates, and just as the tree is known by its fruit, it is buried within my wish for you all, that when you leave my class and conquer your monsters and slay your dragons, when you find yourself standing on the precipice of indecisiveness, you will speak your truth with a fleck of the knowledge taken from our time in this room. It is the humility of my profession that I shall never know if any of you fly, my only recourse is that I teach you how."

Everyone clapped and somewhere within me I found a shred of tenderness for him. When the clapping began, I raised my hand and asked to speak. "I know that in our first weeks of instruction, I acted in accordance to my nature and made something easy, difficult." A few with well served memories laughed. "And you told me I could have until the end of the semester to come up with a truth that we were willing to die for. And, Um…It is to my own great embarrassment that my true self, who makes things difficult, that I have to admit that I have not completed the assignment that was asked. I still don't know what it is I'm willing to die for but I can tell you that because of you and your class, I will never stop searching for the answer, but I promise that when I do, I'll send you the letter postscript and thank you," I sat down and touched my head where the heat was rising over my face and then quickly rejoined my pen with its cap and just stared at my desk.

"Well, unless there are any final comments… I will, in the spirit of Mr. Shrader's final words, bid you all farewell in the hopes that you never stop searching. À bientôt. Class dismissed."

There was a moment of stillness when I felt like the rest of the class. We didn't want to leave, nor the moment to end. Maybe if we stayed quiet and still, we could remain frozen in this feeling forever. And for a few fleeting moments I think we succeeded in suspending time. It wasn't until the first book closed, the first pencil snapped, and the first buckle clasped, we were all reminded the final moment of class was gone. We knew we had to move on.

"Oh, and one more thing before I lose all of you. Grades will be sent out, but if anyone wants to know their final grade before the holiday, come see me in office hours before the week is out. Now, off with you!"

Leaving was hard, but promptness put speed in my step. I had a single-spaced paper to write and submit. Straight to the bibliothèque I went, which was nearly empty with the sounds of the semester that had already passed through the hourglass. I had a rough draft done within the hour and then a final draft within the following hour. I felt rather accomplished by the end and stood back from my work with a sense of pride I hadn't felt since I first came to university, which seemed like a vague lucid dream. Seeing the time, I realized I didn't have much of it left and made a dash for his office. When I arrived, my illusive apple group was just leaving. I asked them what they had gotten, and both said 7. You see in France they don't give letters; they give you marks on a 1-15 scale. 7 is passing and no one ever gets a 15 because that is perfection so if you're going to improve, then the highest given, which is hardly ever, is 14. Placing even the brightest and most gifted student one grasping digit away, so they don't rest on their laurels or get a swelled head. I liked the principle of the grading system but as an American, I was not so easily humbled. Nevertheless, before I put my hand on Professor Hubert's door and I prayed that if I got a 7, I would be forever grateful even if my pride didn't believe it.

I opened the door, and he looked up and smiled as if pleasantly surprised. "What can I do for you Mr. Shrader, or are you here for your marks?"

"Well, first, I wanted to turn in the paper from the first assignment, so I understand if you don't have my grade ready."

He took my paper, lifted the first page before slapping it down on the top pile on his desk and said "7."

"But you haven't read it."

"I know. You wanted to know your grade for the class, and I told you 7."

"But you didn't…well, how did I do on the final?"

"I don't know. I haven't read it."

"Are you mocking me?"

"Not at all. I haven't read yours or anyone else's in the class."

"But I just ran into…"

"I know, and they told you 7."

"But you didn't read theirs?"

"That's correct. And just so we don't beat this to death, I haven't had, I don't plan to, I never have, and I never will."

I sat back in my chair. Bewildered. I would smile as if to laugh and then a frown of reasoning would appear on my face.

"I'd offer a cigarette, but as I've been told before…"

"Oh, you and I know you never believed me when I said that."

"Quite right." He said. "So, let's have one now." He put two cigarettes in his mouth like Bogart and then handed one to me. I hesitated to take it because I detested clichés like that but I, of course, took it.

After a deep inhale and exhale, I decided to fill the silence and smoke with a question he was already waiting for. "Okay, so facts as they are, we write papers and take finals and you don't read them?"

"Yes." He smiled.

"Why are you telling me this? Should you be telling me this?"

"To answer in order, because you asked me, probably not, but it doesn't jeopardize my job in any way technically."

I sat quietly.

"You seem angry and disappointed," he said.

"The answer is yes, yes both. Wait! No! God Dammit! I am …pissed off!"

"Good and you should be. Especially at the buffoons who require me to give tests. Which I do. The point of any exercise is to teach you. By doing the assignment, you learn something. You told me what you got out of my class today and then you went and put it on paper. Did you get something out of it?"

"Yes!"

"Fine, so why do you need me to put a number on what you learned or what you took away?"

"I…"

"Because you've been conditioned to expect a reward for the acquisition of knowledge instead of being taught that knowledge is the reward. I give assignments that force you to work with the material and the university requires that I ritually test you. Ultimately the level of intercourse that you choose to engage in with the material, the class and my instruction determines what knowledge you walk away with, and the true test is how you use it. I am not a prophet. I am a man. I cannot make every person feel and retain the knowledge the same way. More importantly, where and when you use it is up to you. Therefore, how can I give you a grade before you've even taken the biggest test? Life. So, because of the reasons aforementioned, I can only give you all passing 7's because I'm required to give you something. If it were up to me, you would all get nothing, because you have all been given everything. Therefore, what is a grade? A number. Nothing more."

I nodded, took a drag and put out my cigarette. "Not the first time I've stood corrected in this room."

"It will also be your last. You are no longer my student."

"But I would still like to come visit with you."

"Yes, but surely there are parts of us far more interesting, vast and complex that exists outside the scope of my office, otherwise the taste would grow stale."

I paused with a look of defeat, unsure if I had been told to go away or to come closer. "Yes, I suppose you're right."

"No, no, I'm afraid you are the one who's right." He wheeled himself back into place with his chair and pulled out a piece of yellow card stock and scribbled something on it before handing it to me. "Grades do have a purpose. Your report card Mr. Shrader."

I looked down and then up at him and then down at the bleeding 7 on the page. I reached for it and when I went to take it, he pulled back, causing me to look up. Suddenly he was closer than he had been. "Now you are no longer my student." He said.

"Yes." I couldn't say anything else.

He released his grasp from the yellow card. I pulled back and looked at him which had the effect of feeling like I was falling off a cliff. Suddenly he grabbed my wrist. His eyes flashed back and forth as they looked into mine, searching for an answer. I felt him slightly turn my wrist forcing me to sit just below him as if to get a better glimpse in my soul.

"Henry, Henry." Was all I could mutter.

He kissed me long and hard. Towards the end, his lips quivered, and I wasn't sure if he was trying to control his passions from over taking him or if he was as surprised by what he did as I was.

"Why did you do that?" I asked.

"Because you said my name."

"Professor…"

"No, no, we can't go back. I'm no longer your teacher, You're no longer my pupil."

"And yet I'm sure you have lesson plans laid out in your mind for both of us."

He grabbed me by both shoulders. My card dropped to the floor. "Look at me, don't make this taudry. That's not what this is. So, don't cheapen it with your puns."

"Perhaps that's all I can afford for now. Lines worthy of a poet's romance come at a steep price."

"Then save your pennies. I can speak for both of us. But before we proceed I must ask, have my feelings fallen upon false hope built by me, or have I set them upon something firm and real? In which case do you feel as I do?"

"You'll forgive me, but I'm not used to this. What I'm feeling. I don't know how to respond."

"What I'm asking for is your consent. If you're unable to speak then you must show me. Kiss me Antony."

"Alright." I said the words, but I wasn't moving.

"Place your head in my hands."

"Here, help me." I took his hands off my shoulders and placed them around my head. They were warm and smelt of aftershave and tobacco. His fingertips were rough, but his palms were soft. For a moment, I laid my face against the palm of his hand. I closed my eyes and allowed myself to drift up towards him. His olive skin glowed the closer I got. The setting sun beating through his window made him glow like the face of God. When I kissed him, my lips quivered with his like it was our first time, as if it was our bodies' way of deciding whether it could accept the placement of another's soul in its host.

When we parted, my eyes opened, and I could see him staring at me. I couldn't help but smile and then put my hand over my mouth.

"What is it?" he asked.

"I don't know," I said. "I…I think I've swallowed something."

He put his hand over his mouth as if to take inventory of anything potentially missing. "Do you know what it could be?"

I let my hand fall to my lap. "My pride."

CHAPTER FORTY-ONE

Saints And Cigarettes

The next few days were quiet ones that I used for myself to dwell and conceal my secret. We consummated the beginning of something, of what I couldn't say, only that it felt different, apart from anything else I had felt before. It made me forget entirely about anything that had come before. More effective than any drug I was taking. It made me want to use the memory sparingly. I wanted a mind that could think again and a body that could taste and feel again. In the height of her cold, I felt like I was actually getting to know Paris. I found myself sneaking away to find undiscovered roadways and cafes where I could write, people watch, and think. One day I was down in the third by the St. Michel fountain, I wandered into a bookstore whose rafters I could not tell if they were supported by the building or the books themselves. In the bookstore, I saw a tiny blue plastic camera with a flash bulb. It was so cheap I was sure it would break by simply pulling the shutter. They called it Diana. Can you imagine?

A camera made entirely from plastic? But there was something charming about how ugly it was. So naturally I bought it with the

120mm film that cost almost as much as the camera itself and went to work. From the Fountain, I stole away to the Spanish Quarter that I would describe as being the most aromatic section in all of Paris. Every corner was marked either by roasted chestnuts, crepe carts, or rotisserie vendors that carved lamb or a side of pork right off the spit. Each building was ornamented in an English Tudor style, and etched glass. The intimate proximity of all buildings to each other created the sense you were in a Grimm fairytale. The closeness of all the little shops and buildings themselves were like portals to different worlds. I found myself getting sucked into all of them. Crullers rolled in sugar crystals, assortments of hand knitted gloves, hats and scarves, varying trinkets, imported wine and every flavor of tobacco imaginable. There are a few places in this world that when you reflect back on your life, your mind allocates sacred space for. Moments or places of pleasure, preserved for you to revisit whenever you find yourself lost. I've gone back to those places in times of solace and reflection. Sometimes we can't remember if the life we lived was worth it when we are faced with the impossible, but then our mind takes us to those frozen moments that force you to keep going as you search for those seconds of fleeting perfection. When I think upon the life I could have led, I hoped that I would take with me the memory of this book shop. A shop of beautiful leather bound, encrusted, embroidered books. Metal latches thread and bound spines, some dipped in gold leaf paper, shining from the tips, begging to be filled.

The treasure of this place was that all the books were blank. This place appeared in its humble elegance as if to say, "From here, you shall write your story." In addition to beautifully bound blank pages, the shop offered the various quills, pens, inks, and leather goods consisting of hand-stained leather bags, wallets and day planners. In the back there was, under a brass lined glass case, an assortment of hand carved pipes made from various materials. Cherry, sinew and bone etched or accented in gold and silver displayed on a crushed velvet sash. Tobacco was displayed on the wall behind it, in exquisitely painted stained glass scenes from Notre Dame and the St. Louis

Cathedral, sprinkled in with some oil canvases from previous artistic periods. I walked past the case, back towards the collection of blank loose leafs and books, passing in a somber drift until I found the one that spoke to me. The bell above the door chimed. I heard footsteps head towards the back near the pipes and tobacco but wanting to remain alone and uninterrupted in my little world, I moved myself behind a spinning tack of painted postcards. They were a collection of reproduced Monet's, each one signed by the artist who copied it. I noticed that all were painted by a Jean or a Claude of some sort. I spied over the counter at the little old man who acknowledged me and noticed him working away on the same postcards I was holding in my hand. "Are you Jean or Claude, I wonder?" I asked myself.

The old man looked up from his work and directly at me as if he had heard my thoughts. He rose from his work, and I froze before realizing he had headed towards the back to help the person who had entered previously. I turned back to my painted post card and held it up in front of my camera. Having taken the picture, I uttered a small laugh at my theft of his recreated art which was stolen from its original master. However, his use of "detournement" to recreate an iconic image into something else was what drew me to it originally. I just didn't want to pay for it, as embarrassing as it is to admit. But from the grainy image I captured you could see the language of art through interpretation. That is how art is kept alive. This image had traveled through the ages from its initial conception as one thing, only to become many other things while still being exactly what it was before. Proof that the alpha and omega of this realm begins and ends with art. This painting along with every version of it here often shall be as it was while not being as it was. I suppose people are like that in a way as well. Perhaps it is for this reason they create art, because it's the process they can control, while keeping the artist eternal.

I continued to move my eyes over the shop as I had done before but through the eye of the camera. Through a delicate pirouette, I looked across this hidden gem, snapping a few stills along the way. I turned the zoom lens and focused on various objects and points. Light bulb, arm of coat rack, spine of book, the transept shared tobacco tins with raised medieval designs on them. My eyes moved up to the man holding it, who by the time I reached his shirt collar turned to me and smiled. For a second I froze, but I let my fingers do the talking and pressed the shutter.

"Nothing newsworthy here. Just picking out my tobacco."

"I can see that Professor. I should have known you'd buy the source of your habit from here."

"Naturally, I would not support such a habit unless I was killing myself slowly with the most delicious poison."

"You're the only person I know who can make a slow and assisted suicide sound appealing."

"I think I'll take that as the first compliment from you to date…I think." He smiled from the corner of his eye.

"Pardon, Misseure?" Claude or Jean interrupted with the two open containers of tobacco waiting for the professor to decide. I realize of course that I have continued to refer to him as the professor, but I admit it's not out of respect or propriety. Truthfully, it turned me on.

Henri held the two cannisters in each hand, smelling each before turning to me, "Your pick. Either Christina the Astonishing, patron saint of lunatics and mental illness, or this Delaroche."

I smelt them first before I spoke. "Well, to be honest, the differentiation in the tobacco themselves are so subtle that I don't feel as though I could make a decision based on their nuances. But pardoning my superficiality, I must say the Delaroche is gorgeous."

"So, you like Le Jeune Martyre? Alright then, I'll take it. C'est la bonne; si vous plait. And you can have it when I'm done."

"Bon," said the clerk.

Then Henri turned to me. "So, I understand that you haven't seen our young martyrs in person."

"No, I haven't, But I see it here. It's remarkable and haunting."

"Merci Monsieur. À bientôt! Alright then, come with me."

"Where are we going?" He was pulling me by my scarf, and I could barely keep up.

"How about this?" His voice bounced like a cacophony of pennies against the thatched buildings as he raced through the Quarter. "A riddle to see if you can guess otherwise you'll have to wait."

"Is stop and think an option?"

"What do you think?" he shouted back.

"Ok, then tell me."

"Alright. I am all prepositions. I am time past and present. Look through me and you'll see nothing. Walk through me and you might see everything."

"Wouldn't a cab be faster? Sorry, I have to catch my breath." Something was making my heart race. The unknown or the exercise.

"It would be faster but then you'd know where we were going. Besides, part of the answer lies in the journey." He smiled and we dashed underground while I prayed for air and answers.

"Was that part of the answer or part of the riddle or both? Or were you even referring to the riddle? Were you talking about us?"

He laughed, "I'll make you hate me and say all of the above."

"Fine. Let's see. All prepositions. So over, under, through, around, out, ok. So, all of those things. Fuck it. Around the post, over the past, at the present. Okay, ways to go through, but if you look through me, you'll see nothing. So, you have to go in, around, or under… Fuck! But why can I see through you? Can I see through you?

Wait, is it through you like pages of a book or look like I see through your bullshit?"

"You know the rules of riddles?"

"Never attempt while drinking?"

"Um no. Yes or no questions only."

"Oh, professor. Do you mean "look as in touch?"

"No."

"So, you mean, look? As in sight?"

"Yes."

"So why would I have to walk through if I can see through you? That's rhetorical. Um, Okay. So, by looking through you, I can't see what's inside."

"Yes"

"But I can still see through you?"

"Yes"

"Can I also see myself?"

"Yes."

"Well, you're not a mirror, like looking through a mirror you only see what's behind. You look into a mirror, not through it. And you can't go through it."

"So, you know that it's not a mirror?"

"Well, I'm trying to eliminate it."

"Then you have to ask me 'yes or no' once you are finished and we get off here before the transfer. No pressure, but you're running out of time."

"Fine! Are you a mirror?"

"No."

"But I see myself?"

"Yes!"

"This was easier with apples. But I can through…"

"Is that a question?"

"Make it one."

"Fine, yes!"

I looked around for the first time for the answer on the floor, his shoes or even in his eyes. The metro doors opened and closed leaving me alone with my reflection.

"Glass!" I shouted. Everyone turned and glared at me like the stupid American I was.

"Keep your voice down Antony."

"Are you glass? Tell me if you are."

"Yes."

"But then why do I have to go inside to see if I can see through you?"

"Yes or no, remember?"

"I know! I was thinking out loud. All prepositions, ways in, like right now we are going under, and you have to go through to see everything. But you're glass. Unless, is just a portion of you glass?"

"Yes."

"Past and present, are you a museum?"

"Yes."

"Museum made of glass! I got it!"

"Tell me, now this is our stop!"

"You are the Louvre."

"Yes! And you can go in it, under it, around. Above ground. This stop is called the carousel, from here we can go anywhere and bisect all those clamoring tourists from above."

"Is this where they keep…"

"The Delaroche? Yes. I want to show it to you. I want to show you a lot of things."

He took me by the hand and led me through a catacomb of refined pop-up shop windows, cafes and eateries sitting pressingly behind what looked like cave rock. I knew when we were getting closer because the stone ground changed from gray stone to marble. Henri just flashed his school badge, and we went in. Although underpaid and underappreciated, the world of academics still came with its perks.

"Shall we go straight to the Delaroche, or would you like to see the Mona Lisa and Napoleon Crossing the Alps?"

"I don't know. You decide. I'm overwhelmed and embarrassed that I haven't been here yet, having lived here all these months."

"But we never stop learning so we can always start somewhere."

"Alright. You lead."

"To the ancient world then."

And down we went to walk the hallways of marble masterpieces, golden cacophobia sarcophagi, and mosaics that looked as if they held within each fragment a piece of the universe. We left and moved down the line to lesser known but remarkable pieces like Haarlem's Le Baptême du Christ when the portrayal of Jesus was a muddy illusioning silhouette. As if he were saying he had no right to speculate on the appearance of the divine and left the true identity in the eye of the beholder with minimal lighting, acting in accordance to the claim made by Pontius Pilate, "ecce homo" behold a man. Then the great disappointment. The Mona Lisa. The ropes that keep the public back draw more sensation than her half smile, which makes the public clamor to see a woman who far surpasses the lowest expectations. Yet to her credit, a woman who can still draw a crowd after 400 years should prove to all youth seekers that beauty does not lie within the drawing but within the mystery. And then we came upon the Young Martyr. So alive and yet so quintessentially still as if given life by the flow of water itself. A glow illuminated the head of the martyr to show he died for the purest cause as two passersby wept by the shore.

"There's something wonderfully morbid about it. Almost cruel how beautiful he makes death look. We all hope for immortality and here he's given it away so freely." I found myself enamored by its beauty, unable to break away.

The professor stood back and took a breath, "I suppose but many have debated the sex, origin and identity of the martyrs. Some say his wife or a lover. Others point to religious persecution of his time, whether it be a man and woman or both."

"But regardless, immortal they are, before us, in death, preserved in youth and beauty forever. How many people can point to something that says, 'look how much I mattered.'" The tears forming in my eyes over personal frustration and anguish forced me to turn away from our fallen martyr.

"Sometimes we look to the others we left behind and wonder, how much we matter?"

I looked at him and smiled. "Oh, how nice would that be?" He touched my shoulder and removed it as I drew a breath.

"Now that we've seen it, we can go now," Henri said.

"No, just a few more moments, I want to pay my respects to the one left behind."

"Alright, but I wouldn't worry. If you look closely, our young martyr is in eternal peace and smiling at us."

"Smiling at us all because she's the lucky one."

"Do you find your own incessant morbidity insufferable or is this your own version of flirtation?" the Professor asked.

"As soon as I know I'll fill you in. But I'm sorry. You've been so kind, offering to take me on this spontaneous adventure. I loved the painting. I do. I'm so good at self-sabotage that you'll find me abysmal in the flirtation department."

By now there was a small crowd circling around us like sharks that could smell blood in the water.

The professor leaned in, "You are also abysmal in the quiet department."

"On the contrary, far worse than abysmal in the quiet department if there exists such a thing."

He touched his forehead to mine. "Then come with me."

"I think we should save our next adventure for when we both have strength."

"This will just be a methodical stroll. Perhaps planning for our next adventure."

"Then I'll follow," I agreed.

"Let the record show that my constant endeavor will be to make you follow and for you to feel you always have reason to."

"We are born with legs, sir, we are taught reason. It is the heart that pulls us. For now, I'll let you take the heart strings and play the song of my heart."

We left the Louvre through the glass top and so above we saw a glowing orange disc and a tired fading star. Towards it we walked into the garden, nesting into it. The Tuileries Gardens. The culmination of ideas and billiards boards as nobility courtiers and bourgeois circulated the fountains and flower beds to anticipate the move and motivations of opposing worlds and classes were visions passing through me like memories resurfacing from a forgotten past. Now we walk to forget but one can't escape the geometry of the gardens. It's intentional walkways that force you to look across fountains and through statues at the carousel gardens, especially the Louise Bourgeois welcoming hands stretching 30 inches wide and high. It was as if the granite was the stone of solidification and love in a world that would never die. I found this part of the gardens most fascinating.

For a while we were quiet, and I could tell he was letting me enjoy myself. Refraining from showing me various species of flowers and historical placement of certain statues. He knew it all, but knowledge is the religion of humility and means nothing except in practice. I admired his temperance and how he resisted from coming off as a know it all. Out of benevolence I pointed to a few sites, he kept his explanations respectfully short. He was a very patient man and out of courtesy he waited for me to talk.

"Henri," I said.

"I like when you say my name. Yes Mr. Shrader." He goadingly smiled.

"I'm feeling a lot of things; tranquility, happiness, but I keep thinking something of a different nature."

"Go on."

"Right now, walking with you, I'm happy, but I keep thinking, well, I can't tell if I'm losing you, if we are getting closer or if you're pulling away."

"Really?" He exclaimed, "Well, now I'm perplexed."

"Really? How? I'm just asking a question."

"Alright, I hear you. You can't tell if we are growing closer or if I'm pulling away because you're unsure of where you stand after your museum outburst."

"Yes, that's what I'm thinking but that doesn't answer…" I stopped talking only to realize Henri wasn't standing next to me anymore. He had stopped and was standing several yards behind me.

"What are you doing?" I asked and squinted.

"I'm pulling away, and now…" He ran to catch up to me. "I'm beside you. You don't have to wonder whether we are together or whether I'm pulling away. You'll know."

Henri continued, "I've realized something in the limited time I've spent with you. That two people aren't together until after a kiss and one date."

"You speak as though you've already doubled down."

"You are correct Antony, usually a couple goes through several dates, interludes, and perhaps some fornication while playing the game of who can act as if they care less, and with all the humility I know if we went down that road together, you would win. You'd run so far and so fast it would be too long before I even realized what I did to bring you back. Just so you know." He grabbed my hand and held it in his like the lullaby that could put the sun to bed. "I'm putting my heart in your hands. I won't leave you because I don't want to give you any reason to leave me. I'm in this. I can't put you out of my head. I used to think some cruel trick of nature put you in my class but then I began to realize you were put in my care not just for your sake but for mine. This old breed of which I'm composed withers at the first sign that our vintage starts to show, and then we are alone. You've given me life and now I'm going to save yours."

CHAPTER FORTY-TWO

Where You Carve The Initials

We continued in secret and silence and with each day I spent with him I could feel that hot heat of the past breathing on my neck lessen, but it was getting harder to regimen my high throughout the day. I wasn't trying to be high but trying to maintain a homeostasis, completely sweating through all my clothes and trying not to take all of them off in the middle of a French café. When it got very hard I would always have to excuse myself to go to the bathroom. There wasn't enough time to swallow a pill to suppress the side effects, but crushing the pill on the lid of the toilet tank was enough to stop the cold sweats. Sometimes I would come back and wonder if he knew but he was always so kind. "Shall we go dear?" He would pay the bill and we were off. One day we were sitting at a cafe, and I was scratching away in my leather-bound journal with my charcoal pencil when he called to le garçon "L'addition s'il vous plait?" and he took me to a special shop next to Le Procope, which was the oldest restaurant in the world, and he brought me to this little shop decorated in silk scarves and beeswax candles. On the front table, next to the register they had an arrangement of fountain pens either gold or silver tipped that were as heavy as the price was.

"Henri, that's ridiculously expensive. I'm fine with my charcoal pencil."

"Men of the world, men of conviction, men of history write with instruments worthy of their practice. I write and sign with nothing less." He said, pulling out his lapis and gold-tipped fountain pen. "For the sake of your craft and all future philosophy, please choose an instrument worthy of your work."

I sighed, "Are you sure? Are you sure it isn't too much too soon?"

"I think to wait any longer would be a disservice to humanity." He wrote on a piece of paper and handed it past me to the merchant who looked at him and back at me and brought out a burnt-red orange and silver-tipped pen. It had the initials H.H. written on the side of the cap. "I had it made, and I was planning on picking it up. But if it's too hard to choose, I should insist you take mine."

"I can't argue with you anymore. I'll take it."

"Come on, let's get out of here."

We walked out of the shop before he whipped around and told me, "I want you to write about us. Everything you want and desire. Put it to paper and do it with my pen. I have to go but I will come see you again soon. And so, on our next adventure I want to hear all you've written.

"Why?" Was all I could think to say.

"Because I have to go and I have so much to write about today and I can't wait to tell you all about it."

"Do you forget I was there? We were there Henri. We are here now!"

"I was too. And I wasn't. Because I went everywhere else in my head, through every junction to another trance with yours and then to the future, and there was this shore and a house, and we were there. We were old and at the end of time. It was the warmest I'd ever felt. I'm going to go there and find it again in the pages." He was off and down the cobblestone streets.

"You're absolutely mad!"

He whirled and shouted back. "Oh, you can't help that. We're all mad here."

"No, I'm not!"

"You must be, or you wouldn't have come here."

I stopped following him and watched him disappear down the rabbit hole, determined not to follow despite this pull like an undercurrent running across my feet. "Curiouser and Curiouser" I wondered.

CHAPTER FORTY-THREE

The Last Temptation of Caduceus And The Emersion Of Aesculapius

I t's called a philosophical elephant for a reason because we could all be touching a different part of the elephant and have a different perspective and neither one is more or less true because the truth is governed through the merit of the experience. The man who touches the trunk believes he is touching a snake, the man with the legs a tree and the belly a boulder and neither is less correct except when you put all those perspectives together to get a fuller picture, a larger truth. This could also be true for different fields of study, science, philosophy, history, even pragmatists are a piece of the elephant. As small as humans appear in the scheme of everything our desire to see the entire picture, the elephant is undeniable and unmistakable.

I responded with perked interest to the topic Henry had introduced, "Our endeavor is a lost cause when you consider that you can't know everything. We are at all times only ever seeing pieces."

"Time is the enemy. If we had eternity, then I would say you were being lazy, but you're right. We don't have forever, and we can't know everything. Rather than considering something as fantastic as the universe, and if we set aside our elephant, let's consider something of equal complexity on a smaller scale." Henry paused for a moment to allow for me to ponder before opening with his answer. "I'll open. How would the concept of the philosophical elephant change if we analyze something as paradoxically smaller and possibly even more complex, if we make our elephant the inner child at the center of every human soul. He is as complex as the answers to my question. He is as ubiquitous as the image we may never get to understand completely, even if he sits before me."

I was thrown off this unsubtle and not so slight amendment to our original discussion of topic and could only respond with the thoughts of someone else. "The Cartesian approach would say that only our own souls and minds are the things we can know in their entirety and be sure of complexity."

"I would like to amend that. I think we are given two tasks when we are put on this earth. The first is to know thyself. The next, and this is just a theory, one of which I'm testing and learning about as I go along. Our second task is to spend our life trying to learn a person's soul as well as ours. This venture we take up as humans is our own philosophical elephant. Looking at anyone. I see elements and pieces of your soul, but is what I see is who you really are? When it's all laid out on the table, are we really the sum of our parts or are we all greater than the parts we are given ?"

"And have you figured me out?" I asked while I played with a cigarette between my fingers.

"First, I must ask, are you going to light that or put it back? The longer this goes on the more un-French you appear. Sitting in a public café it is important to maintain some of the traditional customs out of respect." He curled his hair between his fingers awaiting my answer.

"Light me professor." I insisted.

"Moving along, you asked what I have figured out. That's an enterprise of monolithic proportions all on its own; trying to figure you out. What I have been able to figure out has been based on three components. What I see, What I know to be true, and the hypothesis I've drawn from there, which until now, I've been unable to test."

"You may test them now." I said.

"You mustn't become angry with me." He inhaled deeply, dabbed his eyes and laid back.

"I think you'll find I'm more perceptive than I've led you to believe." I took the cigarette from his lips.

"That too is just a theory. Now we'll decide how perceptive you are." He began to roll another cigarette, allowing me to keep his other for myself. "I'm immune to your perceptibility. I can see it in the moments when you love the way I carry myself."

"I might also be immune to you extraction of an accurate perception. I also know it to be one of the reasons you love me as being part of the way I carry myself." I took in another inhale and let the smoke drift up into my nose before quickly blowing it out as he began to change with a look of seriousness.

"Well, that's the trouble I find myself in. Certain conclusions have kept me at a distance while others have drawn me closer to you all while trying to reconcile how I feel when I'm just with you. Perhaps the enigma that surrounds you is what draws me to you. It's when I begin to deconstruct the riddle is when I cannot decide what part of the elephant I'm touching, or if I'm even touching an elephant."

His look of bewilderment was causing the smile to trail from my face.

"For the sake of sticking to one metaphor, let's just say that I am." He inhaled a huge breath staring at the ceiling. Before he could answer, I interjected.

"Alright, you're an elephant and these are the pieces I see. You're beautiful." He then opened a notebook he always carries. I guess he was serious when he said he was going to write. I don't know why I would ever doubt a man who does everything he says.

As Henri scribbled, he wrote, "He is beautiful. But he is vain because he doubts his own beauty. Vanity is prideful and pride is compensation. What is he compensating for?" Then he paused, "To whatever I've just read, I was hoping you could answer the rest."

I turned, "I didn't realize we were writing our story line by line. Repeat the question."

He smiled, "Alright, moving along." He took a big inhale from his cigarette like it was his first. "Okay, he's brilliant, speaks with full intention and like his arguments arranges his sentences like an improvised Jazz musician. Therefore, speaks only what he knows. He is the only sure of what he knows and nothing else. Through our courtship he becomes less sure of everything and speaks less. Either he is afraid he'll say the wrong thing, or he knows intelligence is the only card he has to play. Despite possessing the ability to run circles in certain subject matters, he has abstained from his own opinions to maintain equilibrium and ensure he won't make a mistake."

"Is there a question coming?" I was at the end of my cigarette and found myself reaching for the other as I licked my scorched fingertips.

"Yes, does he think intelligence is all I like him for? Or is that all he thinks he has to offer?" He passed a freshly rolled fag to me.

"My turn again? Alright, I've never thought about what to give to someone, what parts to lend to someone as we decide if we will continue the saga of knowing someone's soul. What will they take?

What will they give? I don't know what to give, probably because I don't know what you want. I have some inclination of what you want but that idea terrifies me, because it goes to the heart of the questions I can't answer for myself."

"What is it you think I want?"

"Me, myself in all of its entirety."

"Do you think drugs prevent you from knowing who you are or is that why you take them? Have they helped you come to any conclusions about yourself through self-medication?"

"But I'm not… I don't know what to say now."

"It's one of the pieces of the elephant I've struggled to place. One might see that piece and think self-fulfilling indulgent narcissist, incapable of feelings but then I see a person who feels everything, internalizes the world a bit too much. I have vices, I do, but my mind has limitations to justifying their use as being necessary. And of course, the question of truthfulness is raised. First, one must lie to themselves to allow the behavior with the conclusion, 'No one will understand.' So you keep it secret and then lie to everyone else. Seems like an awfully large amount of effort with little return unless the secret behind your reason for continuing is so severe you're willing to dance until something gives out."

"How many PhDs do you have again professor?"

"I told you to call me…"

"How many?" I asked again.

"Three, with a master's in physics."

"And you think the extensive time spent in labs, classrooms and archives have prepared you to navigate the depths of the human soul?" I stared him down and ashed the end of my cigarette.

"No, just curiosity. The same curiosity all humans possess to know another soul as well as their own. It is such a long journey to knowing another soul that we begin to love it and the body it inhabits."

"I don't think you could ever understand." I rose from my chair as if to leave.

"I won't allow you to make it that simple, because we are human. We aren't simple. We're messy and complicated. Sit down please. I insist. Here, have a glass." He said as he pushed the glass toward me.

"Henry, Old man. I haven't seen you since you took over the department. Do you ever come down from your perch to visit those you've left behind?" A scruffy Englishman came up to us, aged, older than he was, his fingers were brown from his pipe tobacco, his vest didn't match his trousers, neither did his socks, and the soles of his shoes were caked in the muck and grime of Paris, stretching the battle of wear for 10 years at least.

"There's a reason I dislike you, the English bastardization of my name is one of them."

"Would Doctor Henry suffice, or do you need more tender care than an already bruised pear?"

"Your unsubtle comparison of me to fruit is really getting to be quite old."

"And obviously, we agree with stereotypes Henri. The cause of your department's inability to publish anything with originality." The old Englishman stood, cold, as if over a chessboard waiting for the next move.

"Should I go?" I had my bag in hand ready to make a dash for it.

"Not at all." Henri said. "In fact, I want you to meet the self-employed professor of metaphysics Dr. Joseph Westin."

"Charmed," he said. "Henri and I go back, you see lad. Prep school, then Cambridge. I've seen him at his highs and lows, and he's seen mine. You're looking at one of the movements right now."

"Lose your way in the absinth bar again Dr.?" Henri asked while staring at the smoke of his cigarette.

"Filled me up to the tits they did. So…" he said looking down at me before putting his hands on my shoulders. "Is this one-off limits? To you as well as to me or just to me?"

Henri shot up out of his chair. "Dr. Westin, do you need some coffee?"

"He means business when he says Dr. Tell me, what does he call you?" Dr. Westin breathed into my ear before taking in a breath of my essence, trying to figure out what I was to the Professor, smiling for the answer as if I were prey.

"Joseph, I'm not kidding. Leave the kid alone."

"Kid?" I exclaimed.

Dr. Westin smiled. My dear Henri. I'm sorry chap. Really I am. You forgive me? Please don't fire me." Dr. Westin put their heads together and whispered very intimately, "Please don't fire me."

"You know I won't Joseph."

Dr. Westin smiled and kissed him, "I know," he said.

"Leave us please, now Joseph."

"I will Professor, but I did, now that I've run into you, the faculty, this dying breed of philosophers and decrepit thinkers are getting together at the Parish and attendance is mandatory. No exceptions."

"We really need to stop having faculty meetings like this," Henri said in a half smile as he pulled out his pocket watch to assess the time, the position of the sun, and his life choices leading up to this moment.

I took this lull in conversation as an opportunity to inquire, "What's the Parish?"

"A safe haven for the last and only Irish pub in Paris, or at least the only one worth going to," Dr. Westin took out his pipe.

"Perhaps you could sober his thoughts, leave me the brochure on why one should go."

"Because you love whiskey don't value your life and enjoy life or death situations."

I tilted my head, waiting for my next thought. Dr. Westin smiled. I looked at Henri, "Whiskey and harlotry. Sounds like something an academic would seek."

"Afraid not. This venue is retired of harlots and whores. We are washed up and crippled and go to be with the other lepers, and you have the Professor here who just comes out like Jesus to bless us."

"Joseph, don't start again." The professor glared and blew smoke through his nostrils like a dragon being awoken.

"I'm not. I'll save it all for tonight." Dr. Westin sneered.

"I look forward to it Dr." Henri put out his cigarette.

"Oh, look, I've agitated the Savior. I'll go light a candle at St. Germain before I head over there." Before leaving, he pivoted on his heels to say to me, "Was nice to have met you and remember to beware of strangers." Then stumbled away into the fading light just before the Paris lights changed for the Parisians. Daylight was for tourists and outsiders. Le Soir was for the Parisians.

"What the fuck was that?" I asked.

"An abscess," he answered. "A beloved abscess that can't be removed."

"Why keep him around?"

"Because he's not the man you met today. He's lost, gone, somewhere else. Some of that I'm partial to blame. That was a long time ago." He rubbed his hands over his face, finished his drink and let out a large sigh.

"Are you going tonight?" I asked.

"Of course. Who else is going to make sure they make it all home alive?"

"And give them shit for it in the morning?" I asked.

We both laughed, then quiet fell over us like someone had to go but no one wanted to move.

"Shall we consider today a scratched surface then?" He asked with the severity of a physician.

I nodded.

"Alright then, I'll see you here tomorrow. Noon. Perhaps we'll explore Irish pubs ourselves, take a boat down the river, anything you want."

"Why does that sound like an apology?"

"It's not. It's a promise."

We rose from our seats and looked around at the general public. We stared at each other, unable to say goodbye. I tilted my head in a sharp jerk to the right and he disappeared behind the corner. After a few seconds, I ran after him and called out "Sir, sir, can I have a cigarette?" I went right up to his face and took one. Looking out to the right again, I turned and kissed him before disappearing once more.

CHAPTER FORTY-FOUR

Poets Are Patriots

"Well, you have to fucking go!" Ci was elated with the drama of the café threesome.

"Ci, you don't have to scream, because I'm not. I wasn't invited."

"Maybe Parish is code for sex club." Her mind was a vessel for dirty channels.

"Afraid that's not his style. He actually didn't even want to go himself. I told you. That man is like his wounded project."

"More reason for you to go and support him, rather, save him from drunk imbeciles."

"I heard that." Jane said, propping her body against the doorway.

"What do you think I should do Jane? Assuming you no longer hate me, that is."

"I still hate you, but I'll help you."

"You don't have to."

"You haven't killed each other. That's more progress than I would have given either of you credit for." Jane said as Ci rolled a fag and put on her satin robe.

"He's going to the Parish."

"Oh. Yeah, you can't go. You need a password to get in. An English password. They are an exclusive establishment." Janes poured herself a drink.

"You mean they hate the French?" I asked.

"Precisely. Which is ironic because in the center of the establishment they have stacked to the ceiling a heap of twisted broken chairs piled high, purported to be from the barracks of the July Revolution, on top of the heap an aged Irish Whiskey bottle and shot glass. Suspended from the ceiling is a liberty bell. At the last call, the most obscene nationalist drunkards try to climb the debris to see if they can reach that bell to pay 100 pounds for a shot, or a 1000 pounds for the bottle of Three Crown Whiskey of the Royal Irish Distillery in Belfast. And yes, some have died and broken their necks in this pursuit but for those of us who have reached the top, the view and the spirits are worth it I hear."

"I gather you've been there?"

"Yes."

"So, you know the password?"

"Yes."

"Are you going to tell us?"

"Yes, and non-regrettably I have an angle." She chuckled.

"Which is?" I turned as my neck strained so it might crack.

"I need you to tell my brother to remove me from his roster for next semester. The damn French love their bureaucracy so much that apparently, I noticed too late to formally request a change myself and the only one who can is the teacher himself. And since our recent not speaking is basically all your fault anyway, then I would appreciate your help in exchange for the password and my inevitable forgiveness, to be taken from his roster. Forgiveness is something I'm working on. It seems to be something the British are not used to."

"What's the password?" I asked as soon as she took a breath.

"Do I have your word?"

"You have my consideration, that's all you get. You should add humility to your bucket list."

"Just promise you'll talk to him."

"PASS-WORD!" I demanded.

She pursed her lips and breathed her fire through her nose before rolling her eyes to the ceiling where she threw up the password "Poet and Patriot" Then she left the room.

I turned to Ci, "Now that we know, I think we should go."

"I honestly think that sometimes people want you to do things without being asked. Sometimes we surprise people when we surprise ourselves. I think we should go.

"We?" I turned to her with a face twisted in horror.

CHAPTER FORTY-FIVE

Justify

"Y ou do what you like but at last call, that ball and whiskey are mine." She smiled

On the outskirts of the Spanish Quarter, a hovel reminiscent of an English Tudor, faded etched glass, and a rust red door, hanging above it, a faded mustard yellow sign with a raised cast iron mold of a bell with Celtic writing which presumably spelled "Parish." I lifted the rusty iron door knocker, looked once over to Ci before dropping it against the door. Immediately the top sections of the viewing portal opened, and we spoke the password, which was followed by a non-subtle eye roll from the door keep, the like that suggested, "how the fuck did these two get the password," before he opened the door to let us in. The door led us into a world of green velvet tufted chairs, reclaimed wood bar stools, cigar smoke, where all entered to pay homage to the July rebellion tower of chairs. It wasn't until I gave the room a once over when I realized how out of our element we were.

I decided to dress up. What a mistake. I chose to wear a long chiffon white oxford with leather tights and platform boots. Underneath my shirt, I had a bullet shell belt garter that I used to hold my cigarettes in.

I failed miserably to blend in and Ci... in her blood red fox fur coat, with ruby flapper headband adorned with feathers. Underneath the dead fox, she wore a sequined gold slip and that was all.

Dr. Westin leaned back in his chair, pipe in teeth with his thumbs tucked under suspenders, he raised his eyebrows and cocked his head to alert Henri.

Henri put his hands in his hair as the faculty pushed their chairs out, legs apart waiting to see how this would play out. I walked right up to him and threw my arms around his neck, pulling his ear close to my mouth, "I know I fucked up, don't say anything that could make me feel any stupider then I already do now."

"Fine, but now? Right now? I hate you."

"Understood."

We walked over to the table of aging brilliance, and I paused to sit down having realized I lost my fellow saboteur to the bar as she began collecting a harem of Irish alcoholics.

One of the senior professors leaned over to me and said, "Don't be intimidated, the young ones always arrive later." In a few moments, we were joined by two junior professors, one man of Indian descent, and one pixie haired feminist studies associate professor who preferred women but who was currently scheduled for an abortion in the morning to make a point.

"Point taken," I said.

"It's very Simone de Beauvoir of you."

She smiled and we took a drink trying not to look at her uterus.

"Do you guys have an agenda for these meetings?" I asked.

"Oh, let me explain," Dr. Westin poured a glass of bourbon and slid it in front of me. "The faculty and I are allocated a budget for meetings that benefit the department. Only we never meet because we disagree so violently against the study of the other that the money sits until the end of the year. But the only thing we can agree on is this night to meet to spend the money and drink the entire budget before the end of each academic session in a place no ordinary idiot can come into."

I nodded in understanding before speaking. "I had already concluded in my limited education that this was not a 'sanctioned' faculty meeting but what exactly do you all do?"

"Well, sometimes we try to wear shirts that aren't enemies to back lighting like a chiffon," Dr. Westin remarked before taking back the bourbon he poured for me and knocking it back.

"I'm sorry, I was worried it was going to be hot in here." And I was right. It really was very, very hot. I looked around and saw the barkeep coming to the table with pitchers on a tray for the table, one was water. I reached for the small pitcher tankard of water and dumped it over my head, slicked my hair back, pulled my shirt up to pull a cigarette from my garter and lit it before smoking the entire fag to the filter. My pixie haired counterpart pulled a cigarette from my thigh and winked, "Nice nipples."

"Je pourrais avoir une carafe d'eau s'il vous plaît?" Henri Said.

"What's your name, professor?" I turned to my feminist star.

"Taylor. Tonight, I'm Taylor. Because gender and title is bs. and I'll be someone else in the morning."

I turned to Henri, "It's just water, it will dry. Calm down professor."

"I think it might be time for a game." Dr. Westin suggested.

"The game?" Taylor asked in sudden excitement.

"It's not fair that we do this every time." Dr. Hadid voiced in protest. It ruins the prospect of winning as the fear of heights is a real thing."

"That's just a mental construct." Taylor said from the side of her mouth.

"Well, you think everything is a construct." He snapped.

"Because it is!" slamming her hand on the table she almost choked on her inhale.

"Save it for the game my dear Dr. S."

"There are a few extra of us here," I pointed out. "Is it going to work with an odd number or a holy number?"

The table seemed confused.

"What the fuck?" Taylor asked as she put her cigarette out in Dr. Hadid's drink.

"Sorry, just tell me, what's the game?"

Taylor lit another cigarette before explaining the rules. "The game is called 'Whiskey and Spit.'"

"For some, it's whiskey and sickness" Dr. Hadid was the only one I felt like would tell me the truth at this table. It was hard to read the table with Henri not even looking at me.

"Anyway, no interrupting unless you're adding something useful. Anyway, someone starts with a person, word, phrase, construct."

She looked around the table and found no one to object, "And then the next person has to come up with something that will relate support or is the extension of that relevant thing. This goes clockwise around the table until someone can't think of the next thing in which case they take a shot of whiskey. Now, being this is a table of academics, some of us like to spin bullshit, in which case, if the person preceding you doesn't agree with the logic of your answer, then they can say 'Justify.' If you can't justify the reason for the placement of your answer within the round of the original topic, you have to take a shot and then you have to pick a different topic right away or risk taking another shot."

"I'm assuming the last person standing is the presumed winner?"

"Yes but the winner has to at least try to climb the mountain of chairs to try to get the shot that sits on top, or risk being called a little bitch and just a smart-ass alcoholic instead of an academic badass unlike Dr. Hiatus over heights right next to me."

"How many times do I have to tell you, I didn't ever think I'd win." Dr. Hadid looked almost defensive to tears.

"Trust me, no one thought you would either. It made the let down all the more disappointing."

"I thought no one ever makes it to the top?" Every question I asked made me feel even more new to everything than I was willing to appear but unfortunately it was the only way to learn.

"I mean people try, some die, as far as this game goes, sometimes we all lose by drinking each other into a wasted stand-off, but should one rise above us, then they at least have to try, otherwise the notion tying academia to social justice and revolution becomes meaningless Dr. Hadid." Taylor was being relentless towards him although it was sadistically amusing.

"Well, why don't we start with the sacrificial lamb and see how far we get?" Dr. Hadid motioned over to the barkeep for the whiskey.

"I'm not a drunk!" I insisted.

"You are when you're among wolves, Antony." Henri whispered.

I leaned close to Henri, "Is that man being tattooed by that other man over there?"

"Yes."

"Is that legal?"

"I imagine legality is not why they do it."

I leaned closer. "I think I'm fucked."

"Oh, don't think, believe it."

"I think we should abandon the ancient regime rules for the evening and invoke the Thermidorian rules for our special guest." Dr. Westin suggested.

"Agreed." Said the table.

"Agreed," Henri said. "I would ask the Lord to take mercy on us but seeing as the church has been obliterated by the table in the dismantling of the l'ancien régime, I move this to be the year one of the annual meeting of this .... Cult of supremely drunken beings, Commence!"

I grabbed Henri's leg from under the table and leaned into him speaking through my teeth.

"Unless I'm already plastered, you didn't explain the Thermidorian rules, did you?"

"Nope, but the objective is the same."

"Which is?"

"To get very, very drunk." He clinked my glass and said, "Bottoms Up."

"Wait! What was that drink for?"

"Everyone starts the game buzzed as the Thermidorian rules stipulate. Also, everyone who hesitates to take their poison has to take another shot. Here you go." Dr. Westin was eager to test my tolerance, at whose expense, mine or Henri's, I wasn't sure.

"While you're at it, why don't you start us, Antony?" Dr. Westin insisted.

I partially threw up in my mouth and was trying to keep my stomach from rising up inside my throat and muttered the only thing that seemed relevant. "Water," was all I could mutter as I reached for the carafe.

"Ocean."

"Pond."

"River."

"Aqueduct."

"H20."

"Physics."

"Chemistry."

"Justify." Called one of the senior professors.

"What? You're not even next!" I shouted.

"In these rules anyone can say justify. Tick Tock."

"Because H20 is the chemical compound of water. Now drink."

"My pleasure young sir."

"Tasteless."

"Organic."

"Justify!" I screamed a little too enthusiastically before hitting the table.

"Excuse me, because it's in nature, it's life."

"Yes, in a hippie dippie euphoric notion of water, but water exists, as a polar inorganic compound." I looked at Dr. Hadid who was frozen and shifted his eyes to Henri.

"You have 3 PhDs. Have you the answer Henri?" Dr. Westin teased.

"While there exists great debate in the scientific community over whether to classify certain compounds as organic or inorganic, the majority agree that the organics classification portends to the compounds containing carbon. So…"

"Well…" Dr. Hadid said in haste. "It means drink up idiot, carbon and water, non-existence."

"Je vis maintenant don le magnifique pay de non-existence. Merci Henri."

Then Hadid rolled his eyes and knocked back the shot. "Continue."

"Odorless."

"100'c."

"Amphoteric."

"Wet."

"Solvent."

"Slippery."

"Organic." Dr. Hadid hissed, "Because solvents can be, like in dry cleaning so fuck you all."

"Don't self-justify – it breaks the flow. I'm old but stalling is stupid."

"Homogenous."

"Pharmaceutical."

"Diagnose."

"Cure."

"Disease."

"Justify." Henri called.

I glared at him but found my way out of that predicament, "Typhus disease, stemming from unsanitary drinking water."

"Fine," He turned to the next opponent.

"Organism."

"Microbe."

"Fuck it," Ci said.

"Excuse us?" Spoke the professors in unison. "What? Oh, you two are like the Magi? I'll take my poison now to declare this section dead." Ci slammed down the glass to dare anyone to challenge her. "Water? Really? For Christ's sake. I'll start. Deliverance."

"Islands In Stream."

"Crystal Cave."

"The Bluest Eye."

"Male rape."

"Justify," said Dr. Westin to Taylor.

"Deliverance. The male rape scene."

"Continue." said Dr. Westin.

"Squeal like a pig!" Laughed Hadid.

"Banjo."

"Inbred."

"Albino."

"Savant."

"Justify." Said one of the old Magi to Henri.

"Lonnie the inbred albino banjo player, though mentally deficient, a savant."

"But while he might be in one aspect, that does not make him a savant on the whole. He is, as you say, mentally deficient. Sorry my darling, you should have said musical savant." I pulled a cigarette from my thigh and lit it with confidence and with regret for having helped to kill my lover's argument stone dead.

"I'll drink to that." Henri said, taking his shots. "And while we are on the subject, the stakes for this game are too low. Would you all care to make them more interesting?"

I paused for a look of general consensus, as smoke was filling the bar, and the Irish music was beginning to drawl and drown out our intellectualism into utter debauchery.

"What do you suggest?" I asked.

"I'm invoking a new rule. Begin again. It is a new rule that anyone can invoke. Any person who has preceded the next can call 'justify' or 'begin again' to the person whose turn it is next. If the person is commanded to, 'begin again.' That person has to recall all the connections made prior to declaring their new addition to the list. The last two standing will enter a lightning round to determine who will climb Le Montagne De la Révolution, and the loser has to get a tattoo from that charming sack of cuddles and smiles in the corner over there." He smiled and waited for the group's consent.

"That man use to tattoo inmates in prison. I'm pretty sure he was a resident of the L'île du Diable." Dr. Westin said.

"Joseph, what are you saying? Are you really afraid of a man who wears a butterfly tattoo on his chest?" Henri grabbed one of the shot glasses from the table and raised his eyebrows.

Dr. Westin turned to the two emeritus corpses. "I know you both are close to retirement or death, whichever is closer, how much money do you have between the two of you?"

The one looked to the other and then down at the place below each of his pocket watches with a monocle glass. One of them pulled out a leather fold and thumbed through the paper bills.

"Enough." They said in unison.

Joseph reached for the leather parcel and walked over to the barrel chested Papillon and in a few moments, was back. The Papillon raised a glass in acknowledgement of our Jacobian club.

Taylor turned to the table. "What shall it be?"

"Yes, for Christ's sake! Something I can bring home to my wife." Hadid squealed almost at the brink of impending loss.

"Oh, shut up! Your lightweight ass is lucky if it makes it to midnight." Taylor was the ideal reality check for a table such as this.

"I think it is appropriate to pick something that the loser should be able to loath for eternity as well as by his colleagues but appreciated by the masses." Ci slid in her suggestion like a knife into a cutlet.

"You have something in mind?" Henri looked almost content at her orchestration, then to me like watching a social experiment in action. As the ones who rise are usually the least likely and yet when they perform, the results of their vigor are self-evident, making all previous doubt seem futile. Yet, having an entire group of intellectuals willing to engage in depravity at the cost of my own personal discovery was intoxicating. I think Henri could see that.

"I do! Let it be…" pausing for dramatic effect…

"Vien libre ou mourir." I think Ci was more excited by her memory of the words than the cleverness of the phrase.

"Live free or die? It's so pretentious and self-satisfying. I love it!" Taylor raised her glass.

"Antony, it's your turn. I'll accept Cecilia's suggestion as the choice phrase for my own victory."

"Fine! Henri, I will take 'survivalism,' and accept the same fate!'"

"Self Sufficient."

"Sustainable living."

"The individual."

"Indivisible."

"Empiricism."

"Metaphysics."

"Kierkegard."

"Because… of fuck, I meant his two philosophies bridged."

"You still have to drink Mr. Shrader." Henri said whilst pursing his lips as if to hold back laughter after my blunder.

I took my medicine and swallowed my pride.

"Lockean theory."

"Justify," I screamed.

Henri interjected to mediate my point which was quite out of turn. "The two schools of thought, the last one was metaphysics, and John Lockean theory flies in the face of that Taylor."

"But the basis of this stream was the individual and the social contract between rational beings as the cornerstone of the individual as a doctrine of philosophy...Fuck... Humanity even." She did have a very strong argument.

Henri looked at me with raised brows, "Your argument Mr. Shrader?"

"The doctrine of the individual is based on the concept that all humans enter the world as a tabula rosa, a *blank* slate that is shaped by experience, the external, nothing to do with the metaphysics." I looked around the table that remained silent with no objections.

"Kant." I hissed "Would be the appropriate logical placement as he is the marriage between the two schools of empiricism and metaphysics."

"Fuck, after this, I'm going to throw up." Taylor chased down her shot and then rose from her seat and slapped Dr. Hadid on the back. "You are the great hope."

"Fuck you all and your idealism. Hegelian theory." Dr Hadid felt strong about this new added dimension to the argument.

It is unclear when it started but Justify, moving in a circular fashion became Justify, ping pong style. The few standing, who could continue drinking were calling justify on every single point made or added to the duties of related topics.

I started up again and offered up Kierkegaard.

Dr. Westin turned to me and laughed at Kierkegaard. "I find your suggestion laughable because he reflects the Hegelian notion that individuals are subordinate to history's forces. Humans can choose their own fate."

" I agree. That as humans, we choose our own fate." Henri turned to me like he had his pistol drawn and he was ready to start walking ten paces apart.

"Are you calling to justify?" I asked him with scotch soaked breath and false confidence.

"Hey Marley, Scrooge, look, I'm on a roll. Don't try to stop me." Henri didn't like being challenged.

Dr. Westin leaned back in his chair and pulled on his suspender straps, "Fuck this should be good."

"What? If we come into his world *blank*, then from infancy we learn very quickly, that power is like a finite specimen in what we are all competing for. Some are crushed in the race for it; me included. That's why they call it the human race. Maybe it's not something we are all not a part of but a path we are all born upon with no alternate courses." I felt confident in my conclusion of human nature.

"The willpower is manifested in all types of ways, perhaps those crushed under the stampeded are impeded by their own psychological disturbances and therefore are not equipped for this "race." Westin placed insight like a tower of Babylon.

I felt as though Westin was speaking through me and not to me and I could not speak.

"Scheripenhauer would contradict that," Henri said.

"For every human, and I believe this myself, is born with a will to live."

"And for those of us who don't care and would rather die?" I asked before continuing.

"Well, Joseph, I would say then that they had the will to live taken from them." I finished speaking to Dr Westin and turned to address Henry with silence.

"Probably on that race you were talking about." Hadid said under his breath.

Taylor came back to the table bare breasted with her necklace hanging over her nipples. "I'm sorry but my blouse did not survive, and if the Papillon can do it, fuck it."

"We teeter between both at all times and yet there are those individuals who fall to one side with no recourse because the universe does not take that into consideration." Henri punctuated his point in a cloud of smoke hiding his face.

I heard his point, and I didn't. I found myself talking only to Henri, unable to separate my eyes from anyone else. "Most organisms are not born of intellectuals. A lion nurses a cub and slaughters its prey but derives pleasure from neither. It is for survival."

"I'm officially commencing this as the lightning round." Dr. Westin raised his glass in approval.

"Shut up, Joseph!" Henri was talking through his teeth to hold back anger. Dr. Westin snapped his fingers for the barkeep and a new bottle was opened and only two glasses remained on the table.

One of the emeriti rolled a fag for the other and the rest of the table watched.

"He can't help it, Dr. Westin, there's only a finite amount of power in this brothel for him to stomach. And to your point, a man devours a man every day."

"But a gazelle does not choose to be prey nor the lion to be the predator. It is we who are born with the choice."

"A victim does not choose to be a victim; however, a predator chooses to prey and therefore victims are made, and predators are what? Sorry?" I felt smart in this remark but could feel a challenge coming.

"Can the predator not also be a victim? Perhaps he was and chose not to be any longer." This was a point Henri planted but felt no fault in saying it.

"Did you?" I spoke.

Henri retorted, "This is not about me."

"Then give me an example."

"Israel. Ashkenazi Jews returned to their homeland and founded a state of their own but not before almost being wiped from the face of the earth."

"It was Palestine before it became a Jewish State. Clearly you, like most, forgot about the people already living there, who are now treated as invaders in their own country, destined to be folded in this intractable conflict over who controls a spit of land less than the size of the state of New Jersey. All this, because that land of milk and honey and who controls it is all that matters."

Henri took his drink and paused before cutting the silence. "That state was created as a badly executed experiment orchestrated by a number of European actions. Germany created the problem and England botched the solution along with the French who see minorities as pawns in their own power play."

"Then you admit…" I started.

"No, no, I do not because the pretext for this conversation was the individual and not nations."

I took a drink.

"Touché, but are nations not individuals and do individuals not make up nations? Therefore, the will of the nation is expressed as the will of the individual?"

Henri took his drink and then filled mine.

"Yes, however, nations are constituted by the will for the majority and not every individual and any further platitudes of nations and individuals is reductive." He smiled, knowing I had nothing to say.

I took my poison and the room along with my head were both spinning.

"Fine, but you have yet to reconcile the conflict derived between the relationship between cruelty and pleasure as it relates to power. The pleasure derived from cruelty increases as power does and crushes the nature of pleasure derived from goodness or pleasure itself."

"That is utter nonsense when plenty of people mutually and exclusively derive pleasure from pain." I smiled and took a drink as a sacrifice. I rolled the dice and saw how he would swallow my argument.

"However, the will to power is much stronger than the will to survive. In fact, the desire for power increases as power increases and life becomes less meaningful. And once again you are left with predators and victims. It's the master and slave dialectic before us."

Henri took a drink, beginning his monologue.

"The master and slave are driven by different motives. Consequences and morality respectively are not mutually exclusive and yet one needs the other to exist, one to subjugate and one to be subjugated. In fact, it is the presence of the slave that keeps the master moral. The Master can't exist without its subject; therefore, the master must keep his subject alive. The slave teaches the master to be just and moral even though he is motivated by power. We see this in characters like Oskar Schindler who is made moral by those who depended upon him for survival."

I knocked back another shot of whiskey, watching the walls spin as the Papillon prepped his needles and ink. I looked around the bar and at Ci, and wondered if I was in checkmate myself. Then I looked at Henri and he was smiling, as if he had helped me arrive at the end of some cruel irony.

"There does exist one exception to your notion, one in which the oppressor is made more moral and also destroys the oppressor in one fatal swoop."

"Are you stalling or are you going to tell us?" Henri asked.

"I only pause, as I have great respect for you despite being a man who is about to be betrayed by his own profession."

"All men in my profession find themselves this way at some point. We call it learning. Do you have something to teach?" I took a deep inhale and waited for a retort.

The words hummed and teased my lips. "Lolita."

"Humbert is obsessed with Dolores and is driven to his own destruction to save her from a fate he would have inflicted upon her himself had Quilty not attacked her first."

"But then Quilty is the catalyst who is amorally driven." Henri held his breath for my response.

"Humbert wouldn't have known about Quilty's crime had Dolores not told him, thereby saving herself from two predators. She has zero power! None! Yet manages to win, escape their clutches, apart from the mishap of childbirth." I breathed a sigh of relief.

"Begin again." Henri smiled.

"Survivalism, self-sufficient, sustainable living, the individual, empiricism, empiricism, metaphysics, Kierkegaard, Locke, Kant, Hegelian dialectic, Kierkegaard again, determinism, will to power, Schopenhauer, cruelty versus pleasure, survival of the fittest, free will, predator versus prey, moral predator, moral victim, nations as individuals but we scrapped that, back to cruelty and pleasure, cruelty increases power and pleasure derived from cruelty is mutually exclusive to people who derive pleasure from pain but necessary. They seek power because pain can be self-created, master and slave dialectic consequences and morality, master and slave binary with the exception that while the master seeks power, they are the inevitable cause and effect of dialectic cycle, whereas the desire that drives the master becomes his own undoing, the resounding irony that the slave remains as he was, all powerful and powerless at once."

My heart raced and Henri slammed down the remaining shot in front of him. Dr. Westin motioned over to the Papillon, the bottom front of Professor Hubert's shirt ripped open to a tangle of coarse hair and supple olive flesh to be branded by the persistence of myself to make my mark before his. I sat on top of the table as the Papillon scribed Henri's shoulder like the spirit of Yahweh on Mount Sinai as I plucked a cigarette from my thigh holster and set a flame to my lips to breathe its sweet smoke into my lungs before passing it to the lips of my love. "Congratulations Professor." I breathed into his throat for that was all my lungs could sustain without passing through my lips, the fruits of a whisper yielding "I love you."

He swallowed my exhale just the same, metabolizing all that could not be said in a pub, concealed in a kiss and like the martyr of wisdom against well-worn parchment he was, the black ink permeated through his skin like a broad tipped quill. I separated myself from the Jacobinism to relieve myself in the restroom while wading through a fog of smoke and dust. The whole place numbed me to joy and silenced the outside world to form a quieter bliss amongst our little band of chaos. When I resurfaced from that poorly tiled interstice of excrement, I walked straight into Joseph Westin. He pushed me into the wall as if to examine me the way the coyote does a carcass.

"Do you find me intolerable?" He breathed.

"I don't think sir, you understand the world. To be intolerable would mean the rendering of my life at a full stop, unable to move forward because your effect upon it is immeasurable, therefore you have made a gross miscalculation of your own importance to those around you."

"You wield your tongue like a scythe." He pressed his words into me like a knife to the skin without breaking the surface.

"With the same accuracy, your lips have for the bottle."

"Son, I'm Cain and he's Abel. He's Jacob and I Esau. Well, if you saw what I saw, then you would see what he's really like."

"You're drunk."

"Abel, that must be that razor perception he finds so alluring. Although in all the years I've known him, we've had the same taste in youths and the mind has nothing to do with it. We've even shared the same ones until we shared the wrong one. A Hungarian aristocrat, whose son was so pure and pink I thought it too selfish to keep him for myself. His father had us followed. These men broke in just as Henri had finished decimating this young blonde imp. And they tried to castrate him, but I fought them off while Henri fled, sparing him and leaving me crippled. But sometimes if I get just drunk enough, I stay at a hotel and order a scotch and pink lemonade. They always send up a Swedish looking waif like you, holding a bottle for me to empty, while I fill the other fleshy salver, if I time it just right. Ever since that last rendezvous between Henri and I, it just doesn't always work but you're welcome to try."

He grabbed my hand and pressed it against his crotch. "I used to always let Henri go first to warm them up so as not to leave them completely annihilated."

I grabbed his crotch back and gave him a hard squeeze. Before I released him, I laughed and smirked, "I'm not sure why you only ever succeeded at making miscalculations but," Then I sized him up and down with my eyes, "still, less than tolerable." I released his cock. "On all counts." He gasped and Henri approached.

"Everyone being civil here?"

"Yes, just discussing how the stunted growth of certain nations as it relates to the failed maturity of manhood. Excuse me."

I brushed past both of them and out the back door, holding it cocked open as I threw up. I was wondering what I was doing here and whether or not I had accomplished anything but then I was high and wasted and all I really wanted was a cheap crepe. In the back there was an old pump. I rinsed my mouth and threw water around my neck and looked up at the sky, wondering how I got here and how I was going to go inside with a straight face. I walked back to the fountain that resided in the back of the courtyard threw the water on my face and spit the residual bile from my teeth. "Should I offer you a glass?" Henri was standing behind me.

"How's your arm?" I tried to conceal my laughter behind my hand.

"Can you feel hepatitis?" Henri asked.

"You'll have to tell me."

"So, you tried to kill me then?"

"Sometimes I think that I will if I let you get too near."

"Is that why we're walking around this fountain like predators in a standoff?"

"I don't know what we're doing out here!" I screamed.

"I thought you'd want to see my fealty oath to you. The ink that has pierced my flesh at the behest of your genius. Can't you see that I bow before your mental prowess? I'd do it again if only you'd do me the honor and allow me to kiss you before I sink my teeth into your flesh."

"You find pleasure is the way to connect sex to carnage?" I asked.

"I'm just following the logic of your argument. As I recall, you don't have a choice."

I skirted away from his advances but found him too quick, his blood was now flowing and mine was curdled with booze and pills.

"Let go of me, please." I breathed out my protest like a whisper knowing he was all I dreamt of and it scared me how much he knew it too.

"I can't help it. I'm just a victim in my own want for power. The fact that I can crush you between my fingers is incidental."

"It was just a game." My breathing grew sparser as I leaned my head back further.

"Was it? You played some really hard talking points that lead us all to believe you were honey dipped in paper and all your peers are bees who fly down wind. Well you've caught me. Do I have it straight? Do you want me?" He looked for a flicker in my eyes resembling validation. I couldn't breathe nor answer before I heard our reconciliation resembling my heartbeat. It made its way up into my mouth that felt like the acceleration of time, surpassing every moment since the sands of time first began to fall until to now.

"I don't know." It was all I could say.

"Do you know what I think?" His grip never wavered.

"I don't care what you think. I thought you were hiding some piece of yourself from me, and I had to come out here. That's all."

"So, because you found nothing you had to create something?"

"I don't know. You're hurting me." I tried to pull away from his grasp.

"My feelings aren't nothing! I will not be made less of a man to pursue another. I will love you now until the heavens break before I follow my lust through the gyres of hell. I will adore you before you taunt me like a dog who chases a bone. For the love of God, love me before you pull both of us into the fiery pit."

"I don't want to break you. Henry. How do I know if I am strong enough? How do I know if I am strong enough for us? "

Henri removed his hands from my shoulders and wrapped his thick coarse tobacco-stained fingers around my neck. For a moment I lost my breath, not because of him but because of fear. He kissed me and I drowned in the strength of his gaze.

CHAPTER FORTY-SIX

The Carbon Paper Is Made Of Skin

I awoke to the stain on his shoulder. I read it about 100 times before he awoke. He rolled over like a bear onto his back and yawned with outstretched arms, looking for a cigarette.

"What?" He looked with surprise as I stared at him with my mouth open.

"I thought your smoking was more of your façade. I didn't think you smoked in bed."

"Are you really surprised, or would you prefer I not? Or would you prefer I roll you one for yourself."

"Make it look like that?" My eyes moved down to his penis.

"I haven't the tobacco to come close." He turned away from me to grab his lighter. "And I'm not a pimp. I don't use cigar paper."

I turned red and laughed, turning over and unable to look at him.

"Should I dress?"

"No, no, but now that's all I can think about. I'm rather fixated. You are the first."

"Lies and flattery make strange bedfellows. That's the price of pleasure over pain."

"No, I … you're not white."

"Your regret or surprise are not your ally."

"Neither of which I'm expressing. I'm just stating."

"But aren't we better than the obvious?"

"I was merely noting the surprise at my own delight and part of that is just you." I smiled and held out my hand.

He handed me a cigarette, "as lovers we fetishize each other, but I hope yours extends beyond the surface of pigmentation."

"Of course, it does."

"For example, my interest in you might start with your youth and supple skin as a foundation, but I enjoyed you and our time well beyond the sum of your years, partly due to your overwhelming enthusiasm."

I let out a small laugh. "Should I now take offense in the insinuation of my enthusiasm like I'm some prostitute?"

"Not at all. You're not dead behind the eyes, a person who just lays there and trades sex as a commodity, you're anything but."

"Have you much experience in this field?"

"Only to the extent as it was explained to you by Dr. Westin. It was a period in my life and like a season, it ended."

"Seasons repeat." I said.

"In some people, yes. But when I decide something, the decision is as final as death in everything except in matters concerning you."

"I will wait until time will tell us whether I can bask in that as a compliment or not." I took a deep inhale and ashed my cigarette.

He took my cigarette from my hand and put it out on the nightstand, placing himself in between my legs, growing before me as he spoke into the side of my neck. "We have nothing but time and the time I spend with you I will shelter all the confines where your mind likes to run and hide until you beg me to return you to this world."

I looked inside my mind and found nothing. With each plunge, he pulled me back into his escape. It felt like running away from the finish line of a race, not wanting it to end. I wanted to stay there before the memory would fade. I tried to stay behind in that other world until I though my lungs would burst, before I came back, I was pulled forward by his parting breath, punching through the air, along with this sweat and spit that fell into the hollow circle of my ear, and like Lazarus, I rose from beneath him in awe of him and the power of my own breath. Every time we flew, all we had was our breath.

CHAPTER FORTY-SEVEN

The New World

I don't know what I should tell you," he began. "What is it you would like to hear? If I start at the end, you'll think I've learned nothing, or you'll think I'm a liar. Starting at the end of my own life, I've often told myself none of the other stuff matters, yet it is central to how I see the world now."

I must be honest in all these precious moments; I did not know I loved him. I look back and some part of me must have but I didn't know it. I was too numb to be aware of anything. I didn't know I loved him until much later. We were driving through a coastal town in Provence, and I was low. I tried to space out the poison, but it slipped through my fingers like sand. I told Henri that I wasn't feeling well. I think he knew why. He pulled off the dirt road into a little town in the car Dr. Westin told us not to bring back. He was right. What use could he have for it with no use of his driving foot? Henri found a tavern with rooms, and I demanded we leave the bags before even going to the room. We should just get a drink.

I ordered something with a sugared rim to help cut the cravings but as soon as Henri left to use the toilette, I knew it was curtains unless I figured something out. Dumping my tote onto the tavern bench, I looked for anything, gum, Imodium, even a fucking Tylenol, nothing. Then I remembered the hole in the cotton lining I used to smuggle drugs and cheat sheets into tests. I found nothing except a small bag with two caplets. Remembering not what they were, I opened one and sampled it with my wet pinky. It was ecstasy.

"Fuck!" There's no way I can take this without him noticing. I would definitely appear "off." I said to myself.

So, I drugged us both and washed down my deed with a bottle of bourbon. If I timed it right, we could float between a nice medium of serotonin and O2 depletion. We arose from our table and paid the bill. Ignoring the request of our patron to return to our rooms. Instead, we wandered beyond the outskirts of the town, through the fields of sleeping flowers to a belt of trees. Henri, who was so sure of everything was sure of nothing, I felt nothing except sorrow at the man who was feeling everything. I felt pulled into the magnetism of his gyre of emotions.

"I'm afraid!" he screamed.

"Of what?" I pleaded.

"That you'll decide not to love me, not because you don't, but to spite yourself from feeling everything. In order to feel love, you have to feel everything else. And I worry. I worry you won't be strong enough, that you'll be too afraid too."

"I'm not afraid now. You make me not afraid."

"Not now. What happens later? What if I get too close?" He reached out and grabbed my face.

"How?" I pleaded.

"Don't make me say it. You can hate me instead!"

"Just say it!"

"No!"

"Say it." I screamed.

"Make it real for me, damn it!"

"I know!"

"I know what he did to you."

I couldn't breathe.

"I'm sorry."

"I was 11." I said.

"I was 14." He exhaled.

At first I backed away then he. We both backed away until we were about 20 paces apart. Only our face and hands could be seen clearly in the moonlight. I ran towards him. He held out his arms for an embrace, but I pushed him. He stood with tears in his eyes. I pushed him again. The tears began to fall.

"I hate you." I spat.

"I know."

"I hate you."

"I know."

"I hate you! I hate you! I hate you!"

I hit him as hard as I could against his chest.

"I know. Please come here." He squeezed me with all his might, and I screamed into his chest until we sank into the wet field. I sobbed in his lap as he stroked my hair.

"I hate him." I whispered.

"Me too." He said.

I looked up at him. "I want to write a different story for us my love. I don't want Romeo and Juliet or Hamlet. I want 12th Night. I want magic and joy that overthrows the constructs of love, that brings the very foundation of love to its knees, not even the walls of Jericho could withstand the fury of its sound."

"And what happens after the walls fall?" He asked.

I rose from my knee-soaked pants and took him by the hand, leading him to the dark wood where the straightforward path had been lost. "When the walls fall, then the sound will continue on, and on until the ends of the earth."

Deep through the forest we ventured until he laid me down in the center of the thicket where we laid all night until the owl screeched the dark away, the moon rose, and the stars faded until the trumpet wailed and the walls fell. And I loved him.

I loved him.

I loved him.

I loved him as we slept to the trumpet's sound.

CHAPTER FORTY-EIGHT

Why I Hate Mirrors

After we returned from the woods to Paris, those next few weeks were the happiest times I can remember. Being in that city, it was new and exciting to see the world as he wanted it to be for me. He planned our days with militant diligence and a Hollywood flair. Café in French quarter, dinner at Le Procope, followed by boat rides on the Seine, climbs to the Eiffel tower. In the city of love, we were invisible, like everyone else was to us. That was the true magic of Paris. You could make your own world out of a world that existed apart from the rest. That magic of invisibility went with us no matter where we went. At every shop and street corner, we moved in or out of one world and into another. If you sit at a café and ask for cognac, le garçon brings it to you, and you never see him again until you raise your hand for the check. If we kissed or laughed or held hands, we were as invisible to the other patrons as they were to us. It was this privacy that allowed me to grow close to him. I had only ever been gay in the dark. It was like having a part time job, you couldn't tell your friends about, so you simply lived differently and secretly. I thought love would be different for me and to my surprise it was not different from any other version of love I had ever read. It was just as beautiful as it had been described to me in books. This was a fact I held close to my heart.

And then I ran out of everything I had taken with me. There was nothing left for me to use to try and keep up with this man's false ideal of me, who had all but given up on love until we met, and now, he wanted to see and reset the world he had known before in every facet with me by his side. I could barely get through lunch on aspirin and mouthwash.

I would get home, having made some excuse to leave him and find nothing except demons hiding in the dark around every corner.

Mirrors are clocks in disguise. They record the passage of time, and you can't change or alter the ledger they keep because they do not keep track of day or light, but every moment missed by the owner. We find our image trapped in a permanence of the present, frozen in glass, recorded in the failing eyeballs of the witness aware of the deficit accrued in times wasted, until the viewer is aware time is not something you view. Time is your only witness, watching you, as it hangs on your wall, while you miss every look because you only care how it sees you once you're aware of glances missed. They are symptoms of the reality of mortality and the cause for looking, framed in a reflection. My distaste for the honesty I saw made me want to hide from every source of reflective glass, bearing witness to the reality of my demise.

We look at the clock because it possesses the hands we think we can control, but even the last drop of water from a dried-up lake that has seen the passage of time, knows it will return from the clouds above or from beneath the earth. When you shake and hurt and throw up, you curse yourself for having sought relief from your past and curse yourself for needing something man-made when addiction's curled fingers come to dig themselves into your shoulder. The reflection was like staring into the abyss of someone else's life as I stood screaming into the void, wondering how the course of my existence, culminated into recognizing pain only as a familiar bedfellow. Looking back, I could see this wasn't entirely true, but anger was the only feeling that seemed to temporarily cancel out physical pain. I loved Henri. My teacher, confidant and friend, but there was no love that could make me look into the mirror and keep me from wanting to rip my face off, tear my hair out and gouge out my eyes from their sockets.

This need to hurt the physical, is my habeas corpus plea for euthanizing, presented before the alter of God as the sole perpetrator and prosecutor, that has been denied conviction and pardon for the very mind that seeks to destroy the housing of the soul. These failed attempts hurt above all. To be sent down from heaven and put in a vessel, forced to live inside a coffin made of flesh that felt everything the soul could not turn off. And so, the soul tries to escape. "Free me from this prison, O' God, or I will decimate this body and consecrate this soul to hell for being forced to live as a thinking, feeling thing." But there are no guarantees of neither hell nor of God. No stamp or initial on our forehead to let us know who gives a fuck! So, I will separate my body from my soul and my mind. The two shall never know the extent of the suffering on behalf of the other. Whether I could hide this fact from Henri or explain my determination to burn away this vessel was an afterthought.

I picked up the receiver and turned the rotary for information to find Leon's club in Paris. I found Leon and unapologetically gave him the price for my body. I knew there were people who lived lives who didn't have to trade drugs for sex. It seemed like a role I was resigned to play. I would have to double the dosage to block out memory of days when drugs were for fun and not for underlying pain.

The first time you lie to your lover, it's easier than you can ever imagine. They believe you with the utmost sincerity when you have to stay up late for that paper, and when you say, "You make me so happy, I don't need that stuff anymore." The lie is so much better than the truth, anyone would be willing to believe the former. It must be how mediums, politicians and clergymen make a living.

But then I got sloppy. My want for ups and downs was greater than the effort I was willing to put into keeping the ruse up. And that moment you decide to say, "fuck it," it won't be pretty, clean or planned, rather it will feel like the splitting of an atom.

We had returned to Henri's apartment after having a nightcap with Ci and her beau at an absinth bar. I had consumed much of the green elixir and chased it with Italian soda to cut the Joneses. I thought, if he gives me one good fucking then I'll probably pass out and be in Leon's bed by brunch.

But demons never sleep. They reside in the space between this world and eternal peace. And when the body has been weakened by the task to protect the soul, there they will come to rip you through the other side. I used to salivate in the darkest night for quiet, as I cursed God asking why the remedy for absolution could always be found in my nightmares and never on my knees on a Sunday.

They tricked me. When I didn't have it, the nightmares came, and if I couldn't have it, I wanted to die. It started with a need for money and that was the beginning of the chain I forged to hell. Cuffed to its immeasurable weight, his love alone could not pull me back but only rip me apart like William Wallace. At first it was night sweats, I tried my hardest to escape to the other side of the bed, but the sweat bled out of me like my secrets onto him. He knew. I cried first silently, and then uncontrollably. I couldn't stop the ungovernable terrors from coming into my mind every time I closed my eyes. God help me, I tried but it was too late. The entire house was on fire. True to instinct, he begged me to let him take me to the hospital or call a doctor.

"So, they can pump me with more fucking drugs? How many PHD's do you have again?"

"You lied to me." He sat silently by my bedside.

"Obviously! You, Fucking jerk off! Seems rather trivial at this particular moment."

"I don't know how to help you. Trust you. You'll just lie to me again."

"Probably. I'll go now."

"You can't live like this." He pleaded.

"I can't live like THIS either. And I don't want to die but each day is like a tale that keeps getting harder and harder and I know how it ends."

"All it takes is faith. You have to trust me."

"The saddest realization is that it's probably a symptom of my drug-addled brain, but I can't tell."

So, clad in tights, knee length chiffon tank and white fur, I left to join the land of the in between where silence has insurance.

CHAPTER FORTY-NINE

The Architect Of Hell Has No Map

On the fifth day, I awoke on a futon next to a cat that had turned from white to grey. I rose with the enthusiasm of a corpse dipped in ether and moved into the other room. I saw nothing but travesty. Drug addled corpses of various youths strewn about like dish rags getting fucked and infected by fat ugly French patrons with hair in their ears, razors on their backs and claws for nails.

I just stood there trying to remember my life and I could see no good things, only evil. But I know there have been good things. I just couldn't see them there. I closed my eyes to try and remember Henri. My mind started to paint us like a scene from a Renoir, but the bottom of the canvas began to burn, and up from beneath our beautiful world, a nickelodeon featurette worth a thousand pictures of me fading in and out of myself, unable to speak out only able to lay there and be fucked. And when I saw the hand reach for the dish soap because there was no lubricant left, I ran like Dante down the stairs, like sliding down the belly of Satan, the world invested on my race to the bottom and instead I emerged out into the light.

I ran. I just ran. Through the streets of Paris, through the underground of the metro. I turned down Rue Reaumur onto the street of virtue where he resided. I waked for the rest of the way down the street, thinking of what I would say. I saw a figure walking with a weight about him with only the residual strength remaining with him, his love and his pride. He had been out all night looking for himself and for me. When we caught eyes of each other, we ran, but I began to slow halfway, my knees buckled, and I fell to the street.

True to nature, he rushed over and tried to pull me up, a truth wrapped in metaphor, disguised as a weight I could no longer bear.

"I'm so sorry! Please! Please don't look at me."

"Get up, please! Darling, I love you. I don't care what you've done. Only please get up."

"I can't. Just leave me here in the gutter where I belong."

He let go of my arms and let me drop.

"You're right! You probably do belong there. You know what I think?"

"What?" I asked.

"I think John Locke is full of shit!"

For a second, I thought, and laughed, not remembering the last time I did either and asked, "Why?"

"Because I don't think we are born on a blank slate. I think we are dropped in the gutter and it's our job to pull ourselves up and start anew."

"I'm so tired, Henri."

"You can lean on me. You can always lean on me, but only you can stand."

"Henri."

"What?" he asked.

"Nothing. I'm just glad to be able to say your name."

He smiled, even though his eyes carried with him the weight of all I had done to him and all that could still happen. Helping me up he asked, "Would you like some breakfast? Eggs Benedict, and coffee?"

"So much coffee." I gasped.

In the middle of my look he said, "I've never loved you more, hearing you say that."

"My family has a place on the coast. We need to talk about getting you to a place where you can dry up and have some quiet. I have a colleague, she's a psychiatrist, I can pay her to come after to stay with us for as long as you need."

"I've never known someone to be so kind. And I know I don't deserve it."

"That's where you're wrong. You deserve the world. And I'm going to give it to you, as soon as you're well; as long as you want to be well."

"I've never known what that means. It rather sounds like being someone else though I know it isn't. I would like to give it a try."

"Thank you, my love. As long as you believe it, it shall be so."

When we returned from breakfast, I found standing at the entrance of the apartment a familiar and foreboding figure.

"Good morning, my eyes either deceive me or my favorite stray has taken a lover." Leon appeared like a serpent seeking sunlight.

"I'm not yours. I never was. How did you…"

"Address book amongst the other things you left behind though I neglected to bring them."

"Why are you here?" I shouted.

"10,000 dollars say there are about 10K worth of favors in the pocket of that jacket."

Henri whipped around and reached into the pocket of my coat, fished out the bag and pushed the contents against his chest. "Here, now go."

"Don't tell me he's entrapped you as well. He is a pretty thing but believe me when I say it won't pan out."

Henri grabbed him by the folds of his jacket and slammed him against the doors of the building. "It will because I'm willing to break your fucking neck for him and you're not. If you're not willing to do the same, I implore you to move on or drugs won't be the only thing they'll be feeding you through a straw. Now leave while you can still feel your legs."

He disappeared down the street. I never saw him again, except as a warning in my memory.

"Come! We leave for Marseilles in the morning."

I realized I was a captive to my own recovery, with some different wardens holding the keys.

CHAPTER FIFTY

Who Guards The Ruins Guards Heaven

I sat up in the empty space beside me in bed and reached to the side only to find nothing but air. Then he emerged from the room, wet, but focused.

"How are you feeling? Do you want some breakfast?" Henri asked.

"Just coffee. Extra brown sugar."

"You know what tomorrow is. How are you feeling?"

"Like I'm about to be beheaded."

"Think of it as a transplant."

I turned quiet, looking for my shirt.

"I didn't mean that. I just want you to heal." He kept his eyes reaching, deep in mine as they searched.

"I know, I just…every time I do this, it's like sending myself away from my body. And my soul goes to a place where I don't want to go back to."

"I'm going to take you away, somewhere safe."

"That's what the pills promised."

"I want you to sail into me, with open arms away from the person you want to be and into the arms of a man I know you to be as you say to me, 'I'm yours forever more.'" He said.

I fell into him and forgot for a moment. He lifted me like a corpse he plucked from the vat of ether, waiting to be taken out into the sun and dry out in the pursuit of the light.

In a dream, I saw myself, like a plant out on a windowsill of a copper vessel where my master planted me, I found the light and grew outwards from ashes to the prestige of dusk and looking away from the ground, I pointed towards the light.

In the morning, I told him, "I only wish to be with you for the day; with you by my side. Let's dive into something real where I remember sitting in your lap on a beach; while I'm retching on some toilet waiting to come back to you is not what I want for us. Let's create a memory unfettered by the burden of my disease so that I may carry it through the darkness."

"Where shall we go my love? Say it and it is done." His eyes were fixed and as firm as glass.

"Back to the shore, where all things go to pass."

We left the cottage and walked the path whose conception began with the impression of human steps and where life yielded to the passage of people over time. We followed it until the dirt and pebble path turned to weeds and jagged stones that lead to the feet of a castle that had succumbed to the elements, standing only as a memory of its former glory.

Stepping through its collapsed archway, a garden flourished in the stead of the eroded floor and fallen stones. A patch of heather grew along the steps leading to a turret that held onto the ramparts like an outstretched arm, jeweled in vines and thorns.

Standing atop this sprawling callus of history, I felt as insignificant as the stones I stood upon, which were left honor to guard the view of this long since forgotten fortress overlooking the port town.

"Come down from the clouds and tell me what you are thinking about?" Henri held me close while whispering in my ear.

"I was thinking of how I would describe you, to myself."

"What did you come up with?"

"Well, that he has the body of a bear, the hands of a titan, the prowess of a sultan, the mind of a stoic and a heart made of whipped lemon meringue and eggshell cream."

"You could devour my soul with your words."

"Do you want it back?" I asked, staring over the rampart that looked beyond the sea.

"What is a man but the sum of his parts and what am I to be? Should I not be the best part of him and him of me?"

Turning to him I said, "I want to be that for you, but I can't go through my life feeling everything and nothing, except I want to feel everything with you."

"You don't have to be afraid to. I want you to be with me always and to never hide yourself from me."

"I had a dream, Henri. I had a dream, at the moment the universe emerged from the eye of god, I reached out, and woke up inside the palm of his hand where he presented me to you. When I woke up, I started to cry because I was afraid it was just only a dream."

The sky was rumbling and growing darker and taking my hand, he turned to the horizon, "Look at those birds. If we are them, I'd rather see these birds perish in my sight, than watch them crash upon the rocks for not being able to fly beyond the storm because they're afraid."

"Look at them. Look at the birds Henri, the way that they dance and tease across the sky. They don't know that the storm is coming. Is that what we are to be Henri; dashed upon the rocks before our lives have begun? We must be like the shore against the waves, to see the sun rise again."

"We will see the sky again, otherwise there would be no reason for us to be standing here now, except to know where you want to be standing when it's over, and who you want to be standing with." He held me close, and a tear hit my neck.

"I know it's time, but I'm so afraid it's going to hurt."

"I will not leave your side. We will stand at this spot again. And we will weather the storm.

CHAPTER FIFTY-ONE

Separation And Reparation

A pitcher of water, a pack of cigarettes and half a bottle of aspirin later and I had not moved from the seat in front of our cottage window. Waiting for withdrawals to kick in was like waiting for the rush of the first time you get high. First you feel the adrenaline of waiting for the high, then the effect takes over and you sort of fall into it, like falling into bed. Detox was like having your head on a chopping block waiting for the ax.

I stared out at those tiny little aspirins and thought about the man who first decided to put relief into tiny capsules: so clean, so efficient and so powerful. They were pretty much everything I felt life wasn't. I found comfort in knowing something perfect existed. Now I felt as though I was learning a different lesson; that things that we think appear perfect are not. The things that we love in life are messy and mysterious, like a code we have to crack on the road to discovering why it is that we love the things we love.

Henri put his hands on my shoulders. The sweat had soaked through my sweater. By the window, I sat looking out to the sea, unable and too afraid to move, cold and wet at the same time.

"You must come and lay down. It's starting, Antony, you can't stop it." He clasped my hand where the cigarette had burnt to my fingertips.

I reached around and grabbed his hand, pulling it to my face. "I'm frightened. I'm frightened! I don't want to do this anymore!"

"Here, get up and take off this sweater and you won't feel so cold."

I got up and tears began to roll down my face. Every limp node in my body swelled like a balloon, my joints locked up, even the act of standing was painful.

Taking my sweater off felt like being skinned alive, I doubled over onto the bed and wailed, "Oh God, help me. I feel like I'm coming apart."

Henri tried lying beside me, I just cried out in pain.

"Oh God, don't touch me! Please!" I shot up out of bed and tried drinking a glass of water, but the water just rolled down my face.

"I want my mother, I fucking hate her, but I want my mother!"

"I know you must be in so much pain right now, but you have to lay down."

"I don't want to lay down. I want you to fucking leave!"

"At least take some ice chips! You're dehydrated!" He handed the pewter dish of ice chips, and I smacked them out of his hand.

"Get the fuck away from me! I hate you! You're a fucking rapist! You don't even deserve to live!"

"Antony! I know you're in there! Lay down. You're hallucinating. It's Henri. No one else is here!"

"But someone else is there, in here, will always be there! I need to go! If you stop me, I will fucking kill you!" I ran for the door, when I opened it, Henri was right behind me to slam it shut. I screamed and he put his hand over my mouth and lifted me by the waist. I kicked against the door, he swung us around and threw both of us onto the bed.

"Help! Help! Help! Help!" I screamed.

Over my mouth his hand went. I screamed into his plate sized hands until my vocal chords tore. He squeezed tighter and tighter, kissing the top of my head until my fighting and screaming had worn me out. "He's not here!" He whispered. "You're safe. He's not here." A tear fell from his face and onto my cheek like the bell from a trance and I fell asleep.

When I awoke, I was alone and cold in sweat-soaked sheets. I felt a pain, like a residual reminiscent pain of rape returning to my body. It started from the bottom and moved its way up into the inside of my throat and made me want to throw up. I shakily picked up a glass of water and tried to drink only to see a familiar and twisted face staring at me in the mirror. It was probably a hallucination, but I could feel this lingering presence of evil still trapped inside of me, that was projecting him into my reality. I threw my water at the mirror sitting above the wet bar to wash away the image, but it grew stronger and more persistent with each breath until he was standing behind me through the mirror! With a scream that ripped my gut open, I hurled the glass into the mirror causing the image to fizzle. Then I picked up the pitcher sitting beside the glass bar table, and threw it, shattering the face of the monster I had hid and loved and despised for more than a decade and it was gone. Henri came bursting into our own one bedroom to find I was crying hysterics. The abscess had been cut out. The demon purged. The walls had fallen yet I was standing. At last, I had finally put the earth down and could stand up straight. I thought I had to destroy the temple to free the spirit, but there was only room inside for one. No demon could linger in a vessel conceived in perfection. Body and spirit made whole again, I collapsed under the weight of the miracle that restored me. Laying on the floor in a heap of tears and glass, I cried as Henri rocked me, my arms wrapped around his, I looked over at a shard of the mirror and saw only myself.

CHAPTER FIFTY-TWO

The Last Baptism

The worst had passed as I laid in bed for three days and nights until I rose from my bed on the fourth day, wrapped in linens and walked to the edge of the sea. The shrouds fell from my body like the Pentecost, as their owner moved from their folds into the icy water, I waded in until the sea came up to my navel. I turned around to the sound of Henri's voice yelling for me to return to the shore. I laid my arms out to each side, pointed towards the sky and fell back into the wave coming overhead, allowing the wave to swallow me up in the will of the tide.

A gruff hand reached in the sea and plucked me out. Henri could hear nothing but white noise as he dragged me to shore.

"Stop Henri, please! I'm alright."

We fell into the sand, Henri's eyes were bloodshot, his breathing strained, and he was crying. Henri then looked at me. "I'm sorry. I didn't mean to frighten you. I went into the sea to be reborn, and I no longer want to die. I only want to live with you in this world for as long as my body shall let me. And no matter in what manner of what world our souls reconvene, I swear mine shall find yours, or I shall not rest, until time stops."

"That's why I've never been afraid for us, no matter how many times doubt tried to dissuade me. I knew I should have you in this life or the next." Henri said while shaking.

"Take me inside Henri. It would be a terrible irony to die of cold in this life, having come so close to it before."

We looked at each other and laughed.

"I'm so glad you've become a humorist when facing life," Henri said as he wrapped me in crumpled linens.

"How can you say that when I've always been a realist?"

"Those aren't one and the same thing."

"Aren't they? Now hand me a cigarette before you dampen them with your false sense of humor."

"The greater irony being that we continue this habit having acquired such a fresh perspective on life."

I stopped for a moment and inhaled, "I won't stop if you won't," and we journeyed on.

CHAPTER FIFTY-THREE

Chariots Of Fire

While drugs created chaos, there was a routine and planning that went into fucking up your life. Now my days began differently, light benzos and anti-nausea meds for breakfast with a little late afternoon tea and therapy, followed by long walks on the beach accompanied by deep thought.

On our last night at the cottage, I decided to take Henri with me on a walk, told him about my progress and how I was writing all my thoughts in therapy down, "But now I feel anxious because soon we'll be back to the real world and what will we be once we are back in it? Right now, I'm happy here with you. But what will we be once pain, emotional and or otherwise cravings come creeping back in?"

"We'll be together. Neither one of us ever has to face anything alone again. We've come so far and that's what we've earned."

I shook my head and stared into my hands. "I got off the phone with the admissions office. After a year stay on my undergrad student visa, there's a one year wait before you can apply for a student stay."

My eyes were beginning to well. "I don't know what this means. It's as if someone else is writing our story now."

"Antony Shrader, you look at me! At times, I thought it seemed farther away, but even when I didn't want to see it, I've only ever seen a finch die in the sky for us. Now I know this would happen, I have applied for positions in the US, but there is paperwork, interviews and bureaucracy that has to take its course." He was quiet. "This all could very well take a year."

I stomped my food and rolled my eyes to the sky, trying not to let the tears roll so hard, but with no effect.

"You will be fine. This is the end of the race. You don't have to run. We have fortified your constitution with love and stability and you have never known them to serve as your sustenance on your next journey. That is why the last bird to fly at sunset is the most beautiful. While the others fly away to escape twinkling stars, this one answers to its own curiosity. Searching for what lies beyond the light, beyond speech, beyond air. He flies by the will of his strength until he finds peace, less he perishes into the sea." I had a look of certainty that I had never used before.

"You talk like a dead poet."

"Because I fell in love with one." I smiled.

"And what was forged within the nature of my being, I fought to crush it under the weight of my agony, not having the wisdom to see it, knowing it could lead me to you."

"And what we must pause to think on is the blind luck that we enjoy this brief moment when the universe blinked and pushed us together as the happy few, the happy stupid few." Henri dropped to his knees, and I stepped back and back…

"What you say speaks volumes and is echoed as scripture. Those city lights flicker like its inhabitants from within begging to be noticed. Any doubts I had now stand wavering above wind and water to be swallowed in the sky by God as a path forged in fire runs straight from your heart to mine." I reached as I fell to the ramparts giving way, having gone one step too far. Henri reached for my hand, pulling me back to him, falling into his arms, I looked into the face of God and kissed him, seeing the image of grace lay across his face, disappearing like an apparition down the drain anchored in his pupils

He pulled away. "Shall we have a bit of a summary now?"

We went chasing after the sun, suspended above the first solitary star of twilight, anchored in the sky. We collapsed into the folds of the night that shielded us from the eyes of God, where we explored each other blindly through the darkness that was guiding our passion.

We returned to Paris like strangers in a land that found each other because the strain of knowing nothing but pain was too great a weight to follow the other without fear of taking the other down with their own anxiety.

I don't remember saying goodbye to him as he opened the door for me to ascend and collect the remnants of my old life. Had he gone up with me, I don't think I could have left. I walked through the door of our old one bedroom apartment.

I walked through the door of our own bedroom apartment and saw the scattered remnants of panties, wine, bottles and discovery. I was so removed from the women of my life I forgot that the reason I was even in this country was because of them.

I sat in the middle of the apartment like I had been there for the first time. The flower beds that lined the balcony had grown to be a reminder of something that was beautiful that had been forgotten wilting in the sun. The air in the apartment was congested like the blood flow to a varicose vein that needed to be severed. I had taken advantage of the quiet and missed the life that could have been a part of its high vaulted ceilings and meandering light of the narrow alleyway that was pertaining to our street.

I sat in the quiet of lingering smells and quiet anticipation of something that would happen in the lull of the quiet that was our tiring home I had abandoned.

The door creaked to the cry of a knock that I thought belonged to a courier or a postman. I was thrilled to interact with a human I thought had no knowledge of me, who I could use as a catalyst to integrate myself into the atoms of society, formed to the complexity of electrons and connecting, the spur of the brain cells popping.

I heard Henri open the door and his feet descend down the stairs. I turned the corner and my mother appeared. When I saw her, she was bowing her head in the vestibule of the unknown of a son who was more estranged than the dish towel she clung to as her salvation from a life of poverty. There she was before me like she had discovered something only her and I could be privy to before the lights shattered like a realization of invention that extended beyond the hopes of any Edisonian realization.

I had no words for her. It was a little like I was a corpse delivering the status of its own lifeless state. Being a parent was a privilege and a reward I had no idea how to reciprocate, viewing her as viewing me as a body on the slab before the stone rolled away to illuminate the Son she birthed from my conception to the one that stood before her, standing somehow taller and translucent to the mystery surrounding the person she already knew.

I loved being able to stand before her, victorious against her quest to destroy me and there she stood, seemingly destroyed and pale.

The denial of her own cancer had rattled her body to the brink of unrecognition. Her eyes were heavy with the acceptance of seeing me intact despite my unclenching desires to survive the reflection of a whisper of scrutiny concealed in the folds of her own sorrow, at last safe in the folds of the lost tribe.

"I'm sorry and I promise it will never happen again."

I stood frozen, unable to respond.

"If you continue to stand there hurt, then your face will freeze." She said.

"I'm too afraid to move, let alone speak. I can barely imagine why you are here." This was my only response to her.

"Because I'm dying and before you speak, it's not your fault. I had a feeling I was not well for some time but was too scared to admit it. And now, here I stand before you and all I can think of, is the time we lost because of my own stubbornness."

"Mother, you don't have to…"

"No, I do. I will never know if I was right or wrong for the way I loved you, but I only know what time we had was destroyed in my stubbornness to see you as anything other than the child I gave birth to. And now I laugh because I'm too late. I feel as though your life rather than mine might flash before me. Yours is one I can be proud of. You may love me, or you may not, but my time is the same despite what I have left to live for. I only hope it is long enough to know I tried. I tried." She paused for a moment to remove herself from the pit as being past and ended with plea for my future.

"Why now? It's too hard to even look at you and yet all I want is to save you, which seems to be beyond my power." I said.

"You don't have to save me. We are very different, you and me. The first time I gave birth to a son I wanted to love you, more than the man who helped create you. But my time with you is near the… and all I have is to give you this, and hope it serves you more than I would while I was healthy and strong with the vitamin of disillusionment, as the hourglass waits for me to nod."

"Is there nothing anyone…"

"No, there isn't. And I don't want anyone to help me. I'm going to go to a hospice clinic, surrounded by family and tranquilizers. But I have to give you this before I leave to retire in the arms of my mother."

"I didn't even know you were alive." Truth be told, I forgot she was until I realized that everyone needs their mother.

"I don't know what to say." She sighed.

"I know you leave tomorrow to go back to life without a man who has supported you more than I could under the gaze of your father. But when you land, I want you to read my last wishes as though they were the blessings of a mother giving her son away to the arms of someone wiser beyond the ability of a mother who loved you too late and too little."

"Why do you think I shall not read what you have put to paper before you perish from the earth?"

She opened her heart and spoke her soul. "Because He is in everything. Because He loved you, even when I couldn't and because He will love you beyond what I can before the cancer takes me."

"But I don't want to see you go."

"Where you go, I follow in the light that shines from the window that has eluded me. May your steps travel with my blessing."

"When will I see you again?" I was fighting back the sobs of a face that mourned the loss of time that could not be recuperated from a promise sewn in birth and lost in adolescence.

"But please, for the love of all that I have done and not done, do not read it until you have reached home." She never looked more sincere than now.

"I want to love you without having to walk away from you." I pleaded.

"Away from me you shall not stray. I shall love you, even when God takes me, I will love you." She grasped my hand.

I thought I would ride with her in silence to the airport, wishing I had Henri to squeeze as I boarded on an early flight to avoid seeing him cry at my departure. I knew it was cruel to leave him, but it was all I could bear before I could travel the air without leaving my heart behind with my soul intact.

"Mom, I don't want to go back knowing I'm leaving you here."

"You're not leaving me. I'm sending my heart and my love back with you. Now leave with this gift. I just want to remember you like this. Happy to see me before leaving, rather than hating me. No matter what any of you have done or begun, I have loved you as all my children."

"Take me to the airport?" I asked.

"Alright, let's go."

Down we went into the car, and I looked up to the Haussmann apartment building and wondered why looking at it as we drove away, why I couldn't feel us, Henri and I in it anymore. Perhaps I was taking it with me, about to drop it into the sea as I flew over because the curtain was coming down on our play, and neither actor could not have the heart to end it on the world's stage. As we drove out of Paris to the airport, I searched for a sign of him in the air at familiar sights and spots we had visited, with any trace vanishing from the background of a fading Paris that mimicked an Impressionist painting. I recall now, why the painters of Paris painted the way they did. How She made them feel instead of how they saw Her because she leaves you no other choice when you're saying goodbye.

CHAPTER FIFTY-FOUR

The Ocean Is Where Farewells Are Buried

As we got closer to the terminal, I knew whatever I was going to say goodbye to before slamming the door was the last memory I would have of her. I often go back and wonder how many times we receive gifts as both a blessing and a curse. After all, this was worse for her than anyone.

Before I left, she grabbed my arm and kissed my cheek before shoving an envelope in my waistcoat. "Open this on the spot. Goodbye my sweet boy. I love you." She nearly pushed me out of the car as she drove away.

When you're sober, you remember everything as if it were a second frozen in eternity. When you're high, it's like being stuck in a prison, in solitary where you have no memories and time becomes meaningless, feeling like an eternity. That last sight of my mother is like a bittersweet pill that I have to swallow every day until time runs out.

I clutched the envelope in my pocket tighter than my passport, waiting to get to a place to begin my chapter in cultivating your minds as I expanded my own. Suddenly the things that mattered most didn't matter at all, just the final words I said to Henri before my mother.

"I honestly can't bear to look at you while I pack. It feels like a cruel punishment coupled with a reward."

"Harvard was your dream. Not mine. But I would feel worse if you turned down this fare. I don't want to be your replacement for something else. If I could come with you I would but maybe we are supposed to be apart like this until you learn how to walk again like that ball of fire that ripped through my classroom the first time."

"I don't know if I can."

"You won't know until you try. I'm coming after you. I just can't come with you."

"I know you're right. There was some lingering fear that the months would go by, and I'll be staring at a door that will never open."

Henri walked over to me and grabbed my hands. I dropped whatever I was holding. "That's the disease knocking on your brain begging you to turn time off because it wants your desires for it to be more powerful than us. My promise to you and the promise we made to each other. As a formal teacher and mortal, I will not lie to you when I say there is no more powerful weapon forged in our species than doubt or fear of the unknown. I believed that until I met you. There's nothing more powerful than doubt except for love. Which paradoxically, is about as unknown and undiscovered as you can get."

"I would not dream of stepping through the looking glass if I didn't believe you were following suit. So, I'll plunge into the abyss and reach out with my extended hand until I feel it enclosed in mine again."

He smiled and kissed me as he always had, each laden in a promise and a sunrise.

"Let's get you packed. When we're done, I'll leave you so you can adjust to being by yourself before you fly away."

He turned and began to sort things. I grabbed his hand with the intensity of a bridge jumper, "You cannot leave me, except in devastation." The garments remained on the floor as they were until morning, when I awoke to a scene of strewn chaos and a piercing quiet in search of a sound that could no longer be found.

CHAPTER FIFTY-FIVE

The End Of The Siege And The Surrender

Those final moments of our time in that apartment before he left, came back to me in waves because it was a time when I surrendered myself to total uncertainty of whether I would ever see him again but I gave myself to him knowing the pleasure given to me from that evening would either haunt me like the high I would never feel again or stay with me as a soothing memory to pull me into the next dawn if the night went on too long.

The present was all fading so fast. Cecilia, Jane, the apartment, the Eifel, the Arc de Triomphe, every cobblestone was fading away. I would never live to speak to my father again and my mother was going off to die. My sisters, I had kept in sparse correspondence with a patchwork of postcards, but I was truly left alone on this path forward.

The lines through the airport moved as time does in observation but fast in motion until I was sitting at a window like an amnesia patient returning to the home I'm supposed to remember. My mind has already taken care of those memories and hid them from their host.

I hadn't felt the lift off of the plane; from that departure. It pulled from my gut into the base of my body to let me know that I was no longer on solid ground. I was truly shedding the weight from the person I had become and killed before getting onto this flight. Seated at the window, I prayed for sleep to wash over me before I woke up in my home country that no longer felt like home. Home was somewhere else, and now that my feet were standing on E pluribus unum, I had to find myself again. I walked from my gate and sat down like those musicians from the Metropolitan who wait until they are bored enough to play Chopin or Christmas Carols on the airport piano.

I didn't find a bench, but a marble statue of Saint Agatha outstretched as if to offer me a seat or a confessional. Staring at my feet in comparison to the massive marble pillars and how they looked next to mine, compelled me to want to do something. While I hadn't forgotten the letter she gave me, I imagined it full of contradictions begging for forgiveness through condemnation. Sitting beneath the patron St. of Nurses, I thought any sting verbally inflicted could be softened by the presence of this healer.

I opened the letter and smiled at the recognition of her familiar hand. Then my eyes moved to the words themselves.

"Dearest Son,

I have seen you and as you read this, know that I knew I would regret this being our last. While time is the enemy of most, I knew you would look as beautiful as the day I bore you. I still don't understand everything about you, but in the limited time I was granted, the only thing my mind could bring back to me was how much I loved you. How much I love you. While you cannot go where I am going, the only thing left for me to do is to send your love back to you with all my love. He is waiting for you as will I be at the end of time.

Love, your Mom."

I felt my hands fall to my side and the weight of a letter that felt like one thousand pounds slipped through my fingers to the floor of the airport to become carbon and ash with its words seared to my brain, in the annals of my heart, buried in the pit of my soul.

I rose in parallel to outstretched hands that loomed above me and looked for something to head towards. I saw baggage claim, what should have been more appropriately named as a command, "Claim your baggage." But doesn't possess the same inviting ring. I walked with turned out hands towards the neon sign. First, in a slow shuffled walk, then into a fully escalated tear-streamed run. I could feel him, crawling across the top of my heart as I grew nearer, until I was sure I could taste his name in my mouth and spit it out for him to catch it in mid-air to the part that connects the ears to the heart strings.

"Hen…Henri!" I cried.

I searched but could not see, so I kept running, jumping over any obstacle in my path until a wave of force came towards me like ripples in the ground. Across from the revolving doors a turbine of flesh and desperation was making its way through the sea of people towards my gate.

I stopped to see the source of this commotion until I locked sight on a pair of lost eyes, full of hope and doubt. I cried for his name and only air came out. Smashing my way through the swinging iron and glass doors, my foot acted like breaks to the rubber pads lying on the other side that sent me falling only to be upheld by a pair of strong arms that I pulled on like the side of mountains until I was staring into the face of God and kissed him for showing a glimpse of himself in a man who was a pawn in being my own savior. He would be my king and captain for as long as we remained together in this world.

I laughed as I cried looking for the answer in his eyes that I already knew. "How are you possible? How are you here?"

"It was all her. She used her name and pushed my paperwork though. When she landed in Paris, my colleague gave her the name of the hotel I was staying at because I didn't want to return to an empty apartment until I was ready. She called out my name in the lobby as if she already knew me. She had seen my name written a dozen times on postcards she intercepted intended for my sisters. As an acting donor and Harvard board member she was immediately notified of your application. On top of that, when it came time to vote on prospective associate professor applications only one name stood out to the dying woman, at her behest, my name went to the top. University contacted the visa bureau to push my paperwork through. When she called my name, she placed a copy of my visa and my appointment in my hands."

"What did she say?"

"She said, 'I've come to pay the ransom you have placed on my son's heart. Death is tapping me on the shoulder, and I don't want to be wrong. I fear I have been. You have his heart, so you have to take care of him, because…'"

"I… I know the rest." I whispered.

"Come with me," he said, "and let's carve a little place for the two of us in the world."

The Speech, The Gospel And The Epitome

I seldom do these, not because I'm afraid to speak, but because I don't know what you'll hear when I speak, how you are feeling today and the effects my words will have on you in this moment.

A small part of me fears, what I will say will have no impact, for we have all been a victim of vanity.

How you are feeling now, my words are meant to provide you with some road maps to the next step. I am here to tell you, when you get to be as old as I, you realize there never were, nor will there be any road maps. Despite what you believe or don't believe, believe me when I say, all of our births or either accidents or works of art, left on this planet with no way to fix it, guide the interpretation for the soul placed in the landscape of your body.

So, you come here because someone told you to. Some of you might even have been told you'll find the answer to answers. Having sat where you are, I know you have more questions than answers. Sometimes circumstances trick us into believing we were born with a plan others were not privy to. But even that plan has an ending with no more story, because it was written by someone else, for someone else.

Whether it has already happened or will happen, there's a point in your life when you say, "Now what?"

Prodigy does this to us sometimes. It wasn't in the plan but happened anyway. And now what?

I can tell you this much, these things happen because we are born on this earth with choice so that we overturn the plane of eminence we were born upon. That's why there's no script. No plan. Each of us, regardless of profession, is writing a living record on how they contributed to the overturning of that plane.

This world was created in the equivalent of a moment in eternity and whatever forces or theories played out leaving us to decide what this world shall be. Surely those choices will have an impact on what the next world shall be.

This world for now is mine and my colleagues for a little while longer, we know what the world means to us and how we want it left. What it will become, will come from you. I leave it to you. Now, I know some of you are thinking, "How can I know what I want for the world when I don't know what I want for myself?" My answer to you is to first stop asking that question. Ask what you want for the world and the world will follow. Because as I have said, there is no plan written so how can you know? If you want bigger answers for yourself, then you're going to have to ask bigger questions. What world do you want?

What world do you want to leave behind?

There was a time when my partner and I were split halfway across the world, and when we found each other, we had nothing to say because we didn't have answers.

The love of my life said, "come with me and let's carve a place for the two of us in this world…"

And that's what we did, and as I look over all of you, I say to you with as much love as it was said to me, "Go and carve your place in the world." The visionaries of your own nations, the leaders to your own garden so that somewhere in the index of the annals of your own history and time itself, there will be a place within this place of eminence upon which we live that you can look at and say that space and time was yours, you see, we are all kings of this earth. Walk from this place now and claim a space in time and build upon it your own nation that will sit upon eternity. You are not your accomplishments; your accomplishments are not you. They are signatures of your time in this world written in the essence that is you. That is something no one can take away, not even time. Thank you." My speech ended and I looked across the crowds to smile and take my seat.

"I saw many faces in the audience that day, some there and some not."

"Like whom?" Henri asked.

"Lucien was there, my sisters, Jane, Ci and her husband, the one she met in Paris. I suppose we both got what we wanted from that city."

"And what did you get?" Henri came out and set a tray down, nestled between the two of us like our house nestled by the sea. It was unclear whether he was aware of the overwhelming magnitude of safety I felt every time he sat beside me. Looking back, I realized I never had to ask.

"Looking back, I suppose I got everything from Paris. Everything that matters sits with me now."

"And at your commencement speech; who did you see?"

"Just my mother. I couldn't tell but I think she was smiling."

"Any monsters?" Henri asked.

"No darling, no monsters."

"Good." He rose from his chair, extending his hand to pull me up from mine. The wind from the sea blew his hair into his face which made me laugh. I moved aside the pieces with delicate and admirable affection.

"You too will see the eyes of God," I smiled.

And then he smiled back, "I already have."

Cheek to cheek we looked to a vast ocean of mystery and adventure that lay before us, while for me, the memory of our youth played for me like a moving picture across the sky, sent from heaven, residing always in my heart.

(If birds forever fly, love shall never perish. It is under this very promise that carries them upon the wind, until they see heaven. .)

True or not, I put it on his tombstone because he asked me to. The same will be on mine when I will leave my body to find him again in the next world or in another sky.

NEXT CHAPTER

The Speech

I seldom do these, not because I'm afraid to speak, but because I don't know what you'll hear when I speak, how you are feeling today and the effects my words will have on you in this moment.

A small part of me fears, what I will say will have no impact, for we have all been a victim of vanity.

How you are feeling now, my words are meant to provide you with some road maps to the next step. I am here to tell you, when you get to be as old as I, you realize there never were, nor will there be any road maps. Despite what you believe or don't believe, believe me when I say, all of our births or either accidents or works of art, left on this planet with no way to fix it, guide the interpretation for the soul placed in the landscape of your body.

So, you came here because someone told you to. Someone might even have been told you'll find the answer to answers. Having sat where you are, I know you have more questions than answers. Sometimes circumstances trick us into believing we were born with a plan others were not privy to. But even that plan has an ending with no more story, because it was written by someone else for someone else.

Whether it has already happened or will happen, there's a point in your life when you say, "Now what?"

Prodigy does this to us sometimes. It wasn't in the plan but happened anyway. And now what?

I can tell you this much, these things happen because we are born on this earth with choice so that we overturn the plane of eminence we were born upon. That's why there's no script. No plan. Each of us, regardless of profession, is writing a living record on how they contributed to the overturning of that plane.

This world was created in the equivalent of a moment in eternity and whatever forces or theories played out leaving us to decide what this world shall be. Surely those choices will have an impact on what the next world shall be.

This world for now is mine and my colleagues for a little while longer, we know what the world means to us and how we want it left. What it will become, will come from you. I leave it to you. Now, I know some of you are thinking, "How can I know what I want for the world when I don't know what I want for myself?" My answer to you is to first stop asking that question. Ask what you want for the world, and the world will follow that. Because as I have said, there is no plan written so how can you know?

If you want bigger answers for yourself, then you're going to have to ask bigger questions. What world do you want?

What world do you want to leave behind?

There was a time when my partner and I were split halfway across the world, and when we found each other, we had nothing to say because we didn't have answers.

The love of my life said, "come with me and let's carve a place for the two of us in this world…"

About the Author

Garrett Garland

Garrett Garland is a California bay area resident who studied at the University of Santa Cruz and Sciences Po. in Paris. Drawing from his extensive travels abroad this is his first novel. He currently resides with his husband Sam next to the sea in Half Moon Bay. Their long walks on the beach and love of the ocean are where he draws most of his inspiration. The ocean is home, but Paris is Garrett's hometown.